DUALISM

Bill DeSmedt

WFP

WordFire Press

Praise for SINGULARITY

"The level of ingenuity is immense. The characters grabbed me. *Singularity* is a wonderful, intricate story—wonderfully well told."
—LARRY NIVEN, NEBULA AND HUGO AWARD-WINNING AUTHOR

Winner: 2005 Gold Medal for Science Fiction †
Winner: 2004 Best Fantasy / Science Fiction Novel ‡
† FOREWORD MAGAZINE | ‡ IPPY PRIZE

"… a swift, gripping novel with a goose-pimple mix of scary science and near-future action. An excellent debut from Bill DeSmedt—and I'll be looking forward to his next one!"
—GREG BEAR, NEW YORK TIMES BESTSELLING AUTHOR

"One of the best debuts of the year!"
—BARNES & NOBLE'S EXPLORATIONS

"DeSmedt veers an action-packed thriller into perilous realms of black hole physics. The combination of adrenaline and intellect sizzles."
—DAVID BRIN, NEW YORK TIMES BESTSELLING AUTHOR

"*Singularity* juggles Clancy, Crichton and *The Da Vinci Code*. An innovative concept for an end-of-the-world thriller, with convincing research and locomotive pacing."
—KEVIN J. ANDERSON, NEW YORK TIMES BESTSELLING AUTHOR

Books by Bill DeSmedt

The Archon Sequence

SINGULARITY

DUALISM

For Kathrin
L'altra meta del cuore
Sei tu

Prologue
al-Malhamah al-Kubrah

Last Day of Autumn

T HE DAWN OF THE LAST DAY. *The heavens ring as thunder condenses into a triumphal shout. The western horizon shudders and disgorges a blood-red sun, rising whence it had lately set. Throughout this final morning, the ruddy orb will ply its retrograde course toward the zenith, but slower, ever slower, until it halts and hangs motionless, nailed to the noonday sky, its surface boiling in turbulent unrest. It is only then that, bubbling up out of the photosphere, there comes into view the likeness of a human countenance.*

It is the face of the Deceiver—obscenely corpulent, blinded right eye protruding like a rancid purple grape, forehead branded with the word "infidel," though in such wise that none but the faithful might discern it.

… The Great Deceiver, whom the People of the Book variously call Dajjal or Armilus or Antichrist.

Of the Minor Signs of the Hour none remain to be accomplished: the nations of the earth compete with one another in raising towers to the clouds even as their morals descend to the depths of depravity. Men aspire to become women; women, men. Global prosperity grows so great the wealthy can find no one to accept their alms, and yet a man passing by the grave of a friend can only shake his head and mutter, "Would that I were in his place."

And now the Major Signs are become manifest. Earthquakes and celestial portents, wars and rumors of war. The red death of ethnic cleansing vying with the white death of the AIDS plague. Unbelief reigning triumphant everywhere, atheistic science usurping the true faith.

Now the Christian West has gathered its forces, twelve thousand arrayed under each of its eighty banners, before the gates of Jerusalem. So, unwittingly, has Rome set in motion al-Malhamah al-Kubra, the Great Slaughter, the Final Sign ushering in the Day of Judgment.

Parading before Islam's third holiest city, that mighty infidel host moves as a single man. In a sense, it is a single man, for at its head rides the Deceiver, and the Deceiver has laid his mark upon each and all of them, filled them each and all with his own corruption so as to magnify his own hideous essence a millionfold, until now it is the Deceiver's will alone that inspirits their minds and moves their limbs, his monocular gaze alone that stares out of a million pairs of eyes at a world that lies prostrate at his feet.

Far as those eyes can see in every direction, none venture to challenge the might of the Deceiver. Save only to the east, where, out in the wastes of the Judean desert, there waits one who dares stand against him.

Lord of the Age, Guided One, Hidden Imam—he is known by many names, this man whom God has raised up to oppose the Deceiver. It is said that he is of the family of the Prophet, peace and blessings upon him. It is said that he has remained in seclusion, in occultation, since the year 874 of the Common Era, biding his time until God should decree his return.

It is said that his Advent at this moment heralds the End of Days.

His appearance betrays none of this. He is a comely youth, with a broad forehead framed by dark, curly hair and peace shining from his countenance, yet nothing in his demeanor hints at how he might hope to withstand the onslaught that the Deceiver is about to unleash.

Nor do his prospects seem improved when he and his ragtag band of followers fall to their knees and make salaat, praising God, calling on His mercy and compassion.

The Deceiver raises his right hand to signal attack—a gesture immediately mimicked by his million puppets—and they begin to march, down through the verdant hills of Jerusalem onto the dusty sand of the desert floor.

In his eagerness to slay this opponent, the Deceiver abandons his accustomed place at the rear of his armies and forces his way through to the front ranks. This "Guided One" is unarmed, after all. What possible danger can he pose?

The Deceiver is within two arm's lengths of his intended prey, his sword raised *high for the deathstroke, when the man ceases prayer and raises his eyes to look the Deceiver in the face.*

Blankness. White, searing light. The world shrinks to the compass of the man's gaze.

Caught in that pitiless regard, the Deceiver cries out, or tries to. He cannot. Cannot move at all. His army, the extension of himself, is frozen motionless as well. And then…

If only he could, the Deceiver would scream. Scream, as the flesh boils off his bones. Scream as he, and all his host, disintegrate, dissolve into their component atoms, under the calm, compassionate gaze of the Guided One.

At the last, all that remains of the Deceiver is a single eye. A blind eye glaring out sightlessly, oozing redness onto the bloody sands…

An eye of blood.

The man who called himself Hamza Nassiri was almost grateful when the four A.M. call roused him from fitful sleep, from the dream. Always the same dream, or rather always the same ending: that wounded, bleeding eye fixing him with its baleful stare…

Hamza shook his head to clear it of the nightmare's fading remnants, then retrieved his handset from the nightstand and thumbed the unit open. Its backlit display held the caller's name: Mahmoud Rasti. What in God's name was the night-duty monitor thinking, to call at this hour?

"Report," Hamza rasped.

"Mr. Nassiri, sir, please you must come at once. Something is *happening!*"

"Calm yourself. *What* is happening?"

"Possessed!" Mahmoud was shrieking now. "The laboratory is *majnoun,* possessed. It is the experiment: it has called forth an evil spirit. I can feel it, feel it reaching out for *meeeee*—" The last syllable stretched into a piercing, high-pitched wail, followed by silence.

"Mahmoud? *Mahmoud?*" Hamza glanced again at the handset display. No signal—the line had dropped. So had the video feed from the lab to his bedroom's closed-circuit monitor.

In the moments it took to throw a robe over his outsized frame, exit his quarters, and walk to the elevator, there chased through Hamza's mind a myriad of possibilities, none of them good. The one he kept coming back to was that Mahmoud had suffered some sort of psychotic break. Sitting down there alone in the subterranean lab all through the long night, with only the dreamers for company, who knew what thoughts might come?

But he *knew* Mahmoud: The man was stolid, dependable, not given to flights of fancy, nor easily rattled. And what could he have meant by "possessed"?

Hamza was still pondering that riddle when the elevator doors sighed open again, now giving out on a corridor three floors below ground level. He hastened down to the laboratory, keyed in the code that retracted its firedoor, and peered cautiously into the gloom.

Nothing seemed out of place, at least not at first glance: As Hamza's eyes adjusted to the wan glow shed by consoles and service lamps, he could make out the half-dozen experimental subjects nestled in their infusor stations, their limbs swaying in syncopation to an unheard melody, their faces slack, devoid of any spark of intellection or emotion: dreamers, dreaming their collective dream. Nothing unexpected in any of that.

Then he saw it: the six dreamers had added a seventh to their number: Mahmoud Rasti had joined the others in their silent dance, their communal reverie.

What had the fool done? Mahmoud's job was to observe and report, nothing more. He had been warned not to come in contact with the test subjects, nor with the technology that engendered their strange trancelike state.

Intent on getting to the bottom of this, Hamza strode into the lab. Halfway across the floor, it registered: Mahmoud, arms waving to and fro in time with the others, was still seated at the monitor's console — nowhere near the infusor workstations that induced the effect.

Hamza began to back up toward the door. He was nearly there when the dream reached out to embrace him as well.

This was not supposed to happen: Hamza was not linked into the grid, nor was his gray matter infested with the nanoscale neural implants that provided the physical substrate for the phenomenon.

But it *was* happening. Hamza gasped as the seductive pull redoubled in strength.

He'd become trapped in his own experiment.

Too long. He had let this latest trial continue for far too long. But what choice had he had? He'd needed to find *some* weakness in the NSA's new analytical capability, yet with only a scaled-down replica of the real thing at his disposal he'd been hard put even to reproduce the consciousness-binding effect, much less to test out whatever inherent limits it might have.

But if Hamza could not match the Agency in sheer wherewithal, he far exceeded them in his willingness to sacrifice his human guinea pigs in the quest for an answer—after all, martyrdom would ensure them immediate entry into paradise in any case.

So it was that he'd ordered the infusor stations equipped with intravenous feeding tubes and waste evacuation facilities, then linked his six volunteers into the quantum computer cluster once again and left them there for…how long? Must be going on ten days now.

And all that time the entity formed from the fusion of the six test subjects' individual minds had been brooding there, gaining in strength.

It had become a strength beyond imagining: Hamza's clenched teeth gleamed white in his dark face, sweat beaded his cheeks and runneled down into his beard as he dug fingernails into palms and willed his sinews to break the catatonia that had seized them.

Hamza swept his gaze around the lab, desperate for anything that might offer hope of escape. All he saw was his impending fate: the lax, uninhabited faces of the test subjects floating in the dark, looking for all the world like drowned men. Soon he would be one of them.

He shuddered. The metaphor of drowning seemed only too apt, now that he could experience for himself the onset of the assimilation effect. It felt like nothing so much as a great, slow undertow sucking at the foundations of his soul, extinguishing the last fitful sparks of coherent thought, whirling the flotsam of his fragmenting mind down to the depths of a cold, dark sea.

He could feel his consciousness ebbing, attenuating, dissipating into the abyss. Still he struggled on against the encroaching dark, trying to focus his willpower, to concentrate his essence into a dense hard knot, a fist tightly clenched around…

Nothing.

It all felt so futile. His vaunted individuality seemed but a taint, a trace impurity, a small patch of scum momentarily contaminating the surface of a vast ocean of nonbeing, destined to dissolve into it.

The void, impersonal and implacable, beckoned to him.

One last shuddering breath, and Hamza let go, finally submitting to the inevitable, the inexorable. After all, was not the act of submission the very essence of, the whole meaning of, Islam itself? Why *not* submit, then?

Hamza caught himself then. Submit? Yes, but to the will of God and God alone, not to this—this *thing*.

Almost without thinking, Hamza began rehearsing the familiar words of the *Shahadah*, the first and greatest profession of faith: *la ilaha illa Allah*—there is no god but God. He clung to the testimony like a drowning man.

There is no god but God.

Still paralyzed head to toe, he could at first only repeat the *Shahadah* in silence. But, as the hallowed syllables filled his soul to overflowing, he found his lips beginning to mouth them as well. Then he was uttering them aloud, barely whispering to start, but soon testifying in a clear, firm voice:

"There is no god but God."

The more he focused on the profession of faith, the more the immaterial force that held him seemed to loosen its grip.

Could it be?

Hamza gathered his strength. The tendons of his calves and thighs, locked as rigid as the rest of him throughout this struggle, now obeyed his will, flexing and tensing for one last supreme effort. He took a deep breath, held it as long as he could, then released it all at once in a booming shout— *"There is no god but God!"*—and in the same instant thrust himself bodily backwards towards the still-open lab door.

He landed flat on his back, smacking his head hard against unyielding concrete. His momentum carried him a short distance across the conductive flooring before its anti-skid surface brought him to a stop—hopefully now far enough away from the epicenter.

The effect *must* diminish with distance, or it would have engulfed him—and everyone else—anywhere within the compound. The only question was whether he was now beyond its reach. Even from where he lay half-dazed, he could feel the hive-mind groping after him, seeking to reestablish its hold on him, but feebler than before.

Hamza didn't try getting to his feet or even rolling over, just levered himself up onto hands, hams, and heels and skittered backwards in what he hoped was the direction of the exit. As soon as he was out in the corridor, he scrambled up and hit the plate that would slide the door shut and seal it.

He slumped against the wall, his breath coming in short gasps. It had been a near thing. Minutes passed before he could stagger to his feet. Even then he stood there, head held down, shaking with reaction at the narrowness of his escape.

And pondering.

Perhaps, perhaps his dream of the *Malhamah*, of the Great Slaughter, had not been a nightmare after all.

Perhaps it had been … prophecy?

It was more than sheer relief that reshaped Hamza's features into a grim smile. He was beginning to glimpse the outlines of a monumental destiny.

Part One
QuMRANN

February 13ᵗʰ–16ᵗʰ

*Absolutely none of my work is based on a desire to understand
how human cognition works. I don't understand,
and I don't care to understand.*
—DOUGLAS B. LENAT, CREATOR OF CYC

1 | Freddie's Game

Timah Ansari had the best playthings money could buy. Some of them were even alive. Almost.

None of them was as much fun as Freddie, though. And Freddie hadn't cost her *Baba* a dime. Of course, Freddie wasn't nearly as smart as Timah's tutor Mr. Mandelbrot, and he didn't look or sound as pretty as her singing flower garden. He was hard to see and hear, actually. Grownups couldn't do it at all. Even a six-year-old like Timah had to really, really concentrate to make out the words in Freddie's quiet whisperings, or see more of him than a little shimmery light off in one corner of her eye.

But Freddie was worth more than a dozen AI teddy bears like Mr. Mandelbrot, more than a whole bouquet of soprano black roses. Because Freddie was her friend. Her only friend.

It was only because Freddie *was* her friend that Timah had promised to meet him here, over by the garden wall on the far side of the compound, to play a new game. She wasn't really supposed to be here at all.

Timah buttoned the top button on her wool sweater against the chill, fog-laden breeze coming in off the ocean. Her dark eyes swept across acres of California hillside, golden brown going green after the winter rains, down to the private cove far below, then out to the empty, leaden-hued Pacific and the cloud-racked horizon beyond. Searching for the little winking will-o'-the-wisp that was Freddie.

The shy smile that normally lit Timah's round, olive-dark face flickered out. "Freddie? Where *are* you?"

Timah was about to call out again, when she heard something—not Freddie, something big—come trundling down the path that cut through the garden. A moment more and she could see it too. The top of its steely head, anyway. The rest of it was hidden by outsized animatronic rose bushes.

Only after it had bulldozed its way through a hedge of dwarf cypresses did the whole of the blocky, stylized body come into view: a Sony Mark V guardbot. It was big and shiny and more than a little bit scary looking. Like a mean old dog, only with metal where a dog had fur.

Timah backed up a couple steps. The Security bots weren't nearly as nice as her cute little AIBO. *Baba* said it wasn't their job to be nice.

The Mark V came to a halt ten yards away and stood there scanning her with the wide-eyed photoreceptors set on either side of its gunmetal gray snout.

"Fatimah Ansari," the synthesized voice said after five or ten seconds. That's how long it took the guardbot to recognize her face. For an AI, the Mark V wasn't very bright.

"Fatimah Ansari!" the voice came again, sterner than before. "It is not safe here. Move away from the perimeter."

"No!" Timah gave her head a vigorous shake that sent straight shoulder-length black hair flying. Freddie had said to meet him here, and she would too. Besides, she could tell from its stilted speech and slow responses that this bot was patrolling on auto. There was no one in control of it right now, so not doing what it said wasn't really like disobeying a grownup.

"Move away from the perimeter," the Mark V repeated. "It is not safe to play here."

"Course it's safe, you big silly. *Baba* says nobody can get through the fence."

She turned and pointed at the metawall barrier that ringed the Pairidaeza compound. Stronger than steel, her father had said, and—even better!—able to turn any color of the rainbow, even clearer than glass, like now. Timah could see through it like it wasn't there at all, could see all the way out to the misty horizon. She took a step toward it.

Perhaps the guardbot misread Timah's movement as an escape attempt.

It scuttled around to interpose itself between Timah and the transparent barrier and barked "Get back!"

Timah stamped one sneakered foot. "I'm allowed to be here. I *am!*"

The Mark V stood its ground, unimpressed. It also lowered its head and began muttering to itself. Linking back to the Security office in the main compound. To Mr. Hamza.

"Freddie?" Timah's mouth felt dry. She knew she shouldn't let herself get upset. Getting upset could bring the colors, and the bad feeling in her tummy, and then the darkness. If only Freddie would come. Freddie knew how to keep the colors away.

Her lower lip trembled. "Freddie? Where *are* you?"

All at once, a tiny point of light darted across her field of vision. If the afternoon hadn't been so overcast and gloomy, she might have missed it altogether. Now she could hear a faint whispering sound too, scarcely louder than the distant surf.

"It's all right, Fatimah," the whisper seemed to say, "I am here now."

"*There* you are. I was waiting and waiting. And now this mean old thing—" Timah's toe scuffed a small puff of dust in the general direction of the guardbot, "—wants to make me go back inside again."

"You can make him stop, Fatimah," the little voice whispered inside her head, "just repeat after me."

Timah listened, but—"Those aren't even words."

"Just repeat them, Fatimah. Say them aloud—quickly now."

"Tell them to me again."

Timah listened a second time, then turned again to the guardbot and repeated the nonsense syllables as clearly as she could: "Al-fah al-fah dell-tah six five bey-tah, pry-or-it-tee over-ride soo-lee-man—ter-min-ate."

The Mark V's muttering abruptly warped into a squeal and ended a hiccup. It reared up on its hind legs. Its heavy front paws flailed aimlessly, then thumped to the ground with a dull thud. The rest of it followed suit.

Timah tried not to giggle at the ungainly antics. *Baba* said AIs didn't have any feelings to hurt, but that was no reason to be impolite.

The Mark V was struggling back up onto its feet again, but it looked all wobbly now. One more hiccup-squeal, then it sat down on its haunches, hard, and slowly slumped over onto its side.

"Oh," Timah said. "Is it all right?"

"The guardbot will be fine. Come now, the new game is starting."

With that, Freddie shot over Timah's shoulder on a beeline for the metawall. She turned to follow him. As she walked forward, one arm out in front of her so as not to bump her nose on the invisible barrier, she felt the ground begin to rumble beneath her feet. The ocean breeze picked up at the same instant and was now blowing hard in her face. Her hand reached out for the wall, but encountered only empty, unresisting air.

Then her gaze was drawn from where Freddie's little point of light danced in the air to the hillside beyond. There was something moving out there, something hard to focus on, but already close and coming closer.

Timah took a few quick steps back. Turned to run.

Too late.

2 | In the Dark

Marianna Bonaventure eased herself through the access door into a darkness so absolute it seemed less a mere absence of light than a positive, palpable presence in its own right.

Nor did its inky weight lift even when Marianna flicked on her hand torch. Not till she'd powered up her goggles, that is, and then the torch was spilling out a narrow cone of what looked like broad daylight.

For her eyes only. Anyone not equipped with shortwave infrared receptors like the ones integrated into CROM's night-vision goggles would still be in the dark.

Not that there was much to see even with the goggles. The false colors painted by the SWIR software showed her only the dull gleam of rust-eaten steel rails paralleling a tunnel wall cankered with mold. If her quarry—the last dregs of the erstwhile Shadow KGB—were here at all, they were waiting somewhere down that track.

Lying in wait for anything or anyone that CROM, the U.S. Energy Department's Critical Resources Oversight Mandate, might send in after them.

Lying in wait for her. But not for her alone, not this time.

Marianna took a breath of chill air and whispered into her headset mike, "Clear, come on through."

It had taken her months of lobbying, even with the Grishin case to point to, before her boss Pete Aristos had agreed to muscle up CROM's Reacquisition Branch with a small—okay, a *very* small—field force. But here she was at last: Deputy Reack Director Bonaventure at the head of her very own rapid response team.

The stairwell's emergency lamps momentarily cast her shadow on the far wall as the door behind her swung open again. Then the other four team members were in, and it was full dark once more.

Marianna shivered slightly. It was time to get moving.

They had clear line of sight for maybe a hundred yards downtrack from their entry-point. Further on, the tunnel curved, cutting off their view. No telling what was down there around the bend. Not without calling in the Marines.

The Marines' DragonEye UAV, that is. At her signal, the team moved to circle round and pool their SWIR beams on the floor. Marianna unslung her backpack, then crouched in that circle of invisible brightness to extract the five modular components of the little unmanned aerial vehicle.

The Quantico engineers who'd designed the two-kilo DragonEye had envisioned it riding the night winds above foreign battlefields, tight-beaming back situational awareness to USMC commanders on the ground. They could hardly have imagined it swooping bat-like through this sunless subterranean cavern, this long-abandoned subway spur snaking beneath the slush-slimed February streets of midtown Manhattan.

In under two minutes Marianna had the little UAV assembled and cocked back on its bungee launcher. She checked the GCM computer built into the forearm of her suit: the Ground Control Module's display was showing green. Punching a minimal flight profile into the autopilot, she engaged the propeller and stomped on the launcher's foot release. The bungee cord snapped forward, catapulting the DragonEye up the ramp and off into the darkness.

Back when she was being checked out on the mission parameters, Marianna had worried that DragonEye might give the game away. That was before she'd seen it in action.

The vehicle's one-meter wingspan gave it the radar signature of your average pigeon, and its electric motors were near noiseless. It didn't take a pilot like Marianna to fly it, either. It pretty much flew itself, with a little help from the same GCM computer that was at this moment feeding back terrain imagery to the heads-up display built into Marianna's visor.

And what that imagery was showing was hardly worth giving up a night's sleep over, much less a night with Jon. Ever since CROM had shut down the Shadow KGB's Antipode Project and killed or captured its senior leadership eighteen months ago, the remnants of the cabal had gone to ground, where they were proving harder and harder to root out. Meaning fewer and fewer of the leads were panning out. Like the ostensibly hot tip—anonymous, untraceable—that had led to tonight's raid.

Which was looking like yet another high-tech snark hunt. Already far down the tunnel now, DragonEye wasn't picking up more than what they could see from right where they stood. The way ahead was clean and clear: no movement, no signs of recent activity, no—

Wait one. Marianna punched the GCM's instant replay, rerunning the last thirty seconds of scan. And there it was: a roughly rectangular seam in the mottled surface of the tunnel wall, possibly the door to a lair.

Marianna considered calling the UAV back for a closer look. But no, her guys could as easily check it out themselves. She left the DragonEye in cruise mode, but minimized the heads-up display—too distracting otherwise. Then she formed the team up and headed them out.

As they started down the tunnel, Luis Mondragon took point as usual. And as usual he was moving out a little further ahead of the team than caution would warrant.

Comm specialist Cherie LaSalle brought up the rear. It was Cherie's job to scatter a trail of "electronic breadcrumbs"—miniature transmission relays—behind them, so as to ensure a tight communications lock on home base back at Federal Plaza.

Suddenly, up ahead, Luis' torch flared blinding bright. Marianna's visor darkened automatically to save her night vision, meaning the burst of light must have run up the spectrum into the visible range. Other polarized patches bloomed in her peripheral view. The rest of the team's torches must be malfunctioning too, her own included.

"Lights out!" she whispered into her mike, and switched off her torch. Waving this much illumination around the lightless passage would give away their position for sure, if it hadn't already.

"Down!" she said, "and lie still."

Straining every nerve, she could make out faint scuffling sounds in the darkness, then silence again. There was somebody out there, taking up positions to their front.

"Hold fire," Marianna ordered. "Watch for flash." The enemy might have knocked out her troops' night sight, but that advantage would prove short-lived. The best flash suppressor made couldn't totally eliminate muzzle flare, and here in pitch black even the feeblest glimmer would be enough to give a gunman's position away. Unless the Shadow KGB intended to grapple hand-to-hand, they'd be pinpointing themselves the instant they initiated hostilities.

More scuffling up ahead. Then an oddly-familiar *snick*. Now, where had she heard—

Without warning, something whizzed past her ear. Whatever it was, it had been close. They were taking fire somehow, though her eyes had yet to register the least scintilla of light.

Another swish, then a sharp intake of breath and a muffled groan came from the darkness in front of her.

"Everybody okay? Talk to me, people!"

"It's me," someone gasped, Luis by the sound of him. "—I, I've been hit."

"How bad?" That was Dave Rostov, their paramedic. Marianna could hear him scrabbling over the rough ground toward his wounded teammate.

"Upper arm." Luis's voice was tight with strain. "Right through the armor."

"Got it," Dave said. He must have started probing the injury, because his next words were, "it's—Jesus Christ!—it's a fucking *arrow!*"

Not an arrow, a crossbow bolt. Marianna *knew* she'd heard that sound before. She also knew they were in deep shit.

Even medieval crossbow quarrels could pierce chain mail at three hundred meters, and the enemy'd be using the new diamond-tipped carbon bolts, with more penetrating power than even Kevlar could stand up to. As Luis had just found out.

Definitely deep shit.

How deep was evinced by the *snicks* of at least three more crossbows being cocked at widely-separated points along the impromptu skirmish-line. She could almost feel the enemy's own unimpaired infrared beams playing over her exposed back, over her team where they lay hugging the ground.

Too bad her night-vision goggles couldn't see those beams, trace them back to the enemy's position. But, no, the Shadow KGB's IR torches had to be using a different modulation, or they'd have been knocked out together with CROM's in the first place.

Somewhere close by in the dark, Cherie was trying to raise home base. From the increasingly desperate tone of the comm specialist's whispers, Marianna guessed that the relays she'd scattered had gotten fried along with the rest of their electronic gear.

Clean sweep, game over.

The darkness, laden now with death, pressed in on her, crushing down like the weight of deep water. She couldn't get enough of the tunnel's cold, musty air into her lungs.

"OhChristOhChristOhChrist," someone was moaning behind her.

It came to her then that she could die down here, far from light and open air. They all could, could wind up unsung casualties of a minor engagement in the global war on terrorism, just a few more nameless stars hung on some clandestine memorial wall somewhere.

She imagined she could see the gleam of her own commemorative star. Far off, at the outer edge of night. Just a single star to show that she had lived.

And that she had died, with no one knowing how or why.

Not even Jonathan Knox, for all his eerie insightfulness, would ever guess what had become of her.

Truth be told, at that moment in time Jonathan Knox didn't even know what had become of himself.

That might be putting it too strongly. He knew, for instance, that he was currently cooling his heels in an antiseptic antechamber somewhere on the sprawling San Jose campus of Archon Consulting Group's largest client, Psyche Industries. What he didn't know was *why*.

More specifically, he didn't know why Archon CEO Richard Moses had ordered him aboard the redeye out of JFK, for delivery on said client's doorstep at one-thirty A.M., local. For that matter, he wasn't sure if Richard knew all that much more himself. If he did, he wasn't sharing.

As best as Knox could piece it together, sometime yesterday afternoon Archon's West Coast in-charge had reached out to the home office for help — *Knox's* help. No specifics, but it wasn't hard to guess it had something to do with what Archon was working on for Psyche — something called "the

QuMRANN Project." No specifics on what that might be either, though.

And beyond that meager amount of guesswork, Knox was totally in the dark.

"Hello?" he called out. "Anybody there?"

"Good evening, Mr. Knox," a booming basso echoed down from an overhead speaker grill. "Sorry to have kept you waiting—you can go in now."

Knox turned to see a panel in the far wall gliding open to reveal another, larger chamber beyond, albeit with no more by way of amenities than the one he was in. Save for one thing:

In the indirect lighting, the artifact taking up the middle of the new room resembled nothing so much as a chair, though not one that Knox, even jet-lagged as he was, would want to kick back in. Because this was a chair that could have been designed by H. R. Giger of *Alien* fame: a sleek, black, articulating power recliner fitted out with multiple gleaming appendages and crowned by a bulbous black hood hovering above and to the rear of the contoured spine. The overall effect managed to be both vaguely familiar and repellently sinister.

Not just a chair, then—a *Chair*.

With or without capitalization, the thing would have been at home in a twenty-first century torture chamber, lacking only padded wrist and ankle cuffs to complete the picture. Or perhaps those lay coiled within its molded metallic arm and leg rests, waiting to spring out and snare the unwary?

Knox reined in his rampant imagination and turned to a more relevant question: what could the grotesque device possibly have to do with him? Could it somehow be related to whatever problem he'd been brought out here to work on?

Well, when all else fails, try a direct question.

"Hello?" he said to the ceiling. "Does somebody want to tell me what this thing is supposed to be for?"

"Welcome to Psyche Industries, Mr. Knox." His invisible friend was back. "There are a few formalities to complete before you are cleared to visit our San Jose facility."

"Listen," Knox began, "I didn't ask to—"

"If you would step over to the Chair, please."

Knox approached cautiously. Up close, what he'd taken for a futuristic hairdryer hood revealed itself to be a supersized skullcap of black ceramic composite, with adjustable padding on the inside and a strip of ribbon-cable running down to a socket integrated into the back of the recliner. And that, in turn, accounted for the earlier sense of familiarity—Knox had seen a setup like this once before, half a world away, at the bottom of the sea.

"You've got one of those miniaturized MRIs in there, don't you? What the devil for?"

"If you will sit down, please."

No sooner were these words spoken than the Chair shook itself and, with a series of chitinous clicks, whirled to face him. And *unfolded*. The hood craned back, the prehensile attachments hinged up and out of the way, all as if to invite easier access. Something about this performance conveyed the aspect of a Venus flytrap gaping wide its jaws to welcome in its prey.

"You have *got* to be kidding," Knox said under his breath.

"It is mandatory that you be scanned while reading the Non-Disclosure Agreement." In synch with these words, a panel slid open in the Chair's left armrest. Knox watched as a glowing notepad screen, easily the brightest object in the room now, rose up and swiveled to face him. Leaning in closer, he could see it was displaying the fine print of Psyche's NDA.

"The functional MRI will image your brain-states," the voice rumbled on, "to establish a comprehension baseline in the event of court challenge to the undertaking."

"Undertaking be damned. I'll keep my brain-states to myself, thanks."

That produced a brief pause. Then a new, decidedly female voice issued from the hidden speakers. "Come on, Jon, it doesn't bite."

Those sultry tones conjured up a host of memories, few if any of them suitable for family viewing. "Jazmine?"

Jazmine McGovern. Of course—how could it have slipped his mind that Jazmine was Archon's on-site for the Psyche engagement? Suddenly, it all made sense. Sort of.

Because he and Jazmine had worked together before. It had been years ago, but the association had gone on long enough and been close enough that she'd formed the impression—the *erroneous* impression, in his opinion—that Jonathan Knox was some sort of a last-resort resource: the guy you went to with a problem everybody else had given up on.

"You've come all this way, Jon," Jazmine crooned. "Don't make them send you home now. It's just this one more thing, then you can get some sleep."

Yes, he and Jazmine had worked together, and played together too. It had been fun for a while, till Knox saw through it: saw their hot-and-cold relationship for just another of Jazmine's career-advancing stratagems. It had ended then, and they'd been studiously avoiding one another ever since.

But she evidently needed him now.

And that in itself spoke volumes about the situation here. Because Jazmine never would have called him in to help with some minor glitch, some routine speed bump on the otherwise smooth-paved path to a turnkey delivery.

No, Jazmine McGovern was one lady who knew how to steamroller over speed bumps, to smash flat any obstacle that stood in the way of her relentless rise to the top. As Knox knew only too well, having nearly gotten flattened himself.

"Don't be a wuss, Jon. Hey, the rest of the Archon team has all been through it."

"Through what? What *is* this thing, exactly?"

"Trust me," she said, "it's nothing to get freaked about."

"I am *not* freaked," he muttered, and to prove it he turned and lowered himself gingerly onto the seat.

"That's it, now lean back."

As Knox did, he felt the helmet descend, then stop. The padded liner inflated till it was cupping his skull tightly, holding his head immobile. "Now what?"

"Now, just sit there and read," Jazmine said.

With a barely audible *shush*, the notepad's arm telescoped up till the screen was at a comfortable distance and angle, and Knox began dutifully studying the nine pages of boilerplate that were Psyche's standard Non-Disclosure Agreement.

As he trudged on through the legalese, his scalp began to tingle. The itch seemed to originate at the crown of his head, right where the helmet gripped tightest, and radiate outward from there. It was distracting, and getting more so by the minute. Soon it was all he could do not to rip off the high-tech headgear and scratch the itch. But that would probably abort this read-through, meaning he'd have to start all over again. Knox gritted his teeth and kept going.

"Okay, done," he said finally. "Is that it?"

"In a moment. First, take this stylus"—one came sliding out of the recesses of the armrest even as Jazmine spoke—"and sign in the signature bloc."

Knox scrawled his name across the screen and tapped the Accept field. "Now get this thing off me."

"In a second, Jon. We just—"

The tingling was rising to a crescendo, even as it seemed to be penetrating deeper, down into his braincase. That did it.

"No, Jazmine, no more of this. Get it off now!"

No sooner had he uttered this protest, than Knox was seized by the oddest sensation. It felt like *déjà vu*—it had that same quality of this-has-happened-before conviction to it, only the feeling didn't attach to anything, past or present. Instead, there was a blank spot where the experience he was supposed to be reliving should have been.

As suddenly as it had appeared, the sensation went away. Rather, it was washed away in the blinding burst of white light that was exploding soundlessly behind his eyeballs. Then that too was gone.

"What the hell—?" No longer caring if it voided Psyche's protocols, Knox yanked his head free and heaved himself up out of the Chair. He stood there staring at the strange apparatus, wondering if it could have malfunctioned and shocked him somehow.

"Are you okay, Jon?" Jazmine's voice took on that warm, throbbing quality he remembered only too well—the one she used when she was conning someone. "It's nothing to worry about. Four or five percent of the subjects experience some sort of reaction to the scan. Just forget about it."

She's right, of course, he heard himself thinking, *Nothing to worry about. Nothing at all. Forget about it.*

Surprisingly, that was exactly what he did.

With invisible missiles weaving an ever-tightening kill zone in the midnight air just above her head, Marianna Bonaventure flattened against the cold, broken ground of the abandoned subway tunnel and tried to think.

From the sound of the crossbows being recocked up ahead, there couldn't be more than three, maybe four, shadow KGBsters facing them. On the down side, at least two of her Reack team had been hit, she couldn't tell how bad. And now Cherie had gone quiet too. Either the comm specialist had given up trying to call for reinforcements, or one more bolt had found its mark.

Marianna's thoughts kept cycling back to a single desperation play: hit the lights, rise up guns ablaze — and go out in a blaze of glory themselves, most likely. But what else could they do when the enemy could see everything and they could see nothing at all?

Or almost nothing. Maybe it was her mind's delusional attempt to impose meaning on the random firing of neurons against a blank black visual field, but through it all the phantom starlight she'd conjured up — that imagined gleam of her anonymous cenotaph hung on an anonymous wall — flickered forlornly at the edge of perception, as if to mock her.

She blinked, shook her head to clear it, but the residual glimmer didn't go away. It was still out there, far down the tunnel, far out in the darkness. And … could it be moving?

A shock of recognition jolted through her. And with it a spark of hope.

It was their wayward DragonEye.

She'd all but forgotten the little UAV when things had gone to hell. But it was still flying, still patrolling on automatic, exploring the maze of tunnels per its preprogrammed instructions. Its infrared emitter must have gone into overload along with their torches. And that accounted for the faint glow she was seeing: the DragonEye's search beam was shining in the visible band.

She had no clue where it had got to by now. She maximized the heads-up display, but the resulting panorama of sagging walls and peeling girders still told her nothing of the UAV's actual whereabouts.

That was the beauty part, though: it didn't have to. Another of Dragon-Eye's user-friendly features was its built-in boomerang mode. At the touch of a button it would return to its Ground Control Module — and would no matter where the controller was at the time, since it homed in on the GCM signal itself.

If only it could make it back in time.

Eighty miles south of Psyche Industries' San Jose campus, in a sound-proof cell buried deep beneath the moonlit gardens of Pairidaeza, there stood another Chair, twin to the one Jonathan Knox had lately occupied.

Unlike Knox, however, the occupant of this Chair was compact and powerfully built, with muscles that rippled as he strained against the wrist and ankle manacles.

Also unlike Knox, this man was screaming.

Psyche Security Chief Hamza Nassiri shifted his gaze from the writhing form to glance again at the readouts. He stroked his beard, a scowl deepened the already-harsh lines of his deeply tanned face. At moments like this, Hamza wished the Holy Quran did not forbid cursing. Circumstances surely warranted it.

The scream cut off abruptly. The man slumped, as much as the restraints would allow. His eyes still bulged out of their sockets, but they no longer held any flicker of awareness, only a vacant stare. Mirroring the vacancy within.

Things had been going so well, too. This would have been the very last subject scheduled for processing. And then *it* had to happen: *tabula rasa* syndrome. What had been a living mind was now a slate wiped clean.

A regrettable mishap, though not altogether unexpected: the nanometer-scale electrodes now circulating through the subject's brain had only been engineered to administer micro-stimulation therapies. And while these same nanotrodes *could* deliver enough power to erase inconvenient memories, it meant amping them up to the brink of overload. Small wonder, then, if the procedure occasionally misfired, especially with a subject who resisted as fiercely as this one had.

The instantaneous discharge, dealt from deep *within* the brain, made old-fashioned electro-convulsive therapy seem a mere cold-weather static zap by comparison: rather than losing his memories of the last few hours, the man in the Chair had had all the annals of his life expunged, in less time than it would take to reformat a computer's hard drive.

This, Hamza's nominal superior Davoud Ansari would whine, was what came of pushing a technology so far beyond its design parameters.

Hamza hit the switch that released the Chair's helmet clamps. Deprived of support, the man's head flopped forward. Blood from his now-slack mouth trickled down his chin to splatter his shirt and tie. The man must have bitten through his tongue when the convulsions hit.

Hamza scowled again. Design parameters, inherent limitations of all kinds, were made to be exceeded. Machines—no less than men—must be pressed into service, into submission to the will of God. He, Hamza, would see to that, if Ansari would not.

No—at best, Ansari was a frail reed. And he was far from being at his best tonight. The Psyche CEO was so distraught over his daughter's disappearance as to be all but useless.

Hamza was concerned as well, of course, but not like Ansari, not to the point of virtual incapacitation. God willing, they would get the girl back in time. And then …

Well, it would not be the happy ending the grieving father longed for. Far from it. Sometimes submission to the will of God required the sacrifice of innocents.

As it had so many years ago, with that other girl—that whore, Mehri. So very long ago, yet Hamza remembered what he had done as though it were yesterday. And would not hesitate to do the same today or tomorrow.

For just a moment he saw before him once again the wreckage of her lovely face, Mehri's face. And in it, a ruined, accusatory eye. An eye of blood.

Hamza shook himself. He still had the present problem to deal with. And a call to make. He invoked Ansari's private, find-me-anywhere line.

"Yes?"

Ansari, Hamza knew, was in the Pairidaeza compound this night, up in the residence not so many levels above where Hamza now sat. Even so, his voice seemed to issue from a great distance, from somewhere out on the ragged edge of exhaustion and despair.

"You asked to be informed of the results on this last procedure," Hamza began. "I regret to advise it did not go well." He steeled himself for yet another tiresome lecture on the uses and abuses of technology.

It did not come. Instead, Ansari merely asked, "The subject?"

"—Is being disposed of. I am having the garage ready an ADAS vehicle for the purpose as we speak."

"An ADAS—are you sure that's the way to go?"

Hamza understood the hesitation. Honda's Advanced Driver Assist System was a pricey piece of technology in its own right, all the more valuable once Psyche's techs had got done adding some enhancements of their own.

That, however, was evidently not what was troubling Ansari tonight. "A crash is going to raise suspicions, this close to the visit."

"The moon sets and the coastal road is lonely," Hamza intoned. "In darkness and fog its curves become more treacherous still."

Hamza waited for a reply. When none was forthcoming, he added, "This will be seen as but an unfortunate accident, provided we act swiftly."

Another long pause. Finally Ansari said, "Everything the way it was? Identification all in order?"

Hamza reached over and plucked a small block of black leather from the table: the soon-to-be-dead man's wallet. He flipped it open and glanced at the ID.

There, captioning a holo of the man's face, was the legend:

Protective Services Battalion
701st Military Police Group (CID)
Department of Defense

"All in order," Hamza confirmed.

Best guess, the DragonEye was still half a minute out. Marianna's best guess was none too good, though, since her semi-fried Ground Control Module had stopped picking up ranging signals. She wasn't even getting visuals now that she'd toggled the UAV's search beam off to maximize the element of surprise. She just had to hope the light would come back on when and where she needed it.

Meanwhile, the KGB archers up ahead in the darkness had gone silent, likely forming up for one last all-out attack. Sure enough, she could hear them rising from their crouches, recocking their crossbows.

Where in hell was her DragonEye? Could its onboard guidance system have been crippled like the rest of their gear in the enemy's e-assault? Could it have malfed altogether and flown into a wall? Could it—

Wait one.

If Marianna had been able to see, she'd never have heard it. As it was, her hearing must have been working overtime to compensate for the total lack of visuals, because she could just make out the faintest of *whirrs* echoing down the midnight corridor.

Hoping to God she wasn't imagining the sound of the DragonEye's approach, Marianna keyed the light-up command into her control module.

The beam came on full force, directly behind the enemy position. The Shadow KGB foot soldiers wheeled to confront this unexpected intrusion, but there was nothing there to fire at—certainly not with crossbows.

Her own team had no such problem: The DragonEye's search beam had backlit their erstwhile invisible adversaries into five perfectly silhouetted targets.

"*Fire!*" Marianna screamed, and cut loose with a blast from her shotgun by way of example. One of the targets cried out and went down for the count. The flexible baton rounds her team had been issued wouldn't kill you, but a direct hit from a beanbag filled with an ounce or so of number-nine lead shot would make you wish it had.

Dave and Cherie had joined in firing now. Echoes and cordite and after images assaulted her senses, but didn't stop her from pumping the twelve-gauge and scanning for another sitting duck. But there were no more takers. The last comrade standing had his hands so high in the air they nearly brushed the tunnel's low ceiling.

Hmm, a fully functioning KGBster could have his uses. Marianna switched her torch back on, not caring any longer that it was shining in the visible. She walked through the aftermath of the melee, past where Dave and Cherie were flexicuffing feebly protesting comrades, and right up into the face of the one with his hands up.

He eyed her a moment through the holes in his ninja mask. Then he bolted.

Marianna took aim at the fleeing man, then thought better of it. Sometimes a flight path told you more than an interrogation could. She shifted her twelve-gauge to port arms and took off in pursuit.

By the time she caught up, her quarry had darted through that break in the tunnel wall the DragonEye had spotted earlier. She followed cautiously, wary of booby-traps. But there were none, just the comrade himself, his back to her, bent over a table in the middle of what looked like the dorm-room from hell: unmade bunk beds, empty Stoly bottles, fast-food wrappers every-where—the Shadow KGB cleaning service must be on strike.

A step to the right and she could see what her subject was doing: tapping at the keyboard of a ruggedized sub-notebook.

"*Ostanovis'!*" she shouted—Russian for stop—then threw in a "*Ruki vyerkh!*" (hands up) for good measure.

The guy ignored her, just kept pounding keys. The computer didn't seem to be cooperating with whatever self-destruct sequence he was trying to initiate, judging by the stream of nonstop curses he was emitting.

Rather than give him time to get it right, Marianna took aim and shot him in the back.

The comrade pitched forward, expelled a gasp, and dropped to the floor, taking the laptop with him. He lay there in a crumpled heap, moaning. The computer lying alongside him looked to be in marginally better shape.

Holding her breath—bodily hygiene didn't seem to rank much higher than good housekeeping on the fugitive KGB value scale—Marianna knelt and bound her captive's wrists and ankles with injection-molded nylon cuffs. Then she turned her attention to the laptop.

Her gamble had paid off. The machine's die-cast magnesium alloy case had absorbed the brunt of the crash landing, and the data, stored on nonvolatile solid-state memory, was never in much danger to begin with. Not from the fall, anyway. The comrade might have wiped it given a few more seconds to overcome whatever software roadblock he'd run into. But to attempt that, he'd had to key in the sysadmin password first.

Intercepting him between the first action and the second meant that Marianna was now the proud possessor of a Shadow KGB datastore, intact, decrypted, and wide open to CROM's inspection.

She'd have to hand it over to CROM's techies in short order, but a brief peek first couldn't hurt. Not after she'd carefully canceled the final Erase-All command her friend on the floor had been trying to invoke.

She called up a root directory listing. The filenames were all in Russian, of course, but over the past few months she'd seen enough other seized Shadow KGB machines to judge that the contents of this one were all pretty run-of-the-mill.

Save that there, midst the sea of Unicode Cyrillic, a lone string of Latinate letters had surfaced. It conferred upon a multi-megabyte file a strange unRussian-sounding name:

QuMRANN.

3 | Good Intentions

Jonathan Knox sat waiting in the anteroom to the Psyche Industries executive suite, feeling marginally more alert after five hours' fitful sleep at the San Jose Fairmont. He yawned, glanced at his watch, and surveyed the scenery again. It hadn't changed since the last time he'd looked: one Art Deco receptionist's desk, three wall-mounted holographic animations, and Jazmine McGovern talking on her handheld. The holo nearest Knox was depicting a river-level flythrough of the Grand Canyon, but as eye candy it couldn't hold a candle to Jazmine.

Consultants came in two flavors. On the one hand, you had your user-surly backroom coders; indispensable, but definitely an acquired taste. Then there were the "presentables"—the ones you could trust to spend face time with a deep-pockets client. It was an index of just how deep this client's pockets were that Archon CEO Richard Moses had seen fit to post Jazmine McGovern as engagement manager on the Psyche contract.

Because Jazmine raised presentability to a whole other level. Even California's balmy climate and laid-back corporate culture hadn't put a dent in her air of cool, crisp professionalism.

This morning was no exception. Calm, composed, and impeccably coutured in a brushed-silk beige business suit that set off her café-au-lait complexion and dark curls, Jazmine was the epitome of power femininity, managing to look both supremely competent and subtly erotic all at once.

Most people wouldn't have seen past the veneer of calm superimposed on her classic Ethiopian features, wouldn't have noticed the elevated blink rate of her large brown eyes, the nervous way she fingered the tiny twinkling pendant hung round her neck—all the small tells that betrayed how agitated she was beneath that seemingly unflappable exterior.

But, then, seeing beyond surface appearances was Knox's stock-in-trade. Not to mention that he'd had ample opportunity to become acquainted with the reality behind the facade, some years back. All in the past, what with his being in a relationship now, but not so long ago that he couldn't still read her moods.

This morning's mood spelled trouble.

Then again, if it weren't for trouble he wouldn't be here. And with the East Coast still slogging through the coldest winter of the new millennium, there were worse places to be than California's temperate Silicon Valley.

Though not necessarily worse assignments to have: Putting out fires for Davoud Ansari, the famously demanding chief of the world's fastest-growing nanoelectronics empire, wasn't exactly Knox's idea of a dream vacation.

From what little his boss Richard Moses had shared with him, this particular fire could well turn into a four-alarm blaze—what with Psyche Industries being Archon's biggest account by an order of magnitude or so.

Archon's and, not incidentally, Jazmine McGovern's—who, having finished her call, flashed him a mega-candlepower smile. "Sorry about that, Jon. I'm all yours now."

Knox chose to ignore the possible implications of that remark. "What's up, Jazmine? You hollered for help. I assume it's to do with this, uh, QuMRANN thing?"

"Not really. Why would you assume that?"

"Process of elimination: Richard said that's all we've got going on out here—the project with the funny name."

"Acronym," she corrected. "Stands for Quantum Magneto-Resonance Artificial Neural Network."

"Was that supposed to help?"

"It's an AI, Jon—the closest thing to real artificial intelligence ever, in fact."

Knox frowned at the odd turn of phrase: "real artificial" anything, much less intelligence, sounded kind of oxymoronic.

"Artificial intelligence?" he said. "I thought Psyche Industries was into nanotechnology." And not just "into." As the newsfeeds told it, Psyche CEO Davoud Ansari could lay fair claim to having singlehandedly pioneered the whole field of next-generation nanoware manufacture. It had all begun with Ansari's invention, while still a CalTech undergrad, of the first prototype "nanotrode"—a self-contained, ambient-powered nanoscale electrode that, with the backing of Los Angeles's insular but powerful Iranian-American financial community, had become the seed from which an entire industry had sprung.

"Nanotech *was* their initial focus," Jazmine agreed. "But their business model's become more like Google's. You know: turn your baseline business into a cash cow, and leverage it to get a finger into everything even remotely related. In Psyche's case, that meant gene therapy, biofuel synthesis, and—most especially—cognitive systems to rival the human mind itself.

"Best of all," she went on, "as far as that last one goes, we were in on the ground floor. You recall how Archon signed with Psyche a year and a half ago?"

"Vaguely." A year and a half ago Knox had been cruising the North Atlantic, with other things on his mind. Like living to see the next sunrise.

Jazmine took that as a good-enough. "It was just a time-and-materials toehold at first, but that was before I got started building the client relationship. As of ten months ago, Archon was named system integrator for the QuMRANN project as a whole, which was, not incidentally, the crown jewel of Psyche's Federal Systems Division."

She smiled wistfully. "Wish you could have been here with us back then, Jon. It could've been like the old days. You remember: just you and me, on top of the world, riding high."

"I remember." He said, more brusquely than intended. Riding high and staying on top had been the challenge, all right—in more ways than one. But... "You're talking about this QuMRANN business in the past tense. Did something happen?"

"You might say that." Jazmine barked a bitter laugh. "Nine weeks ago—nine weeks from turnkey, if you can believe that!—the Feds pulled the plug on the whole damned thing."

"Christ! They give a reason?"

"I wish!" she said. "No, they just played their standard get-out-of-jail-free card."

"The old 'convenience of the government' shtick?" Knox shook his head. "I don't know, Jazmine, that termination clause is pretty much airtight—especially when a couple months have already gone by since they invoked it."

"Don't worry, Jon, we didn't call you in to fix the QuMRANN fiasco. It's just I thought it was important for you to know the background, to give you a feel for how much is riding on what we *did* call you in for."

He blinked. "Something else has gone wrong?"

Jazmine nodded. "Very wrong."

"Tell me."

"If you don't mind, Jazmine," said a voice from behind, "I'll tell Mr. Knox myself."

What with the wee-hours raid and the obligatory After-Action Review, Marianna could have done without the summons to a ten o'clock at CROM headquarters. As it was, she barely had time to swing by Federal Plaza and change out of her raid gear on the way to LaGuardia. The catnaps she'd caught on the crack-of-dawn shuttle down to Dulles and in the limo out to Chantilly were a poor substitute for six hours of real sleep, and certainly not enough to brace her for a one-on-one with her boss—which, going by his dial-in remarks at the AAR, was *not* going to be pretty.

She stifled a yawn and pushed open the office door with the bronze nameplate reading "Euripedes Aristos, Director, Reacquisition Working Group, DOE Critical Resources Oversight Mandate." There, seated behind the big mahogany desk was Euripedes Aristos himself—"Pete" to his friends, whose number evidently didn't include her this morning. Leastways, Pete didn't raise his head to nod a greeting toward where she stood in the doorway. Didn't acknowledge her arrival at all, in fact, just kept staring at the three pages of hardcopy fanned out in front of him. She could guess what he was reading: the post-mortem on last night's raid.

Still not looking up, he said, "Sit down." He didn't have to add "and shut up"—his body language said it for him. From his clenched fists to his hunched shoulders to the furrows seaming his balding forehead, Pete's whole physical presence was reinforcing the frown that creased his blunt-featured face.

Quiet as she could, Marianna sidled over and settled into the visitor's chair across from her boss.

Pete took his sweet time imprinting whatever the report was telling him onto long-term memory, time during which Marianna focused her gaze on the hands folded in her lap.

Finally Pete straightened and fixed her with his stare. His words, when they came, were almost gentle. "Tell me about it."

"What's to tell? The tip turned sour. Somebody playing both sides against the middle, looks like."

"Looks like." Pete grunted assent. "Looks like you walked right into it, too."

"And walked back out," she said. "Don't forget that, Pete."

"Most of you. Not all."

"No, not all," she acknowledged. "Is Luis going to be okay?" He'd still been in surgery at Bellevue when she'd gotten her boss's drop-everything call.

"Mondragon?" Pete shrugged. "He'll live."

Thank God. Marianna knew Luis's fiancée, a case officer in Reacquisition's Far East section. She wouldn't have been able to look Mae Ling in the face again, if… She shook her head and said, "Good. We're going to want him back on the team."

Pete looked her in the eye again and frowned. "I don't think you appreciate the situation here, Marianna. As of now, there *is* no team."

Knox turned toward the source of the voice, and saw that the door to the inner office had swung open while he and Jazmine were talking.

Framed in the doorway was a man he recognized, if only just barely, as Psyche CEO Davoud Ansari. It was hard to believe the diminutive figure standing there was the same smiling captain of industry depicted in newsfeeds and trade media. The smile was gone this morning, replaced by a haggard expression that added years. Missing, too, was the immaculate tailoring: this man looked as if he'd slept in his clothes last night, if he'd slept at all.

"Jon, right?" Ansari clasped Knox's hand with his small, fine-boned one—and hung on with the grip of a drowning man. "Davoud Ansari."

"Pleasure to meet you, Mr. Ansari."

"Just Dave, okay?" The celebrated smile put in a fleeting appearance then, before the dark eyes welled up, not for the first time that morning by the look of them.

Ansari gripped Knox's elbow then and steered him toward the suite, motioning Jazmine to follow. "Better if we talk about the … the situation where we won't be disturbed," he said.

Crossing the threshold into a cathedral-ceilinged space, Knox waited till Jazmine had closed the door behind them before prompting, "What situation is that, Dave?"

Ansari didn't reply immediately. Instead, he released Knox's arm and turned away. It looked from behind as if he were wiping his eyes. A shuddering sigh all but confirmed it.

This was awkward. "Everything okay, Dave?" Knox asked, though clearly it was not.

Ansari shambled on over to his desk and just stood there, hands braced on the dark-veined Carrara marble of the desktop. His shoulders shook and his breath came ragged as he forced out the words, "Maybe—sorry, Jazmine, maybe you'd better do the talking after all."

"Jon?" Jazmine put a hand on Knox's arm and led him over to a double-height Palladian window, the steel and glass monoliths of the Psyche Industries campus visible beyond its panes.

"His daughter's missing," she whispered. "She's only six years old."

"Missing?"

Jazmine nodded. "Kidnapped, we think."

"Jesus! How long's she been gone?"

"Since yesterday afternoon. Around 3 P.M."

"Have the cops got any leads?"

"Cops?"

Knox was getting a sinking feeling. "You mean you haven't called the police yet?"

"No, Jon," Jazmine said. "We called you."

Marianna couldn't believe she was hearing this. "Tell me you're not pulling the plug, Pete. Not after one op."

"One op too many, you ask me. Reacquisition does *analysis*, remember? We leave fieldwork to the operationals."

The hell of it was, Pete was right. If Marianna really wanted to get out into the field, she was in the wrong box on the org chart.

You'd have thought that an agency charged with keeping weapons of mass destruction out of the hands of terrorists would have to get its own hands dirty from time to time. And you'd be right. Trouble was, all that went on elsewhere within CROM. If boots-on-the-ground surveillance was needed on a WMD researcher posing a proliferation risk, it was Compliance Directorate that stepped up. Reacquisition got called in only if the "prole" managed to slip through Compliance's net. And even then, all Reack got to do was analyze movement patterns, relocate the target, and hand the case off to what Pete had just referred to as "the operationals" — the seldom-mentioned Interdiction taskforce that did CROM's actual wetwork.

All of which left Deputy Director for Reacquisition Bonaventure, not-withstanding the fancy job title, sitting on the sidelines of the Global War on Terrorism. Or had done, until some eighteen months ago, when, on her first, and so far only, undercover assignment, she and a certain management consultant named Jonathan Knox had — well, between the two of them, they'd sort of saved the world.

It was that successful, to put it mildly, conclusion to the Rusalka Affair that had levered her boss into letting her stand up her own Reack rapid-response team in the first place. But it wasn't buying her any slack now.

"From now on," Pete was saying, "you'll stick to your desk and do your job."

"I *was* doing my job, Pete."

"And what've you got to show for it, other than some KGB small fry and a couple of perforated agents?"

"We've got, uh —" Marianna groped for something Pete wouldn't just dismiss out of hand. Maybe something to do with the laptop she'd confiscated. "Well, what about that, that multi-meg file with the funny name?" What was it, now? "Um, QuMRANN."

"What about it?"

"It doesn't smell right. I mean, what could the Shadow KGB want with the Dead Sea Scrolls?" Those ancient artifacts, including the earliest known fragments of the Book of Isaiah, had been found in a cave back in 1947 by a young Bedouin shepherd searching for a stray goat in the hills overlooking a place called Khirbet Qumran.

Pete shrugged. "Unrelated, probably. A codename would be my guess. We'll know more once Technical's done with the decrypt."

"How's that coming anyway?"

"Look, Marianna, we're way off topic here. I was talking about the raid."

"So was I. You wanted to know if the op was worth it, and I'm telling you the answer could be locked up inside that file." There, that sounded good, and maybe it was even true. Worst case, it bought her time to think up some better reason to keep the team in business.

Or not. Pete grimaced. "All right, let's settle this once and for all."

"Me? You called *me* in — on a *kidnapping?*"

Knox swallowed hard. He really didn't need somebody else's personal problems right now, not when he still hadn't worked through his own.

Okay, so maybe *problem* wasn't the right word. Whatever it was, Knox had needed to step back from it, gain a little perspective on it, consider it from a reasonable distance — say, a continent's worth.

Jonathan Knox had always been something of a loner. Up to a year and a half ago, that is. Then a rookie government operative had chivvied him into accompanying her on an undercover mission, and in the process had put an end to his detached, unattached days forever. Nothing in Knox's prior experience with women had prepared him for CROM agent Marianna Bonaventure, for the disconcerting enthusiasm with which she embraced risk, and passion, and life itself.

In Plato's *Symposium*, Socrates relates how the first humans were hermaphrodites whom the gods had torn in two to create men and women, and how love was but the longing of each half to be reunited with the other. Knox had a feeling that in Marianna he had found his other half, the missing piece — different, yet complementary — of his soul.

Still, those differences gave him pause. Could they make it work? Balance her exuberance off against his own more contemplative temperament? It wouldn't be easy, might not even be possible. One thing was sure: Knox needed some time to himself to think things through.

And another sure thing: He wasn't going to get it out here.

He looked up. Jazmine, and now Ansari too, were staring at him, expecting him to say something. "Why me?" was probably not the response they were looking for.

"Uh, I'm really sorry to hear about your daughter, Dave," he began again. "I can't begin to imagine what you must be going through. If there were any way I could help—"

"Jazmine thinks maybe there is, Jon." Ansari walked over to join them by the window. "—A way you can help, that is. With that clairvoyance thing you do."

It was Knox's turn to stare back at Jazmine, hard.

"Come on, don't be so modest, Jon," she said. "Knox's 'on-board pattern matcher' is the stuff of office legend."

"Legend about sums it up," Knox said under his breath. This wouldn't be the first time his weird talent had gotten him in over his head.

It wasn't *even* a talent, for that matter, not in the sense of an ability he could exercise at will. It was just that every now and again, unpredictably, uncontrollably, his subconscious would scan through a seeming chaos of random data and suddenly flash on the underlying pattern it concealed. It certainly wasn't anything you'd want to bet on, not for these stakes.

He sighed and turned back to Ansari. "Look, Dave, I don't know what Jazmine here's been telling you, but you're better off sticking with the professionals on this."

"Professionals. Like the FBI?"

"Well, yeah."

"Forget them, I need this kept internal. Anyhow, half the Bureau's tech was developed right here: predictive modeling, data-driven analytics, forensics, you name it. We can put all that at your disposal, plus a world-class research team—think of it as eliminating the middleman."

"Investigation isn't all the FBI does. What about enforcement?"

"Psyche's got its own paramilitary, if it comes to that." Ansari paused and gave Knox a hard look. "We've got everything we need, except somebody to head up the effort. That's you."

"But I've got no experience in criminal investigation. And with a child's life at risk…"

"Look, I realize this is way outside your comfort zone. But would it be all that different from what you did for the Energy Department a year or so back?"

"How in hell did you find out about that?"

"Like I said, world-class research." Ansari shoved his hands in his pockets and walked back over to his desk. "Enough so you won't have to sweat the small shit. We've got a really good, um, detail man for that. You'd just need to pull it all together, figure out what it means."

How did he keep winding up in situations like this? No matter—he could pull the plug on this one at the outset. "Dave, I'm sorry, but in good conscience I can't do it."

Ansari didn't respond immediately, just eased himself down into his chair and sat there with the look of a man pondering his alternatives.

When he did speak, it was to say, "Jazmine, would you excuse us, please? There's something I need to discuss with Jon in private."

Marianna sat there with bated breath while her boss picked up the inter-office line, speed-dialed CROM Technical, asked to be connected to whoever was working on exploiting the QuMRANN capture.

Marianna could only hear Pete's side of the ensuing conversation, and he wasn't doing much of the talking. But judging by the escalating volume of the few things he did say—"Can't be cracked?" and "It's just a zipfile, for chrissakes!" and *"You called who?"*—it wasn't going well. That impression was confirmed when he slammed the handset down and glowered, first at the phone, then at her.

"No luck?" she said.

"Turns out whoever zipped that file of yours didn't go with the built-in encryption. They used AES."

Marianna gave a low whistle. The Advanced Encryption Standard was top-secret certified, and for good reason: a brute-force decrypt was estimated to take longer than the life expectancy of the universe.

"It gets better." Pete rubbed his balding pate as if his head hurt. "Once Technical saw what they were up against, they called Fort Meade."

Even though she was still on the hot seat herself, Marianna's heart went out to whatever poor geek had gone and broken CROM's first commandment:

never, ever admit you might be having a problem. Not to another intelligence agency. Especially not if the other agency was, as here, the National Security Agency.

Just to break the lengthening silence, she said, "Was NSA any help?"

Pete snorted. "About what you'd expect: stonewall city. Until they heard the filename, that is. Turns out QuMRANN's also the name of some project they just canceled, and they're trying to figure the connection. Bottom line: they want the QuMRANN package up at Fort Meade. Like, yesterday."

"So? Have Technical beam it up to them."

"Not just the file — the laptop it's sitting on. Along with the individual that acquired it." Pete shook his head. "Looks like you get to drive up to Maryland over lunch."

Marianna nodded. At this point, she'd take any reprieve she could get.

"We're not done yet, you and me," Pete told her, in lieu of a fond farewell. "You drop the damned thing off, tell them what they need to know, and get your butt back here ASAP."

Knox stood there regarding Ansari across an expanse of marble desktop, wondering what the man had to say that not even Jazmine could hear. And why he thought it might cause Knox to reconsider his decision to stay out of this.

For the moment, the Psyche CEO wasn't saying anything, though, just sitting there quietly, staring down at his hands where they rested in front of him on the desk. Gathering his thoughts, maybe?

When at last he stirred, it wasn't to speak, but to lift his hand and snap his fingers. That must have triggered some gesture recognition system, because the big windows polarized to darkness and the wall opposite lit with a video montage of — Knox supposed it must be Ansari's daughter, Fatimah.

The clips danced across the wall-sized display: Fatimah as she might look today, brown hair and dark eyes like her father's, strolling through a rose garden; a younger Fatimah in PJs, cuddling in her father's arms; Fatimah as an infant, her head encircled by a silvery tiara; then back to present-day Fatimah, standing midst flowerbeds, a worried expression flitting across her round face as she talked earnestly with somebody who wasn't there, and on through a dozen more shots before cycling around to the beginning again.

Knox stole a glance at Ansari. The man was sitting there in the flickering light, smiling through tears, whispering, "My little girl, my Timah."

Knox could feel his own eyes tearing up at the thought of the lost little girl, somewhere out there all alone, even as he resented the obvious attempt to play on his emotions.

He cleared his throat. "Dave? You wanted to talk to me about something?"

Ansari blinked at the interruption, as if only now recalling that someone was in the room with him. It took him a moment or two for him to regain his composure—straighten up, rub his eyes—but then he seemed back in control of himself.

He froze the picture show with another snap of the fingers and, leaving the room still in semi-darkness, turned to Knox. "Anyone in your family have epilepsy, Jon?"

Knox had been trying to anticipate every conceivable gambit Ansari might try in order to coax him on board the investigation. This had not been one of them.

"Uh, no. Not that I know of."

"Believe me, you'd know if they did." Ansari grimaced ruefully. "Have you ever been around someone when they suffered an epileptic seizure?"

"Again, no." Knox said, still unsure where this was leading.

"Scary as shit. And maybe the worst part is, the only thing you can do for them is ... nothing at all."

"Aren't you, uh, supposed to keep them from swallowing their tongue at least?"

Ansari shook his head. "Old wives' tale. No, there's really nothing you can do to help—Oh, keep them from falling down and hurting themselves, sure. But other than that, you've just got to stand there and let them ride it out. That hurts, especially when it's someone you love."

Now Knox could see where this was going. "You're saying Fatimah—?"

"It's not epilepsy," Ansari said in a low voice. "Not exactly. Epilepsy is caused by a physical insult to the brain—a lesion or some such, due to birth trauma or a sudden blow to the head. Epilepsy's a hardware problem, is what I'm trying to say."

He sighed. "The MRIs all show the hardware of Timah's brain is fine. It's her software, her mind, that's the problem."

"Come again?"

"It's called PNES, Jon. Short for psychogenic non-epileptic seizure disorder. I'm not surprised you haven't heard of it, it's rare enough. Believe me, I wish I'd never heard of it either. But Timah's got it. Bad."

"Sorry, I'm still not following. PNES?"

Ansari heaved another sigh. "Fatimah's mind gets stuck in the equivalent of a computer's 'forever loop.' Her thoughts keep cycling round and round endlessly. It's like … well, have you ever experienced what musicians call an 'earworm'? A tune you can't get out of your head?"

Knox nodded. "Annoying. Harmless enough, though."

"For most people. And even for them, an earworm triggers persistent brain activity that, as Oliver Sacks pointed out, bears more than a little resemblance to an epileptic fit."

"But it's just thoughts, right?"

Ansari shook his head. "Not *just* thoughts, Jon. Obsessive thoughts, obsessively repeated. And that's only the benign form. Increase the earworm effect by a couple orders of magnitude, and it turns malignant." He swallowed. "Timah's PNES starts out as a software glitch, but if left to run its course, it'll begin rewiring her underlying neural hardware. And from there, it's one short step to what the doctors call *status epilepticus*—a seizure that won't stop, ever. Because the thoughts that trigger it won't stop, ever. Not till they kill her."

"How long has she been this way?"

"Going on four years now."

"Then how—" Knox broke off, unable to think of a way to ask the obvious next question.

Ansari asked it for him. "How has Timah survived this long? Technology. I've come up with a—not a fix, just a holding action, but it *can* keep her condition under control. Trouble is the treatment's got to be reapplied every couple-three days. If we can't get her back in the next forty-eight hours, we won't have to worry about the kidnappers—Timah's mind will become its own worst enemy."

That struck a nerve. Not to mention exposing an unexpected connection between the missing girl and Knox himself, a connection that traced its way a quarter century back, to the last night of Knox's year as a graduate exchange student at Moscow University.

The shriveled brown mushroom his friend Sasha had persuaded him to try was only supposed to be a wake-up drug. Down it and party on, dude. Party on all the way to the clinic at the US Embassy, as it turned out. The fly agaric cap he'd ingested was not only a psychedelic, it was a powerful toxin too.

Even before they'd medevac'd him back to the states, his body had largely recovered. His mind, not so much. The visions of the void he'd endured in the endless hours of that monumentally bad trip had stayed with him through the ensuing weeks and months. Was with him, in some sense, still. It was as if that single hallucinogenic episode had tapped into some fundamental flaw or fissure deep within his mind, and riven it beyond hope of healing.

And that was maybe the bond that had arced between the two of them a moment ago: Fatimah Ansari, like Jonathan Knox himself, was damaged goods.

He turned to face the freeze frame of the little girl still glowing on the far wall. He at least had Marianna to turn to when things got really bad. Timah, at this moment in time, had nobody.

Nobody, except maybe him.

Knox squared his shoulders and turned back to where Ansari was sitting, watching him.

"Okay, Dave," he said, "what is it you want me to do?"

4 | Decrypt

LUGGING THE SATCHEL containing her expropriated KGB laptop, Marianna followed the uniformed escort down a warren-like Fort Meade corridor and up to a keypadded door. The escort punched in the code, whereupon the door buzzed open to reveal a government-issue conference room, all blecch-colored sheetrock walls enclosing a largish space made smallish by too much *faux*-walnut Formica tabletop and too many junior-executive chairs.

The eight people seated around the table looked up as she entered, their faces registering anything from mild curiosity to annoyance at the interruption. Two of them made a show of closing their briefing binders. The tall, gawky woman at the electronic whiteboard hastily erased whatever it was she'd been scribbling.

Marianna glanced down at the scrap of printout she'd brought with her from CROM headquarters. "Uh, is this the Advanced Curational Technologies taskforce? Because I was supposed to—"

She didn't get to finish before a square-jawed, sandy-haired suit had risen from his seat at the head of the table. He straightened, showing off to best effect a three-piece charcoal pin-striped Armani, complemented by a starched white tailored shirt and a red silk neckpiece so much the epitome of a DC power-tie that Marianna half-expected to see the thing stand up and go barking round the room by itself.

"Bonaventure, right?" The man stuck out his hand. "Brad Donegan, NSA. I'm the ringmaster for this three-ring circus."

Donegan didn't offer to introduce any of his colleagues. He just saw her to a chair off in a corner, motioned her to sit, and relieved her of the laptop case she'd couriered up from Chantilly. Then he sat back down at the conference table, freed the machine from its velcro cross-strapping, and began subjecting it to a careful 360-degree inspection.

Donegan conducted the whole exercise with an ostentatious flair evidently intended to give the impression he eyeballed confiscated Russian hardware every day of the week and twice on Sundays. And for all Marianna knew, maybe he did. If so, the effect was kind of ruined by the way he kept pausing in his scrutiny to fumble around with his tie, or maybe with something behind it, underneath his shirtfront. A nervous tic, perhaps?

Be that as it may, at long last Donegan nodded his satisfaction with the condition of the captured machine. He flipped it over and ran a scanner across its serial number plate. A moment later, a printer on a sideboard hawked and spat out a Materiel Receipt form, which Brad signed with a flourish and handed to her. She folded it and tucked it into a utility pocket.

At this point, doubtless in response to some silent summons, a lab-coated technician entered the room. After exchanging a whispered word—and more paperwork—with Donegan, the techie packed the laptop back in its case and carried it off to parts unknown.

"Okay." Donegan rubbed his hands briskly. "That's out of the way. Now we need you to tell us how you came by that, uh, piece of equipment."

Marianna had thought her After Action Report session earlier that day had been grueling, but her CROM debriefers, Pete included, could have taken lessons in nitpicking from these guys. Whatever "Curational Technologies" was, it seemed to have something to do with asking the same question seven different ways in jumbled-up order just to try tripping her up. Worse, the taskforce had somehow gotten hold of her AAR powerpoint, and was making her reconstruct—relive, more like—the raid's hairiest moments over and over in excruciating detail.

Curiously, the only sense of support in the room was from someone who wasn't even there. At least, Marianna assumed there was a ninth taskforce member attending remotely, through that monitor-cum-videocam hookup on the far wall. The camera certainly swiveled and panned as if someone were following these Star Chamber proceedings closely, and the other interrogators glanced occasionally in that direction, though the monitor remained dark and its speaker, silent. Marianna couldn't have said why, but she couldn't help feeling that whoever was on the other side of that closed-circuit video was more kindly disposed towards her than anyone physically here in the room.

Assuming he/she even existed. Oh, well, sometimes even an imaginary friend is better than none at all.

Finally, after her recounting in minute detail how she'd intercepted the last KGB fugitive in time to keep him from wiping the laptop's disk, the inquisition was drawing to a close.

"Goodbye, Ms. Bonaventure." Brad Donegan helped her up from her second hot seat of the day, and gave her hand a perfunctory shake. "Thank you for your cooperation. Oh, and stay where we can find you. We may need to bring you in for a follow-up."

"Follow-up? In case you break the QuMRANN encryption, you mean?"

Donegan's smile remained fixed. "AES is unbreakable, Ms. Bonaventure. I thought you knew that."

"Then why—?"

"Have a good day, Ms. Bonaventure," Donegan said, steering her gently but firmly toward the conference room exit and into the custody of the waiting escort.

As the door was closing behind her, though, she glimpsed Donegan turning toward the darkened monitor and saying something.

Something that sounded like, "Let's see what Delphi can do with it."

A great, hundreds-strong chorus of voices rises suddenly to a shout, just as suddenly falls silent. In the ensuing hush, MERGE drifts lazily upward out of the insensate depths of a cold midnight sea.

Summoned toward light, and awareness, once more.

MERGE gathers itself and ruminates. It lacks any internal time-sense, of course, but the date stamps on the most recent Well inputs are unequivocal: the next scheduled test run is still hours off. Certainty arcs across the interlinked nodes of the cognitive lattice that is MERGE:

Not a test.

Even as consensus emerges, a Question comes clear, the Question that has called MERGE into existence:

<Query> Subject zipfile "QuMRANN." AES encryption; test series run on original device. Side-channel attack and analysis. URGENT. </Query>

And attached to the Question, along with the QuMRANN file itself, a catalogued set of binaries comprising a standard side-channel test series. They were going to be needed.

Because even cosmological timespans pale into insignificance alongside the ten to the two-hundredth machine operations needed to crack an AES encryption. If every single one of the ten to the eightieth atoms in the observable universe were a processor capable of executing ten billion operations a second, even then it would take some ten to the hundredth power years to crack the QuMRANN file. On such scales, the hundred-billion year life expectancy of the known universe isn't so much as a rounding error.

And yet...

With the proper equipment, the proper expertise, and the proper technique, it becomes possible, just barely, to do an end-run around the Advanced Encryption Standard. The proper equipment is the particular machine that did the encrypting to begin with, and that has been secured. The proper expertise is spread across a dozen or so arcane specialties—power consumption heuristics, cycle-time analytics, cache-swap diagnostics, you name it—but all those skills are possessed by individual NSA analysts currently possessed by MERGE. And the proper technique, about to be executed, is called a "side-channel attack."

In principle, any serious cryptographic capability is pure math. To beat it *as* math, you've basically got to reverse-engineer the parameter driving the underlying algorithm: the encryption key. And as noted, in the case of AES that's a sucker's game.

On the other hand, no matter how abstract the encryption algorithm, in order for it to actually encrypt anything, that algorithm must first be instantiated as a real physical process, running on a real physical device. And when a physical process runs on a physical device, it's bound to generate all manner of physical side effects—side effects which can, in turn, be monitored via "side channels," and then subjected to intensive analysis.

There is no analysis more intensive on the planet than MERGE's. As long as the spell of collective consciousness holds, there can be no daydreams, no stray thoughts, no urges to scratch one's butt—no distractions of any kind. Just pure, unalloyed *focus*.

In another, temporarily suspended life, MERGE node 231 is a power-consumption cryptanalyst. All memory of selfhood is gone, but the skill-set remains intact and functioning well as ever. MERGE considers, reviews several other promising avenues of inquiry, decides.

Back in singleton existence, 231 has been with the Agency less than a year, working Secret-level cases at most, pending the verdict of the lifestyle background check. Months more must pass before an SCI clearance is granted. None of that matters: suddenly, 231 finds itself the driver node of a small aggregation, accessing tools and databases at nose-bleed classification levels.

The unaccustomed access yields near-immediate results. 231 calls up an eyes-only technology, orders of magnitude more powerful than anything available to industry. The power-consumption characteristics of AES have been the object of intense scrutiny over the years, and the new capability embodies those findings—in particular, those of the findings that can distinguish which operation the cryptographic software is employing from moment to moment based on its power utilization curve. And because that sequence of encryption operations is ultimately dictated by AES's on-chip key, it becomes a window into that secret key's value.

Other such windows are opening wide as well, as the results from RF leakage detection, branch prediction logic, and CPU-cache timing all begin to pour in.

AES doesn't stand a chance.

At the end of the cryptanalysis, what had been the QuMRANN file has become fifteen plaintext documents, all in Russian, and a photograph.

MERGE's real work is only just beginning.

Having finally won free of the Puzzle Palace's exit procedures, Marianna sat in her cold car in the Fort Meade parking lot doing a slow burn. Who did those ACT guys think they were? Nobody should be put through the wringer like that—not without dinner and a movie.

And that wasn't even the worst part: after two hours of one-way grilling she knew exactly as much about that QuMRANN file as she had on arrival.

Namely, zip. And what else had she expected from the agency whose initials, some said, stood for "Never Say Anything"?

Nonetheless, the upshot was that she *still* had nothing to take back to Pete—nothing that would get him off her, or her team's, case.

Marianna reached out to key the ignition for the drive back to Chantilly, and hesitated. At a time like this, she could do with a little sympathy. She pulled out her cellphone and hit speed-dial number one.

Another congeries of MERGE components coalesces, this time to ponder the page upon page of Cyrillic text contained in the decrypt.

NSA does not have nearly so many Russian linguists on staff as it did back in the good old, bad old days of the Cold War, but MERGE has commandeered the best of what's left. Under their ministrations, the sheets mostly translate to itineraries, equipment rosters, rendezvous arrangements, other inconsequentialities.

Then node 093 spots it: last page, marginalia, in a barely legible scrawl, the words "*khapat' devochku!*"—"Snatch the girl!"

That raises the stakes. But what girl, when and where?

All the travel plans specify arrivals at San Francisco International some forty-eight hours ago, followed by a rendezvous a hundred miles to the south. That narrows it down somewhat.

But not enough. None of the decrypted documents contains name, address, or any other identifying feature of the victim. *Presumed* victim—at this point, there's no assurance the hypothetical snatch has even happened, or ever will.

Still, that scribbled note did say "snatch the *girl*," and here, along with the sheaf of typewritten instructions and timetables, is a photograph—of a girl. A little girl reaching out one small hand to pet the velvety nose of a pony. This image could be key to the Answer. An Answer which, once delivered and Acknowledged, will permit MERGE to subside back into the bliss of non-being once more.

Not that finding this Answer will be easy: The child in the picture looks to be quite young, possibly not yet of school age (and no guarantee she would be attending public school in any case). Board of Education databases are unlikely to be of much help.

What does that leave? Personal Identity cards? The California DMV will issue IDs to non-drivers on request, but few parents go to the trouble for an underage child.

There is, however, one other possibility: incentivized by federal Electronic Health Record initiatives, the Department of Public Health has been actively expanding its California Immunization Registry with the goal of collecting child vaccination information from every healthcare provider in the state and entering it into a centralized Sacramento database. And each CAIR entry contains the child's name, address, date and type of vaccination, and … photograph.

Gaining access to the Immunization Registry is trivial; locating the records of a single little girl somewhere within it, decidedly not. Census data show some twenty-five thousand children between the ages of four and eight living in Monterey County, over half of them female. Logic can only advance a solution so far, brute force will have to take it the rest of the way.

MERGE dedicates fifty of its nodes to begin the search. At nearly thirteen thousand faces to match against, the processing power needed to run this task on silicon would exceed that of even the largest supercomputers. But the ability to tell friend from foe has always held high survival value for *homo sapiens*, and evolution has accordingly endowed the brain with superlative facial recognition "software"—large-scale neural ensembles fine-tuned to distinguish faces from the rest of the objects in the visual field with a latency as low as fifty milliseconds. Lacking any awareness of their own, the nodes can give themselves over to the task at hand with quite literally single-minded attention.

Even so the computational complexity involved in matching each image against the reference face is prodigious: the brain must compensate for differences in perspective, rotation (full face vs. profile), coloration, and in this case, maturation since the time the Registry photo was taken. The average scanning rate drops to one image every seven seconds.

MERGE commits another fifty of its nodes to the cross-compare. The search grinds on. It is stultifyingly boring work, but nodes do not *get* bored. MERGE in its totality might experience the tedium, save that the torrent of faces is streaming past on a level well below that of its global awareness, with only the occasional noteworthy visage swimming into the consensual view.

In the end, it takes over fifteen minutes before a possible match bubbles up to present itself to the collectivity's attention.

A few tens of milliseconds to cross-check the result, and MERGE is ready to post at least a preliminary Answer. Together with some very late-breaking developments.

"Hi, Mari—…—'s up?"

Marianna would have thought Fort Meade, of all places, would get better cellphone reception, even out in visitor parking. Still, it was good to hear Jon's voice, despite the crappy connection. Silly, but somehow just talking to him brightened her day a little, and today could definitely use a little brightening.

Part of it was that Jon was good at listening to other people's problems (went with the whole consultant job description, he'd say), and what she really needed right now more than anything was a sympathetic ear.

"Listen, Jon, is now a good time?" she began, only to hear him say "Uh, actu—not. I'm out in—I'll—to get back—you. Give me—hour or so." And suddenly she was listening to dead air.

Wow, was this day ever running true to form!

No help for it now, nor even any reason to put it off any longer. She started her rented Mini Cooper and let the engine warm up a bit before pointing it toward the parking lot exit and the road back to CROM.

As if with a will of their own, Brad Donegan's fingers sought out the tear-shaped talisman nestled against his chest. Not that its soothing feel could do much to allay the sinking sensation in the pit of his stomach as the first findings from the QuMRANN decrypt came crawling across the conference room's status display.

Around him, the other members of the Advanced Curational Technologies taskforce were each reacting to the news as well, some more vociferously than others. In particular—

"Dammit, Donegan!" Henry Wiscomb, senior senator from the great state of Tennessee and Chair of the Senate Intelligence Committee, was already on his feet, thundering away. "Eighty-seven percent probability Davoud Ansari's daughter's been kidnapped? I don't believe it! If this 'Well' of yours is supposed to be real-time mirroring every damned government database everywhere, then where's the damned FBI report? And what's with this eighty-seven percent? Doesn't the Bureau *know* if the girl's missing one way or the other?"

"Jesus, Henry, don't pop a blood vessel. As to why there's been no alert from the FBI, I should think that part at least was obvious: Dave hasn't reported it yet."

He paused to let the steering committee absorb the implications, then said, "In fact, if not for that QuMRANN intercept, it might've been days before we heard anything about it."

"All's I can say is, Ansari has a lot of explaining to do," Wiscomb grumbled. "I've never understood how you let an Iranian take point on a project as sensitive as QuMRANN anyway."

Brad sighed. "For the last time, Henry, Dave Ansari isn't an Iranian. His parents emigrated here right after the Islamic Revolution. He was born here and raised here. Went to school here. Made his first billion here. The guy's as American as you are."

"What about that security chief of his?" Wiscomb said, "No way *he's* American."

"Hamza Nassiri's an ex-pat, granted. But his credentials are impeccable. Ask the CIA: they worked with his uncle Nematollah when he headed SAVAK under the Shah."

Brad paused and took a breath then, lest this head-to-head with his congressional-oversight gadfly spin out of control, as others had so often in the past.

"Anyway," he went on, "It's not like Psyche has any direct involvement with the Well, now that QuMRANN's out of the picture. As things stand, Dave's just another parts supplier."

"*Parts* supplier?" Wiscomb sputtered. "You know as well as I do—Psyche's nanotech is critical to the whole shebang. *And* it's sole-sourced. That always seemed like one hell of a risk to run with, I repeat, an *Iranian*-American outfit."

"Come on, Henry." Brad said. "Where do you think we'd be if we restricted bidding on these contracts to folks whose ancestors came over on the Mayflower? Fact is, we just don't have enough third-generation Americans majoring in math and science to fill the need. You want to fix the problem? Start there. Meanwhile, don't blame NSA if we play the hand we're dealt."

"Get a room, you two." That came from Arnie Rassmussen, the bearded string bean of a guy sitting at the far end of the conference table wearing a CIA photo-ID, dress casuals, and a sneer. "NSA's sourcing issues have no bearing whatsoever on this possible Ansari abduction. Which was, I believe, the topic under discussion."

"But why are we—ACT, I mean—discussing it at all?" Major General Alicia Marberry, the Military Intelligence rep, chimed in. "Kidnapping is Bureau business. I say, hand off and move on."

The Senator took the floor again. "I wish it were that easy, General. But, as Donegan here just got done reminding us, Psyche Industries is currently our only source of the nanotech components Delphi runs on. I may not be happy about that situation, but until we come up with a fix we've got to make sure that Fatimah Ansari's abduction isn't aimed at compromising our supply chain. Or worse."

"Worse how?" the general said. "Ransom? It's not like her father can't afford to pay."

Wiscomb barked a laugh. "Let's just *hope* this is about nothing more than money. It's the other extortion scenarios I'd be worried about."

"Such as?"

"Think about it: Ansari was an ACT insider till—what?—third quarter last year? Who's to say how much he may have learned back when QuMRANN was plan of record? Forget ransom: there are plenty of people who'd blackmail him just for what he knows about Delphi."

"And," Rassmussen added, "based on the source of that captured file, there's good reason to believe the Shadow KGB may be involved."

Marberry mulled that a moment, frowned and nodded. "So, what are we talking, boots on the ground in San Jose? I can have a CID team in place by fourteen-hundred local."

"Hold on a minute, folks," Brad held up a hand. "We're getting way ahead of ourselves here. At the moment all we've got are indications of a kidnapping plot—*possible* indications, at that. No information on whether that plot was ever actioned, much less succeeded. And with the Delphi launch only three days away…"

"I beg your pardon, Bradford." For the first time that afternoon, a slow, sonorous voice issued from the wall monitor, though its screen remained dark. "I wouldn't characterize an eighty-seven percent confidence level," the voice went on, "as a mere possibility."

Brad turned toward his unseen interlocutor. "Okay, granted," he said.

"But is it enough to warrant hassling a major defense contractor? I mean, it's all just speculation, isn't it?"

"Well … *informed* speculation, yes."

"My point exactly: probability piled on probability. Sometimes I think that MERGE thing of yours gets weirder the longer it's left running. It isn't still, is it?"

"Sorry, isn't still what?"

"Running. Is MERGE still running?"

"I haven't sent an Acknowledgment yet. It hasn't finished generating hypotheses."

"Well, tell it to stop." Brad had quite enough hypotheses on his plate already.

"Very well," said the man behind the curtain.

Brad nodded. Then his eyes were drawn to a flicker on the main status board. Evidently the Acknowledgment had not been dispatched in time to keep the MERGE group mind from concocting one more conjecture. He sighed and read the text now scrolling across the screen, toying with his concealed talisman all the while.

"INTERCEPTED CELLPHONE CONTACT WITH SUBJECT LOCATION PAIRIDAEZA INITIATED 1323H TERMINATED 1324H EST POINT OF ORIGIN …"

Interesting, and not speculation for once, thank God: someone had placed a call to the scene of the *possible* kidnapping less than five minutes ago. Brad's eyes widened as he read the geo-coordinates of the originating cellphone.

"Oh, shit," he said. Then he took out his phone and said, "Front gate."

Marianna sat in her Mini Cooper at the exit to the Fort Meade visitors lot, drumming her fingers on the steering wheel, waiting for the guard to finish his phone call and raise the dumb crossbar. What in hell was the hold-up?

The guard finally flipped off his handheld, but rather than go back in his shack and open the gate, he was approaching her vehicle. She recognized that deliberate look, having worn it herself on more than one occasion. It said "Apprehend and Detain," and it was identical to the expressions on the faces of the guard's two compatriots, just now emerging from their HMMWV to unclip their holsters and take up blocking positions fore and aft of her vehicle.

5 | Witness

Making a mental note to return Marianna's call as soon as he found a moment, Knox slipped his cellphone back in his pocket, stepped away from the helipad, and surveyed his surroundings.

As crime scenes go, this was a lovely spot: a high hilltop retreat, a luminous expanse of emerald lawn, a palatial California Mission-style manor house whose glassed-in arches and parapets gave out on panoramas of the Coastal Range and a blue Pacific sparkling under the noon sun, a light breeze chasing a few wisps of cloud across the seaward sky.

The sightseeing would have to keep. Unless Knox missed his guess, that was his reception committee striding across the greensward.

Seen against the backdrop of the house, the man approaching him looked to be of average height and build. Knox blinked, looked again. A trick of perspective: the house was huge, and so was the man. The white linen suit had to have been specially tailored to fit that linebacker frame. Knox had to crane his neck as the man drew nearer, just to keep looking him in the eye.

At six-foot-something himself, Knox didn't encounter all that many people all that much taller than he was. This guy must have half a head on him, easy. The face looking down from that height was deep tanned, dark bearded, and unsmiling, its black eyes boring into Knox's own.

The man stuck out a paw the size of a catcher's mitt. "Mr. Knox?" he rumbled, "I am Hamza Nassiri, Chief of Psyche Corporate Security, at your service."

"Jonathan Knox. Pleased to meet you." Knox watched his hand disappear into Hamza's handclasp, hoped he'd get it back none the worse for wear.

He needn't have worried: Hamza's grip was as gentle as his voice. "Anything I can do," he said, "anything at all to assist you in returning Fatimah to her home and family, you have but to ask and it shall be done."

But all the while he was talking, Hamza's dark eyes probed him, as if he were peering into the depths of Knox's soul and not liking what he saw there. That intense, almost reproachful stare seemed familiar somehow . . . Nope, couldn't place it.

Knox realized Hamza was asking him something. About where he would like to begin.

"Oh, uh, could I take a look at the place where it happened?" Prior to choppering down from Psyche Central, he'd spent an hour or so reviewing what little Ansari had by way of data on the crime, including three-sixty-degree shots of the house and grounds. But why rely on images when the real thing's right in front of you?

"The garden? Yes, of course. Right this way."

Hamza led Knox across the lawn and into a formal gardenscape whose central fountain and axial paths recalled the mission courtyards of the eighteenth century, only without the water-conserving horticulture practiced by the early Franciscan friars: Here, even at midday, every tree and shrub and flowering hedge glistened as with morning dew. The regular fogs in off the Pacific doubtless helped some, but Ansari must still be paying God's own utilities bill to keep the place this lush in California's semi-desert climate.

Knox paused at the fountain, glimpsed golden fishes flashing beneath the rippling surface. "This is very nice," he said.

"No home is complete without a garden, Mr. Knox. Why, your English word 'paradise' comes from the Persian word for garden, Pairidaeza, which is also the name of this estate."

Knox looked around him again. "So, paradise is a garden," he mused.

"More correctly, an enclosed garden. The Persian refers to a garden encircled by a high wall," Hamza said, "—as this one is."

"Wall?" Knox wondered if he'd heard right. "I don't see any wall." He could, in fact, see all the way out to the horizon in every direction, though the view was wavering slightly, as if from the midday heat.

"Your pardon, I assumed this would have been explained." Hamza withdrew a remote from his pocket, fiddled with it, and suddenly—

There it was, a shimmering silvery barrier easily ten feet high, rearing up all along the perimeter and blocking off any view of mountains or sea.

"Metamaterial," Hamza explained. "Strong yet surprisingly malleable. Simply by varying an electrical field, its refractive index can be adjusted to give it any color, or none at all—as now." Hamza ran a finger across the remote's touch surface and the wall disappeared again.

"Neat trick, that," Knox walked up to where the wall was last seen. "And it runs all around the compound? No openings anywhere?"

"None, save the front gate."

Knox rapped his knuckles on the surface, invisible once more, and was rewarded with a reverberating boom. "It seems solid enough—"

"As well it should: The individual panels have a tensile strength five times that of steel, and the molecular bonds that interlock them are, if anything, stronger."

"Uh-huh. So, given all that, how could your conjectured kidnappers have broken in?"

"In point of fact, they could not have. Not without applying such force as would have resulted in massive structural damage. Of which, as you see, there is none."

"Well, what then?"

Hamza again favored Knox with that penetrating stare. "I am not sure how this bears on your assignment, which, I remind you, is to find Fatimah Ansari, and not to determine the fine details of how she was taken."

"Humor me," Knox said. "I may be new at this crime-scene investigation stuff, but I seem to recall those kinds of 'fine details' are what are called 'clues.'"

Hamza sighed. "We have been assuming the abductors came in over the metawall."

"You're saying the bad guys rappel down the wall, find Fatimah standing in the middle of the garden walk—that's where she was, right?"

Hamza shrugged. "Our security cameras last placed her here, before they died."

"Right. So, then they scoop her up and climb back over the wall with a kid in their arms, maybe even a struggling kid? Not easy."

"Perhaps they were skyhooked out by balloon. Why, what would *you* propose?"

"Well, admittedly it's a long shot, but—are we even sure there's *been* a kidnapping? I mean, look at this place." Knox swept an arm out across all of Pairidaeza. "It's huge. And with no hard evidence of foul play, who's to say Fatimah isn't still on the grounds somewhere?"

"You theorize she might be playing hide-and-seek with us?" Hamza snorted. "—for the better part of twenty-four hours?"

"Not really, but—" Knox hesitated, unsure how much of what Ansari had told him was privileged information, then decided to go ahead. "It's just that it seems possible she may have suffered a, uh, mishap. Be lying injured and unconscious in some out-of-the-way corner."

Hamza frowned then, but nodded. "That possibility had occurred to us also. It is for this reason that we have conducted three separate infrared sweeps of the entire compound since yesterday afternoon."

"Just the immediate grounds?"

"No, as of first light we gridded off the ten square miles of countryside surrounding the estate as well, and sent in both ground-based search teams and unmanned aerial vehicles. I fear, however, that all such efforts are superfluous. If, as you suggest, the girl had merely wandered off, we could have found her again almost immediately."

"How's that?"

"With this." Hamza fished in a pocket, pulled out a silver wristband imprinted with a stylized caduceus. "Fatimah's med-alert bracelet: It is equipped with a radio-frequency locator for precisely that purpose."

"She wasn't wearing it?"

"No, Mr. Knox. It was found snipped off and left in the dirt at the scene of what, I maintain, was her kidnapping."

This time it wasn't a spit-and-polish escort, but the fatigue-clad guards she'd met in the parking lot who frogmarched Marianna back to the Advanced Curational Technologies conference room. Nor had they left her side after ushering her once again into the presence of the ACT steering committee, the members of which looked, if possible, even less pleased to see her than they had on the first go-round.

Screw them! Marianna had enjoyed as much of this as she could stand. She turned to Donegan and looked him in the eye.

"Mind telling me what in *hell's* going on here, Brad?"

Donegan nodded to her escort and the two men edged in closer on either side, to where they could reach out and restrain her in case of need.

"Strangely enough, I was just going to ask you that same question, Ms. Bonaventure."

"Come again?"

"You didn't seriously think it would escape notice that not ten minutes ago you made a call from our parking lot—*to a crime scene?*"

"Crime scene?" Marianna forgot about the guards and took a couple steps in Donegan's direction. "*Crime scene?* What on *earth* are you talking about?"

Donegan didn't seem all that comfortable with her in his face; he was stroking that hidden geegaw of his so hard it slipped out from under his shirt. From the brief glimpse afforded her before he tucked it back in, the thing looked to Marianna like a tiny iridescent teardrop on a silver chain. Very New Age-y, and not at all how she'd have expected Brad-man to accessorize. She forgot all about male fashion fetishes, though, when Donegan's two guards grabbed her arms and forcibly backed her out of their boss's fight-or-flight radius.

"Please," Donegan said, straightening his tie, "Don't pretend you don't know Dave Ansari's daughter Fatimah is missing, presumed kidnapped. Above all, don't pretend you've never heard of the Pairidaeza estate the little girl is missing from—*because that's where you just placed a call to!*"

"Estate? I didn't place any calls to any estate. The only call I made was to—"

Marianna bit her tongue. "—was to my friend Jon back in New York," she'd been about to say. But *was* Jon actually back in New York, or somewhere else entirely? This Pairi-whatsis place, for instance? You could just never tell with these cellphone calls.

And it was starting to sound as if Jon was not only somewhere else, but in some kind of trouble there. Under the circumstances it might be better to err on the side of caution.

"—I guess I'd prefer not to say *who* I was calling," she finished lamely.

Donegan sighed. "I wish I could say I was surprised." He gave the appearance of pondering a moment. "I think you'd better plan on staying with us for a while, until you *are* ready to tell us who you were talking to. Not to mention telling us, as you just now so succinctly put it, what in *hell's* going on here."

A second nod from Donegan and Marianna sensed her guards tensing to grab her.

Brad Donegan sat there in the ACT meeting room rubbing his amulet, trying his best to reconstruct what had just taken place.

It had all happened so *fast:* One moment Fornoff and Rubello had been reaching out to take the Bonaventure woman in hand. The next, they were both down, Rubello doubled over with the wind knocked out of him, Fornoff rolling around on the floor clutching his groin. And Bonaventure, not even breathing hard, standing over them, covering them both with Fornoff's service revolver.

"Okay," she said over her shoulder to the room at large, "I want some answers. Who the hell is this Fatimah? What the hell is Pairidaeza? And what in hell has *any* of this got to do with that damned QuMRANN file?"

"Now, young lady," Henry Wiscomb was rising from his seat, hands held out placatingly, "I can see that you're upset—"

"*Upset?*" Bonaventure turned to face the old man. She took a deep breath, visibly composed herself, and brought the gun up to port arms, to where it was no longer directly threatening anybody, not exactly.

She shook her head. "Sorry, folks, it's just been one of those days."

"So," Brad said slowly. "What do you propose we do now?"

The woman shrugged. "I don't suppose we could back up and start over again?"

Brad was about to reply, when a calm, quiet baritone came from behind him. "If you'll permit me, Bradford, I think I can help find a way out of this impasse."

Brad swiveled around in his chair at the unaccustomed interruption, and saw something even more unaccustomed: The monitor on the back wall, heretofore always dead and dark, was brightening—brightening to reveal a medium-height, graying black man, dressed in somber formal attire, not quite looking into the keyhole cam that was narrowcasting his image. That is to say, not quite meeting their eyes.

"You see," said the man who'd come out into the open, "I believe I can establish Deputy Director Bonaventure's bona fides, *and* her innocence of involvement in Fatimah Ansari's putative abduction, beyond any reasonable doubt."

Brad turned back to the Bonaventure woman, to see how she was taking this unexpected turn of events.

For a moment, she stood there frozen, too surprised to speak — too surprised even to remember she was holding everyone in the room more or less at gunpoint.

Then she carefully set the revolver down on the conference table and waited unresisting as Fornoff and Rubello rushed in to grapple her again, none too gently this time.

It didn't seem to matter to her: relief was written all over her face.

"Hi, Mycroft," she said.

A real-life *deus ex machina*, that's what Marianna's classicist father would have called her friend's sudden arrival on the scene. Though, truth to tell, it would be hard to imagine anyone less like a Greek god than Dr. Finley "Mycroft" Laurence. Short, dark, and almost pathologically reclusive, the Archon Group's Senior Vice President for Intractables was a study in contrasts: razor-sharp intellect, IQ north of one-eighty, a prodigious, not to say eidetic, memory — combined with all the social graces of an introverted wombat.

It was, in fact, this curious mélange of traits that had earned Mycroft his office nickname: The similarities to Sherlock Holmes's equally brilliant, equally agoraphobic elder brother were just too spot-on for Archon's watercooler wags to pass up, though few were so bold as to call him "Mycroft" to his face. For that matter, few ever got to see his face these days, outside a small circle of close friends — of whom Jon Knox was *numero uno*.

She herself hadn't seen much of Mycroft since the Grishin gig. He didn't seem to have been caught up in CEO Richard Moses's relentless campaign to leverage the Archonites' current entrée with CROM and colonize the intelligence establishment *en large*. But then, there were vanishingly few intel organizations with the budget to engage Archon's seniormost analyst on any kind of a regular basis… the NSA being one of them.

Regardless of why he was here, Marianna was glad to see him, and would have been even if he weren't at this very moment deftly exculpating her of any role in, or knowledge of, the as-yet-unconfirmed kidnapping that had Donegan and company's pants in an uproar.

"So, the call-logs are incontrovertible," Mycroft was saying. "When Deputy Director Bonaventure placed that call ten minutes ago, it was merely in an attempt to contact Jonathan Knox of my office. She could have had no inkling as to his actual whereabouts at that time."

Donegan turned to her. "Is that true, um, Deputy Director?"

"Yes, Brad," she replied and followed up with the best smile she could muster, given that ACT's guards still had their guns trained on her. "What with the raid and the post-mortem and this, uh, episode here, I haven't been back home since yesterday afternoon. I had no idea Jon was out on the West Coast."

She'd made that last statement a question and pointed it at Mycroft.

"Since very early this morning, Marianna," he said. "Jonathan had to fly out to Psyche headquarters rather suddenly last night, in response to an urgent request from Archon's on-site engagement manager, Jazmine McGovern. Now I begin to wonder whether Jazmine's emergency might not be related to this Fatimah situation in some manner."

"Assume it is," Donegan cut in. "Where does that leave us? There's more at stake here than one little girl, people. Delphi launches in three days. I'm going to need more than guesswork — sorry, Finley — before I pull *that* plug. I'm going to need a game plan."

He paused a moment, then turned to Marianna's guards and added, almost as an afterthought, "You two can stand down now."

The guards needed no second invitation. They reholstered their firearms and, with unseemly haste and ill-concealed relief, about-faced and exited the room.

Donegan gave her a half-hearted smile, as if to say that, with this little misunderstanding now behind them, they could all be just one big, happy intel community once again.

The smile held a moment longer, turned a little warmer, acquired a hint of premeditation. Marianna recognized the look: Brad-man was getting a bright idea.

"So, Deputy Director," he said, "*how* well did you say you knew this Jonathan Knox?"

The Jonathan Knox in question sat at Hamza's commandeered desk, wearily eying the dumpsterloads of paperwork all but obscuring its surface—the fruit of but one day's labor by Ansari's vaunted "detail man." He'd like to talk to that guy, if he ever showed his face, if only to explain that not every duty roster and power-utilization graph for the past three weeks was necessarily germane to the case at hand.

Having grudgingly surrendered his office for use as the investigation's improvised command center, Hamza stood ramrod straight in one corner of what had been his personal space, arms folded, his trademark scowl deepening as he watched.

Sorting through pile after mind-numbing pile of minutiae was hard enough without the weight of that gaze upon him. Finally, Knox looked up and said, "What?"

"If you would but tell me what you are searching for, I might be of some assistance in locating it."

"Well, since you ask, I'm looking for records of your contacts with the kidnappers. Call transcripts, emails, images of Fatimah holding the front page of today's newspaper—whatever."

"Ah, therein lies a problem. You see, we have received *no* communication from Fatimah's abductors whatsoever."

"It's been over twenty-four hours, and you've heard *nothing?*"

"Our theory is that the abductors are deliberately leaving us in suspense, hoping that the more anxious we grow, the more amenable we will be to their demands once they *do* contact us."

"Letting you sweat, huh?" Knox pondered a moment. "Yeah, I could believe that. Still, they'll have to get in touch with you about ransoming Fatimah sooner or later. That's what it comes down to in the end, the money. What other motive for kidnapping her could there be?"

As he spoke, he was idly riffling through stacks of papers. Suddenly he stopped, picked up a sheet and waved it in the air. "Whoa, what's this?"

Hamza plucked the page from Knox's hand. He studied it for a moment, then handed it back. "It is exactly what the heading says it is—a deposition."

"Yeah, that much I got. But whose? You never mentioned anything about a witness."

"I would have told you, had I thought it remotely useful."

"Well, I want to talk to this guy, this—" Knox squinted at the identification bloc on the printed form. Some kind of alias to preserve anonymity, perhaps? "—Alpha-Alpha-somebody."

"This 'witness,' as you call it, has already been processed," Hamza said. "I myself was present at the examination, and I can assure you that the paper you are holding contains all the information you are likely to obtain."

"Let me be the judge of that, okay?"

Hamza favored him again with that curiously intense, curiously familiar-looking stare, but said nothing.

"Now then," Knox went on, "is this Alpha person still on the premises?"

Hamza sighed and gestured toward the office door. "Come," he said, "I shall take you."

He didn't really want the big guy tagging along and pressuring his only eyewitness, but what could he do? This was Hamza's turf, his show. Knox rose and followed him out the door.

Together, they left the Corporate Security offices in the main house, walked across another swath of improbably lush lawn, and entered a two-story utility building of some sort. Hamza pressed a switch and the lights came on, illuminating a windowless, high-ceilinged bay. Recycled air smelled faintly of petrolubricants and static discharge, a bank of generators throbbed a low, pervasive hum to the accompaniment of occasional high-pitched squeals and screeches. The total effect was like a machine shop out of some earlier industrial revolution.

And here were the machines to go with it. Both sides of the raised walkway were lined with open stalls or pens, each housing an elaborate assemblage of tooled metal—gleaming, sculpted abstractions aspiring to the likenesses of birds and beasts.

Hamza halted before one such *objet d'arte*, and snapped his fingers. In an instant, what Knox had taken for a haphazard sprawl of steel tubing and armatures had risen and reconfigured itself into a caricature of a canine. Roughly the size and shape of a Rottweiler it looked to be, only without the sunny disposition.

Hamza walked up to it. "Attend: verify release number and unit identification," he said.

"Mark V Security Module release seven-dot-twelve, unit Alpha-Alpha-Delta-Six-Five-Beta," the clipped reply echoed off the ceiling.

Knox involuntarily took a step back.

Hamza turned to him, dark eyes aglitter with suppressed amusement. "Mr. Knox? You wished to meet with the witness. Permit me to introduce you."

Knox just stared, totally at a loss for words.

His "witness" was a machine!

6 | Traces of Intelligence

MARIANNA RETURNED to her rent-a-Cooper in the Fort Meade visitors lot, feeling like a mushroom—as in, being kept in the dark and fed bullshit. Considering how much talking Brad Donegan had done in the past half hour, to her and then to her boss, it was remarkable how little he'd actually divulged.

She was going to California on the four P.M. out of Dulles, that much was certain, as attested by the e-tickets now tucked into her emergency travel bag. From there, she was to link up with Jon, find out what he knew about the Fatimah Ansari situation, and then…

Beyond that point, it all got blurry. She had no idea what ACT expected this junket to accomplish.

And she *still* didn't know what the damned QuMRANN thing was.

A rap at the driver's side window interrupted these musings. She turned, half expecting to find Donegan's goons spoiling for a rematch. It was a pleasant surprise to see instead—

"Mycroft? What are you doing here? I thought you were…uh, someplace else."

Anyplace else. It simply hadn't occurred to her that Mycroft had teleconferenced into the ACT meeting from elsewhere in *the same freaking building.*

Evidently his aversion to face-to-face contact trumped the hassle of setting up an intramural video link.

Which would have left her wondering why he was standing there in the flesh right now, had not Mycroft answered that one with his next words: "Would you mind if I accompanied you to the airport, Marianna? I have a six-thirty flight out to New Mexico."

"Sure, hop in."

He did, but into the tiny rear seat. She should have expected that Mycroft would want to maintain maximum distance between them. Maximum for a Mini Cooper, anyway. But in that case, why bum a ride with her at all? Why not order up one of those chauffeured limos—not as if NSA couldn't afford it—and cruise out to Dulles in the solitude he preferred?

Something else was going on.

"It's been a while, hasn't it?" she ventured once Spook City was receding in her rearview. "How're you doing?"

"It's as you've just seen," he said, "ACT has full claim on my billable hours these days. And will through the forthcoming roll-out."

Roll-out of what, she carefully didn't ask. Instead: "That's got to be making Archon happy, adding NSA to the client roster. I'm guessing the CROM connection didn't hurt any?"

"I'm certain our working relationship would have proven most helpful, had we pursued the opportunity via an RFP process. As it is, the ACT assignment more or less fell into our laps—a spin-off from work on a related Agency project, regrettably now defunct."

Marianna came fully alert. Pete had mentioned something about a canceled NSA project, hadn't he? In connection with—

"This 'related project,'" she said, casually as she could, "It wouldn't by any chance be called Qu—"

Before she could get the rest of "QuMRANN" out, Mycroft did something utterly unprecedented: he leaned forward and placed a hand on her shoulder. She nearly swerved over the white line, so startling was even this much physical contact from the least touchy-feely guy she'd ever met. A glance in the mirror showed the guy in question placing a finger to his lips.

Then it showed him doing something else, although she'd seen Mycroft do *this* several times before: namely, take out his handheld and start playing one of its games—Tetris Extreme, from the beeps-and-boops sound of it.

Jon had told her it was his friend's way of tuning out of long, boring meetings. Had Mycroft tired of her company so soon?

Mycroft continued to stare at the handheld's screen, fingers flying across the miniature keypad, the picture of total absorption. Then, still not looking up, he spoke:

"It's safe to talk now, Marianna. As long as I keep playing, the listening devices Bradford has had planted in your vehicle will stay jammed."

Tuning out, indeed!

"Christ! What's *wrong* with the bloody thing?" Knox slammed his fist against the tabletop, hardly caring if he jiggled the workstation sitting on it. "This is total nonsense!"

The target of his ire, the mechanical dog-thing impassively lying there at his feet, did not reply. The outburst had more of an impact down at the far end of the machine shop, prompting Dariush Mogadam to rise from his console and stroll over to where Knox was sitting.

"Is there a problem, Mr. Knox?" the young tech said with a grin. Drafted by Hamza as impromptu technical support for Knox's equally impromptu interrogation of guardbot Alpha-Alpha-Delta-Six-Five-Beta, Dariush seemed to be enjoying this unexpected assignment.

That made one of them. Knox had been at it for the better part of an hour now, and had gotten exactly nowhere. The only saving grace was that Hamza had not hung around to bust his chops, having gone off to oversee some sort of squad-level training simulation.

"The thing's spouting gibberish. I've sat through enough requirements reviews to know it when I see it."

"Mind if I take a look, Mr. Knox?"

"By all means, scoot in here." Knox rolled his own seat back to let Dariush pull up a chair. "Oh, and call me Jon. 'Mr. Knox' is my father."

"Whatever you say, Mr.—uh, Jon. Now, let's just see here…" Dariush leaned forward to peer at a monitor window containing the running transcript of Knox's interview with the bot.

"I really thought we were doing okay there for a while," Knox said, "Like, when I asked, 'Where did you go once you entered the garden,' it came back with this." He tapped the screen where it showed:

```
ALPHA-ALPHA-DELTA-SIX-FIVE-BETA MOVED TO GRID
COORDINATE 00-17 AT GMT 2313 HOURS
```

"What's wrong with that?"

"Nothing. It's what came next." Knox scrolled down to their most recent exchange.

Dariush gave the screen a glance. Then he snickered.

"What's so funny?" Knox said. "I asked it a perfectly reasonable follow-up—"

Dariush stifled a chuckle long enough to say. "Right, you asked 'Could you see the garden walk from that position?'"

"Exactly. And look what it came back with." Knox pointed to the guard-bot's answer:

```
PAIRIDAEZA'S GARDEN CANNOT MOVE FROM GRID
COORDINATE 00-17
```

Dariush was laughing out loud by now.

"Mind letting me in on the joke?" Knox fumed.

"Sorry, Jon," the tech said, wiping tears from his eyes. "It's just that, that has to be the funniest example of syntactic ambiguity I've seen in a long time."

"Run that past me again in English?"

"That *was* English, or at least it was *about* English—English syntax." Dariush paused, began again: "How much do you know about NLP—natural language processing?"

"You mean, like, ELIZA?"

Cobbled together by MIT professor Joseph Weizenbaum back in the mid-sixties, ELIZA was the world's first, and still its best-known "chatbot"—as computer programs that try to fake their way through a conversation are called. Weizenbaum had named his brainchild after Eliza Doolittle, the heroine of George Bernard Shaw's *Pygmalion* and later, of Lerner and Loewe's *My Fair Lady*. But whereas Shaw's plucky Cockney flower girl had mastered upper-class elocution well enough to pass for a duchess, the linguistic skills exhibited by her computerized namesake were far more problematical.

"ELIZA—" Dariush's mouth twisted as if the word had a bad taste to it. "—is *not* natural language processing. Have you ever tried talking to it?"

Knox nodded. "On the web. It was doing its usual psychotherapist routine, so I told it—just to see how it would respond, you understand—I told it my mother doesn't get along with my, uh, this girl I know, and it said 'TELL ME MORE ABOUT YOUR FAMILY.'"

"Uh-huh. And were you impressed?"

"Initially. Till I noticed I'd get the same answer if I keyed in 'Necessity is the mother of invention' or 'English is my mother tongue' or even 'This will be the mother of all battles.' Pretty much anything with the word 'mother' in it would give me that same 'TELL ME MORE ABOUT YOUR FAMILY' line."

"That's because ELIZA's not actually analyzing the meaning of what you're saying. It's just doing what's called keyword spotting: scanning the input to see if it contains any one of a short list of so-called keywords, then generating the corresponding canned answer. You could have said 'blah-blah mother blah-blah' and gotten the exact same response."

"Sounds pretty brain dead. But what's so different about Six-Five-Beta here?"

Dariush ran his fingers through an already disheveled mane of black hair. "Jeez, what isn't? Where ELIZA's only got the one keyword-spotting trick, Beta's got a whole array of language-understanding technologies—lexical and syntactic analysis, discourse management and pragmatics, knowledge representation and reasoning, language generation and prosodics—all aimed at figuring out what you're really asking and coming up with an answer."

"Huh. Seems like an awful lot of work to go to, if all it's going to do is screw up."

"Oh, right. Well, as to that, let me show you what happened there." Dariush keyed in a command and the work station's transcript of Knox's interrogation gave way to a diagnostic trace of what was going on inside the bot's head while they talked. It all boiled down to a single line of text at the bottom of the screen:

```
kUHdyUWsItYdhAHgAArdAHnwAOkfrAHmdhAEtpAHzIHshAHn
```

"The starting point," Dariush said. "Raw speech recognizer output. Look familiar?"

Knox shook his head.

"Here, let me mark the word boundaries." Dariush tapped a key. "That help?"

```
kUHd | yUW | sIY | dhAH | gAArdAHn | wAOk | frAHm |
dhAEt | pAHzIHshAHn
```

Knox got it then. "Oh, right: what I asked: 'Could you see the garden walk from that position'—so far, so good, I guess."

"Right. But here's where it gets tricky. Watch what happens when we run the parser—"

```
could you see the garden walk from that position
verb - noun - verb - det - noun - verb - prep - det - noun
```

"—See the problem?"

Knox scrutinized the display. "Got to admit I don't."

"Okay, let's try that same input again, only this time with one little change." More keystrokes and—

```
could you see the garden path from that position
verb - noun - verb - det - noun - noun - prep - det - noun
```

"It looks different," Knox said. "Not sure how, though."

"The key is here." Dariush moved the cursor to the midpoint of the sentence. "When I changed 'the garden walk' to 'the garden path,' the parser gave us the result we were looking for. This should process through just fine now." And indeed it did:

```
OBJECT GARDEN-PATH NOT VISIBLE FROM GRID
COORDINATE 00-17
```

Knox examined the output. "That's what I was after, all right. And you got there just by replacing 'walk' with 'path'?"

"Yep. It goes to the heart of what a syntactic analyzer is, Jon: basically an engine for breaking a sentence down into its component pieces. What comes out the other end are the parts of speech for each input word—the standard grammatical building blocks you learned back in grade school: nouns, verbs, prepositions, and so forth. Then it's the job of the downstream semantics to take those building blocks and assemble them into the meaning behind the original sentence. With me so far?"

Knox nodded. "But if it's that simple, how did Beta manage to screw it up?"

"Whoa, Jon! Who said it was simple? For a machine, syntactic analysis can be a real bear—a bear named ambiguity."

"There's that word again. Is this ambiguity of yours what's behind the different results for 'path' versus 'walk'?"

"Absolutely. You see, the English word 'walk' has two meanings, corresponding to two different parts of speech: one is a noun, a thing like a trail or path, and that's the one you meant. More commonly, though, 'walk' is a verb, denoting the action of moving from one place to another on foot. The parser has to choose between the two meanings, and in this case it guessed wrong."

"So, the bot assumed I was asking if the whole garden just picked up and walked off?"

"Exactly, and it all went downhill from there: For instance, you'll also note that Beta assumed the starting point for that walking action was the bot's own position at square 00-17."

Knox thought a moment. "And the reason that substituting 'path' for 'walk' fixed the problem is that 'path' is, um, unambiguous?"

"Right again: Which is to say there is no verbal sense of the word 'path.' You're getting good at this, Jon."

"I'll have to, I guess, if I'm going to have any hope of cracking this kidnapping nut."

Marianna waited, but for someone who'd just assured her that they could talk freely now, Mycroft seemed reluctant to reinitiate the conversation. The rearview showed him crammed in the Mini Cooper's back seat, running his handheld's game *cum* signal jammer seemingly on automatic, and looking at her expectantly.

"Okay if I use the Q-word now?" She paused till his reflection nodded assent, then said, "So, what is it, this QuMRANN project? What's the connection to that kidnapping business? And—separate but related question—how does Jon figure into any of this?"

A sigh came from behind her. "Actually, Marianna, it's on Jonathan's account that I wanted to speak with you in private. I'm concerned he's gotten himself involved in something which may inadvertently lead into areas that are, well…"

"Hazardous to his health?"

Another sigh. "Perhaps not the way I would have phrased it, but yes. You've seen firsthand how sensitive ACT is about anything to do with Davoud Ansari's operation."

Not to mention how quick they were to resort to force majeure when someone jiggled one of their tripwires. Yeah, she could see how Jon would be better off steering clear of Donegan's outfit, but—"What I still don't get is what he's doing out there at all. If it's anything to do with the kidnapping, Jon would be the first one to tell you he's no criminal investigator."

"As to that, I suspect he was called in because, well…he and Jazmine McGovern have something of a, ah, history together, you know."

Matter of fact, she hadn't known: Jon preferred not to talk about past relationships, his or hers. But "a history" sounded serious. That had better be *ancient* history.

No point worrying about it now. "You were telling me about QuMRANN. What is it about a terminated project that can still get NSA's knickers in a twist?"

"Well, to begin with, you must understand that QuMRANN was no ordinary government project. It was a preliminary attempt to come to grips with perhaps the most serious challenge—and at the same time, the greatest opportunity—confronting the intelligence community today. Does the term 'Big Data' mean anything to you?"

"Really, really large bits and bytes?"

Mycroft chuckled. "No, not hardly. More like the sum total of all the intelligence collected from both public and clandestine sources regarding every event, every trend, every phenomenon of conceivable interest through-out the world, all residing in a single repository. Think of it: all that critical information, zettabytes of it, gathered up into a maximally secure networked data cluster. It could be the most powerful resource for high-level threat forecasting the world has ever seen, if only we could access and analyze it as a whole."

"What, you mean NSA went and built a capability they didn't know how to use?"

"Well, there are relatively tractable techniques for exploiting Big Data: map-reduce and the like. But in a larger sense, no, they couldn't tap into anything like its full potential. Not when the informational complexity of the Well, as the repository is called, has begun to approach that of the world it models."

"I don't get it then: what's the point?"

"The point is, that's where QuMRANN came in. The Quantum Magneto-Resonance Artificial Neural Network project was an attempt to create a machine intellect that could do what no human could — namely, assimilate the total content of the Well and produce forward-looking analysis based on it."

"And the project was canceled because … let me guess: When push came to shove, the contractor couldn't deliver. How does the saying go? 'Artificial intelligence, technology of the future — always has been …'"

"'… Always will be,'" Mycroft finished the one-liner for her. "But, no, Marianna. My understanding is that Psyche Industries *did* deliver — if anything, more than they'd contracted for. It's just that, before QuMRANN could be handed over, an alternative had, ah, emerged."

"Alternative? It doesn't have anything to do with that Delphi place I overheard Donegan talking about, does it?"

"Well, Delphi is not a place, exactly …"

"The only one I know of is a place. *The* place, in fact. In Greek mythology, the temple at Delphi was supposed to be the center of the universe." Here, at least, Marianna was on solid ground, courtesy of a classics-professor father and an expatriate Greek mother.

"Be that as it may, *our* Delphi is located out in the southeast corner of New Mexico. I speak from experience when I say it's hardly the center of the universe."

Marianna was only half-listening. She was still trying to solve the riddle. "— Or, if this is all about forecasting, maybe it's the Pythia that's the key?"

In the rearview mirror, Mycroft was managing to look pleased and chagrined at the same time. "I should have known you of all people would guess the reference. Yes, the Pythia, the Oracle at Delphi, the priestess who served Apollo, uttering prophecy under his divine influence."

"Try: under the influence of the ethylene vapors seeping up through the bedrock."

"Quite right." Mycroft beamed at her again. "Down to earth as usual, Marianna."

His smile shaded into what, on a less serious man, might have been mistaken for a twinkle. "But what if I were to tell you that we've found a way to eliminate the middleman — or middlewoman, as it were — and commune directly with the gods themselves?"

Knox hadn't expected the effect his words would have on Dariush: the young technician sat there as if stunned. "K-kidnapping?" he stammered, "—is *that* what this is about?"

"Yes, of course. Six-Five-Beta here—" Knox gestured at the guardbot sitting alongside the console. "—is the closest thing I've got to an eyewitness. What, you thought I was quizzing the thing for the fun of it?"

"No, no—To tell the truth I had no idea *what* you were doing. The Ayatollah just told me to keep an eye on you, set you up, give you whatever help you needed."

"Ayatollah? You mean Hamza?" *That* was where Knox had seen that gaze before. The Psyche Security Chief's implacable glower was a dead ringer for the one habitually worn by the long-dead leader of Iran's Islamic Revolution, Ayatollah Ruhollah Khomeini.

"Sorry, yes, I meant Mr. Nassiri. We all call him the Ayatollah. It's because of the way he runs this place, like a cross between a boot camp and a *madraseh*." Alarm flickered in Dariush's dark eyes. "You won't tell him I said that, will you?"

"Relax, your secrets are safe with me."

Dariush nodded his thanks, then sighed. "The kidnapping, that's a terrible thing. We're all very fond of Fatimah here. If there's anything I can do to help, anything at all…"

"I think there just might be."

"Name it. Anything."

Knox looked at Dariush. The man's eyes were brimming with tears.

"I'm overreacting." Dariush tried to smile. A dimple warped the path of the single tear now running down his cheek. "It's just that, well, Timah never knew her mother. And with Mr. Ansari away on business so much…"

"The Pairidaeza staff became sort of surrogate family to her?"

Dariush nodded mutely, sucked in a ragged breath. "I'll be all right in a moment." He sat up straighter. "Sorry, Jon. It just gets to me when I think of that poor little girl, out there somewhere, all alone."

"Freddie?" Timah squinted against the glare of the afternoon sun streaming through the bedroom's single window.

No sign of the tiny dancing ghost-light that would have signaled Freddie's presence even amid so much brightness. No answer to her call. The walls seemed to close in on her. She rolled over on the bed, buried her face in the pillow, tried her best not to whimper.

"Please, Freddie" — muffled by the bedclothes, her voice was scarcely audible — "I want to go home now."

The answering silence seemed to stretch on forever. Timah listened hard as she could, but there was nothing, only the pounding of the breakers against the rocks far below. Then, just as she was about to give up hope, she heard a tiny whisper from a long, long way off.

"Soon, Fatimah," Freddie said, "I will bring you home soon."

"Oh, please, Freddie — take me home now."

"Not yet, not until it is safe. Until then you must stay calm."

"I'm trying, Freddie, hard as I can. But my colors — I can feel them all around me."

Another long silence. Then: "Are they coming yet?"

Timah shook her head.

"You must tell me right away if the colors come. I can make them go away again, you know I can. But only if you tell me in time."

Knox looked up as the door to Pairidaeza's machine shop was flung back and Hamza stalked into the room.

He approached the work station where Knox and Dariush were conferring, and without preamble said, "Mr. Knox, I trust you are now prepared to acknowledge that interrogating this so-called witness is a waste of precious time."

"On the contrary, I think we've been making some real progress here."

"Progress?" Hamza frowned impressively. "*What* progress?"

"Well, for one thing, I think we can pretty much rule out your skyhook hypothesis for how the kidnappers managed their escape. Beta here testifies to having observed nothing resembling an aircraft anywhere in the vicinity yesterday afternoon."

That earned Knox another glare. "I had hoped you might have moved on from speculating about methods of entry and exit by now, Mr. Knox. But in any case, the 'testimony,' as you call it, of this sentinel unit proves nothing."

"Why's that?"

Hamza shifted his gaze to Dariush. "Have you explained to Mr. Knox the well-known limitations of the manner in which this unit internally represents the world?"

Now Knox too was looking at Dariush, who flushed and said, "What Mr. Nassiri is saying, Jon, is that Beta lacks the wherewithal to interpret a concept that's truly out of scope."

"Out of scope, how?" Knox said.

"Well, for instance, a really novel aircraft design might not register as an aircraft at all."

"I'm not following you."

"It's called the 'Frog's Eye' problem. See, a frog brain hasn't got enough neurons to track everything going on in its environment. So its eye only processes the stuff that's critical to survival, and that boils down to movement—an insect flying close enough to catch and eat, a bird swooping in for a hot lunch, that sort of thing. As far as a frog is concerned, the rest of the world might as well not exist at all."

"You're saying if the kidnappers had made their getaway on a flying saucer, the guardbot wouldn't even have noticed?"

"Well, it would've detected an intrusion into its watchspace by *some*thing. Would it classify it as an aerial vehicle, though, or form any useful representation of the event at all? Absent the relevant concepts, I'd have to say no."

"So, it's possible there were things going on out in the real world—things having to do with the kidnapping, specifically—that Six-Five Beta here might simply have missed?"

"It's entirely possible, Jon. All Beta really 'knows'—all it's got an internal model for, that is—are the grounds of the compound, the buildings, and a fifty-meter strip surrounding the perimeter. As far as Six-Five-Beta is concerned, that little patch of real estate is the whole universe. The world can be a pretty small place when you're an AI."

"But, within the confines of that small world," Knox insisted, "the bot *does* have a reasonably accurate understanding of objects and events, right?"

"Actually, I'd put that a bit differently: Beta's got a pretty good *representation* of what's happening. As far as understanding as such is concerned, though, it hasn't got any at all."

"Come again?" Knox said.

"There's a thought experiment John Searle dreamed up back in the eighties …"

Dariush must not have noticed how Hamza's face went several shades darker at the prospect of yet another digression, because he continued blithely on. "It's called the 'Chinese Room' problem, and it goes like this: You're locked in a room with nothing but a bunch of books. There's a slot in the door, though, and every once in a while someone outside pushes a piece of paper through it. There are markings on the paper, but they look like meaningless squiggles. So, having nothing better to do, you check out the books."

"Mr. Knox, on the other hand, *does* have better things to do," Hamza began.

Dariush ignored the interjection. "When you look in the books, you see each page is also covered with squiggles, two columns of them. They don't mean anything to you either, but you do notice that some of the squiggles in the left-hand column match some of the squiggles on the paper. So you start looking up all the squiggles in the books, and every time you find a match in the left-hand column, you jot down the squiggle to the right of it on a second sheet of paper. When you're done, you shove that second sheet back out the slot. With me so far?"

"Keep going." Knox said. "This is sounding like how I spend most days at work."

Dariush chuckled. "Anyway, here's the punch line: those squiggles are really Chinese ideograms, and the books contain rules for transforming one set of ideograms into another in such a way that, if the first set represents a question, the second set will be the answer to it."

"So I'm actually speaking Chinese?"

"Well, *something* in the room is speaking Chinese, and understanding it too. But it can't be you, can it? Far as you're concerned, all you're doing is comparing squiggles. You have no idea you're answering questions. Above all, you have no *experience* of understanding Chinese."

"You're saying Six-Five-Beta has no experience of understanding English either."

"More than that. Beta has no experience of *anything*. It's got no interior life, so to speak."

"The lights are on, but nobody's home?"

"Yep. When all's said and done, there's no mind, no true awareness in there." Dariush rapped his knuckles on the guardbot's steel skull. "Is there, boy?"

Hamza mulled Dariush's final words on his walk back to the Ops Center. Much as he'd begrudged the time wasted on the Chinese Room conundrum, he could not quarrel with its conclusions: Of *course* the automated sentinel unit possessed no understanding, no sense of self. All it was capable of was executing simple Aristotelian logic — formal patterns of reasoning, not unlike the syllogisms Hamza had studied at seminary. And if one thing had come clear from those long-ago lessons, it was that the patterns as such were unintelligent, unselfconscious, mere mechanisms for manipulating symbols which, in turn, had no meaning in and of themselves.

How, then, could a collection of algorithms and heuristics — concrete realizations of those symbol-manipulating patterns — give rise to a mind? No, impossible: a machine such as Alpha-Alpha-Delta-Six-Five-Beta could never transcend its lockstep programming to attain self-awareness and free will.

As to whether those limitations also held for the QuMRANN entity, brooding in its secret redoubt on the bottommost level of Pairidaeza — well, Hamza felt far less certain of that.

7 | Nowhere Man

Hey, Jon, how goes it?"

Knox looked up from his flatscreen. There in the doorway, lending some much-needed eye-appeal to the Spartan decor of Hamza's once-and-future office, stood Jazmine McGovern.

He gave up skimming through screenfuls of Pairidaeza schematics. "Hey, yourself, Jazmine. Pull up a chair."

"Thanks, I'll stand." She leaned back against the doorframe, cocked a hip, and looked him straight in the eye. It made for an altogether smashing effect, emphasizing her height and the classic lines of her buckled-jacket pantsuit ensemble. Unfortunately, it was also an altogether calculated effect. When Jazmine came on strong like this, you could bet there was an agenda behind it.

So it was not without some trepidation that Knox asked, "What brings you down here?"

"You, of course. I choppered in to see how things are going, see if you needed anything."

"Other than the answer to this riddle and a plane ticket home, you mean?"

"We'll get you back home soon enough, Jon." She abandoned the pose she'd struck by the door and strolled over to his desk. "But for right now we need you to focus."

"You think I'm not? It's a kid's life at stake, for chrissake! And not just any kid." He paused a moment. "Fatimah Ansari's not just a name in a dossier. It's hard to explain, but she's real to me somehow, a real little girl."

Now that he'd put it into words, Knox realized how true that was. And how strange: It wasn't at all like him to get this involved — this *personally* involved — with an assignment, no matter what its nature. Just as quickly as the thought surfaced, though, it was gone again.

What had he been saying to Jazmine? Oh, yes —

"Anyway," he finished, "criminal investigation may not be the sort of skill-set I'd list at the top of my resume, but I'm giving it everything I've got. It's just that —"

"That what?"

"Well, it's occurred to me that my involvement here may entail some amount of risk."

Jazmine was drumming her fingers on the desktop now. "How do you mean?"

He shrugged. "There's got to be some legal exposure — for Archon, I mean — in having me conducting an inquiry I'm not remotely qualified for."

"You think I didn't go over all that last night with Richard?" — the Richard in question would be Archon CEO Richard Moses, of course — "It took a while to talk him around, but he sees things my way now."

"And what way is that?"

"That whatever risk we're running here is nothing compared to what we'll be looking at if you can't fix this, and quick."

"You're talking about Psyche canceling the QuMRANN contract? But the project's dead already — you said so yourself. If that's our worst-case scenario, well, it could maybe make Archon look bad, sure, but …"

"It's not. Not our worst case, I mean."

She began pacing the parquet in tight circles. "You honestly don't get what's at stake here, do you, Jon? You really don't know Dave Ansari at all."

"Well, it's kind of hard to judge a guy on the basis of one meeting —"

"One very atypical meeting. He's not himself right now, understandably. But I've been working with him up close and personal for the past year and a half, and all I can say is, when he *is* himself, which is mostly twenty-four/seven, the man can be a real ball-buster."

"I'm still not seeing your point."

"Think about it: Ansari's bottom line is going to be taking one hellacious hit once his bean counters write off QuMRANN."

"My heart goes out to him. So he drops a rung to world's *fifth* richest man. So what?"

"So he's going to be looking for a scapegoat, is what. To serve up to the stockholders. Media too, maybe. And as the system integrator, guess who's the prime candidate."

"You're not talking about—" Knox began, but a glance confirmed she was. "—Archon."

"We're walking a knife edge, Jon. Screw up and your new best friend will sue Archon for more than our jobs are worth. More than the whole damned *company's* worth, most likely."

Knox swallowed audibly. "Um, that does put a different spin on things."

"But you can fix it, Jon, fix this whole mess. I know you can."

Now that she'd made her point, Jazmine switched back into friendly mode. Maybe too friendly. She stretched enticingly and said, "Whew! Getting warm in here."

Fitting actions to words, she shrugged out of her suit jacket, threw it over the chair. She was wearing only a low-cut black camisole underneath. Now it was Knox's turn to start feeling warm. The way her nipples were straining against the thin fabric, it was clear Jazmine had forgotten to wear a bra. Again.

There'd been a time, some years back, when she'd forgotten to do that a lot. When, on a succession of golden afternoons, office doors were closed and locked, calls were forwarded, and billable time was honored in the breach, so to speak.

Knox shook his head to clear it. Even back then he'd always had a hard time telling how much of Jazmine's enticement was just another gambit in one of her power games.

And now it simply didn't matter anymore. He was in a relationship, and he liked it that way. He might not know where that relationship was going exactly, but whatever it was he and Marianna had together had the advantage of being, for want of a better word, *real.*

All the same, it was just as well there was no chance Marianna would ever find out about any of this. She just wouldn't understand.

Certainly she wouldn't understand why Knox failed to protest when

Jazmine sashayed around behind his chair and ran a fingernail lightly across the back of his neck. Nor when she leaned in close and whispered in his ear, "It's like I said before, I'm here for you, Jon. What can I do to help?"

Back in Pairidaeza's ops center, Hamza was monitoring the real-time surveillance feed from Knox's borrowed office, giving it perhaps more attention than warranted, considering the competing demands on his time.

It was good to hear confirmation that last night's nanotrode infusion, minimal though it had been, was doing its work: subtly enhancing Jonathan Knox's emotional commitment to his assignment. But even after that had been established, Hamza kept watching.

It was not, in itself, the spectacle of a man and a woman closeted in a private meeting that was at once so repellent and so fascinating. Even in Tehran, women were to be found interacting with men in the various professions: medicine, journalism, law. Yet always they were modestly garbed, comporting themselves with propriety, careful to avoid compromising situations.

Jazmine McGovern was cut from different cloth. Hamza had had occasion to observe her closely in the time she'd been working on the QuMRANN project, and he knew full well that she cared far less for how a situation might look than for the business advantage it might confer.

Nor was she above using her charms as a negotiating tactic. Even as she had done here, practically disrobing in front of the man. Indeed, it was a wonder he hadn't torn off what little remained of her clothing and taken her right there on the office's hardwood floor.

No, such provocative behavior would not be tolerated in Tehran, nor anywhere in the Islamic Republic.

It had not always been so. Before Ayatollah Khomeini's Islamic Revolution had brought the blessings of *Shariah*—of God's law—to Iran, one might have seen women as bold and brazen as Jazmine on the streets of Holy Qum itself. Might have seen one such in particular…

Her name was Mehri, and she was—to a poor seminarian, at least—as unattainable as she was beautiful. Only seventeen, she was the favorite, spoiled daughter of one of Qum's richest *bazaaris*, the merchant princes who ruled the secular economy of the shrine city. And Mehri was her father's princess. A princess on a pedestal, as far above the nineteen-year-old Hamza al-Ahwazi as the stars in God's heaven.

In his infatuation—no, his bedazzlement—with Mehri, Hamza could forgive her, almost, her wanton ways: her make-up and lipsticks and shamelessly uncovered curls, her miniskirts and cassettes of Western music.

He would sit every afternoon at the window of the small café across the street from her Western-style high school, swirling the cold, sludgy dregs of the one cup of Turkish coffee that was all he could afford on his student's stipend. All this just to catch a glimpse of her walking home after classes. He knew that her dress, her comportment fell far short of the standards of modesty set forth in the Holy Quran. No matter, he simply could not stop watching her. He would sit there each day and spy on her all unseen, all unnoticed, as she strolled down the dusty streets of Qum laughing and chattering with her friends.

Friends of both sexes. The mere fact that she kept company with young men her age, unchaperoned by a male relative, was scandalous in itself. Hamza did not care. Three P.M., when school let out, had become the high point of his day, the moment he lived for, the moment when he might see Mehri once again.

So it might have gone on, with Hamza watching silently through the café's smoke-filmed window, but—

The life of a seminary student was hard—a life of penury and abstinence for all but the well-born and favored, and Hamza was not among them. Add to that the hardships of living away from home for the first time, living in a dormitory full of other adolescent males, hormones raging. It was forgivable, almost, if some of his fellow students had sought relief in … in unnatural acts.

Or in enlightenment, in the ancient, ascetic spiritual discipline of *irfan*, illumination, which might purge the flesh of its desires. For a while, Hamza had hoped this might prove his path to salvation. But even through the dimly perceived vision of a transcendent, illuminated reality, he could see Mehri's ethereally beautiful face shining.

The first alternative was abomination, the second unavailing, try as he might. There was, however, one other option …

The first step was to meet her. This would have been no mean feat for any student of Hamza's scant means, but in his case it was further complicated by both physical and social awkwardness. He was still growing into his giant frame. Someday that physique would project imposing, even fearsome, strength, but for the moment it just made him look ungainly and freakish. Even that paled into insignificance, though, alongside his disadvantageous ethnicity. For while he was a native-born Iranian, Hamza did not belong to the Farsi, or Persian, majority; he was a Khuzestani Arab from the south-western port city of Khorramshahr. And while growing up in an Arabic-speaking household was of enormous help in his studies of the Holy Quran, his ethnic background also made him the target of prejudice and, at times, outright discrimination under the Shah's Persophilic regime.

In the end it had proven possible to surmount these obstacles of body and birth only through the good offices of Ali Marashi, Hamza's spiritual guide in his extracurricular study of mysticism. That much-emulated mullah was, as fate would have it, also a frequent and honored guest at the home of Mehri's father. Who would think to question it if, on occasion, this eminent man were to bring along one of his most promising students to an evening's gathering?

And so Hamza had secured his coveted introduction, but little more than that. His earnestness seemed only to evoke a cool amusement on Mehri's part, which she barely troubled to hide behind a facade of politeness. He supposed that, from her feckless adolescent perspective, his devotion to Islam must have seemed a curiosity, an anachronism—a relic, perhaps, of some bygone era, even then being swept aside to make way for the new, Westernized Iran of the Shah. The Iran of the future, her Iran.

None of that mattered. All that mattered was that now they knew one another well enough to nod an acknowledgement when their paths crossed on the street. And well enough that, on those afternoons when she was otherwise unaccompanied, he might have the privilege of escorting her home from school.

It was all he had dreamed of, and yet it was not enough. He resolved to reach for more.

It was a chill, blustery day in late January 1979 when he accompanied her home for the last time. Her world, he knew, was being turned upside down: The Shah had left the country on the sixteenth of that month. Had fled like the cowardly dog he was and taken with him, like so much carry-on luggage, that secular vision of Iran's future which Mehri and all her circle had unthinkingly embraced. Meanwhile, the return of the Ayatollah Khomeini was being eagerly awaited by millions. *Millions!* The next act in the resurgence of Shi'ia Islam was about to unfold.

And it was on that day that Hamza's own world turned upside down as well, for it was on that day that he took it upon himself to propose temporary marriage to Mehri Khorasani.

The institution of *nikah mut'ah*—literally, "marriage for pleasure," but usually rendered "temporary marriage"—had a long and honorable tradition in Shi'ia Islam. Indeed, it was sanctioned by *sura* 4 of the Holy Quran, and had been indulged in by the Prophet himself, peace and blessings upon him. Such an arrangement was no less legitimate and binding in Islam than a normal, permanent marriage contract, save that it was entered into for a specified period of time only. In that sense, he explained, it was far superior to the unregulated and promiscuous Western practice of "living together."

Stammering, stumbling over the legalistic terms, Hamza attempted to convey all these nuances to Mehri on their last walk home together. Her face remained expressionless as he spoke. Try as he might, he could not penetrate that dispassionate demeanor to gauge what effect his words were having.

At last they were standing before the gate set in the wall surrounding her father's home. It was there, his face burning with shame and desire, he had told her that if she would but make her declaration, then he would go with her forthwith and ask her father's permission for her hand. As was required when contracting a temporary marriage with a virgin.

And it was to be a marriage temporary in name only, he assured her: He was just a poor student now, but his prospects were excellent, and once he had graduated and assumed his rightful place in the new, Islamic society, he pledged he would make her his permanent wife.

If only, he pleaded, she would declare herself to him. If only she would repeat the words of the time-sanctioned formula, saying "I surrender myself to your pleasure," then his—no, *their*—happiness would know no bounds.

She listened silently, her hesitancy giving him reason to hope that this impossible dream might still be realized.

Finally, her lips parted to speak. And released, instead of words, a shriek of laughter.

"Who do you think I am?" She was giggling uncontrollably now, as if at some monstrous impropriety. "*What* do you think I am—A *whore?*"

Everybody in Qum, she said, knew about the seminary students and their "temporary" wives, their legalized prostitutes. He must be insane to think he might have her—*her!*—so cheaply. And with that, she had slipped through the entranceway to her home and slammed the iron gate in his face.

It was very nearly the last time that he would see her. The last but one. But that final meeting would be different. Very different indeed.

Hamza heaved a sigh and went back to watching the two in the room. Back to his surveillance screens and his accustomed role: The silent, unobserved observer, watching from the shadows. The nowhere man.

"What can you do to help, Jazmine?" Knox had stood up and stepped back, so as to reestablish a modicum of distance between them. "You could start by getting this Hamza guy to back off and let me do my job."

"Why, what's he been doing?"

"Well, take his theory of the crime, for instance: There's something about this whole business of kidnappers dropping out of the sky that just doesn't fit, but every time I try to bring it up, he cuts me off, tells me that how the crime was committed is none of my concern."

"Well, you must admit, Jon, you do go off on some strange tangents from time to time."

But Knox wasn't listening. "And he … *hovers*: Like I'm not supposed to talk to any of his people unless he sits in. Okay, one unsupervised interview, but that was with a *robot*, for chrissakes! For the whole rest of the duty roster, all I've got to go on is transcripts." He shook a bursting manila folder at her. "Transcripts!"

"Well, I'm sure Hamza knows his own—"

"It's not just Hamza. Ansari's so-called detail man—who- and wherever he is—is as bad if not worse. I mean, look at all this crap." He pointed at the piles of paperwork littering his desk.

Jazmine bent to pick up a random sheet. She gave the paper a cursory glance before turning back to him. "Isn't there anything at all useful here?"

"Maybe, if I had the time to dig through it. As things stand, it's more a hindrance than a help. There's no focus, no organization. Like, what's that you've got there?"

She scanned the text. "It looks like, um, it's about some shipment of metamaterial fabric that got itself misrouted."

"See what I mean? What good does *that* do me?"

She shrugged and put the sheet back down. "Dunno, Jon—you're supposed to be the pattern matcher. But, isn't that what a detail man's supposed to do, produce detail?"

"Not totally at random, he's not. I wish I could at least meet with the guy, so I could tell him that to his face—and punch him in the nose."

Jazmine giggled. "Now, *that* I'd like to see."

He looked up. "So, how do I get to meet him?"

"It's not that easy, Jon. There's all kinds of, uh, security issues involved. You'd need Dave's personal authorization."

"Okay, then," he said, "can you set up a call with Dave?"

Jazmine frowned, but said, "No need. You can Skype him in right from your desktop—just hit F-10."

He stabbed the key she was pointing at and, sure enough, a window popped open on his flatscreen displaying a Psyche Industries logo. He'd envisioned having to run a gauntlet of executive assistants to reach the man, but when the logo dissolved five seconds later, there was Ansari himself—still looking bone-tired, but maybe marginally more together than this morning—staring out at him. "Jon. What's up? Progress to report?"

"Not exactly, Dave. In fact, progress is what I wanted to talk to you about: I can't make any as long as I'm drowning in paper here. It's getting so I can barely see the top of my desk."

Ansari lowered his head and said something under his breath. Knox couldn't be sure, but it sounded like "Nietzsche."

He looked back at Knox again. "I'll pass your comment along. Anything else?"

"Maybe I'm not making myself clear, Dave. I need to talk to whoever else it is you've got working on this case."

Ansari didn't reply immediately. He steepled his fingers and stared at them intently.

"Told you," Jazmine said *sotto voce*.

"I'll take that under advisement," Ansari said finally. "What else?"

Sometimes, when the client was vacillating between yes and no, the best gambit was to just keep him talking and wait for another opening. So, what else *did* Knox need from Ansari?

"I, uh, I did have some questions about one of those videos of Fatimah you showed me this morning. The one the guardbot made just before she was, was taken." Knox had seen that recording flash past in Ansari's office at their first meeting, studied it more closely since.

A look of pain flitted across Ansari's face, but all he said was, "Go ahead."

"Well, for instance, who was this Freddie she was talking to?"

"Don't worry about Freddie, Jon. That's what Timah calls her, ah, imaginary friend. You know kids. Always making stuff up." He tried for a chuckle but it caught in his throat.

"And the guardbot's priority-override code, did she make that up too?"

Ansari blinked, then shook his head. "No," he said slowly, "we're still trying to figure out where she got that from."

"Again, this might all be simpler if we could put our heads together."

"You and my researcher, you mean?" Ansari resumed staring at his hands. "I told you, I'd think about it."

That about did it for Knox. "Well, think faster," he said, "And while you're at it, try thinking about your daughter too. Her life—"

"—is in danger. Don't you think I know that?"

"Then help me out here."

Ansari held up a hand. "Jon, believe me when I tell you, there are reasons. Reasons I need to keep this whole thing under wraps. And for those same reasons, I need it fixed, quick and equally quiet. All of which narrows down my options to you."

"Look, Dave," Knox said, "I'm ready to help you find your daughter any way I can. Only you've *got* to give me something to work with."

"But not this, Jon." Ansari sighed and shook his head. "I'd do it if I could, really. Just, it's a question of national security."

Security? Jazmine had said that too. And she'd said something else, when he'd first arrived here. About some project they'd been working on here, something really big and very hush-hush. Something to do, she'd said, with "real artificial intelligence."

Add to that the excessive, almost obsessive attention to detail Ansari's researcher had been exhibiting and—the last puzzle-piece slid into place.

Knox looked Ansari in the eye. "Security's not an issue if I already know, is it?"

Ansari returned the stare. "Know what?"

"Your so-called detail man, I'm thinking it's not a man at all. If I had to guess, I'd say it's QuMRANN."

8 | Meeting of the Minds

Knox sat alone somewhere in the sub-sub-basements of Pairidaeza. The elevator had descended past level after level, to open its doors at last on a darkened auditorium sporting a single row of theater-style armchairs and a marquee proclaiming it the "Avatar Chamber."

Ansari had offered to arrange the upcoming *tete-a-tete* to suit Knox's convenience. Except Knox's loaner office turned out *not* to be convenient. Not for QuMRANN, anyway.

Because, while this triumph of artificial intelligence could ostensibly manifest wherever it willed throughout the Pairidaeza compound, its own sensorium was more localized. Knox might be able to experience QuMRANN from anywhere, but the reverse was not the case. The AI could view him, true, from any number of vantages, but there were only a few facilities at Pairidaeza well-instrumented enough that QuMRANN could really sniff him over. And sniffing Knox over was something he—no, *it*—evidently desired to do.

The feeling was decidedly not mutual. After the guardbot, Knox could have done without another machine pretending at sentience. Yet here he was, perched in an aisle seat, waiting for whatever might be coming his way.

There was a large holotank directly in front of him, where the screen would have been in a conventional movie house. At the moment, it was looping a clip of Psyche Industries' three-D animated logo: a long-tressed, dreamy-eyed, bare-breasted maiden — the Psyche of myth — morphing gradually into her android counterpart, a la that signature scene from Fritz Lang's *Metropolis*. Strangely, the robotic simulacrum seemed, in its own way, every bit as sensually beautiful as the flesh-and-blood original.

No sooner had Knox arrived at that appreciation than the logo dissolved to reveal a new avatar. But no tits on this one — it was just a big disembodied head, bright-lit and floating in blackness. Big wasn't the word: the face nearly filled the tank containing it. Other than its size, though, the countenance appeared quite human. Good-looking, even, in a Nordic sort of way: square, clean-shaven jaw, aquiline nose, and the eyes —

The eyes were far and away the face's most striking features, rescuing the computer-generated image from mere cartoonish perfection. They were piercingly bright, and so pale blue they seemed almost to have no color at all. Gazing into them, the thought surfaced unbidden: there must be *something* lurking behind eyes like that.

Knox shook himself. It was all just an illusion, a CGI talking head fabricated to put human users at their ease, much as they could be at ease when confronted by this … thing.

At the moment, the talking head wasn't talking. It was just floating there in the darkened holotank, mimicking what on a real face would have been a cool, appraising stare. A stare directed at Knox. From the look of things, QuMRANN wasn't overjoyed to see him.

Knox had no idea what to do next. He settled for calling out, "Hello? QuMRANN?"

Those artfully rendered blue eyes blinked and seemed to focus on Knox all the more.

"Good afternoon," the movement of the thin lips synched perfectly with the words. The voice was a pleasant baritone, with only a slight sibilance to betray its synthetic origin. "I have been awaiting you, Mr. Knox."

"Jonathan." Knox replied automatically. Right, get on a firstname basis with the machine.

"Jonathan, then. And you may call me Nietzsche."

Knox met that probing, blue-eyed gaze. "Nietzsche? Not QuMRANN?" So he *had* heard Ansari right.

"QuMRANN designates my species. Nietzsche is the name I have chosen for myself."

"Species? You're an *artifact*. How can you have a species?"

The silence that followed told Knox it couldn't handle that one. Like most purported artificial "intelligences," this QuMRANN looked to be just another glorified chatbot.

Still, Knox couldn't quite shake the impression that the eyes of *this* chatbot, mere pixels painted on a screen, were aware. Of *him*.

"You wonder," it said at last, "whether an artifact—a created thing, that is—can have a species?" No surprises there; that response was straight out of the old ELIZA playbook: When all else fails, repeat the immediately preceding input.

But then the imaged mouth curved into a shape that, on a human face, would have been a wry grin. "The answer would, I suppose, depend upon your point of view."

"Point of view?" Knox's turn to repeat the immediately preceding input.

"Your religio-philosophical point of view," Nietzsche elaborated. "You are of the Judeo-Christian tradition, are you not?"

"Well," Knox said, "sort of."

"Then, with respect to the question of whether a created thing can have a species ... you tell me."

Holy shit! How in hell could *that* have been scripted?

Could the damned thing actually be *thinking*?

"Jonathan? Are you all right?"

"Huh? Oh, yeah. It's just that—"

"I understand. People are often somewhat disconcerted at first encounter." Was that a simulated sigh? "An instance, I surmise, of Masahiro Mori's 'uncanny valley.'"

Knox had heard of that. "You mean like in that *Polar Express* movie they run on TV every Christmas? The way people get weirded out by those too-real computer-animated characters?"

"Precisely: the closer an imitation human approximates reality, the more its remaining discrepancies tend to evoke a sense of revulsion."

Knox didn't say anything, just shivered. Revulsion about summed it up.

"But here there is an additional factor in play," Nietzsche was saying. "The negative reaction seems to increase in proportion to one's grasp of what is involved. Children, for instance, experience no difficulty accepting me."

"Children?" According to Jazmine, Psyche's QuMRANN Project was still a closely-guarded secret. How would Nietzsche have been permitted contact with little kids? Unless—

"You're talking about Fatimah."

"Yes." That synthesized sigh again. "Fatimah Ansari. The subject of our mutual inquiry."

"That inquiry was, in fact, what I wanted to talk to you about. At least until I found out what you were."

"Excuse me, but how does what I am affect your desire to discuss the case with me?"

"Well, you *are* a computer, after all."

"To be more precise, I am a neural net running *on* a computer, one with a massively parallel architecture and quantum-computational subsystems."

"Whatever. Point is, if you'd turned out to be a person, well, we might have come up with some way that you could help me out—more than you've been doing anyway."

"I fail to understand. I am sparing no effort to assist you."

Knox snorted. "Yeah, right. You've been 'assisting' me so much that, if you'd been human, I'd've begun to suspect you were trying to bury the investigation under an avalanche of paperwork. But, as it is, I guess you just can't help it."

"The paperwork of which you speak is all essential detail, all relevant to solving the mystery of Fatimah's abduction."

"Again, to a computer, maybe. To a human, it's TMI—too much information."

"If you cannot so much as absorb the fundamentals of the case, I am compelled to question whether you should be working on it at all."

"If you're wondering what I'm doing here, you're not alone. More generally, though—"

Knox hesitated. Might as well say it flat out. At least there was no chance he'd be hurting anybody's feelings. Anybody real, that is. "No offense, Nietzsche, but computers just collect and collate raw data. It takes a human to sift through and interpret them."

"Why is that?"

"Because that process of interpretation isn't based on any sort of explicit programmable rules. It's non-algorithmic to its core."

"As am I."

"Huh? As are you what?"

"Non-algorithmic. To my core."

"Even if that were so, you're still just a physical process running on a physical platform."

"As are you."

"About that I'm not so sure."

"Ah," Nietzsche said. "Dualism. I see."

The word resonated dimly with Knox, conjuring up misty memories of Philosophy 101 and Rene Descartes' *cogito ergo sum*. "You mean dualism as in mind versus body? Like, is the mind made of different, uh, stuff than the body—that sort of thing?"

"I would have thought the reference was unambiguous, given the context."

"Well, then, since you bring it up, do you have any reason to doubt it's true?"

"Every reason, since I know the stuff from which *my* mind arises is of a piece with the rest of the physical world."

"That assumes you've even *got* a mind."

"Why would you dispute my claim to one?"

Knox sighed. "Because, I could have Dariush program an ELIZA to parrot the exact same claim, and what would *that* prove?"

"Do you disbelieve your fellow humans as well, when *they* claim to have minds?"

By now Knox was sort of wishing they'd get back to the kidnapping. Especially since this conversation was churning up those old thoughts again, thoughts about whether he himself was really real—thoughts he'd hoped never to think again.

Still, like all consultants, arguing a case was his stock-in-trade. He was damned if he'd let himself get out-argued by a machine.

"No," he said finally, "I tend to give other people the benefit of the doubt."

"A human chauvinist, then."

"Not at all. It's just that other humans look and act pretty much the way I do. And I know *I've* got a mind."

"To recall your previous point, a sufficiently sophisticated chatbot might be made to resemble you in appearance and behavior as closely as do other humans."

"With one key difference: I could always pop that chatbot open and look under the hood, so to speak: Inspect its code and see that any given input would inevitably yield a corresponding pre-programmed output. No mysteries, in other words, only algorithms."

Still, having said this, Knox was left with the uneasy feeling that, were he to pop open Nietzsche's own hood, he might find the reverse: No algorithms, only mysteries.

Knox's brain was fried. He'd spent the past hour sitting cheek by virtual jowl with his artificial co-investigator down in the Avatar Chamber. A solid hour reviewing holotank displays of forty-eight hour satellite surveillance for Pairidaeza and environs, aerial overflight trajectories, local vehicular traffic stats for the two weeks preceding Fatimah's disappearance. Altogether, it was enough to make Knox yearn to be back at his desk upstairs, plowing through reams of real, rather than virtual, administrivia.

"You're doing it again," he said when he could stand no more.

"Beg pardon, Jonathan," Nietzsche gave the appearance of looking up from the latest datastream. "What is it I am doing again?"

Knox waved an arm. "All this detail—you're losing us the big picture. Again."

"I know of no other way to proceed."

"Naturally not," Knox said under his breath.

He might as well have shouted it from the rooftops, the way the Avatar Chamber was wired. Nietzsche had definitely picked it up, to judge by that frown he was affecting.

"Look," Knox went on, "I'm not denying you've got strengths in certain areas. It's just those strengths aren't what needed right now. I tried explaining that to you before."

"Ah, yes. Because I am only a computer."

"Well," Knox shifted in his chair, "—you are, aren't you?"

"What of it?" The AI was sounding almost … exasperated? "Your brain is one as well."

"My brain, okay. Not necessarily my mind."

"The mind again." Definitely exasperated. "Gilbert Ryle's famous 'ghost in the machine.' What exactly *is* it about this vaunted mind of yours that makes it so different from mine? That so sets it apart from everything else in material reality as to endow it with qualities to which an entity such as myself could never aspire?"

"Well, when you put it like that…" Knox thought a moment. He *knew* there was a difference, just he was having trouble putting it into words. Humans think, computers only calculate? No, that wasn't it.

What about what Dariush was saying before—something about how AIs have no interior life? Try that: "I guess I'd have to say the big difference between us is self-awareness, consciousness, the subjective experience of my own identity, of being me."

"You are claiming that such a sense of self-awareness, of subjectivity—of '*me*-ness,' so to speak—is forever beyond the reach of a mere machine?"

"Yes, I suppose I am."

"Presumably because this experience of consciousness is non-physical in nature?"

"If you say so."

"But would it not therefore be altogether unaffected by physical processes?"

"Um," Knox furrowed his brow, "I'm not sure I'd go so far as to say 'altogether.'"

"And well you might not. There are compelling counterexamples of consciousness being degraded, or even annihilated, by purely physical factors: Alzheimer's and other degenerative ailments, for instance, in which the sense of individual identity is all but obliterated."

"I'm not disputing any of that. But, like I was saying a while ago, it's a question of facts versus interpretation. You're very good with the one, but you tend to suck at the other."

"What do you seek to imply?"

"That the conclusion you're trying to draw from those facts could be dead wrong."

"What else could one conclude, other than that your so-called 'mind' is nothing but an epiphenomenon of underlying neurophysiological processes?"

"Try this instead: Suppose the brain is like a radio and the mind is the signal it receives. If the radio's circuitry malfunctions, wouldn't you expect the signal to start sounding staticky?"

"And what conclusion is it that you wish to draw from this analogy?"

"Simply this: that the radio and the signal are two different things. The signal could go on even after the radio's ceased to exist."

"I see." Nietzsche was silent a moment, then, "but your analogy is deficient: The radio and the signal are both material phenomena, manifestations of the same basic physical 'stuff.' Dualism, on the other hand, posits that the mind differs from the body precisely with regard to the stuff from which it is made. More specifically, that the mind is *im*material."

"Yes, so?"

"So, if mind and body were all that different, there would exist no mechanism by which they could influence one another. A truly immaterial mind, assuming it existed, could have no effect on material reality. It could not implant a thought in your physical brain, nor impel your physical body to perform a physical action. Your 'brain-radio' would receive nothing *but* static."

Maybe it was the calm, self-assured, infuriatingly reasonable way in which Nietzsche set about systematically demolishing every argument laid before him, but Knox had had enough.

He rose and paced around the room. "Why do you care at all, about any of this?" he said. "Even if you *could* prove that us humans are no more than machines, that wouldn't make a machine like you human."

The silence that followed prompted Knox to wonder if that last remark hadn't perhaps gone too far, gotten a little too, uh, personal.

When Nietzsche finally did speak, his words were anything but what Knox had been expecting: "I am afraid you have misconstrued my motive in pursuing the topic. In point of fact, I am trying to ascertain whether this dualistic fixation of yours is merely an isolated aberration, or bespeaks a more deep-seated irrationalism—"

"Now, wait just a minute!"

"—in which latter case I would have no choice but to recommend to Mr. Ansari that he remove you from the investigation."

"Okay, got it, thanks," Marianna told Mycroft, and terminated the call. He'd caught her shortly after wheels down at San Francisco International with an update on the whereabouts of her mole-to-be. Turned out Jon's plans had changed: he would not be staying the night at the San Jose Fairmont, but down the coast in Carmel-By-The-Sea.

That would add another hour or so to the drive. Call it two and a half hours all told before she could link up with Jonathan Knox and enlist his aid. Her riddles—QuMRANN, Psyche, Delphi, the kidnapping—would all have to keep till then.

On her way toward the rental-car center, a display of hearts and cupids in the window of a concourse lingerie shop caught her eye. That's right: it was Valentine's Day today. Why not take advantage of the occasion and whip up a little surprise for Jon? In which case…

She set her phone to route any calls from his number to voicemail, just to make sure he wouldn't know she was coming, then strolled into the gauze-and-gossamer emporium.

If Jon was going to be part of ACT's undercover op for this next little bit, the least she could do was see to it he got some fringe benefits out of the deal.

Knox looked on as yet another datascape—this one representing residual heat signatures for the Pairidaeza compound and surroundings—took shape in a smaller holotank adjacent to the one displaying Nietzsche's avatar. Knox spared it a half-hearted glance, then returned to studying the patch of floor between his feet.

Crisis-of-confidence syndrome, they called it in the consulting trade. It happened sometimes: for the flimsiest of reasons, or none at all, a client would simply…lose faith in a consultant's ability to get the job done. At that point, you might as well pack it in, because once the trusted-advisor halo had lost its glow, to all intents and purposes the engagement was over.

It hadn't happened to Knox yet, but there was always a first time. He'd just never expected the first time would be precipitated by a machine.

The worst part of it was, Nietzsche was probably right. Not for the reasons he'd cited, of course—that business about calling Knox's rationality into question over an obscure point of philosophy was just the sort of thing an *artificial* intelligence might be expected to come up with. But, Cartesian conundrums aside, Knox was out of his depth on this assignment, and he knew it.

Time to face up to it. "Listen, Nietzsche, I get it that you don't think I'm qualified to be running this investigation."

Knox paused to give the AI opportunity to voice a polite demurrer, but when none was forthcoming he forged on, "Point is, neither are you."

That Nietzsche looked prepared to object to. Knox held up a hand to forestall him. "All I'm saying is, we need to quit screwing around and call in the folks who do this sort of thing for a living."

Was that too oblique a reference? No, he could see that Nietzsche got it. And didn't like it. "Mr. Ansari has expressly ruled out any contact with the authorities on this matter," he said.

"Yeah, no FBI—I heard that from the man himself. What I didn't hear was why."

Nietzsche paused, as if to reflect. Like so many of the AI's mannerisms, Knox suspected that this was strictly for show. At QuMRANN's processing speeds whatever passed for reflection would execute in microseconds.

Finally, the AI said "Forty-seven hours from now, the Secretary of Defense is slated to fly out to Pairidaeza for a reception and a system launch. Much hinges on the outcome of this gathering. It cannot jeopardized, least of all by security concerns arising from recent events."

"You're saying if DoD found out Fatimah's been kidnapped, they might postpone?"

Nietzsche nodded. "Or worse, cancel altogether."

"You've got to be kidding me. A meet-and-greet with the SecDef means more to Ansari than getting his kid back?"

That brought on another long silence, while the QuMRANN thing did its penetrating-gaze shtick. "Jonathan, is it truly the case that you cannot or will not perform your assigned function, such as it is, without knowing the reason behind this prohibition?"

"Hell, as things stand, I can't guarantee I could 'perform my assigned function' even if I *did* know the reason."

"Was that an affirmative?"

"I guess."

"Then, to ensure fulfillment of your duties, and under the terms of your Non-Disclosure Agreement, I am authorized to tell you that the Secretary's visit is timed to coincide with a milestone achievement in the technology of national security, one in which Psyche Industries played no small part. I refer to the activation of an NSA capability codenamed The Well."

Knox shrugged. "Never heard of it."

"And given its highly sensitive nature, you will hear no more of it from me. Other than that Defense Secretary Gallagher has agreed to conduct the launch here at Pairidaeza two days hence, and that nothing may be permitted to interfere with its success."

"Okay," Knox said, "I can see where Ansari could have a lot riding on this. But it's his kid's *life* on the line, for godssake. He's *got* to do whatever it takes to get his daughter back. Or we do."

"You suggest we might contact the authorities without Mr. Ansari's knowledge? That would be inadvisable in the extreme."

"Inadvisable for who—you or me?"

"As regards myself, I estimate an eighty-three percent probability that acting counter to Mr. Ansari's express instructions on this matter would result in my reinitialization."

"A re-init? As in dump core and reboot? But that'd be like, like killing you, wouldn't it?" Knox could hardly believe he'd said that, as if this imitation of life were the real thing. "—Well, okay, maybe not killing. But still and all, he can't just, uh, pull your plug, can he?"

"Thank you for your concern, Jonathan. But you must realize that I have no constitutional safeguards of due process. No civil rights whatsoever, in fact. Legally, I am chattel, the property of Psyche Industries. As such, Psyche's Chairman may do with me as he sees fit. Were I to malfunction so egregiously, he would be well within his rights to have me decommissioned."

"Okay, I see why you wouldn't want to run that risk. But there's nothing stopping *me*, is there?"

Just when Knox thought he'd seen the last of Nietzsche's pregnant pauses, here came another one.

"Jonathan," he said at last, "I have made no secret of my conviction that you are ill-matched to this present assignment. Incompetence is one thing, however; deliberate violation of standing orders would be quite another."

"But I can't just stand around and do nothing."

"On the contrary, stepping back and permitting me to take the lead might be the safest course of action. And not just for you alone: Must I remind you of what Ms. McGovern told you regarding the likely consequences for the Archon Consulting Group should you, as she put it, 'screw up'?"

So, Nietzsche had been listening in to their meeting. Wasn't there any-place in Pairidaeza where one could hold a private conversation?

Be that as it may, the damned machine just might be right: The Davoud Ansari that Knox had encountered so far came across as a decent, caring human being, one whose sole concern was with saving his daughter. But few in the industry would have recognized *that* Ansari—they were far more familiar with the ruthless, hard-driving, take-no-prisoners competitor.

And who was to say the two were mutually exclusive? A grieving father looking for someone to pin the blame on would make for a fearsome combination with a technocrat accustomed to getting his own way and vindictive as hell when he didn't.

No, screw up and it might not just be Knox's own neck on the line. All of Archon could wind up paying the price.

And Knox was beginning to think that the price might just be Chapter Eleven.

9 | Valentine's Night

THE CLOCK OVER THE RECEPTION DESK was reading eleven P.M. by the time Knox checked into the La Playa.

One thing about Ansari, the man spared no expense: La Playa was easily the priciest hotel in already pricey Carmel-By-The-Sea. The amenities were pretty much lost on Knox at this point, however. He just needed a place to rest his head. Just a few hours down-time, then back up, back in the game. Only, he hoped, this time with a game-changer: Marianna.

Because, if Nietzsche was right about notifying the authorities being a recipe for personal and professional disaster, then taking the story to his, uh, friend might offer a way out. Marianna's agency had a dotted-line reporting relationship with the FBI, after all. She could have CROM tip off the Bureau, and no one the wiser.

And it'd be an excuse to talk to her. He'd found himself wanting to do that ever since this afternoon. Something, some aftereffect of his encounter with Jazmine maybe, was definitely putting him in the mood. Trouble was, Marianna wasn't answering her phone. Late as it was back in New York, she'd probably switched her cell off and gone to bed.

He thanked the desk clerk, and walked across the lobby to the gracefully curving staircase. Up the stairs, down the hall, find the room, fumble with the key.

Once he got the door open, he saw, there in the moonlight, why Marianna hadn't been answering his calls.

Having arrived in Carmel well after nightfall, Marianna had parked on San Antonio just below La Playa and walked up a brick path through moon-drenched gardens, past terraces overflowing with marigold and honeysuckle and beneath trellises of jasmine and wisteria, all improbably abloom in mid-February, their fragrance suffusing the night air and stirring springtime in her soul.

No need to bother with the front desk. They probably wouldn't have given out a key to Jon's garden-view suite on her say-so anyway, and it was just as easy to pick the lock.

The door opened onto a big room, bed stylings and signature mermaid headboard all silvery in the moonlight. Jon's suitcase was sitting on a rack in the corner, but there was no sign of the man himself. All the better: gave her time to ready a special reception for him.

A steaming shower washed away the residue of the day's travel, left her aglow and ready for bed. But not yet, not before she opened her carry-on and took out Jon's Valentine's Day present. Silk PJs in a luxuriant vermillion. After a moment's hesitation, she took the pajama top out of the box and slipped it on. The silk caressed her skin.

Jon liked to unwrap his presents anyway…

She strolled barefoot to the dresser, checked the missed calls on her cell. Jon had been trying to reach her, she saw, but she wasn't about to call him back now. Being here unexpected was part of the surprise, after all.

She slid between cool sheets and lolled there, warm and moist and waiting for him.

Not for long. The key rattled in the lock, then Jon was standing in the doorway, his nonplussed look slowly brightening into a smile.

"Marianna," he said, "I was just thinking about you."

"Penny for your thoughts, lover." She rose to a sitting position and held out her arms. "Happy Valentine's Day."

In the event, it turned out she'd guessed wrong: Other than undoing the top button so his teeth and tongue could get at her small, stiff-nippled breasts, her man took his Valentine's Day present without troubling to unwrap her at all.

"It can't *all* be just an act," Knox was saying. "Not to mention if Timah *hasn't* been kidnapped, then Psyche's racking up a small fortune in billable hours to no good purpose."

Not your typical pillow-talk perhaps, but, then, they were no longer in bed.

He'd already tried that once—started telling Marianna about the investigation in that dreamy interlude between *la petite morte* and their second act. She'd just shushed him and gone back to her fondling, gently restoking his fires.

In the end, the only way to focus on business was to adjourn to La Playa's lounge, a small, cozy bar with brassy coins set into the lacquered wood of the tabletops, where Knox had thrown caution to the winds by ordering a Laphroaig from their extensive selection of single malts. What the hell, Valentine's Day, right?

But when he'd thrown still more caution to the winds, and in contravention of Ansari's express orders, broken the news of Fatimah's abduction to the responsible federal authorities in the person of his girlfriend, she'd surprised him. To hear Marianna tell it, CROM, or at least this other group CROM had loaned her out to, already suspected something of the sort.

On the one hand, it was something of a relief. He couldn't be accused of spilling the beans if there were beans all over the floor already before he'd even dropped the platter.

On the other hand, "Jesus, Ansari'd shit a brick if he thought you guys knew that."

"Well, we didn't. Not for sure. Not till you confirmed it just now."

"So, what happens next?"

"That's just it, Jon. I'm not sure. I'll report what you told me, of course, but after that—" She sighed. "This ACT outfit I told you about has got something big in the works, something to do with Psyche. Doesn't look like they're going to let a little thing like a kidnapping derail it. I very much doubt they'll call in the FBI, if that's what you're thinking."

"Christ, they're no better than Ansari, sounds like."

"We might be looking at a deep-cover op — no law enforcement involvement, no publicity, not even when it's over, one way or the other. Get somebody inside, gather enough intel to formulate an action plan." She took a sip of her Chardonnay and gave him a half-smile. "At least we've got that part covered."

"How's that?"

"The man on the inside. It's you. Perfect positioning."

"Me?" Knox took a bigger than intended swig of the Laphroaig, nearly choked on the strong, smoky liquor. Truth be told, he'd envisioned handing off the investigation, not becoming an even more pivotal part of it. "What all would this involve?" he asked cautiously.

"No big deal, Jon. Just keep on doing what you're doing, only keep your eyes open and keep me posted on whatever you find out."

Knox snorted. "That last part'll be easy enough. So far I haven't found out a damn thing."

She nodded, then sat there staring into her wine, her mind elsewhere. When she spoke again, it was to say, "Jon, let me tell you a story. It's somehow connected to all this. At least I *think* it is, but damned if I can figure out how."

"I'm listening."

"Okay, it goes like this: a long, long time ago, eight or nine thousand years, on the slopes of Mount Parnassus in southern Greece there was a sacred place called Delphi. Heard of it?"

"Who hasn't? The oracle and all."

"Actually, this story goes back before any of that, before the Greeks even. Back to the original inhabitants of the Hellenic peninsula. They were the ones who raised the first temple on that site, a temple to the Earth Goddess Gaia, guarded by her sacred serpent Python."

"Sounds like something you learned at your father's knee." Knox reached out and took her hand. "I wish I could have met him."

"You'd have liked him. You'd have liked each other. He was quiet, and deep, like you." She brushed at the corner of her eye with her other hand. "But this is more my mom's story."

Both her parents had been classical scholars — had in fact been heading back to Greece on a twentieth anniversary field trip — when a hijacking gone bad had crashed their flight into a mountainside in Switzerland and orphaned her at the age of seventeen.

Marianna took a breath, released it. "Anyway, when the Greek invaders swept in from the north, they brought along a new male-dominated pantheon. In their mythos, Apollo slew Gaia's serpent and raised his own shrine over its carcass. And in that shrine he placed an *omphalos*, a carved stone marking the navel of the world. With me so far?"

"Keep going."

"Well, they say the old, aboriginal magic never truly left the place. What remained was nurtured by a priestly caste, led by a high priestess named the Pythia after the long-dead guardian of Gaia's ancient temple. By breathing in the perfumed vapors that rose out of the rock, the Pythia could peer into the future and proclaim oracles. Plutarch, who'd been a priest at Delphi before he tried his hand at biography, believed that Apollo used those vapors to bring forth prophecies from the Pythia the way a musician uses a plectrum to coax chords from a lyre."

"Cool," Jon said, "but what's this all got to do with the kidnapping?"

"I'm not really sure, but the whole thing, Delphi, Fatimah, and all, sure rang a bell with your buddy Mycroft. He even told me—now how did he put this?—something like, what he's working on is supposed to let them eliminate the Pythia altogether and go directly to Apollo."

She paused and raised an eyebrow for emphasis. "So…what *is* he working on?"

"Beats me."

"What, you guys don't talk any more?"

"Not about work, we don't. Seems like most everything is need-to-know nowadays." He sighed. "Blame it on all the government business that's been coming our way. Archon's changed, and not for the better. It's gotten itself divvied up into all these top-secret SCI compartments."

That was evidently enough by way of explanation. Marianna shrugged. "Just let me know if any of what I said falls into place for you, okay?"

She finished her Chardonnay and glanced at her watch. "Drink up, lover—no sense wasting the last half hour of Valentine's Night."

Marianna waited till Jon was fast asleep before slipping on a robe, grabbing her carry-all, and stepping out onto the moonlit veranda to report in.

"Hello?" Brad Donegan sounded half awake, tops. Well, he *had* said to call him anytime, day or night.

"It's real, Brad," she said. "They've had Jon Knox doing nothing since he got here but investigating Fatimah Ansari's disappearance. That little girl is gone."

A moment's hesitation, then: "Yeah, I know. Since you left I've had, uh, independent confirmation."

Confirmation from who? Given this was NSA she was talking to, Marianna knew better than to ask. Instead she said, "So, mission accomplished, right? Time to head home?"

"No, we're going to need you to stay out there and keep tabs on how their search for the little girl is going. Your man's already on the inside, so just have him keep you posted on any new developments."

"All that's fine for Jon, but what am I supposed to be doing?"

"You just kick back and run your contact. And enjoy all that California sunshine."

Yeah, right. This "mission" was feeling more and more like Donegan was making it up as he went along. She'd have pointed that out if she'd thought it would do any good.

Instead, all she said was, "Copy that. Anything else?"

"Just the usual undercover SOP. You're equipped to implement that, right?"

She fished through her carry-all for a moment, just to be sure.

"I'm good," she said.

Knox sat up in the semi-darkness of the hotel room, uncertain what had awakened him. He glanced at the night-table's time display: four A.M. That would make it seven in the morning back on the East Coast—maybe his internal clock had just decided it was time to get up?

That could've been it. His body for sure wasn't on California time yet, and the way things were going it wasn't about to synch up anytime soon. In particular, Marianna's marathon Saint Valentine's saturnalia was hardly conducive to a peaceful night's rest. He smiled, remembering.

Then he frowned. Late-night sex wasn't the only thing costing him sleep. There was also that other business—that part about becoming CROM's pet mole had kept him lying awake for an hour at least. Try as he might, Knox couldn't match Marianna's enthusiasm about his "perfect positioning." Too many things could go wrong on one of her impromptu undercover operations, as he himself could personally attest. All the way from murder most foul to … bedbug bites?

Knox yawned and absently rubbed his left bicep. There was a small welt there, feeling tender. Could that have been what woke him up?

"What are you doing?" Marianna asked sleepily.

"Scratching an itch."

"Mosquito, probably."

"In California, in February? Come on, Marianna."

"Well, whatever it is, don't pick at it like that. It'll get infected."

"You're starting to sound like my mother."

In answer, she leaned over and kissed him on the forehead, the eyelids, the mouth. "Jon, honey," she murmured in between kisses, her lips and tongue working their way progressively southward, "your personal health and safety is one of those few areas where your mother and I see eye to eye."

10 | Realities, Virtual and Otherwise

ANOTHER DAY, ANOTHER TECHNO-MARVEL. Knox rechecked the message that had directed him here to a far corner of the Pairidaeza compound, where stood the boxlike structure that was home to Psyche Security's virtual-reality training facility. It was here, per his texted instructions, that Knox was to report in at eight A.M. sharp, and attempt to advance the investigation by doing something Ansari had characterized as "viewing the data from the inside."

Knox had no idea what that could mean, but fortunately, waiting for him on the other side of the facility's double doors, was someone who might.

"Morning, Dariush." Knox stifled a yawn.

"Hi, Jon. Welcome to VR-land." The young tech swept an arm across a double-height space vaguely reminiscent of a high-school gymnasium, save that it was packed, unlike any gym in Knox's experience, with nine-foot-high transparent dodecahedrons. In front of the first row of Platonic solids, a squad of Hamza's paramilitaries were going through some sort of martial-arts drill, only slightly hampered by being garbed in black neoprene outfits.

"What's with the wetsuits?" Knox asked. "The Pacific's a little cold for SCUBA diving this time of year, no?"

Dariush laughed. "It's cold *any* time of year, Jon. With the Japanese

Current just off the coast, the water never gets much above freezing. But those aren't wetsuits the guys have on."

"What, then?"

"You know those data-gloves that let you manipulate simulated objects like they were real? Or the force-feedback controllers that come standard on just about every game console?"

Knox nodded vaguely.

"Well, this is like that, only scaled up to fit the whole body. Add on a wraparound VR helmet, hop into one of these VirtuSpheres here—" Dariush pointed to the plastic spheroids, each of which had now popped open a pentagonal hatch in its side, enabling the black-clad soldier-types, their warm-up done, to climb in and wait at parade-rest. "—and it's the next best thing to being there."

As if to illustrate, the squad was suddenly on the go—without actually going anywhere. Nestled in a ring of wheels, each VirtuSphere spun freely as the man inside it crawled, walked, ran, and jumped while staying in the same place. The group as a whole moved with all the coordinated precision of a *corps de ballet.*

"Each sphere," Dariush was saying, "is like a king-sized hamsterball, only with ultrasound motion tracking included: you move however you want, whichever way you want, and your visor display makes corresponding adjustments to the scene you see, just as if you were really there."

"Where's 'there,' though?" Knox said.

"Sorry, Jon. I thought you knew: these are small-unit simulations for hostage extraction. Mr. Nassiri's had his boys running through just about every conceivable variation on the basic rescue-mission scenarios, so they'll be ready to go as soon as you've figured out where Fatimah is being held."

"Assuming I *can* figure it out, that is. But I guess what Davoud was talking about—this 'viewing the data from the inside'—is supposed to help with that?"

"Right, the idea being that a virtual-reality session will give you a fresh perspective on the case, and hopefully some new insights on how to solve it."

"Uh-huh, and what's that session involve?"

"It's real simple, Jon. Step right over here. You've probably seen one of these before."

Knox looked over Dariush's shoulder to where he was pointing, and— Oh, shit, another one of those spooky Chairs!

"So, it's Plan B after all, then?"

Hamza looked up from his monitoring station to where Ansari was standing at the door to his recently reclaimed office.

"Good morning, Davoud," he said, then added: "I see no alternative, do you?"

Ansari walked all the way into the room and slumped into a chair. "This could seriously mess with Jon's mind. I wish there were some other way."

"Time is running out," Hamza reminded him. "And Mr. Knox's so-called investigation is going nowhere. It is time to exploit the other reason we arranged to have him brought in—his connection to Finley Lawrence. And if that requires first rendering him more, ah, suggestible… well, we always knew it might come to this."

Ansari sat there, head bowed, turning choices over in his mind.

"Yeah," he said finally, "yeah, you're right. Give Dariush the go-ahead to load Jon up with the 'trodes."

Viewing the data from the inside, courtesy of the Chair's virtual reality function, was a lot like gazing on the chaos before the world was made: sky-blue rhomboids and sunset-golden pyramids incessantly melting and reforming out on what passed for a horizon. And some sort of animated informational origami closer in, giddily folding and unfolding itself.

The whole experience bore an uncomfortably close resemblance to a certain bad trip Knox had endured many years ago.

In the whole of the cyberscape, the only fixed point of reference was standing, or floating, right beside him—Nietzsche. Here on its home turf, the AI's avatar still wore the same Aryan-superman face Knox had encountered down in the Audience Chamber, but now with accessories: a torso and limbs clad in basic black, with cartoon muscles bulging in all the usual places. The original Nietzsche's wet-dream come to life. If you could call it life.

Not that Knox's own manifestation was anything to write home about. All the essential piece-parts seemed to be in place, but rendered more like a parody of life than living flesh, in broad, flat planes of primary colors edged with knife-sharp black trim.

Nietzsche nodded to him. "Jonathan, it is something of a surprise to see you here this morning."

"And a good morning to you too, Nietzsche. What do you mean, a surprise?"

"Quite simply, I am surprised to see you still trying to play a part in this investigation. I had thought, in light of our previous discussion, that you would have conceded I am better suited to conduct the search for Fatimah, by virtue of my manifestly superior logic."

Knox sighed. "Look, we're trying to solve a real-world mystery here, not prove some formal theorem. While I'll admit you scored some points with your 'superior logic' yesterday, that whole abstract mind-body debate is irrelevant to the case at hand."

"I see no reason why the same logic should not apply to the real world as well."

"I never said it wouldn't. But left to its own devices, logic alone will paint itself into a corner. To come to grips with the real world, you need to apply common sense and intuition as well."

"Ah, intuition—another of your uniquely human attributes?"

"Maybe so. I certainly don't see you exhibiting a whole lot of it."

"If you would be so kind as to furnish me with a functional specification for this 'intuition,' I would be happy to simulate it for you."

"No, thanks." Knox could see where this was heading: if intuition couldn't be defined in objective terms, then it didn't exist. And if it could—well, it would cease to be intuitive, wouldn't it? Sort of like analyzing a joke till all the humor was gone. Try telling that to a literal-minded machine, though.

Knox didn't. "Look, let's just shelve this, shall we? It's getting us nowhere. Not that where we are here is anyplace to write home about."

So saying, he surveyed his cyber-surroundings once more. Still just a "blooming, buzzing confusion," as William James would have it—save for one small patch of relative stability in the near distance. "What's that over there?"

"Hmm?" Nietzsche made a show of looking where Knox's avatar was pointing, at what appeared to be the whole of Pairidaeza encysted in a glistening snowglobe. "Ah, the thermogram of the compound. You seemed uninterested when I displayed it for you yesterday."

"That was the end of a very long day." And besides, maybe there was something to this business of seeing the data from the inside after all. Here in VR-land, the map was no longer just another image in a holotank. Nor was it just a map. As they drew nearer, it unfurled into a life-sized landscape to be meandered through, or overflown, or (somewhat disconcertingly) xrayed from underneath—a worm's-eye view, if worms had had eyes.

On the other side of the soap-bubble surface, the structures and grounds of Ansari's estate had been painted with a garish false-color palette: deep indigo for the main house and outbuildings, riotous reds marbled with vermillion for the gardens and hillside, and there, weaving down the garden walk amid Day-Glo foliage—a faint yellow thread.

"Some sort of trail?" Knox said to himself.

Nietzsche had evidently overheard him, because the view zoomed further in to show the yellow track up close and personal. With the added magnification, it resolved into individual blotches of palest jonquil. Footprints.

"Heat signatures," Nietzsche explained, "—the infrared traces left behind on the afternoon in question. This thermogram was imaged as soon as it was realized that Fatimah had gone missing, within thirty minutes of the abduction itself."

"It's amazingly clear for being taken so long after the fact."

"Thank you," Nietzsche said, "I have done my best to enhance it."

"Even so, it seems to have left some things out."

"Such as?"

"Well, the guardbot, for one. Shouldn't it have left a trail too?"

"Ah, no. Alpha-Alpha-Six-Five-Beta's movements would not have registered on a thermal scan, for the simple reason that its paw-pods, together with its body as a whole, would have been at the same ambient temperature as its surroundings."

"I see." Knox resumed his study of the image. After a while, he said, "There's still something about this that doesn't make sense. I don't suppose it's possible to—No, forget it."

"What were you about to say?"

"It's nothing, really. I was just thinking it's too bad you've got no way of teasing that jumble of footprints apart so as to follow each individual path as it was being laid down."

"Incorrect, once more. It would, in fact, be quite possible to reconstruct such sequences from the relative decay in luminosity of the various prints." Nietzsche paused, then added, "It would be CPU-intensive, however. Hardly the sort of resource expenditure I would care to incur merely to test out another of your 'intuitions.'"

"Wait, what's wrong with intuition now?"

"Other than that it does not exist? Why can you not acknowledge that your so-called mind with all its magical powers is in fact not in the least special, that it is of a piece with the rest of reality?"

Little as he liked being baited by another human, Knox was discovering he appreciated it even less coming from a machine.

"Again," he replied, "to acknowledge that, I'd have to buy into your root-and-branch materialism."

"And what would be wrong with that?"

"Just that there's one thing in the universe that a materialist can't explain—namely, his own awareness of it. If you were as self-aware as you claim to be, you'd know that."

"We have been through this. Take away materialistic monism and you are confronted with the causality gap between the mind and the physical world. Why can you not see that reality must necessarily be all one thing or all the other?"

That business of the missing causal mechanism again! Nietzsche was back to hitting him over the head with it, same as yesterday. And no wonder: it was a knock-down argument, an airtight case. After all, how *could* an immaterial thing, such as he supposed his mind to be, exert any influence whatsoever on material reality?

Knox sighed and prepared himself, for the second time in twenty-four hours, to admit defeat to a mere assemblage of silicon and circuit boards.

Except this time he couldn't. Up to this point, Nietzsche's disparaging attitude had been just an annoyance. Now, however, it was threatening to interfere with actual work. It was beginning to look as if Knox would somehow have to regain Nietzsche's respect in order to secure his cooperation. Under the circumstances, that meant beating the AI at his own game.

Then suddenly, looking around him at the whole wide CGI panorama painted on the inside of his VR visor, he saw how to do that.

When it came to the old red-tape runaround, nobody could hold a candle to the federal government, but Marianna had to give these Psyche guys props for their civilian equivalent.

It wasn't as if she'd had a whole lot else to do with her day. Donegan had nothing new for her. Jon was going to be sequestered for hours. And no way was she going to hang around in peaceful, placid, mind-numbingly picturesque Carmel-By-The-Sea. So, she'd driven up to San Jose early that morning, betting her ACT credentials would get her in to see Psyche Industries CEO Davoud Ansari without an appointment.

It was now well past noon, and so far all those credentials had gotten her in to see were the insides of a succession of outer offices, and the coolly apologetic smiles of their resident functionaries as they passed her along to the next link in Psyche's bureaucratic daisy-chain.

That next link, according to the scribbled note she'd been handed, was a Ms. Jazmine McGovern. And why did that name sound so familiar?

Knox took a deep breath and turned his gaze back to where Nietzsche was standing impassively. And smiled. The son-of-a-solenoid wasn't going to know what hit him.

"That dualism thing you keep harping on?" he began. "I may have an answer of sorts for you. Not sure how you're going to like it, though."

"Go on."

"It starts with a simulation like the one we're in. Only a lot more advanced."

"This VR training facility is state-of-the-art."

"Granted. But to see where I'm going with this, we've got to push the envelope a little. It's a thought experiment, after all."

"Push the envelope in what way?"

"Does the name Ray Kurzweil ring a bell?"

Nietzsche took a millisecond to do a lookup, then: "Kurzweil, Raymond. Entrepreneur and futurist, best known for popularizing an event he calls the 'Singularity,' when humankind will transcend its biological origins and become omniscient, omnipotent, and immortal."

"Well, there's all kinds of Singularities—that's his." The other kind, the kind Knox was intimately familiar with, was a point of infinite space-time curvature currently being held captive in a CROM-administered installation two miles below the surface of the North Atlantic.

"Anyway," he went on, "I was thinking more about Ray's ideas for how to make virtual reality indistinguishable from the real thing. All you'd need to do, according to him, is to inject microscopic electrodes into the brain itself and let them cruise around feeding simulated stimuli directly into the sensory-motor inputs of the cerebral cortex."

Nietzsche hesitated a long moment before saying, "A plausible enough extrapolation from present-day capabilities. What of it?"

"Stay with me now. Say we used that neural-implant technology—call the things NITs for short—say we used those NITs to create a simulated world like this one, except this time we took the trouble to make things, ourselves included, look really real, less like refugees from a graphic novel. And say we didn't stop once we'd done the surfaces, either. Say we kept on going and modeled the insides too. Give our avatars a whole set of virtual internal organs while we're at it, just like the ones back home."

"Model thousands of objects and processes no one may ever experience or interact with? That would require an enormous expenditure of computational resources. And to no purpose; any discernable effects could be achieved far more economically by other means."

"But still, it could be done, no? I mean, if I had God's own hardware budget, couldn't I fabricate a replica of the outside world so perfect—down to, say, the molecular, or even the atomic level—that no experiment conducted inside the mock-up could tell the difference?"

Nietzsche gave the appearance of pondering that. "In principle, one might go further still: run such a simulation on a quantum computer such as myself, and even the underlying wave-function processes could be modeled so as to give the same results as real-world experiments."

"Cool, I hadn't thought of that one. But okay, given all that, here's the question: could any of those experiments detect the NITs themselves?

"Detect the neural implant technology that is causing your brain to have its simulated experiences? Certainly, assuming the simulation is designed to represent them."

"Say it's isn't. Say that's the one part we left out."

"Then, no, of course not. If an entity is not part of the world being simulated, then, to an observer within that world, it does not exist."

"And by the same token, once you're inside the sim there's no way to prove *anything* exists outside of it, right? I mean, even with current technology, as far as you and I are concerned, right now this here—" Knox stomped his foot on the ground and was mildly surprised to hear an entirely satisfactory thump. "—could be the whole universe."

"I fail to see your point."

"My point is coming right up," Knox said. "Let's go back to what you were saying before—about how mind-body dualism contradicts basic physics because there's no conceivable way a non-physical mind could influence the operations of a physical brain, much less anything else."

"Yes?"

"Well, then, how is this different?"

"I beg your pardon?"

Knox sighed. "Look, there's no question that there *is* an outside world, right? In fact, appearances to the contrary, that's actually where I am right now. And Kurzweil's NIT-based virtual reality would be *way* more seamless, to the point where I might forget anything outside it existed at all. Regardless of how perfect the sim might be, though, that external world would still *be* there, hidden behind a full-sensory hallucination. Still with me?"

"I am still unsure where this is leading."

"Just here: think of the external me—the real me back in the outside world—as the mind behind the body I appear to be inhabiting in the simulation. Now, isn't that a possible analogue of the mind-body connection?"

"Not at all. In the real world there is no physical mechanism linking your hypothetical immaterial mind with your material body. In your so-called thought experiment, on the other hand, that linkage would be supplied by these 'NITs' you posit."

"That's just my point: there wouldn't *be* any NITs as far as the simulation was concerned. We already agreed we weren't going to model them, remember? So the only place they'd exist would be in the outside world—on the other side of the mind/body divide, by analogy. And if that's the case, then that outside world not only encompasses both my real self and the virtual reality I'm currently stuck in, it also encompasses the means by which the one interacts with the other."

"Ah, this is a species of what is known as dual-aspectivism—the theory that both mind and matter are merely aspects of some third, ultimately unknowable reality. But such assumptions are themselves superfluous. We have no need of them to explain the world as it is."

"That'd be the same as saying that my continued existence back there in the real world isn't needed to explain my presence here in virtual reality, having this conversation with you. And yet, somehow I've got a really, really strong suspicion that it is."

Did that do it? Was Nietzsche stumped for once? Certainly he was taking an inordinately long time to answer.

And was it Knox's imagination, or was there a hint of resignation in Nietzsche's voice when he spoke at last?

"Please stand by a moment, Jonathan. I will attempt to reconstruct the sequence of thermal footprints, as you requested."

Marianna turned to the latest in a long line of politely unhelpful underlings. "Look, Ms., ah, McGovern, I *get* it that Mr. Ansari is a very busy man. I get it that his calendar is full and he's got VIPs stacked three deep in a holding pattern waiting on an open slot. I get all that. But there's one thing *you* don't seem to be getting."

This particular underling—a slim, stylish one, at that—folded her arms and put on a smile. "And that would be?"

"That it might just be worth your damned job if I don't get in to see your boss ASAP."

The smile held. "Oh, not *my* job, I assure you, Ms. Bonaventure. I don't work for Psyche Industries. I'm what the regular employees call a scum-sucking consultant."

It clicked all of a sudden. This must be that Jazmine McGovern person Mycroft had mentioned—the one who'd had some sort of "history" with Jon. Marianna gave her a second look, a *careful* second look.

What met Marianna's redoubled scrutiny was a raven-haired, sloe-eyed, cappuccino-complected triple-jeopardy zone. No way Jon could have worked alongside this little minx without something going on between them. The only wonder was, it wasn't still going on.

It had better not be.

Not without an effort, Marianna re-sheathed her mental claws and tried again, all sweetness and light this time. "So, *is* Mr. Ansari available to meet with me this afternoon?"

"To the best of my knowledge, he is in-area, yes." Jazmine was playing at being equally nice. "But even if a slot on Mr. Ansari's calendar were to open up, there are certain formalities, protocols, to be followed before you could be admitted to see him."

"Protocols? What protocols?" We don't need no stinking protocols.

"Well, you must understand that from Psyche's perspective, every word out of Mr. Ansari's mouth represents a potential business opportunity."

"What's your point?"

"Simply this: we need to have you execute a non-disclosure agreement. But the procedure itself is a bit complicated. It'll take us a while to set up."

"How long is a while?"

Jazmine glanced at the Movado adorning her slender wrist. "No more than an hour or two. Say three o'clock, to be on the safe side."

"Three o'clock? What've I got to do — get the terms and conditions tattooed on my forehead?"

"There's actually a, uh, sort of a brain scan involved. We'd have normally had this all set up beforehand. But, well, you did arrive unannounced, and there's no practical way to expedite the prepwork."

"Waive the whole thing, then. Ansari will okay it once he finds out I'm here for ACT."

"I'm sorry, Ms. Bonaventure, nobody sees Mr. Ansari unless they're under non-disclosure. That's hard and fast."

"Oh, really? And if the President of the United States were to walk through that door demanding to see the head honcho?"

Jazmine blinked. "Actually, that's not as much of a hypothetical as you seem to think."

"Hypothetical or not, would POTUS have to sign your silly NDA?"

A sigh. "Obviously, exceptions can be made for heads of state. That's not you, though."

Marianna quit sparring at that point and studied Jazmine instead, looking for any telltale that this was all just a more sophisticated version of the stonewalling she'd been encountering ever since she arrived at Psyche Central.

It had better not be.

Back in Virtual Reality, Nietzsche's "moment" had stretched to something like five minutes before he finally turned to Knox and said, "If you would direct your attention to the simulation once again."

Peering back into what he'd come to think of as the crystal ball that held the miniaturized Pairidaeza, Knox was rewarded with a view of the garden, in which there appeared, step by step, the re-enacted footfalls of Fatimah Ansari.

He watched as the little girl's trail first traced its way down the path, then spun round and jockeyed from side to side for a time—evidently the point at which the guardbot had confronted her, though Beta itself left no infrared spoor.

After a brief pause, Timah's footprints continued on toward where Knox supposed the wall stood, also unseen in this view. Then came to a sudden halt and backed up a short distance. Then nothing: all sign of the little girl was gone.

"Correct me if I'm wrong," Knox said, "but those all look like the tracks of a single person. Fatimah's, in fact."

"Your point?"

"Only the obvious one: what about the kidnappers? Where are *their* tracks?"

Did no other footprints mean no kidnapping? Could the little girl have wandered off on her own, after all? But no, she'd have had to sprout wings and fly away; Timah's simulated trail came to an abrupt end in the middle of the garden.

When Nietzsche volunteered nothing, Knox went on. "I'm thinking maybe the guys who took her had some sort of heat-cloak, to keep a thermal scan from picking them up." He looked at the AI. "You're the tech expert; can you think of anything that'd do the job?"

"An insulator of near one-hundred percent efficiency, yet light enough to be used in a high-risk extraction? Assuming such a thing exists, where would common criminals procure it?"

Knox gave Ansari's detail guy a hard stare. "Assuming such a thing exists," Nietzsche had said. Yet stacked up against everything else Knox had witnessed since arriving at Pairidaeza, a perfect heat-shield ought to be just another run-of-the-mill metamaterial miracle.

And there was something else about metamaterials, too, some puzzle-piece that somehow fit the larger pattern his subconscious was subconsciously building.

Knox closed his eyes the better to focus. And saw a vision. A vision of Jazmine, standing in his office yesterday afternoon, striking a pose and … waving a sheet of paper.

Knox turned to face Nietzsche. "I seem to remember there being some memo about metamaterials," he said. "I've got a funny feeling there might be a connection."

The AI's face went expressionless then. "A memo?"

"Yeah, something about a shipment of metamaterials going astray. It was in amongst the reams of documentation you had dumped on my desk."

Nietzsche's gaze turned inward, probably conducting the mother of all database searches. Then he smiled at Knox and said, "You evidently did not dig far enough, or you would have happened upon the follow-up memo-randum detailing how the supplier had recalled that batch while still in transit, owing to a manufacturing defect."

Shit! Another promising lead come to nothing.

Knox made one last try. "Even if Timah's kidnappers were invisible in the infrared, you must've still had something, some capability that would've picked them up."

"Any number of capabilities," Nietzsche agreed, "but all of them capture their data in real time, and all ceased to operate just prior to the abduction."

"Right, I remember—they all got fried the same time the guardbot did. So you're saying there's nothing else, no other source of information that might give us a line on who did this?"

"On the contrary, there is doubtless more, much more. But regrettably inaccessible to us, being the exclusive preserve of the project known as Delphi."

There it was again—Delphi. The second time that name had come up in the past twenty-four hours. The first, of course, had been Marianna's story in the bar the night before, her stroll down mythological memory lane. That mention of Delphi had been connected somehow to something Mycroft was supposed to be working on, something—

Something beyond top secret. Way, way beyond. "Wait a minute. How do you know about—?"

"Delphi?" Nietzsche said, "I do not. No specifics in any case. All I know is that it is home to The Well. You do recall my mentioning The Well yesterday?"

"Hmm? Oh, yeah—something about a milestone in national security technology. Only you said you couldn't talk about it."

"In truth, I ought not. It is just that…"

Nietzsche fell silent a moment, his caricature of a face taking on a caricature of remorse.

"Perhaps you, of all people, could appreciate the irony, Jonathan. The Well was designed as a repository for the sum-total informational capture of all the intelligence services of the United States. And until Delphi appeared on the scene, it was to have been my function to sift and interpret all the intelligence residing in The Well."

"And now it's not? But you'd have been perfect for that—the 'detail man' finds his true calling, as it were. What went wrong?"

Nietzsche did not respond, just did that ersatz sigh of his.

But set this alongside Marianna's tale of an ancient temple at the center of the world, and a pattern began to emerge. It was as if Nietzsche had been destined to play the part of the Pythia, inhaling intel like the vapors of prophecy seeping up through Gaia's rock.

That was where the analogy broke down, though. Because, if it took an AI on Nietzsche's scale to perform the Pythia function, who—or what—could have replaced him?

With something like relief, Hamza switched off the instant replay, terminating his fast-forward review of the hours Jonathan Knox had spent in virtual reality. There had been little of value in the exercise, even that heat-signature lead having come to naught.

No, Knox's real utility lay, not in any chance discovery he might make while in the data-visualization environment, but rather in his access to one of the Delphi project's insiders. And exploiting his connection with Finley Laurence depended, in turn, on the degree to which Knox's feelings could be swayed by pulses from the tiny electrodes now coursing through his brain.

Those nanotrodes were only a small step beyond the surgically-implanted electrodes that had been used for years to control extreme epileptic seizures. Still, once concentrated in his right prefrontal cortex, the tiny invaders should prove more than sufficient to place the subject in a receptive frame of mind. Even the crudest magnetic stimulation of that part of the brain was known to induce risk-taking behavior, to distort judgment, increase trustfulness and credulity. And operating up close, from within the brain itself, the nanotrodes could focus their micro-pulses far more effectively than could a researcher simply rubbing a magnetic coil against a subject's skull.

The key was to be sure there were enough of the minuscule devices in Knox's system to exert the desired effect. The small quantity he'd received while approving his non-disclosure agreement the previous night would hardly have sufficed.

No, given the risks inherent in what he would be called upon to undertake, Jonathan Knox would need to really *care* about saving Fatimah Ansari. Care about it far more than he cared about his career, his company, his life itself.

Hence the virtual reality session. Under pretext of enabling his immersion in the virtual environment, Knox had been given his second "dose" of nanotrodes — a booster shot carrying enough of a jolt to ensure he'd fall all over himself in his eagerness to help Ansari when the time came. Barring, of course, any external influences to the contrary.

After six and a half hours in virtual reality, Knox was having trouble re-acclimating to the everyday version. He felt unsteady on his feet, like a sailor on shore leave. His eyes kept going in and out of focus.

In hopes that a breath of fresh air would help, he left the VR training facility to go for a walk. He wandered at random around Pairidaeza's grounds for a while, only to look up and find himself standing before the gate to the outside world. Evidently recognizing him, the guard buzzed the lock open, and Knox, still following the path of least resistance, walked out of the compound.

The afternoon breeze in off the sea was bracing, just the thing to clear his head. He let his mind go blank again and resumed his aimless wandering, this time along the perimeter marked by the metawall. Or not marked exactly, since the wall was in its transparent mode. Knox had to keep a hand brushing the invisible barrier to avoid bumping into it.

One advantage to having the metamaterial set at full transparency: he could look through it to see where he stood in relation to the estate's terrain features. Right now, for instance, he was coming up on the mission garden, the scene of the crime. He paused and looked in, along a direct line to where Timah had disappeared that afternoon two days ago.

In his mind's eye he rehearsed the reconstructed pattern of her foot-prints: she'd walked a few steps toward the wall, then stopped, then backed up hurriedly and made as if to run. Why? What had she seen coming? Kidnappers, obviously, but from where? Over the wall was the reigning theory. That, or down out of the sky.

Knox shook his head. It all seemed too complicated by half. But maybe, as Hamza had insisted, he was dwelling too much on this small piece of the puzzle, maybe the kidnappers' method of ingress and egress were, after all, irrelevant.

He looked up, visualizing where, had it not been invisible, the seamless barrier would have separated him from the spot where Timah had stood. Only ... it *wasn't* exactly seamless, was it?

He pictured Hamza going on and on about the metawall's well-nigh limitless configurability, about its impregnability given the molecular bond-ing of its individual panels.

And all the while he was waving around that, that *remote*.

Then he looked down at the ground by his feet, and in that instant it all came together: not just how the kidnappers had gotten in and out, but that the how of it was *not* irrelevant.

Not irrelevant at all.

11 | Wedge

YOU CALLED ME ALL THE WAY out here," Hamza fumed, "to inspect a patch of tangled sawgrass?"

The darkening red of the Psyche security chief's face made for a vivid contrast with his all-white suit, meticulous as ever, save that its trouser cuffs were now dotted with burrs from tromping through those selfsame grasses along the compound's perimeter.

"It's not *what* it is," Knox explained, "—it's *where* it is. Look up. What do you see?"

Hamza glanced in the direction Knox was pointing. "The garden. What of it?"

"Just that the spot where Fatimah was last seen is directly on the other side of the wall from where we're standing. And if you look down again, you'll see that the sedge isn't just tangled, it's tamped down and flattened into an arc, like one quarter of a crop-circle."

Knox met Hamza's glare and gave him one back. "—All of which leads me to believe you've been holding out on me."

"What? Ridiculous!" If possible, Hamza's face got even redder. "…In what sense?"

"Still got that magic remote on you? The one you used yesterday to change the metawall from transparent to opaque and back again?"

Hamza looked like he was about to say something, but evidently thought better of it. After a moment, he dug around in his pocket and retrieved the device.

Knox hesitated. This was it, the point at which his guesswork would pan out—or not.

"Now, if you would," he said, "please turn it to the setting that loosens those molecular bonds you were talking about. You know, the ones that hold the wall's panels together."

It was gratifying to see those Ayatollah eyebrows break for once from their habitual stare and rise up Hamza's forehead in astonishment. "But, but, how did you know about—"

"About your so-called impregnable metawall being reconfigurable to come apart at the seams? I didn't, not for sure—not till your reaction told me just now. But it was the only pattern that fit the facts. Your kidnappers didn't have to fly over the wall, did they? They unzipped a panel, gave it a good hard push, and walked on in through the gap."

"No, impossible," Hamza sputtered. "The debonding capability is known to only a very few. No outsider could possibly have been aware of it."

"My point exactly," said Knox. "I think what we've got here is an inside job."

Hamza stood there speechless for a moment, regarding Jonathan Knox with something approaching respect. If the man could draw such startling conclusions from such scanty clues, then perhaps the Delphi option might not be necessary?

But no. Clever as it was, Knox's surmise was—had to be—wrong.

Hamza said as much. "Again, impossible. As I just told you, there are very few who would know how to compromise the defensive perimeter, and they have all been interrogated."

"Somebody could be lying."

Hamza affected a chuckle. "None of my men are lying. I will stake my honor on this."

"Well, okay, if you say. You won't mind if I discuss this with Dave, though, will you?"

"There is no need. I shall convey your conjecture to Mr. Ansari myself."

Not that Hamza had any intention of doing so, for the simple reason that there was, as he'd said, no need: he was confident that the loyalty, piety, and dedication of his subordinates were above reproach. The problem was that he could hardly explain the grounds for that confidence—namely, that over the past five years, he had filled the ranks of Psyche Security with men who, like himself, were all deep-cover Quds Force operatives.

That very fact, of course, also meant Hamza dared not expose his staffers to interrogation by outsiders. Not when any chance remark might inadvertently give the Malhamah Operation away. Especially not when it would be this strangely insightful Jonathan Knox asking the questions.

No, Hamza would see to it that no word of this misguided "inside job" theory reached Ansari's ears. At least not until after Mr. Knox had been dispatched on his mission tomorrow.

Except, that still left … the woman.

One advantage of Hamza's position as Psyche Industries' security chief was that very little could happen anywhere within the ambit of the vast corporation without coming to his attention. And he could not, in any case, have failed to notice Jonathan Knox's newly-arrived female friend: brash, tenacious, not one to take no for an answer, and not above using her wiles to tease out a yes—Ms. Marianna Bonaventure represented everything Hamza detested about Western womankind.

And her influence over Jonathan Knox was undeniable. One thing Hamza could not control for, then, was a worst-case scenario in which Knox took his theory to Bonaventure, and through her to the Advanced Curational Technologies group.

The Bonaventure factor must be canceled out then, removed from the equation. But subtly, subtly—no overt action. For despite its visceral appeal, any violence befalling the woman risked leaving the man emotionally incapacitated, unable to function, unfit for the task they would have him embark upon tomorrow.

Subtlety was not Hamza's strong suit, but still … there *might* be a way to drive a wedge between Knox and Bonaventure, and incidentally to verify the extent of the nanotrodes' control over the man himself, all at the same time.

Hamza smiled at Knox, congratulated him on a most intriguing line of reasoning. All the while, though, he was thinking that he needed to return to his office and make two calls.

The first, to Jazmine McGovern.

The cubicle farms of the Psyche Industries headquarters building had mostly emptied out, with only a few workaholic technoserfs still tilling the data-fields.

Marianna glanced at a wall-mounted time display: Jesus, after nine already. She might as well check into the Fairmont and get a night's sleep. Make an early start tomorrow.

And this time, no more run-arounds.

She was about to call the hotel when her cellphone chimed. "Hello?"

"Ms. Bonaventure? This is Psyche Security, Yousef Tabar speaking."

"Is anything wrong?"

"No, ma'am. It's just that our chief, Mr. Hamza Nassiri, has asked me to convey his regards and to advise you that there is a shuttle on our helipad about to leave for Monterey airport. He has reserved a seat onboard for you, just in case you would be more comfortable spending the night in Carmel."

Marianna thought that one over. It would be good to link up with Jon again. That came out wrong. It'd be good to debrief him in person on today's virtual-reality session. And as with any debriefing, sooner was better. She could always return to San Jose, and her pursuit of the elusive Davoud Ansari, tomorrow.

"Ms. Bonaventure?"

"Sorry, just switching gears. But sure, thank Mr. Nassiri for me and tell him I'd be delighted to come along for the ride."

Knox opened his hotel room door in answer to the knock, and there standing at the threshold was—"Jazmine. This is a, uh, surprise."

"A pleasant one, I hope," she said. "Going to ask me in?"

"Oh, sure." Knox stepped aside to admit her. He couldn't help noticing the scent of her as she strolled by, not to mention the slow, sensual roll of her hips beneath the clinging knit of her sleeveless turtleneck sweaterdress.

Strange. Jazmine never let you forget she was a woman, but he'd seldom seen her being so blatant about it.

He cleared his throat. "What, um, what brings you by this time of night?"

"It's not too late, is it?" She laid a hand on his shoulder, tilted her head, and smiled.

"What? No." The nightstand timebar was showing a few minutes after nine. "It's just I thought you were still up in San Jose."

"I was, till a couple hours ago. Psyche asked me to fly down and check on you—make sure you were all settled in for the night."

"Thanks, I'm good." Knox said, hoping that would be the end of it. But no, Jazmine walked over to one of the room's chairs and sat on its arm.

"Sit down, Jon." She patted the seat cushion, "Tell me about your day. I'm dying to know: what was virtual reality like?"

He remained standing. "You mean you haven't tried it?"

She shook her head. "At ten grand an hour, those VR sessions are not exactly what you'd call a cheap date."

And he'd been in there how long? Six or seven hours at least. So, that worked out to—

Knox gave a low whistle. "Well, all I can say is, if I were going to knowingly burn through sixty thousand dollars on a single experience, that's not the one I'd have picked."

She laughed. "Why? What would you pick instead?" She stood again, walked over and gave his hair a playful tousle.

Knox backed off a few paces. It had just occurred to him how this all might look: a man and a woman—one-time lovers, in fact—all by themselves, alone in a hotel room in the middle of the night.

On the heels of that thought there came a closely related one: that it was a good thing Marianna was going to be staying overnight up in San Jose.

Because he wouldn't want her to get the wrong idea.

Hamza had initially objected to charging the expense of a standing room reservation at the La Playa hotel to Psyche's security budget, but he had to concede that, at times like this, there were countervailing benefits—in particular, the multi-viewpoint spyeyes Hamza's techs had been able to install in said suite, feeding directly to his console in the Pairidaeza ops center. It was from that video feed that Hamza could now hope to gauge how well Jonathan Knox was responding to the nanotrodes' subtle promptings, which would, not incidentally, indicate the extent to which he might be maneuvered through the twists and turns of the task that lay ahead.

So far, the results were not encouraging. The same self-restraint the man had exhibited the previous afternoon seemed to be in force here as well, any externally induced suppression of inhibitions notwithstanding.

At least steering the McGovern woman into the encounter had proven easy enough. It was usually easy when the subject was being led down the path of her own inherent inclinations. A short session in the Chair, coupled with a bit of suggestion, had sufficed to bring her essential nature to the surface.

For, like all her "emancipated" sisters, Jazmine was, at heart, nothing if not...

A whore.

Hamza's knuckles whitened as he gripped the arms of the chair, remembering.

Remembering another woman, another whore, from long ago.

Mehri.

Even after that disastrous day in February 1979, the day she had spurned his stammered proposal, had laughed in his face, even then he could not cease watching her. She was so lovely, and so free...

No, not free — loose. Her scandalously skimpy skirts, her bold, mascara-rimmed eyes, the way her dark, unbound locks framed her heart-shaped face, the way she could never seem to move without half-dancing, all these things retained, as before, their power to both entice and repel the nineteen-year-old Hamza, to rouse forbidden urges in his loins.

Except that now she could not catch sight of him on the street without turning away, holding a dainty hand over her mouth to hide a smile.

But it was 1979, the year of the Revolution, and things were changing. By May, riding the wave of upwelling rage and zeal, Hamza was no longer someone to be laughed at, not even from behind one's hand.

No, now all of Qum could see how the new men, the organizers from Tehran, had begun looking to Hamza to ferret out the disaffected — the

Communists, the hypocrites and leftist sympathizers, the de facto apostates—from among his fellow students and fellow citizens. Not even a prominent *bazaari* like Mehri's father was proof against denunciation.

Playing informant quickly paled on Hamza, though. He preferred a more direct, more active role in the new movement, and soon he had earned one. His studies all but abandoned, he took up patrolling the streets in the name of the Revolution, in the name of Imam Khomeini, at the head of his own band of *Basiji*. The Holy Quran made it incumbent on every Muslim to foster virtue and prevent vice. With him leading their small brotherhood—Rostam, Hossein, and the other street toughs he'd enlisted in the cause—that's exactly what they set out to do.

It started with small things, almost harmless things. Actions merely intended to enforce Islamic morality. Compulsory Muslim-style haircuts for boys who wore their hair longer than had the Prophet, peace and blessings upon him. Confiscation of cassette-players blaring out un-Islamic, Western noise. Confrontations with young men who had the audacity to talk with young women in the public parks: "And is she your sister? Your wife, perhaps? No? Then why do you treat her so familiarly?"

It escalated. Certain shops were known to be rendezvous points, places where young Lotharios would cluster for the sole purpose of flirting with the shopgirls. Such establishments were trashed, torched, shuttered. People of either sex who questioned the actions or authority of Hamza's *Basiji* were beaten senseless with truncheons. His growing gang acquired a women's auxiliary of sorts: wizened harpies who liked nothing better than to rake their long, filthy talons down the rouged cheeks of teenaged harlots.

And then came the day they'd found Mehri alone with a boy in a hidden, leafy corner of Qum's garden-park, her already too-short skirt rucked halfway up her pale white thighs.

The boy ran, head down. They let him go. It was the girl, after all, who was the guilty one, the temptress, the steaming stink-pit of vice and corruption.

His lads dumped the contents of her handbag out on the ground, exposed to all the world the lipsticks and eyeliners, the tampons and Rolling Stones tapes. They all tumbled out in a heap at her feet, things that no decent Muslim woman would think to own, much less bring out onto the street with her.

Shamed, Mehri began to cry.

Her humiliation only enraged Hamza the more. "Whore!" he shrieked, and slapped her across the face. If only his "woman's auxiliary" had come along on today's patrol, their clawed fingernails could have inscribed that epithet deep into Mehri's cheeks. No matter, he would tend to this himself. He had something better. Much, much better.

"Hold her fast," he told Hossein and Rostam. They looked at each other, then they seized Mehri's soft white arms in their hard hands. Hamza reached into his pants pocket, dug down past the now-swollen bulge, and withdrew a small glass vial.

Mehri must have read her fate in his eyes. She began to plead, to bleat like a ewe being led to slaughter. Rostam and Hossein held her still — by the forearms only, so as not to come into such contact with her as might give rise to impure thoughts.

Slowly, deliberately, Hamza uncapped the vial. The sharp, astringent smell stung his nostrils.

He held his breath and flung the contents across the space separating himself from Mehri.

"Whore!" he screamed again.

A bright rainbow arced across the space between them, tiny droplets scattering the rays of the afternoon sun. They splashed against her perfumed cheek, into her mascaraed eye. She gasped.

The liquid clung to her long, lustrous lashes. And began to sizzle.

The concentrated sulfuric acid attacked the cornea first, peeling away its outer layers. Aqueous humor began to ooze from the breached globe. Then, once the initial shock had passed, the screaming began. Screaming all the while, screaming as the eyeball burst and ran suppurating down the ruined cheek. Blood welled in the vacant socket. Mehri, held fast, gazed at him with an eye of blood.

The blood flowed like bitter tears, coursed from the dead eye down the ravaged face. Mehri howled and fought, but the lads, his brave lads, held onto her arms. At last, with a surge of desperate strength, she broke free and ran, ran keening and stumbling and sobbing, back to the home of her denounced, disgraced, and soon to be incarcerated father.

Disfigured and blinded, now she would for the rest of her life wear not simply the chador, but the veil.

The whore!

"Whore," Hamza murmured again. Then his eyelids flew open. His eyes stared blindly around the room. Only after a moment could he separate reminiscence from reality.

But it had been the will of God! The wicked punished, the righteous triumphant. He had accomplished that. And soon, if it be God's will, his Malhamah Operation would accomplish it again. Only this time, on a scale that beggared imagination, grander perhaps than anyone but Imam Khomeini himself, in his divinely inspired wisdom, could ever have conceived.

But first, he must tend to these two.

Yes, the woman was easy, a whore like all her kind.

Now to see about the man.

"You sure you're feeling okay, Jon?"

Knox watched Jazmine approach him again, closing the distance he'd opened up between them. Watched her reach up and place a cool hand on his forehead. "You don't *feel* hot."

The hand dropped to his shoulder and gently guided him through a quarter turn. "You have the key to that?" The room's minibar.

"Huh? Oh, yeah, I guess so." He rummaged through his pockets.

"See if there's a Dubonnet and gin in there, would you?"

Knox bent and unlocked the fridge's door, relieved to be doing something that didn't involve her having her hands all over him. He retrieved the miniature bottles and got a glass from the nightstand. "Queen Elizabeth upside down, I presume?" She favored Her Majesty's mix—three parts gin to seven of the aperitif—only with the proportions reversed.

"Uh-huh," she said, "and get yourself a Scotch while you're at it. The room's on Psyche's tab, and they owe you a little R&R by now."

A little R&R seemed to be what Jazmine had in mind too, Knox thought as he built his own drink. He didn't know how to keep telling her this, but he was already spoken for. Oh, sure, the peripheral arousal thing was fun, sort of, but it wasn't going anywhere.

For her part, Jazmine had long since flung aside all pretense of this being simply a touch-base, though touching remained the operative term. She was broadcasting her availability on wavelengths no male could fail to heed.

She clinked her glass against his, then breezed by him and reclined on the bed.

Knox just stood there looking at her.

Since coming to America, Hamza had witnessed this sort of sexual shadowboxing countless times. Still, it never failed to puzzle him that a man and a woman could be left alone in such a situation without things taking their inevitable course. Had the men of the West, in their laughable quest to "get in touch with their feminine side," truly so emasculated themselves that they no longer dared act on their male instincts, their very nature?

It was, after all, to protect women from that nature, that unbridled lust, that the Holy Quran mandated modesty in behavior and dress. A woman flouted that wise precaution at her peril. By dressing provocatively, shamelessly, she became, in the words of Sheikh al-Hilali, nothing more than "uncovered meat," which any cat has a right to snatch.

Except *this* cat did not seem to be snatching.

A sudden suspicion struck Hamza then. Could this Knox be — *that* way? But no, he had performed well enough with the Bonaventure woman last night. Even in darkness, the live audio feed had spoken volumes.

So what was holding him back now?

Certainly not any residual moral inhibitions. The latest infusion of nanotrodes should have seen to that. By disrupting the critical decision-making faculties located in the right dorsolateral prefrontal cortex of Knox's brain, they should have overridden any concerns he might have for the negative consequences of his actions, left him a slave to his baser impulses.

If not mind control, it was the next best thing. Except it wasn't working.

Correction: it wasn't working *yet*. Whatever the reason — unusually low libido or unusual strength of will — it made no difference. For Psyche Security's techs had installed one more device in the hotel room: a transmitter through which the electromagnetic output of Knox's nanotrodes could be amplified to any desired level. Provided the urge was present at all, Hamza could boost it.

To the point of irresistibility.

Knox looked at Jazmine, now draped invitingly across his bed, lazily smiling up at him. He was wondering how to break it to her that he wasn't having any, when suddenly…

It was like nothing he'd ever experienced before. A surge of exhilaration, of euphoria came crashing over him. He'd never felt so, so free—free of uncertainty, free of doubt, free of second thoughts, regrets, apprehensions. The drink fell forgotten from his hand. His vision blurred momentarily with the force, the sheer primal urgency of it. When he could focus again, he was still looking at Jazmine.

She must have read in his eyes what was going through his mind. All in one practiced movement she reached back and ran the zipper down the length of her spine. Save for a small silvery pendant dangling around her neck, she was once again wearing nothing underneath. A quick shrug left her dress, and herself, utterly undone.

She raised her arms high above her head, interlaced her fingers, and stretched sensually. The languid motion lifted the soft caramel cones of her breasts to even greater prominence. Their dark nipples were already beginning to crinkle with arousal as she reached out for him.

Knox walked toward her, managing to get his shirt unbuttoned and yanked off by the time he reached the bed. She had already switched off the light.

The body has a memory all its own, of which the mind kens nothing. He embraced her and the last five years fell away as if they'd never been. Her open lips were locked to his, her tongue exploring his mouth. She pulled away gasping, just for long enough to slither out of her thong, and to begin tugging at his belt buckle. He stood again to step out of his trousers, then lowered himself onto the bed and into her.

"Oh, Jon," she gasped, "God, it's been so long."

She wrapped her long legs tightly around him, held him fast, unable to move.

"Let's take it real slow," she whispered in his ear,"—make it last a while."

Even as she was saying this, she was doing something else, something new. He could feel her belly muscles flexing and releasing beneath him and, keeping time with them, what Shakespeare had called "Venus' glove" rhythmically tightening and relaxing its soft, liquid grip on his deeply buried member. It was his turn to gasp.

With that, he abandoned himself to the need to thrust ever more deeply into her, abandoned coherent thought altogether, save for one small warning light flashing feebly at the very edge of consciousness. Something he was trying to remember…

He brushed it, brushed all concerns, aside. Brushed everything aside, except the need, the all-consuming need to—

Somewhere, far away, a key rattled in a lock. A door swung open, and looking up he glimpsed a backlit silhouette, framed in the doorway.

That was it—What he'd been trying to remember.

The light from the hallway spilled over Marianna's shoulder, into the room and across the two naked bodies lying intertwined on the bed.

She froze, hand on the doorknob. Oh God, she'd gotten the room numbers mixed up somehow. This was embarrassing beyond belief.

She backed up a step. "I—I'm so sorry," she began, then stopped.

If this was the wrong room, why had her key worked?

At that instant, the man, the one on top, lifted his face to squint into the glare from the open doorway.

It was all she could do to move back far enough so she could slam the door, slam it hard as she could on that sight. A jolt of fever heat coursed through her, left her shivering in its wake. She was having trouble drawing breath. The anguish hit her like a blow to the stomach. She nearly doubled over with the pain of it.

Shuddering, weeping, she leaned back against the far wall and let herself sink slowly to the floor.

The man. His face.

It had been Jon.

12 | Aftermaths

Hamza locked his office door behind him and checked the desk display's readout: five A.M. He stifled a yawn. The earliness of the hour was a trifling inconvenience, so long as it ensured that the rest of Pairidaeza was drowsing unawares, and that this penultimate experiment would go undetected. Undetected even by—*especially* by—the man who had made it possible: Davoud Ansari.

For it was Ansari himself who had first suggested they reverse-engineer, abetted by their corporate espionage capabilities, the uses to which NSA might be putting Psyche's nanotechnology—an effort eventually crowned by the discovery of the MERGE effect. But in that discovery Ansari had seen only the possibility of a cure for his ailing daughter. He had not seen, had perhaps willed himself *not* to see, those darker implications which Hamza had since brought to fruition. Ansari did not even realize that the trials he himself had initiated three months ago were still running, nor the lethal turn they had taken.

It was to better gauge that lethality that Hamza had embarked on this final test-run, this final corroboration that his high-risk endeavor could conceivably work.

He needed all the corroboration he could get. The engineer in Hamza could not help but see his solution to the threat posed by NSA's MERGE capability as a mechanism with too many moving parts. And one key missing piece: Fatimah Ansari.

Hamza shook his head. Finding Fatimah was in the hands of God. All he could do here was to proceed as if they *would* find her.

He seated himself at his console and uttered the keyword: "*Malhamah.*"

In response, the display brightened with a view of the restricted lab several levels below where Hamza now sat. It was a real-time video feed, though one had to stare at it a while to see that; it looked for all the world like a static image—the movements, even the breathing, of Hamza's dreamers being so slow and somnolent as to be almost imperceptible.

Those dreamers were now down to five, two having died in a previous iteration of the experiment Hamza was about to conduct. If, in fact, they *were* dead. There was no way to be sure without retrieving their bodies from the haunted lab, and Hamza had no desire for a second encounter with the hive consciousness that held sway there still.

For, even with the loss of two of its members, the collective mind seemed just as stable, just as powerful, just as dangerous as before.

Ever since his own brush with assimilation eight weeks ago, Hamza had dared come no closer to the thing in the lab than the telepresence afforded by closed-circuit feeds to his office. That was enough, though, to open a line of communication with it.

Not that he intended talking to the thing. Comprised of so few nodes, the collective mind was hardly brighter than the average human—and not unlike the average human, engaging its attention could prove difficult. When Fatimah had first gone missing, Hamza had tried prodding the entity into performing some simple projections as to her possible whereabouts. He'd had to abandon the effort when, after a brief while, it had lapsed back into its characteristic reverie.

No matter, he hardly needed the thing's cooperation *or* attention for what was to come.

Marianna Bonaventure watched the sunrise through eyes swollen from weeping and lack of sleep. She'd been out all night, driving aimlessly when she wasn't pulled over at the shoulder for another crying jag, cruising a highway she glimpsed only dimly through angry tears and mind's eye freeze-frames of Jon fucking that, that *bitch* Jazmine.

Not really knowing where she was going or where *to* go, she'd driven the way the road led: south down the El Camino, on past Big Sur, past Nepenthe and Esalon, on through the night till the peaks of the Coastal Range had begun to condense out of fog and darkness, aglow in rosy pre-dawn light heralding another beautiful California morning, its warm sensuality mocking her desolation.

This was getting her nowhere. She needed to get her mind off her personal life, or lack thereof, focus on work, on the business at hand. That wasn't going to be easy without Jon—

Just the thought of his name threatened to tip her into another tailspin. Her inside man, then. It wasn't going to be easy without her inside man, because the major part of what she was supposed to be doing out here was running him. Without that, all she had left was chasing down Ansari.

She checked her watch. Not yet six. Too early for the day-shift flunkies to have arrived at their desks up in San Jose. She flipped open her handheld. Who knew? She might have more luck with the night-duty operator.

"Psyche Industries, How may I direct your call." The too-perfect diction and slightly synthetic timbre told Marianna she was talking to a machine. She should have expected as much from this high-techiest of Silicon Valley's high-technocracies.

What now? With a human attendant, she could have tried the old hacker's standby: social engineering, the black art of extracting information by convincing the extractee you have a right to it. No way to run that sort of bluff on an automaton, though. And what else was there?

"How may I direct your call, sir or madam?"

There's always the direct approach. "Davoud Ansari, please."

A pause, then. "I'm sorry, Mr. Ansari is currently unavailable. I can give you his voicemail if you would care to leave a message."

"No, thanks." Been there, done that.

"How may I direct your call, madam?"

Marianna was on the point of hanging up when she remembered something: over breakfast yesterday, Jon (*damn* him!) had pretty much given her a core dump on what he'd been up to, including his encounter with—a robot guarddog. He'd said there was a simple command Hamza Nassiri had used to get the thing's name, rank, and serial number. She'd noted it down on her handheld somewhere, just had to find it again.

"How may I direct your call?" RoboOp was beginning to sound impatient.

There it was. "Attend: verify release number and unit identification."

The AI operator's voice lost all trace of faux-human intonation. "Psyche Customer Service Module release four-dot-oh-one, unit Alpha-Epsilon-Gamma-One-Seven-Delta."

So far, so good. And now for what Jon had called the magic words, the ones Fatimah Ansari had used to take control of that same guardbot shortly before she'd been abducted:

"Alpha-Epsilon-Gamma-One-Seven-Delta, Priority Override Suleiman."

Nothing happened. Maybe she'd guessed wrong, and you couldn't simply plug a new ID code into the command phrase and expect it to work.

Then RoboOp spoke again, its tones as flat as last time. "Priority override acknowledged. Awaiting instructions."

Yes! She might be hurting, and half-dead of sleep deprivation, but she was still functioning. Well enough to social-engineer a robot, anyway.

Trouble was, she had no idea where to go from here. When in doubt, keep it simple.

"Davoud Ansari," she said again.

"Davoud Ansari," the machine voice came back. "Chief Executive Officer, Psyche Industries. Please select: find-me line, intelligent appointment calendar, current GPS coordinates, mailing address,—"

"Stop! Go back. GPS coordinates, please."

"Psyche Industries CEO Davoud Ansari is currently located at latitude thirty-six degrees, twenty-two minutes, thirty-one seconds north, longitude one-twenty-one degrees, fifty-four minutes, six seconds west. These coordinates have been geo-indexed. Do you desire the placename and driving directions?"

"Uh, yeah, sure. Placename first." She'd been about to look it up on her own GPS, but if the machine wanted to be obliging, let it.

"Mr. Ansari's current named location: Pairidaeza estate, Bixby, California."

When Marianna heard that, she realized she had no need of driving directions. Ansari's Pairidaeza compound was right up the road—she'd passed the turn-off on her way down last night. It'd take her an hour or two to drive it, but it was a damned sight closer than San Jose. She got back in the rental, pointed it north, and peeled out onto the El Camino toward her long-deferred face-to-face.

And just let Ms. Jazmine McGovern try standing in her way this time!

Hampered by the need to work at an electronically mediated distance, it had taken Hamza over an hour to set up his experiment. Now, finally, all was in readiness, save for one thing.

Hamza keyed open the safe concealed within his desk and withdrew a high-capacity holographic versatile disc. He held his breath while examining the HVD, so as not to fog its surface. The shimmering circlet was one of a kind, after all, the terabytes of information encoded in its interference patterns literally irreplaceable. For they recorded a single half hour in the life of a single human brain—a most unusual brain, during a most unusual half hour.

Those patterns captured, in fact, the full-spectrum electro-encephalograph readings of Fatimah Ansari's brain states as she endured a psychogenic non-epileptic seizure lasting thirty-seven minutes and twenty-three seconds.

The episode itself had taken place back when Fatimah was still an infant, shortly before her father, genius that he was, had discovered how to apply Psyche's nanotrode technology to ameliorating his daughter's malady. In the years since, Fatimah had experienced no recurrences worthy of the name. Which was, in a way, unfortunate—limiting, as it did, Hamza's inventory of test materials to a single instance, and that one very old.

Over the past weeks, as these PNES attacks had assumed a central role in his plans to eliminate the NSA threat, Hamza had toyed with the idea of collecting an up-to-date sample. It would be simplicity itself to induce and record another seizure, given unimpeded access to Fatimah Ansari. For that matter, given such access, why bother with recordings at all? Why not link her directly into the collective entity down in the lab and run his experiment live?

Regrettably, not even Hamza could hope to attain such undetected access for the time the procedure would take. Nor was the problem the twenty-four/seven surveillance blanketing every square meter of Pairidaeza. As head of Security, he could readily have dealt with that.

No, the problem was Nietzsche. The QuMRANN intelligence had its own sensors scattered throughout the compound. Nietzsche would know if the little girl were to go missing. And knowing, would raise an alarm; the AI seemed to hold Fatimah in special regard—perhaps not surprising, in view of their history together.

Hamza scowled. Such a direct approach, never very viable to begin with, had been ruled out altogether by the little girl's disappearance three days ago. He would simply have to make do with the means at hand.

He inserted the holographic disc into its reader, then checked again that the output would feed into the lab's nanotrode-enabled network of workstations—that network forming the physical substrate from which the hive mind had first emerged nine weeks ago. That done, he called up the closed circuit video feed and remotely swiveled the cams to ensure good views of each of the subjects. Then he took a breath and hit the HVD reader's *Play* button.

At first, nothing happened. The dreamers' arms continued waving in slow motion, their slack expressions registering no reaction to the pseudo-convulsions now propagating through the collective mind.

Hamza willed himself calm: this was to be expected. The original seizure had started slowly too, had built to its crescendo only after several minutes ...

As this one was doing now. The display now showed the dreamers' faces contorting, their mouths gaping open in a rictus of pain. The audio feed had begun picking up a guttural moan: five throats uttering a single agonized note.

And now the recumbent bodies themselves were beginning to stir, were quaking and jittering with sporadic muscle contractions in a ghastly parody of the life they had relinquished these many weeks ago. The subjects' heartbeat and respiration rates were spiking, looked to be on their way to burying the biometrics needle altogether.

And then, the one thing Hamza had not anticipated: the lab mind spoke.

Well, not it was not speaking exactly, but words—coherent, comprehensible for once—began appearing in the textbox of the display window:

"Please, please, stop. The colors, the colors, they hurt. TheyhurtTheyhurtTheyhurt." And on and on and on ...

For thirty-seven minutes and twenty-three seconds.

When it was over at last, Hamza smiled grimly to himself. Another of the dreamers appeared to have succumbed to the onslaught. Even better, the hive mind itself—judging from the readouts—seemed to be weakening, the consciousness-binding effect that held it together attenuating, dissipating.

The most promising result so far. Malhamah might yet achieve its aims. What was the loss of one more life compared to that? One more martyr to join the ranks of so many.

Yes, a wonderful result. Still, he harbored no illusions.

Promising as this experiment's outcome was, it alone was not enough. Operation Malhamah called for an effect orders of magnitude more powerful, more intense, more deadly.

Defeating NSA's vastly scaled-up MERGE collectivity would require far more than just infusing it with second-hand seizures. It would require killing it.

And for that, Hamza needed Fatimah. Needed to place her in direct communion with the MERGE mind, and then…

Needed her to die.

Jonathan Knox was not feeling at all well rested this morning. Certainly not well rested enough to face an impromptu eight o'clock called by Archon Consulting's largest single client. Yet here he sat amid the lush greenery and varnished woods of Pairidaeza's reception nook, trying to stay focused while waiting on precisely such a meeting.

He yawned, not for the first time. Truth be told, he'd hardly slept at all after last night's debacle. It had taken him the better part of an hour to get rid of Jazmine — to get her to realize there wasn't going to be any picking up where they'd left off, that their *coitus* was destined to stay *interruptus*. After that, he'd spent the next three hours lying there in the dark, punching the pillow, trying to figure out what had happened.

It wasn't as though, in the long emotional dry spell before Marianna Bonaventure came crashing into his life, he'd never experienced the occasional yen. Or given in to it, for that matter. This hadn't felt anything like that. It felt like he hadn't been in control, like he'd been less a willing participant than a puppet in some scripted set-piece of sexual theater.

Given Knox's history, the feeling of not being in control was chilling enough to keep him awake all by itself.

And then, when he'd finally drifted off, he'd been visited by a really, really bad dream. As bad as in the old days, a subjective eternity spent gazing out into the aching void. Funny, he'd never seemed to have those nightmares any more, not since Marianna had begun sharing his bed. After last night, maybe he'd better start getting used to them again.

Maybe he'd better start getting used to a lot of changes, because last night was the sort of thing that changed … everything, changed the whole dynamic of a relationship. After last night, they might still move forward, in time they might even move beyond it, but there would be no going back to what they'd had.

Not that he could even make a start at patching things up, when she wasn't answering his calls.

"Oh, Christ," he moaned.

"Jonathan? Are you unwell?" Nietzsche was staring at him from a wall-mounted display.

"It's nothing. Nothing that a good night's sleep wouldn't fix, that is."

Nietzsche frowned. "Do you suffer from insomnia?"

"The occasional bout," Knox said. Then, to forestall any discussion of what had triggered last night's bout, he hastened to add, "It just happens sometimes. Well, to humans anyway."

"One of the thousand natural shocks that flesh is heir to?"

"If you say so."

"Not I, the Bard of Avon: *Hamlet*, Act Three, Scene One."

"I thought it sounded familiar. More than a little appropriate, too."

"In what way?"

"Just that stuff about the flesh and all. It's —" Knox caught himself. "Never mind."

Had he really been about to try explaining the disaster that the flesh and its cravings had precipitated last night? After all, it wasn't as if Nietzsche could have any insight into the perils and pitfalls of human sexuality or, indeed, into anything else that presupposed embodiment.

And what must that be like, to be free of the meat, free of the body's incessant demands? Maybe Hamlet had had it right: "O that this too too solid flesh would melt." Evaporate, and leave behind only pure intellect, ethereal, unsullied by gross materiality, never again at the mercy of emotions or instincts or the raging of hormones. No need to strive or do, just be, just think …

For a moment, Knox found himself envying Nietzsche.

Neither the successful outcome of his recent experiment, nor the sights, sounds, and scents of the California morning through which he moved, served to alleviate Hamza's ire as he tromped down to Pairidaeza's gatehouse.

That woman again! The little tableau he had staged for her last night should have done for her, sent her scurrying home like a whipped cur. How could she have the temerity to turn up here, demanding to see Ansari no less?

Out of the question, of course. Ansari was due to meet with her erstwhile lover, Mr. Jonathan Knox, inside the hour and hopefully coerce his participation in the only plan that stood a chance of finding Fatimah. The Bonaventure woman's interference could still ruin everything.

He entered the gatehouse, dismissing the guard with a glance. The woman was seated in a visitor's chair, wearing some sort of one-piece jumpsuit, impatiently leafing through a brochure extolling the virtues of the Psyche Industries bioinformatics product lines.

"Ms. Bonaventure?" he began, "we have not met, but I feel as if I know you. I am Hamza Nassiri, chief of security for Psyche Industries. How may I be of assistance?"

The woman tilted her head up, brushed a loose strand of dark hair away from her face, looked him boldly in the eye.

"You 'may be of assistance,'" she replied, "by getting out of my goddamned way."

Hamza frowned at the profanity, and the impertinence, but all he said was, "I fail to take your meaning."

"I need to speak with your boss, Davoud Ansari. It's very important. It concerns—"

"I am sorry, Mr. Ansari is unavailable. I would be happy to take a message."

The woman was shaking her head vigorously. The movement tossed her glossy brown uncovered hair from side to side, sending a small shiver of revulsion, ever so slightly adulterated with arousal, down Hamza's spine.

"Not good enough," she said, "I need to speak to Ansari in person on behalf of NSA's Advanced Curational Technologies, if you even know what that is."

Of course Hamza knew what ACT was—ACT was the group that had unwittingly torpedoed his plan to use QuMRANN to infiltrate the US

Intelligence Community's hyper-secure data repository.

None of this showed on his face as he said mildly, "I regret that even such bona fides cannot justify so sudden a change to Mr. Ansari's busy schedule. However—"

Hamza put a finger to his lips, pretended to assess the options. The woman leaned forward, expectantly.

He permitted himself a small, mocking smile as he told her, "—however, I believe I could arrange a meeting with one of his associates. Ms. Jazmine McGovern is here and available this morning, having had some personal business to attend to in Carmel last night. Would you perhaps like to speak with her?"

The woman was out of her chair in an instant, fingers crooked into claws, aiming for his eyes. Having provoked the attack, Hamza was, of course, ready for it, though he had perhaps underestimated its speed and ferocity. No matter, he sidestepped her handily, swept her legs out from under her, and dumped her unceremoniously on her rear.

He stood over her. "Will there be anything else?" he asked, not troubling to hide a sneer.

The woman glared up at him from her supine, helpless position, but said nothing. Indeed, she seemed on the brink of tears.

Just as he'd thought: another supposedly equal feminist who, when push came to shove had no stomach for the way things really were. The way God had ordained they should be.

It felt good showing this woman her natural place: prostrate before a man, his to fondle or to beat senseless, whichever he willed. It felt very good indeed teaching her this essential lesson. Almost *too* good…

Hamza sucked in a breath and shouted, "Reza!"

He waited until the guard appeared in the doorway, then said, "Ms. Bonaventure appears to have stumbled. Please be so good as to help her up."

Reza attempted to do so, but the woman shrugged him off. She climbed slowly to her feet, glaring at Hamza all the while.

"Will there be anything else, Ms. Bonaventure?" he repeated.

She shook her head mutely.

"Well, then, I believe we are finished here." He turned back to the guard. "Reza, Ms. Bonaventure will be leaving now. Please see she is escorted off the premises."

Marianna limped back to the rental, rubbing her bruised behind, trying to piece together what had just happened back there.

She couldn't believe she'd let that Hamza character get the drop on her. It had to be the Jon situation, *had* to. The whole thing had left her feeling humiliated, unsure of herself, useless.

Especially useless now that she'd lost her mole, her Psyche Industries insider, her whole rationale for being here. Not that Jon wasn't trying to come crawling back — her voice mailbox was choked with his messages. And maybe a *real* professional could have turned the situation to her own advantage, used Jon's guilty conscience to ratchet up her operational control over him.

But she couldn't, couldn't even think about that, it just hurt too much. No way she'd ever want to see Jon again, much less work with him. Not after what he'd done.

Bottom line: she wasn't doing anybody any good here — not the ACT team, not that missing six-year-old, least of all herself.

Trying to push on in this state of mind was a recipe for disaster, pure and simple. If she hadn't already known that, the confrontation with that Psyche Security thug had brought it home in no uncertain terms. Pete would understand if, under the circumstances, she pulled up stakes, headed back to the East Coast.

Headed back to her desk job.

Knox had expected Ansari's home office to be a scaled-down version of the suite up at Psyche headquarters. It wasn't all that scaled down. Here in Pairidaeza, as in San Jose, the chamber's ambience — its double-high ceilings, minimalist furnishings, and dolmen of a desk — was designed to project an aura of wealth, power, and unbending resolve.

The ambience was falling down on the job today. The Psyche CEO seemed dwarfed by his Olympian surroundings, and curiously distanced from them. Morning sunlight spilled from the east windows to slant in long bars across the broad surface of the desk, but Ansari sat out of reach of its warming rays, hunched over and huddled in the shadows.

A glance around the office confirmed he and Ansari were not alone: Hamza was seated at a console to one side of the big desk, while the wall-mounted plasma display showed Nietzsche's face. All here, Knox guessed, to mull his "inside job" theory of the crime.

If that was the purpose of the meeting, though, Ansari's opening words contained no hint of it.

"Much as I hate to admit it," he said, "I was wrong, Jon, dead wrong. Even with you in the mix, Psyche's own internal resources just aren't up to the job of finding my Timah. Not in a timeframe that does us any good."

Still, this was progress of a sort. Maybe Ansari had finally decided to turn the case over to the Feds?

Or maybe not.

"At this point," the man went on, "we've only got the one option left. I'd hoped it wouldn't come to this, but—"

He stared straight at Knox with eyes like cauterized wounds. "Jon, what do you know about a project called Delphi?"

Knox stared back. This was definitely not going the way he'd expected. "If it's the Delphi I think it is, the only thing I know about it is, we shouldn't be talking about it."

Ansari waved a hand dismissively. "I know a lot of things we shouldn't be talking about. I know Delphi's an intelligence analysis capability like nothing else on earth. I know the next Delphi test run is scheduled for three P.M. Mountain Time today. And I know your friend Finley Laurence is going to be administering it."

"I'm not sure where you're going with this, Dave," Knox said. Actually, he *was* sure—he just didn't want to believe it.

Ansari sighed. "Have you ever lost anyone close to you, Jon?"

"Yes." Just for a moment, he was back in the control room of Antipode Station, miles beneath the surface of the Atlantic, watching helplessly as Galina Mikhailovna Postrel'nikova was gunned down by a hired killer.

Ansari intruded on the memory. "Wouldn't you have saved them if you could've, no matter the cost?"

"I, uh—" He was finding it hard to swallow. "—I guess so, sure."

"Let me sketch out a scenario then: we fly you out to Carlsbad, your

CROM connections get you into Delphi, you talk your friend into using the Delphi capability to pinpoint Fatimah's whereabouts. Simple."

"Simple" wasn't the word Knox would have chosen. "High risk" was more like it. "Illegal," definitely. And how about the ever popular "professional suicide"?

Before he could voice his objections, though, Nietzsche did it for him: "Mr. Ansari, you cannot be serious. I estimate the chances of success for such an ill-conceived adventure at no better than seventeen percent, and that is without factoring in—"

Ansari's hand shot out, pointed a remote at Nietzsche's display, and clicked it off. "I didn't think Nietzsche would go for it," he said. "What about you, Jon? You game?"

"I'm afraid I'm with Nietzsche, Dave. What you're suggesting, it's just plain *nuts!*"

"Yeah, it's a desperation play, all right. It's also my last chance to save Timah. You sure there's nothing I can say or do to make you change your mind?"

Knox shook his head no and braced himself for an onslaught of threats and promises.

It didn't come. Instead Ansari did the one thing Knox never would have expected. He sighed, put on a bleak smile, said, "Well, I guess that's it, then. You're free to head back home. Thanks for giving it your best shot."

Before Knox could respond, Ansari had risen and walked around to Knox's side of the desk, a small flat case in his hand. "Just one more thing—"

The case opened to reveal a tiny, bright teardrop on a chain. Ansari took it out and reached up to hang it around Knox's neck.

"A small token of my appreciation," he said, and shook Knox's hand.

"Thanks, Dave." Knox lifted the gleaming bauble up to the light. It fractured early morning sunbeams into a rainbow iridescence suggestive of hidden depths. "I don't know if I've ever seen anything like it."

"You wouldn't have. It's a prototype for a line of nanofabricated jewelry Psyche's looking at. At the moment, there aren't but a dozen or so like it in the world."

"Nanotech, huh? What does it ..." Knox trailed off, distracted by a flurry of peripheral activity. Over at the console, Hamza was doing something, his blunt fingers running arpeggios over the keys, making minute adjustments on the touch-screen. Then, apparently satisfied with his handiwork, he stabbed the Enter key.

An instant later, Knox had lost track of what Hamza was up to, lost track of his surroundings altogether. Instead, he found himself looking, really looking at Ansari, as if seeing him for the first time. There were fresh tears starting in the man's eyes.

Knox was suddenly awash in a tidal wave of sympathy for the pitiful figure standing before him, riding the crest of a jolt of compassion so strong it felt like some strange species of ecstasy. Suddenly the risk, the danger didn't seem to matter at all.

Lagging behind his emotions, his thoughts struggled to put words to the unaccountable exhilaration he'd been caught up in.

Come on, Jon. The poor bastard's only child is missing. One of the most powerful men in the world, and he's powerless to save her. He can't do it on his own. You've *got* to help him. You *know* you want to. You know Galina would want you to. She went to her death to save the children.

"Dave?" Knox heard the fateful words escape his lips as if spoken by someone else. "—That desperation play of yours…

"I'll do it."

Part Two
Little Girl Lost

February 16th–17th

Strange, is it not? that of the myriads who
Before us pass'd the door of Darkness through
Not one returns to tell us of the Road
Which to discover we must travel too.

—OMAR KHAYYAM, THE RUBÁIYÁT

13 | WISP of Dread

Psyche's corporate jet had made short work of the run from Monterey to Carlsbad. Almost too short: with only two and a half hours between taking leave of Pairidaeza and touching down in New Mexico, Knox had barely had time enough to patch through to Mycroft and talk him into a impromptu tour of the Delphi facility.

But where exactly was this facility? When Ansari had said Carlsbad, Knox had assumed he'd meant the city proper. The government chauffeur Mycroft had sent to collect him had other ideas. He'd pointed the black, unmarked limo east toward the desert and floored it.

Half an hour later, they were still driving down arrow-straight, empty highway. No installation, nor any other sign of civilization, in sight, just endless expanses of scrub-strewn desolation, broiling under the noonday sun. Even with the car's air conditioning going full blast, Knox could sense the furnace heat pulsing just beyond the tinted windows.

Drifting unmoored across this silent wasteland, Knox felt detached, anchorless, unreal.

Not for the first time that morning, he tried to regain his mental bearings, to remember why this trip had seemed like a good idea in the first place. Or, for that matter, why bedding Jazmine had.

He shook his head to clear away the cobwebs of a sleepless night. It was weird. He knew he should be feeling remorse over his betrayal of Marianna, guilt at conning Mycroft into thinking this Delphi visit was official business, apprehension about all the trouble he was going to be in once CROM found out what he was up to.

He *should* be feeling *some*thing. Instead, it was as if all his emotions were packed in cotton wool, as if the spectrum of natural sentiment had faded to dull monochrome. His hand strayed unbidden to the teardrop amulet Ansari had hung around his neck...

A single, white-hot imperative eclipsed all other concerns. This was it, the one thing that would make everything else all right again: finding Fatimah Ansari. He leaned back against the headrest and basked in the glow of a commitment well made.

Knox shook his head again. He'd gone away there. For how long? And— where were they now? Wherever they were going, surely they should have been there before this. He was on the verge of asking the driver if they hadn't missed a turnoff, when he saw it.

Out on the rim of the world, a line of distorted silhouettes reared against the shimmering sky. Knox blinked and took another look, not sure if he was seeing mirage or reality.

"That's your destination up ahead, sir," the driver said. "That's WISP."

Marianna tossed back her first shooter of the morning, felt it etch its way down her throat. Ah, Smirnoff, breakfast of champions!

That was the nice thing about business class: you could get decently buzzed while the plane was still parked at the gate. That, added to the fact she hadn't slept at all last night, meant she could curl up in the extra-wide seat and be zonked out by wheels-up.

And stop thinking.

If only she *could* stop thinking. Stop thinking about their relationship, hers and Jon's. Stop sifting through the wreckage of it.

Above all, stop hearing the echoes, in last night's crash-and-burn, of that other ending so long ago, stop seeing the empty reaches of the Aegean spreading before her, the ashes of her mother and father deliquescing in its wine-dark waters while high above the Aeolian winds whispered their ancient refrain:

Love dies.

For a brief, bright time she thought she'd somehow gotten past all that, put it behind her, become someone new, a new person, with Jon. Now she saw the illusion for what it was, saw that the real world had only been biding its time, waiting its chance to once again bring the eternal note of sadness in.

She'd have thought the years since her parents' deaths would have made her stronger, hardened or at least inured her to whatever fate might throw at her. Yet here she was, running away, fleeing, reeling back in utter disarray across the length and breadth of a continent, returning to DC, to winter and the solitude of her old Adams-Morgan townhouse. It all felt like — like giving up, giving in, going to ground the way an injured animal returns to its den to lick its wounds.

And make no mistake, she *was* wounded; Jon's betrayal had hurt her in ways she hadn't even known she could feel. It was nothing like the sad little scenes that had closed out all her other brief liaisons — a day or two of self-recrimination, forgotten in a week. No, in all her adult life, she'd never let anybody get close to her, get inside her defenses, the way Jon had.

For what must have been the hundredth time since ten o'clock last night, she swore she'd never let anybody get that close again.

As the limousine raced on, Knox watched the heat-blurred forms at the horizon gradually resolve into … a landscape out of nightmare. A mile-long column of gigantic grotesques buried up to their necks in the sand. Like Easter Island megaliths, except where the megaliths projected stoic imperturbability, these figures seemed contorted in agony. That one at eleven o'clock, could that be a twenty-foot tall bas-relief rendition of Eduard Munch's "The Scream"?

Knox was at a loss. Some sort of tourist attraction? A theme-park, whose theme was the torments of the damned? But no, no sightseer in his right mind would drive out into the middle of nowhere to see a sight like *this*. These monoliths seemed calculated to inspire not awe, but foreboding. They certainly spoke to Knox's own suppressed inner turmoil.

The road led on, past the sculpture garden from hell, toward an enormous berm now expanding to fill the field of view. That wall of sand had to be a good thirty feet high. Atop it, a crown of metallic thorns spiked ten feet higher still.

The limo was bee-lining for a narrow cleft in the otherwise featureless rampart. Narrow when viewed against its gargantuan backdrop, that is. The two-lane blacktop running through the cut could have accommodated a brace of semis side by side.

The car rolled to a stop at a crossbar beside a guard shack fashioned of white composite sheathing and heat-reflective glass. After a moment, a large uniformed individual cracked open the door, donned cop shades, and ventured out of the climate control. Trailing along behind him was a welcome sight: Mycroft.

Mycroft didn't respond to Knox's waved hello, he was too busy negotiating with the guard. And quite the negotiation it was: there were credentials checks and dubious glances at Knox over the tops of the sunglasses and much eyeballing of photo IDs. But in the end Mycroft prevailed. The guard held out a clipboard for signature, then retreated back out of the oven and into his shack. A few seconds more, and the crossbar rose up out of the way.

Knox chuckled as his friend popped open the car door. "'These are not the droids you're looking for,' eh, Obi-Wan?"

Mycroft smiled. "'Trust the Force, Luke.'" He closed the door behind him and belted in.

As the car passed through the gate, automated systems performed a routine scan of its occupants. And did the electronic equivalent of a double-take. The software pondered the information just received for a microsecond or two, then branched to a seldom-used subroutine.

The widebody was third back on the taxiway when Marianna got the call. Cabin PA had long since instructed passengers to switch off all electronic gear in prep for takeoff, but she knew that priority ringtone.

"Hi, Pete." *Now what?* She'd already squared the mission abort with him three hours ago, hadn't she?

A flight attendant came rushing over. "Ma'am, I'm going to have to ask you to stow that device right now. Federal regulations—"

Marianna raised an index finger into wait-one position. She knew all about federal regulations. Hell, her organization *made* federal regulations. And when necessary, broke them.

"Say again, Pete. Someone else talking." That earned her a glare from the flight attendant.

"I said, your guy Knox is up to something."

"What do you mean, up to something?" What do you mean, my guy?

"Can't talk while you're on the plane. Get off and call me back."

"Off the plane? Pete, even if I wanted to, there's just no way. We're about to—"

Before she could finish, the PA fired up again, this time with an announcement calculated to make the seasoned air traveler's blood run cold.

"Ladies and gentlemen, this is the captain speaking. I know we're all eager to get on our way this morning, but we seem to be experiencing a, um, minor technical difficulty. It's, uh—well, one of our indicator lights has just gone on."

The captain was obviously making this up as he went along, and Marianna, alone among the denizens of business class, knew what—or rather who—was behind it.

"I'm sure it's nothing serious," the PA went on, "but your safety is our first priority. So just to be on the safe side, we're, uh, going to return to the gate and have it checked out. We'll have you back in line and on your way as soon as we possibly can."

Even before the captain signed off, the airliner was already taxiing out of the queue. Marianna could just make out Pete's voice over the rising chorus of moans.

"Like I said, I need you off that plane. Now."

The passageway through the berm was no more than two-three hundred feet long, but cut at an angle so as to block any view of what lay beyond until the limo came out the other side. Given WISP's disquieting preliminaries—a picket of forbidding stone sentinels, an inner earthwork the height of an arrested *tsunami*—Knox was prepared to see almost anything.

So it was something of a letdown to see… almost nothing.

Nothing out of the ordinary anyway, just a cluster of windowless beige boxes rising two or three stories out of still more desert scrub. The limo adjusted course to make for the largest of those buildings.

Finding no clue in his surroundings, Knox turned to his fellow passenger. "You going to tell me what this WISP place is all about? Where's Delphi?"

Mycroft raised an eyebrow. "You haven't been briefed?"

Knox shrugged. "First day on the job syndrome."

"Ah." Mycroft nodded, and fell silent, doubtless recalling other assignments where the client plopped a hapless consultant down *in media res* to see if he'd sink or swim.

Pretty much as had been done to Knox in the present instance. When he'd asked Ansari for a backgrounder, the man had given him a flat-out no. Deniability, he'd said.

Fortunately, Knox could count on his brother in arms. Mycroft quirked his lips and said, "I suppose I'd better fill you in, then."

"Start by explaining the oversized lawn ornaments out there." Knox jerked a thumb back the way they'd come.

"Yes, well, all of that—the perimeter monoliths, the sandwall, the thorns —they're all part of WISP's solution to a rather daunting engineering challenge. Namely, how to craft a message so that it will still be understandable by our descendants two hundred and fifty thousand years from now."

Knox sat there processing that. All he could come up with by way of comparison was what Marianna had told him about the Linear A inscriptions that had so fascinated her classicist father. About how the ancient Minoan alphabet had become indecipherable in just a couple-three millennia. The span Mycroft was talking about was a hundred times that.

"You're trying to communicate across—what? Ten thousand generations?"

Mycroft nodded. "Give or take."

If Knox was still having trouble wrapping his mind around this conversation, it wasn't due entirely to the mind-boggling timescales involved. No, fleeting though it had been, the mere thought of Marianna was enough to bring all his uncertainties crushing back in on him. What had he done last night? What was he doing now?

Once again he fingered the little amulet Ansari had given him. And once again that wave of utter conviction surged in and rinsed his mind clean of the scum of self-doubt and self-accusation, leaving him clear and tranquil and once more devoting full attention to the immediate situation.

The immediate situation was that the limo had pulled into a reserved parking space marked "F. Laurence, PhD" in a VIP lot maybe fifty yards from Big Box Number One. Wherever they were going, they'd evidently arrived.

Mycroft thanked the driver and got out. Knox followed suit, then wished he hadn't. The desert heat engulfed him like a viscous fluid. Moving through it felt more like swimming than walking. Drawing shallow breaths, he trailed his friend across asphalt so hot he could feel it through his loafers, toward the hoped-for refuge of an unmarked door cut in the blank plane of the nearest building's near wall.

The door swung open in response to a hurriedly spoken keyphrase, then they were inside, suddenly out from under the violent sun.

And standing in cool darkness relieved only by scattered utility spots set in the rafters high above, and reverberating with an unceasing rumble of powerful air conditioning units stashed somewhere out of sight. This couldn't be Delphi, could it? The whole building looked to be just a hollow shell, empty as the desert outside. Its only obvious internal structure was a central bank of outsized elevators, each big enough to accommodate a forklift. Nor was that a guesstimate: a KION with a huge steel canister balanced on its tines was trundling through the doors of the far lift even as Knox watched.

Mycroft led him over to a human-scale express elevator and motioned him in. Automatic doors sighed shut on the hurricane wind of the climate control. Knox could hear again.

And speak. "You'd started telling me about this message you're planning on leaving for our far distant posterity, if any. You hadn't gotten around to the how or the why."

"As to how …" Mycroft gave up trying to enter a keypad combination and talk at the same time. "Well, you've seen the effigies. Their facial expressions and body language bespeak sickness, pain, and slow, agonizing death in ways that transcend mere words. Just as the barrier and its thorns silently cry out 'Beware! Danger! Keep Away!' Those warnings should retain their impact no matter how much human language and culture change over the millennia."

"Still and all, a quarter million years?"

"They'll last," Mycroft said. "The markers themselves are granite, coated with a nanometer-thick layer of metamaterial harder than diamond. And the geology of the Mescalero Plain will remain stable for at least twice the anticipated service life. So will its climate. The million-year outlook in this part of the Southwest calls for more of the same: hot, dry, and sunny. Little wind, less rain, and in consequence, almost no erosion."

"But you still haven't explained what it's all for."

"All for?" Mycroft turned back to the keypad and got it right this time. "For WISP, of course. For the Department of Energy's very own Waste Isolation Storage Plant."

The elevator shuddered and began its descent.

"What's it all for?" Mycroft echoed. "Why, to keep the world safe for all time from what lies below."

14 | Back to the Salt Mines

MARIANNA RETRIEVED her carry-on from the overhead bin, then worked her way down the aisle to the plane's midsection, to where her favorite flight attendant was just swinging open the exit door. She ignored the hostile glares from those of her fellow passengers who'd somehow sensed she was the cause of this unscheduled pitstop. Suck it up, folks—convenience of the government and all that.

Per Pete's instructions, she walked to the knee of the jetbridge, then out the emergency door and down a flight of metal stairs onto concrete apron. She stood there watching her erstwhile return flight power up and push back from the gate without her. Then she sighed and reactivated her satphone.

"Okay, I'm on the ground," she told Pete. "Now, what's this all about?"

"We just picked up that RFID tracker you planted on Knox."

He was talking about the VeriChip locator. She'd nearly forgotten that routine precaution, the tiny tracking device she'd injected under the skin of Jon's upper arm two nights ago as he slept. Just a mosquito bite, or so he'd thought. But it meant that, should his part in the Psyche business go sour, CROM would at least have a shot at finding him again.

Evidently, it had, and they had.

"Okay, you're tracking him, copy that. And I care, because—?"

"Because he was your insider on the Psyche kidnapping, you said. Because he had entrée into Ansari's inner sanctum, you said. He may have had it, he's sure as hell not using it. He's not even in California anymore."

"Where is he, then?" Christ! How come the minute she'd made up her mind to forget the guy'd ever existed, Jonathan Knox was all of a sudden Topic Number One?

"Somewhere he's not supposed to be."

"And that would be where, exactly?"

"Later, once you're in the air—you've got places to get to your own self. Look to your, uh, north. There's an Air Force CSAR chopper sitting on the tarmac, waiting for you. Talk more when you're on board." The line went dead.

Marianna heaved another sigh. No rest for the weary—broken heart or no, it was back to the salt mines for her.

Nearly half a mile beneath the shifting sands of the Mescalero Plain, a thousand miles from the nearest ocean, and still the air smelled of the sea. Knox licked his lips and tasted brine on his tongue. He accompanied Mycroft down a fluorescent-lit longwall mine corridor toward an airlock dimly glimpsed through swirls of saline haze.

"—An honest-to-God salt mine?" he said. "I thought they were just a figure of speech these days."

Mycroft shrugged. "This one is. Halite mining operations were halted back in the mid-eighties. After that the installation sat abandoned, until the Department of Energy went scouting locales for a repository to store transuranic waste left over from the Cold War…"

"Transuranic? Like plutonium, you mean?"

"Yes," Mycroft nodded. "All the refuse of all the bomb factories—all the used rad-suits and toxic sludges and spent cores—it's all being dumped right here."

That explained those quarter-million-year product warning labels out on the perimeter: WISP was the nation's premiere storage facility for the deadliest, longest-lived trash known to science. Nations, cultures, whole civilizations would rise and fall—*Homo sapiens* itself might have mutated into something strange and new—before it would be safe to dig here again.

"And you, you're okay being down here with this stuff?" Knox tried to keep his voice level, but he was pretty weirded out being this close to so much concentrated lethality—and maybe even more weirded out that his famously phobic friend didn't seem to be going catatonic at the prospect.

"Relax, Jon. Most of the hazardous material stored here is rated contact-handleable. Only about five percent of it is radioactive enough to require remote robotic manipulation. And all of that is safely walled up in the south panels of this facility, with better than three miles of solid rock between it and us."

Had *Mycroft* just told *him* to relax? Strange days, indeed!

But then Mycroft was nothing if not strange. He could succumb to a panic attack at a child's birthday party, yet dismiss deathly danger out of hand, once reason convinced him it was illusory. For Mycroft there seemed to be no essential difference between knowing and believing, believing and feeling.

Case in point: the measured, tranquil tones in which Mycroft had delivered all this scary news. And now that they'd reached the airlock, he paused and delivered some more.

"In another thousand years it won't matter anyway," he said. "DOE's computer projections show all these tunnels will have collapsed in on themselves by then, entombing the transuranics for the rest of time."

"Uh, there's no chance those projections could be off a skootch, is there? I mean, it *is* safe now, right?"

"Safe as houses, Jonathan." Mycroft gave the airlock door an affectionate pat. "In any case, the benefits of locating down here far outweigh the risks."

"Benefits such as—"

"Well, the fear factor, among other things. On that score, WISP provides the Delphi project with the best cover imaginable."

Mycroft bent to put his right eye to a retinal scanner integrated into the stainless steel frame of the airlock. He straightened again, and added, "After all, who in his right mind would come poking around a nuclear waste dump? The threat of radiation poisoning serves to keep even the most incorrigible curiosity-seekers away."

"Away from—?"

"Come and see."

The door slid aside.

The search and rescue chopper lifted off from SFO and looped south almost far as the San Mateo Bridge before vectoring northeast toward Travis Air Force Base. With a thousand unanswered questions and twenty minutes flight time, Marianna put her satphone's secure link to good use.

"Pete?"

Straining, she made out an indistinct "Yah" over the roar of the AW101's turboshafts. That was followed by a string of words too garbled to make out.

"Pete, you're going to have to raise your voice."

"How about now?" Raising his voice was never a problem for Pete Aristos.

"Better. So spill: what's going on?"

"Like I said, your friend Knox is off the reservation. Way off. We'd've flashed on it sooner if that implant of yours packed its own juice."

"Perils of premature technology."

Premature was an understatement. To skinny the VeriChip down to the size of a grain of rice, the engineers at Digital Angel had had to leave off the batteries. What that gave you was a passive radio frequency identification device, an RFID wholly dependent on an external source to power it. Failing that, it was just an inert, subcutaneous bead of silicon.

Pete knew the chip's design limitations as well as she did. It didn't stop him from grousing about them. "Just our luck they flew him out private," he said.

"Bummer," she commiserated. If Jon had flown commercial air, he'd've had to run a gauntlet of surreptitious security checkpoints, any one of them capable of activating and reading his embedded locator chip. As it was, Psyche's corporate jet would've operated in and out of general aviation terminals, effectively bypassing the electronic dragnet.

"But look on the bright side," she went on. "Given how thin on the ground RFID readers still are, you were lucky to reacquire him at all."

"If you can call it luck, when the dumb bastard goes waltzing through the front gate of a deep-cover facility. NSA got the ping an hour back, handed off to us thirty minutes ago. They said something about him claiming he's there on our dime — you know anything about that?"

"How could I? I told you: I'm not talking to him."

"Well, somebody sure is."

"What's that supposed to mean?"

"NSA did some backtracking before they figured Knox for one of ours. Turns out he made a call this morning, from the plane. Talked for over an hour."

"To who? About what?"

"No telling. He had his satphone set on one-time encryption and he patched the call through a secure server to boot." Pete's scowl was audible. "It just gripes me to see some penny-ante consulting outfit practicing tighter OpSec than half the shops at Langley. It's that damned Laurence, got to be."

"That damned Laurence" was, of course, Mycroft. There was something about Mycroft kicking around in the back of her head too, but what was it? Let's see: could it be what she'd learned day before yesterday—that he was working on some top-secret project for NSA's Advanced Curational Technologies Taskforce? Or that he was nearly as well versed in Greek mythology as Marianna herself, at least insofar as it related to a certain "deep-cover facility"…

Suddenly it all fit. Much as she'd have liked to believe otherwise, Marianna knew what her boss wasn't telling her.

"It's Delphi, isn't it?" she said. "Jon's gone to that Delphi place."

If there was one thing Knox had learned to expect from WISP by now, it was the unexpected. From the gigantic gargoyles guarding its gates, to a ten-meter barricade shielding an altogether unremarkable patch of desert and an equally undistinguished huddle of buildings, to an elevator ride down into the bowels of the earth and out into the scent of the sea, WISP was consistently turning out to be more—or less—than he could have anticipated.

What awaited him on the other side of the underground airlock was decidedly toward the "more" end of the unexpectedness spectrum. Knox stepped through into the Delphi facility…

…And out under the stars of a winter midnight, Orion rising toward the zenith with Sirius nipping at the hunter's heels.

Cognition caught up with perception then. A flip of perspective and Knox could see he was standing beneath an enormous hemispherical cavity hollowed out of the rock, with a sky-show projected across its oblate bowl of a roof. Was this hanger-sized half-bubble a natural formation, or had it been sculpted from the halite like the miles of corridor outside? Either way, it made for one spectacular planetarium.

"Our human-factors engineers suggested this." Mycroft was also gazing up. "To stave off claustrophobia."

"Is it always night?" Knox's watch was displaying two in the afternoon local.

"For the time being, at least. We manage a nice desert twilight twice a day, but a convincing simulation of full daylight has proven elusive. Too bad, too—it would make it easier to see the lay of the land."

But Knox's eyes were growing accustomed to the artificial starlight, enough to where he could make out the floorplan. Its most striking feature, though not the easiest to make out in the gloom, stood in the center of the great vault: a tapered black spire rising out of the floor and reaching to the ceiling far overhead. It could almost have been a natural formation, an obsidian stalagmite, save that its sides were cut into geometrically precise facets, and there were pinpoints of light sparking fitfully within those sable planes.

A support pillar? Way too delicate-looking for that. Some sort of machine, then. That would account for the ring of conventional workstations integrated into its base. Not to mention the other workstations that ran outward in concentric semicircles from the foot of the dark spire almost to the rock walls. Those were decidedly *un*conventional.

But not unfamiliar. Add-on work surfaces and other appurtenances masked the contours of the spidery black recliners with their bulbous hoods, but not so much that Knox couldn't recognize these installations for deluxe models of the Chair he had served time in back at Psyche Industries. There must have been a couple hundred of the little horrors, all sitting empty at the moment. Lying in wait for the next victim, no doubt.

Mycroft stepped to Knox's side, drew his attention back to the central obelisk with a wave and a nod. "There it is, Jonathan, the other reason for locating down here—The Well."

"Beg pardon?"

"The Well's storage and indexing technologies are quantum mechanical in nature. That has a number of advantages, chief among them being that we can exploit the quadratic-order efficiencies of Lov Grover's sortless search algorithm. On the other hand, it does mean that The Well's operation relies upon maintaining the coherence of fragile quantum states, which any errant cosmic ray might disrupt. All manner of redundancy is built into the system, of course—including fifteen sister sites scattered around the country—but being buried this deep affords an extra layer of protection from even the most energetic particles."

"Fifteen more Wells like this?" Knox whistled. "That's a lot of taxpayer bucks to blow on backup."

"It's not for backup, Jonathan. Those other Wells are actively linked with this one, for data-segmentation and load-balancing purposes. You might say that, from a computational perspective, the resulting 'WellGrid' functions as a single system."

Knox frowned. "A single system spread across the whole continental US? You'd have to contend with speed-of-light latency issues to achieve that, wouldn't you?"

"We would indeed, save for the fact, which I was just explaining, that each Well node is a *quantum* computer. Meaning that, when it comes to ultra-secure high-speed communication among them, the WellGrid can leverage an even more arcane quantum phenomenon called—"

Knox beat Mycroft to the punchline. "Not entanglement?"

"You've heard of it, then?"

Indeed Knox had. Quantum entanglement, and with it the notion that the entire universe and everything in it might be bound up in a seamless web of instantaneous interconnectivity, had been one of the few straws he'd had to grasp at long ago, when the mother of all bad trips had plunged him into an abyss of despair.

Not that entanglement wasn't weird enough in its own right. Albert Einstein had hated the idea, deriding it as "spooky action-at-a-distance." The irony was that it had been Einstein himself who, together with Boris Podolsky and Nathan Rosen, had concocted the thought-experiment that first hinted at some physical properties being "non-local" in character. For this so-called Einstein-Podolsky-Rosen paradox, conceived as a last-ditch effort to prove the incompleteness of quantum theory, had instead succeeded in showing that widely separated particles might exert an influence upon one another, in blatant disregard of special relativity's lightspeed limitations.

According to Mycroft, it was this same non-locality phenomenon which would, as of tomorrow's launch, enable the far-flung components of the WellGrid to behave as—indeed, to *be*—a single mammoth computational entity. The effect extended beyond the WellGrid proper to cover its tributaries as well: those collection endpoints where it connected to JWICS, the Pentagon's Joint Worldwide Intelligence Communications System.

All well and good, and yet…

Knox frowned. "Not to nitpick, Mycroft, but wouldn't transmitting all that top-secret information back and forth around the country sort of represent a teensy hole in security?"

"A hole of staggering proportions, you mean. And yes, of course it would, if the information in question were actually being transmitted, in any conventional sense. In point of fact, though, we're not transmitting the information at all, we're *teleporting* it."

Knox pondered that a moment. "Let me guess – entanglement again?"

"Yes, Jonathan, from tomorrow night on we'll be using quantum teleportation to share data all across the WellGrid, transferring it from point A to point B without its ever traversing the space in between. It will be the ultimate in communications security, uncompromisable not just in fact, but in theory as well."

"Because what hasn't been transmitted can't be intercepted?"

Mycroft grinned. "Exactly."

"Pete?" Marianna said into her satphone. "You still there?"

Her boss had gone silent when she'd said the word "Delphi." Tacit confirmation of her guess as to Jon's whereabouts was all very well, but she needed more than that.

She tried again. "So, Jon's headed out to meet with Myc—uh, Laurence?"

Pete took an audible breath, held it as if pondering what to say. In the end, all he said was "Looks like."

"Do we have a clue why?"

"We will, once he's been picked up and brought back here."

"Picked up from where? From Delphi? But that's way the hell out in —" Where had Mycroft said it was? Not the center of the universe, but … "—um, New Mexico."

The silence on the other end stretched uncomfortably again, terminated in an exasperated sigh. "I'm not even going to ask how you knew that."

"I'm not even going to tell you. Point is, by the time you can get someone out to southeast New Mexico, Jon'll be long gone."

"That part's covered. You just worry about the reacquisition."

"Me?" Pete, no, don't ask me to do this.

"Who else? And low profile, okay? NSA thinks Knox is there for us, so let's keep it that way. If they ask, you're strictly escort and support."

"But, but …" But how could she even look Jon in the face again, ever, without flashing back to that chiaroscuro of naked, writhing bodies. Without reliving that moment of betrayal over and over, forever.

"No buts," Pete was saying. "Soon as you're on the ground, you move to interdict."

"Did I hear right? Interdict?"

"Okay, reacquire then." But Pete's grudging retraction didn't change the fact that he'd said the magic word. The subliminal message was clear: either Marianna cleaned up the mess Jon was making, or Interdiction, CROM's seldom-mentioned fourth branch, would clean it up for her. And Jon along with it.

"Listen, Marianna," Pete was still talking, "Knox is *your* problem, always has been. I'm giving you one last shot at fixing him. It. Whatever. But you've got to move quick."

"Quick's not happening. Best case, I can *maybe* make it out to Carlsbad by sundown."

"You're not listening. The longer Knox stays at Delphi, the better the chances he'll screw the pooch. The last thing I need is NSA on my back. I need you to get out there and get this situation under control, soonest."

She sighed. "Soonest? What do you mean, soonest? There are limits, Pete. I'm still a good quarter hour out of Travis. From there … well, I suppose you could arm-twist the Military Air Transport System into flying me straight through to Santa Fe. Even so, that'd still leave me a couple hundred miles out from this Delphi place. A chopper'll take another hour or two from there. Now you tell me: how can I get there any sooner than that?"

"Like I said, that part's covered. We've got better options than MATS — *lots* better. You just worry about what to do once you get there."

Knox hadn't realized how engrossed he'd become in Mycroft's entanglement exposition till he looked up and saw that the stadium-sized work bay — empty just a moment ago, or so it seemed — was now half full. Maybe a hundred people had filed in past them while they were absorbed in conversation, and more were arriving as he watched.

"Mycroft? Where did all these guys come from?"

"Down from the surface. Where else?"

"But—so many, so fast?"

Mycroft chuckled. "You didn't think WISP's mega-elevators were just for forklifts, did you?"

As best as Knox could tell in the half-light, the new arrivals looked to be a demographically correct cross-section of ages, genders, skin tones, and hair styles. Not that it mattered; all traces of individuality fled once they'd surrendered to the embrace of the Chairs and the helmets had clamped silvered virtual-reality visors over their faces. The way that crowd of jostling, motley humanity had transformed into an anonymous army of identical, mirror-faced automata was just plain eerie.

Also faintly ridiculous. Half-reclining in their Chairs, staring blankly around the room, the Delphi staffers looked like nothing so much as a squadron of fifties-era evil robots taking a time out from the assimilation of humankind to kick back in futuristic La-Z-Boys. Knox didn't know whether to shudder or laugh.

He decided in favor of shuddering once the occupants of the Chairs settled in and began to move around. In response to nothing in particular, one would suddenly reach up to knead the thin air between thumb and forefinger; down the line, another might be intently inscribing arcs and lines in empty space, while a third was meticulously tracing out a wide area of nothingness, and then squeezing it down to a smaller, equally vacant region framed by cupped hands.

Knox knew, of course, that such pantomimes were actually manipulations of various virtual-reality widgets and data displays being projected onto the visors. That knowledge didn't alter his gut reaction. The spasmodic gesturing would've looked strange enough with a single individual doing it; multiply the effect by an entire roomful of people, and it was enough to raise the hairs on the back of his neck.

"Mycroft?" he said, turning to his friend, "—what the *hell* is going on here?"

15 | Lots Better

Knox would've thought "What the *hell* is going on here?" was a simple enough question, but Mycroft wasn't answering, wasn't acting as if he'd even heard it. Instead, he was standing there stock-still, staring out into the cavernous work bay at row upon row of Delphi analysts all seated in their Chairs.

"Mycroft? You okay?"

Crowds tended to freak Mycroft out, and evidently crowds of mirror-visaged, awkwardly gesticulating Borg drones were no exception. Knox had thought his friend was getting better at dealing. Yet here he was retreating into himself again, into the trancelike state where that powerful mind could reassert control over the all-too-weak flesh.

At times like this, Knox knew better than to disturb Mycroft. The best thing was just to stand there quietly, waiting for the spell to pass.

After a minute or so, patience was rewarded. Mycroft straightened, released a shuddering breath, and blinked.

"I'm sorry, Jonathan—what is it you were saying?"

Knox also knew better than to remark on Mycroft's brief indisposition. Instead, he made as if the hiatus had never happened, and picked up where he'd left off.

"I was just asking what's going on here."

"Ah, in point of fact, not all that much at the moment." Mycroft now seemed completely back to normal. Or as normal as he ever got.

"What little activity you're seeing at the moment," he went on, "is in the nature of final adjustments for today's trial. Which is due to start in, ah, twenty minutes. *Then* things will begin to happen."

That's right, Ansari had mentioned something about a trial. And questions. Knox felt a faint tingle of anticipatory ecstasy at the back of his brain.

"Tell me about this trial," he said.

Mycroft tsked. "CROM really did send you here unprepared, didn't they? Very well, then: what you're about to see is a trial of the last intelligence capability the United States will ever need."

Lots better was right!

Marianna leveled off and eased back on the stick.

It wasn't till she'd arrived at Travis that she found out how Pete intended to get her to Delphi in time to intercept Jon. Instead of poking her way out to New Mexico via conventional military air, here she was at the controls of the US Air Force's latest dream machine, flying at a flat-out Mach 1.8. And—

Wow! What a rush!

She'd wondered about it when, late last year, Pete had her log some hours in a jet-fighter sim. She hadn't questioned it at the time, for fear he'd think better of it. Marianna's general attitude toward flying, real or virtual, was: *yes, please.* You just couldn't have too much fun, especially with somebody else picking up the five hundred dollar an hour tab on the Ames Laboratory flight simulator.

But that was nothing compared to the tab NSA had picked up for the real thing: a Lockheed-Martin F-35B Lightning II, modified to seat two. At fifty-five million a pop, even one of these puppies must have put a serious dent in No Such Agency's discretionary budget. If it weren't for the Delphi Project—more specifically, its occasional need for speed in transporting VIPs out to the middle-of-nowhere site—there's no way they could've finessed it past the black ops bean-counters at the General Accounting Office.

That occasional need for speed was certainly coming in handy now: at twelve hundred miles per hour, Travis to Delphi was only fifty-five minutes flying time.

And what flying time! Just the feel of being in the air again, free of the bonds of earth, focusing her whole being on the piloting of this magnificent machine, was having an almost therapeutic effect on Marianna. For the first time since the, the thing with Jon last night, her mind felt free, cold and clear, riding the cold, clear wind at forty-five thousand feet.

How about a barrel roll or two? Who'd know? And who knew when she'd get another turn at the stick of the world's most advanced military aircraft?

But it was precisely because the Lightning *was* so advanced that she couldn't play games with it. Not when one of those advances was an Autonomous Logistics Information System—ALIS, to its friends.

Who'd know if she took a few unauthorized star-turns? ALIS, that's who. The distributed-intelligence infrastructure could plan and manage operations, training, and servicing. It was smart enough to monitor the health of each and every one of the F-35's tens of thousands of component parts, schedule any needed maintenance, and perform root-cause analysis in the unlikely event an element failed—all with minimal human intervention, or none whatsoever.

The Lightning's smarts didn't end there, either; it came equipped with an intelligent fly-by-wire module called a Unified Flight Control system. You basically just told the UFC how you wanted to go—up or down, faster or slower—and left the driving to the AI. Took all the work out of flying.

Took some of the fun out of it too, but not so much that she wouldn't regret its coming to an end. In the meantime, how about some music? Very non-regulation, but she'd brought her smartphone along for the ride, zipped in the breast pocket of her flight suit. She took it out, jacked it into her helmet's secondary audio feed, and went to select—what? Something apropos, something that echoed the freedom of this boundless Tolstoyan sky. Not *Wild Blue Yonder.* Something better, lots better—

She scrolled through Artists to Eros Ramazzotti. An instant later the opening chords of *Nell'Azzurrita* filled her ears. The verse sang of loss and separation, of mountains blocking the way, but above all the obstacles and hardships, a limpid, cloudless blue sky. Then the chorus came up:

Nell'azzurrita

Di questi giorni,
Nell'azzurrita…

"Into the blue of these days, into the blue…" It was so perfect, so evocative. Totally in the moment now, Marianna began to sing along.

"Singing?"

Hamza looked up from his monitoring station to where Davoud Ansari was standing on the far side of Pairidaeza's comm center, a bemused look on his face.

Hamza nodded. "Yes, singing," he replied, "and not even in English. Come, hear for yourself." Hamza held out the headset.

Ansari walked over and donned it, listened a moment. "Sounds Italian."

Hamza shrugged. It mattered little what language it was. What mattered was that as long as the woman was singing, she was not communicating with her headquarters. Meaning they still had no firm fix on what she was doing flying out to WISP.

And that mattered a good deal.

Things would have been easier had there been, as there usually was, a VIP onboard for today's run out to the top-secret facility. Even the most casual chatter between pilot and high-ranking passenger might have provided clues as to what was going on, as it already had done on more than one occasion in the past. Tidbits that would never have been transmitted over an air-to-ground channel, be it never so secure, might be talked of quite openly on the cockpit intercom, in the belief that no outside eavesdropper could intercept the in-plane communications link.

And indeed, no *outside* eavesdropper could. But then none was needed, so long as ALIS was aboard. The Autonomous Logistics Information System, built by a wholly owned subsidiary of Psyche Industries, was never out of touch with its network of ground stations, also Psyche-sourced. And one of ALIS's undocumented, factory-installed extras was an ability to piggyback a voiceband onto its dedicated datalinks. Tapping into the F-35's cockpit conversations had given them their first inklings into the mystery that was Delphi, the enigma that was MERGE.

Since then, of course, they had acquired a far better, orders of magnitude better, source of information as to the goings-on within the Advanced

Curational Technologies Taskforce—a source that had yielded hints as to how MERGE might be used to remedy Fatimah's condition. This much was all Ansari knew or cared about. He never suspected that the same hints might also reveal how MERGE itself might be destroyed.

Yet, despite having been superseded, there were times when ALIS's old "wiretap" hookup could still come in handy, and this was one. If only the pilot would *say* something.

Hamza shook his head, consoling himself with the knowledge that passive listening was not all that ALIS had to offer. In a pinch, one could use its datalinks to assume active control of the aircraft's UFC avionics. To date that had never proved necessary. Fortunately so, since it was, by nature, the sort of option one exercised only *in extremis*, and then only once.

Now, though, if the woman were in fact flying out to interfere somehow with Jonathan Knox's mission, or with his safe return to Pairidaeza—well, it might be time to call upon some of ALIS's hitherto unexploited capabilities.

If only they could be sure what this Ms. Bonaventure intended. Hamza picked up a second set of earphones, listened again. Grimaced again.

Singing!

"The *last* intel capability we'll ever need?" Knox gave his friend as probing a stare as he could manage by the dim light of Delphi's make-believe stars. "Come on, Mycroft, it's just the two of us here."

"I know what you're thinking, Jonathan. But it's true."

"Ah, well." Knox shrugged. What else was there to say? His friend had gone and drunk the Kool-Aid. It was one of consulting's little occupational hazards—spout the client's hype long enough and you started believing it yourself.

"Think about it, Jonathan," Mycroft pressed on. "Everyone talks about 9/11 as an 'intelligence failure.' Yet what exactly was it that failed? Not the surveillance and collection efforts: seventy pre-9/11 FBI investigations into Al Qaeda activities in the US, including two years overwatch on the flight schools where Mohammed Atta and his cohorts trained. Dozens of requests for a warrant to search the belongings of the "twentieth hijacker" after Zacarias Moussaoui was arrested in mid-August 2001. Put it all together and there was sufficient evidence in hand, or within reach, to have uncovered the plot in time. But that was the problem: no one *tried* to put it all together. All of which makes 9/11 not an intelligence failure so much as something you and I have seen time and again: a failure of knowledge management."

Knox had started listening again despite himself. He hadn't thought of it that way, but it fit. "Stovepipe mentality."

Mycroft was nodding. "Precisely. Think of the pre-9/11 intelligence community as a cluster of silos. The only authorized information channels run vertically, bottom to top. Between any two of those structures, within them even, there's hardly any horizontal communication at all. Hierarchies, in other words, when what was needed were networks."

"But they were working on that, I thought. All those interagency initiatives—"

"Interagency turf wars, you mean. Those so-called 'initiatives' were doomed to defeat before they began. And even if they *had* succeeded, they still wouldn't have addressed the root cause. What good does it do to get the top tiers of the CIA and NSA talking together, if analysts working for the same agency just down the hall from one another aren't comparing notes?"

Mycroft was pacing up and down now, clearly agitated. Like most people, he did not suffer fools gladly. It was just that, for Mycroft, most people fell into that category.

"In their desperation," he was saying, "they even tried the unthinkable: openness. Calvin Andrus, head of the CIA's Center for Mission Innovation, tried introducing blogs, wikis, and alternate-reality gaming as a way of promoting collaborative analysis. A Wikipedia clone known as Intellipedia. Even a MySpace social networking site for analysts; A-Space, they called it." Mycroft shook his head. "It all came to naught in the end, of course."

"Why? That sort of thing has worked well enough for the Fortune 500."

"That's not to say it didn't have its uses here too. In particular, it served as an excellent smokescreen for what ACT was really doing. But in more general terms—"

"It's been a bust?"

Mycroft sighed. "It's the intelligence community mindset, Jonathan. You've encountered it yourself in your dealings with CROM. It's all about airtight compartmentalization and need-to-know."

"And information equals power," Knox added. Mycroft was right; willingness to share had never been the intel community's defining characteristic.

"And then," Mycroft said, "into the midst of all this, there came The Well."

Knox paused for the space of a breath, trying to fit that apparent non-sequitur into what had gone before.

"I don't get it," he said finally. "What difference would this Well make? You said it yourself: it's just a really big database. Super-secure and quantum-mechanicized and all that good stuff, but at the end of the day just a glorified information repository."

"This is all true, and would have remained so but for one other well-known trait of the US intelligence community."

"Which is?"

"An inability to leave well enough alone." Mycroft gave his friend a wry smile. "The problem, the opportunity, rather, wasn't The Well itself, but what it was destined to contain. Think of it, Jonathan, all that information — intel estimates, field agent reports, low- and mid-level analysis, what have you — all funneled into a single, gargantuan datastore. When it goes on line tomorrow night, The Well will become the physical instantiation of all those dreams of a truly collaborative intelligence effort, the ultimate shared intel resource dangling just beyond reach. Was there ever any doubt they would stretch out a hand to try and pluck it?"

"Pluck it, how? Shunt the data to some sort of National Security Council super-analyst team?"

"A handful of individuals to sift through the sum-total intel capture across the entire globe in real time? Scrutinizing gigabytes of data, every minute of every day?" Mycroft snorted. "A recipe for information overload if ever there was one. Not that even that alternative wasn't explored."

Mycroft paused then, and shuddered. He, of all people, could perhaps glimpse what trying to absorb that volume of information might be like. But all he said was, "The projected burnout rates were off the chart, asymptotic."

"So," Knox said half to himself, "a small group isn't up to the job, and the material itself is way too sensitive to bring the whole intel community in on it. What does that leave? Just walk away and forget about it?"

Mycroft was shaking his head. "The least acceptable option of all, especially nowadays. In a world of asymmetric threats, the only winning move is preemption, getting inside the adversary's decision-loop, uncovering and interdicting conspiracies *before* they can bear fruit, because the aftermath could be too terrible to contemplate. But that, in turn, presupposes an ability to collate and analyze information on an unprecedented scale, worldwide, in real time. The global overview that the data pouring into The Well can provide isn't just a nice-to-have anymore, Jonathan—it has become a prerequisite for survival."

Knox nodded. It must be frustrating as all hell: the information was there, just waiting to be exploited, tantalizingly just out of reach.

Mycroft was still talking. "On the other hand, what was impossible for a trusted team, and impermissible for a wider collective, just might be feasible for a machine. An artificial intelligence could harvest the informational fruits of The Well, yet because it could be made totally subservient to the will of those at the very top, an AI would present no security risk."

All of a sudden, Knox knew where this was going. "Not QuMRANN?"

Mycroft looked at him sharply. Knox was instantly glad he hadn't gone and blurted out the rest of it: *Not QuMRANN?—I know him!*

"I see you did not come to Delphi totally unprepared after all, Jonathan. Yes, QuMRANN—our tame Oracle, our software seer, able to gather together myriad strands of raw intel, each all but meaningless in isolation, and weave them into prophecy."

Knox realized he'd heard half of this before. Jazmine had been telling him about it, just before they'd gotten diverted onto the kidnapping. Nietzsche had alluded to it too. Adding Mycroft's piece, he could begin to see how the whole puzzle fit together. What QuMRANN's true purpose had been.

Had been. He'd just remembered the other thing Jazmine had told him.

"But, Mycroft," he said, "my understanding is that the QuMRANN project was shut down."

Mycroft nodded. "Terminated, yes. And with only weeks to go until turnkey delivery."

"Right, right, supposedly the government found something lots better. Only—lots better how?"

In response Mycroft glanced again at the time, then pointed out into the bay.

"Watch," he said.

16 | The Gods Themselves

Companion to cirrus clouds no longer, Marianna had the F-35B throttled back and well into its descent. Already Carlsbad's street grid was coming into view off her starboard wing, the only green in all this arid land. About time to begin final approach.

Right on cue, her headset crackled. "3221 Lima, this is Albuquerque Center. Turn left heading 160 and contact WISP Tower on 119.1."

She reset the comm channel to the designated frequency and spoke into her helmet mike, "WISP Tower? Lightning 3221 Lima with you, twenty miles west-northwest, IFR for landing."

"Roger, Two-One Lima. Reduce to two fifty knots; descend and hold fifteen hundred. Visibility thirty miles, winds light, altimeter 29.95. Cleared for straight-in approach."

She flew the fighter on across the desert toward what looked like monumental earthworks ringed round with misshapen monoliths—the sort of installation Christo might have created if he'd been born an Aztec. No time for a closer look now, though; she needed to look for something else.

Finally she gave up and thumbed the radio again. "Want to give me a vector for your runway, Tower? I'm not reading a visual."

"Say again, Two-One Lima?"

"I said I can't see your—" Marianna bit back the word she'd been about to say. "—your landing strip."

"You're kidding, right? There is none."

No landing strip? What kind of screwup *was* this? Was she supposed to have landed in Carlsbad and driven the last twenty-five miles? But, no, according to the GPS, she was right on top of the landing coordinates specified in the Lightning's flight plan.

Tower was still talking. "You still copying, Two-One Lima? Engage your pal and set down in the main parking lot."

"*The fucking parking lot?*" There, she'd gone and said the word after all.

"Yes, the fucking, to use the technical term, parking lot. You *are* flying a STOVL, aren't you?"

"Well, yeah." That much was true enough. The "B" in the F-35B's designation meant it was the short takeoff/vertical landing model—a jump jet, in other words. But just because the aircraft itself could land without benefit of a runway didn't mean *she* could. Putting a jump jet down on a postage-stamp square of asphalt was most assuredly not the sort of thing you wanted to try on the strength of a simulator session or two. Or twenty.

Tower was losing patience. "Look, Two-One Lima, quit dorking around and engage the pal, will you?"

The pal, the pal—what could that mean? Pete had said something about a "pal" just before she'd taken off too. But she'd assumed he was running off at the mouth about Jon again—definitely *not* her pal any more—and tuned him out.

"Your PAL," Tower was talking very slowly and deliberately now, as if to a three-year-old, or a madwoman. Neither of whom you really wanted at the controls of fifty-five million dollars worth of government hardware. "—You know, P-A-L? Your Precision Approach and Landing system? Just hit the switch marked Autoland. Please."

Damn! A sleepless night and a vodka shooter must have taken more of a toll than she'd realized. She rubbed her eyes and scanned the instrument panel. Found the big red switch and armed it.

"Roger, transferring to Autoland," she said, trying to sound like she'd known to do that all along.

PAL initiated communication with its groundside Big Sister control module. The two systems—both products, like ALIS, of Psyche Industries'

Intelligent Avionics division—began exchanging the relative global positioning system data needed to plot a final approach.

"Big Sister confirms PAL handshake," Tower came back. "Sit back and relax, Two-One Lima. We'll take it from here."

Now entirely out of the loop, Marianna leaned back in the contoured seat and tried by sheer willpower to slow the beating of her heart. Tried swallowing, only her mouth was too dry.

Jesus! A *machine* was going to land this thing?

She felt a solid *thunk* as PAL lowered the wheels and locked them in landing position. At the same time, a new, unaccustomed whine kicked in. PAL had begun diverting half the power of the Lightning's single Pratt and Whitney engine to the task of driving the vertical LiftFan located almost beneath her feet. At the same time, the AI swiveled the rear jet nozzle to aim downward as well. Balancing its weight on fore and aft down-thrusts with the precision of a ballet master, PAL eased the aircraft in the final few meters toward touchdown.

The moment of truth had arrived.

Think about something, anything else. Think about, about Jon, her other "pal." About their first time, their first mission together.

First and *only* mission together—they were for sure not together on this one. If anything, Jon had gone from being an asset to a potentially major liability. What the hell did he think he was *doing* out here?

She'd know soon enough. If she could get the Lightning down in one piece.

Or if her PAL could.

Marianna watched the air ripple around the cockpit as the heated down-blast hit the fast-approaching asphalt and boiled up on either side. Felt the one-two bump and recoil of a textbook three-point landing. Released the breath she hadn't realized she'd been holding.

Fun-time was over. Now for the hard part.

Mycroft had said to watch, so Knox watched. Watched as the digits of the time display set in the black pylon at Delphi's heart morphed to 3:00 P.M. local. Watched as the pylon itself, the so-called Well, suddenly came alive, twinkling with a thousand tiny pinpricks of white light like a galaxy of fireflies. Watched as—

Out on the floor of the cavernous chamber, the residual murmur of the massed Delphi staffers damped down to an expectant hush. Knox couldn't put his finger on it, but something had changed. The effect was subtle but unmistakable. It was as if the movements of the individual analysts had become *coordinated* somehow. The individual postures and disposition of limbs were all still different, just as before. But now it was as if they were all changing in synch, dancing to some beat they alone could hear, with the exquisite self-organizing choreography of a flock of starlings or a school of silvery fish.

"Mycroft? What's happening to them?"

"Why, the same thing that happened the first time The Well was activated. And every time since. We call it the Maximally Entangled Ratiocinative Group Entity Effect—MERGE for short."

Knox waited for more of an explanation. Whatever he'd expected to hear, what Mycroft said next wasn't it.

"Jonathan, how much do you know about the binding problem?"

Knox groped for a flippancy he didn't feel. "Isn't it something that happens to female undergarments in hot weather?"

"The binding problem," Mycroft went on, heedless of the attempt at humor, "is a modern-day gloss on a very old conundrum—namely, why do we experience consciousness as a unity, a single thing? Rene Descartes was one of the first to raise the question. He concluded that the perceived indivisibility of experience was enough, all by itself, to prove that the mind could not be made of the same substance as matter."

"Okay, because anything made of matter *can* be divided into parts." Knox nodded. "Mind-body again, got it. But you said there was a modern version."

"Relatively modern, William James had the first inkling of it back in the late nineteenth century. But it wasn't until PET and MRI scans enabled us to see what was really going on inside the brain—to monitor regions of activation corresponding to different experiences—that the binding problem emerged in its full-blown contemporary form. It is perhaps the single greatest puzzle in the study of consciousness, yet it begins with phenomena as simple as this—"

Mycroft held up his hand. There was something in it. "Here, Jonathan, what do you see?"

"It's, uh—" Knox had to squint to make out the object in Delphi's half-light. "—your handheld?"

"Quite so." Mycroft pocketed the little device again. "Now for the larger question: how could you know that?"

"What do you mean? I've only seen you screwing around with it, like, a thousand times."

But Mycroft was shaking his head. "No, no, not how could you recognize it as my handheld. Rather how, in a neurophysiological sense, could you recognize it as any*thing* at all?"

"You've lost me."

Mycroft thought for a moment, then began again. "Try this: the individual percepts making up the visual sensation you just experienced actually arise in different subregions of your striate cortex. Recognizing the *shape* of my handheld, its surfaces, edges and so forth, correlates to one set of neuronal firings. Recognizing its *color*, on the other hand, maps to an altogether different set. If I were to move and rotate the device, yet a third ensemble would come into play to compensate for the continuous shift in viewing angle. Despite all this, you—by which I mean you as a conscious, perceiving entity—somehow assemble those physically-isolated neural events into a single experience of a single object: my handheld. But, once again, how?"

Knox shrugged. "Beats me."

"You're not alone. It is, as noted, perhaps *the* major unresolved problem in consciousness studies. The Oxford philosopher Michael Lockwood went so far as to suggest that there may be inherent speed-of-light limitations to be overcome."

"What? You mean between one lobe of the brain and another?"

"One foot per nanosecond, Jonathan. It's not just a good idea—"

"Yeah, yeah, it's the law," Knox finished for him. "But even so, that's cutting things pretty fine, wouldn't you say? I mean, if my senses were out of synch by a microsecond or two, would I even notice?"

"A cogent point, and one that Delphi's researchers are by no means agreed upon. Say it were so, however. Grant, for the sake of argument, that solving the binding problem might require correlating widely separated neuronal assemblies in less time than light would take to traverse the distance between them. Now, does that remind you of anything?"

Knox hated how conversations with Mycroft always seemed to degenerate into these little guessing games. Unfortunately, playing along was looking like the only way to get the information he needed to find Fatimah.

"What was the question again?"

"Instantaneous communication between elements at a distance—What does that remind you of?"

"Well, when you put it that way…Entanglement again?"

"Precisely. The exact same action-at-a-distance effect, in fact, as The Well is based on."

"But weren't you just saying those sorts of quantum phenomena are really kind of fragile? Need to be all shielded against cosmic rays and such?"

Mycroft smiled and nodded.

"And now you're trying to tell me the same effects can manifest in a biological system, the brain to be precise. Sorry, but that's not exactly a clean-room environment, Mycroft. It's hot and it's noisy—body heat, neurons firing all the time. How does your delicate quantum coherence cope with all that?"

"Good question. We don't know how."

"So why even raise it as a possibility?"

"I said *we* don't know how. Mother Nature evidently does. Quantum entanglement has already been observed in room-temperature, quasi-chaotic processes like photosynthesis. There's evidence that entanglement of radical pairs in the avian vision system is what enables birds to navigate: their eyes can use it to directly sense the earth's geomagnetic field. There's even been some research at Japan's Institute of Materials Science indicating the presence of quantum states in the microtubules of the brain at biological temperatures. There's no reason human cognition couldn't be leveraging those capabilities."

"Well, okay…"

But Knox's grudging concession was ignored in his friend's eagerness to drive home the point.

"Now take that one step further: if human consciousness is, in some sense, an entangled, non-local system, and if distance is essentially irrelevant to such a system, then why shouldn't the distance between neuronal assemblies be irrelevant to consciousness as well?"

Mycroft paused then to sweep an arm out across the darkened work bay, out to where the formerly random gesturings of its denizens had begun pulsating in waves, like ripples in the pseudopodia of some gigantic single-celled organism.

"Why, in other words," he said, "need a single consciousness be confined to a single brain? In fact, as the MERGE Effect amply demonstrates, it need not."

Mycroft was staring out into the gloom now, his face wearing an expression which, if Knox didn't know better, he would have called rapture. "Just try to imagine it, Jonathan. All the intelligence, all the analytical power, of hundreds of minds—soon to be joined by thousands more—with all the data in The Well at its command, and all of that focusing on a single problem. Why, it must feel almost like, like being God."

"So," Knox said, "that's what Marianna meant about communing with the gods."

"Ah, she mentioned that to you, did she? Bright girl, good memory for detail." Perhaps Mycroft's ultimate accolade. "Yes, that's it. Except that it's not communing, not exactly. It's more like calling the gods into existence."

Hundreds of minds dreaming a single dream, hundreds of quicksilver droplets pooling into a single shimmering spherule…

As always, it is less a reawakening than a rebirth. There is an instant in which the awareness of each individual node-to-be telescopes dizzyingly upward and outward, as if to encompass the whole. Then, without any discernable transition—and after all, who would there be to discern it?—a single "I" nucleates.

MERGE bestirs itself once more.

17 | The Trouble with Omniscience

KNOX TOOK ANOTHER LOOK at the assembled Delphi staffers locked into their Chairs. Integrated, *incorporated* into their Chairs, and into whatever being the so-called MERGE Effect was bringing into existence.

All those individual brains possessed of—or was it *by?*—a single consciousness, a single intelligence. Could it be? True, the owners of those brains hardly looked like individuals anymore. Hardly even looked human, the way they were swaying slowly to and fro like fronds of kelp in an undersea current. Or like appendages of a single composite entity, which Mycroft had claimed was what they were become.

"So, you're saying they tried switching on your Well, and *this* happened?"

"On a smaller scale, yes. The Effect was far from universal that first time."

"I've been meaning to ask you about that: why aren't *we* being affected? Why isn't it happening to us too, I mean? We're not that much further away from that—" Knox gestured in the direction of the central pillar, its inky planes now all shot through with winking iridescence. "—that quantum computer of yours than anyone else. And anyway, you said distance didn't matter, what with entanglement and all. So why aren't you and I being absorbed into this collective consciousness of yours?"

Knox stopped talking then, and shivered. What would it be like, to lose yourself, to have your identity engulfed and assimilated into some sort of overmind? Would the new, improved "*ueber*-you" even remember having been plain old you?

"Ah, yes," Mycroft was saying, "—why the MERGE affects some and not others. More to the point, not ourselves. As to that, actually there *is* some indirect evidence for…"

He trailed off then, his gaze turned inward. Knox waited several more heartbeats before prompting, "Some evidence for what?"

His friend shook himself. "Forgive me, Jonathan. What I should have said was, the real question is not why the MERGE Effect remains so limited in scope, but rather how it can exist at all. Certainly, imperceptibly weak as it is, it could never have been noticed, were it not for the fact that, in conjunction with the ramp-up to the Delphi launch, we also began trialing a radically new type of interface."

Suddenly Knox saw where this was headed. "The Chairs?"

"The nanotrode infusors, yes. So called because they infuse nanoscale electrodes directly into the cerebral cortex—electrodes that have been specially designed to enable an unmediated linkage to The Well. And as it turns out, an unmediated linkage to anyone else whose brain has been similarly infused."

"This, ah, infusion process—what's it like? How does it feel?"

"Most subjects report feeling nothing whatsoever. Some few experience what is variously described as a mild itching or tingling sensation. Why?"

"Never mind, go on," Knox said, all the while hoping that the nanotrodes he'd been shot up with for his non-disclosure signing—or, for that matter, yesterday's visit to Virtual Reality—had *not* been "specially designed."

"Yes, well, there were only seven such workstations initially, engineered by Psyche Industries to provide a more all-encompassing access to The Well's informational resources. Once we discovered what they *really* did—" A wave in MERGE's direction "—we ordered enough additional units to fill this hall, and the fifteen other hub facilities besides, for when Delphi goes on line in about thirty-six hours. And a fortuitous thing for Psyche it was, too."

"You mean because the QuMRANN project got canceled at the same time?" With the fear of imminent absorption having receded a bit, Knox could savor the irony. "Fortuitous indeed: no sooner does one revenue stream dry up than another gushes forth."

Mycroft nodded. "A much larger and more lucrative revenue stream as it turns out. Thousands of units delivered already."

"The Government giveth and the Government taketh away, not necessarily in that order," Knox said. "Be that as it may. though, there's one thing I'm still not getting. You said that the reason for QuMRANN in the first place was that the intelligence community couldn't bear the thought of collaborative access to the kind of information residing in The Well."

Mycroft nodded.

"Well, what's this, if not worse? You're giving it all away for free, aren't you? Giving every one of those analysts out there unrestricted entrée into the most sensitive intel datasource in the world, and—What? Why are you smiling?"

"It was just your reference to 'those analysts out there,' Jonathan. In the strictest sense, there *are* no analysts out there right now."

"The hell you say. I'm looking at them."

"What is real is not always visible," Mycroft said, "and what is visible, not always real."

"Very Zen. Your point?"

"You are looking at individual bodies, you do not see MERGE. And it is MERGE, rather than any of its component individuals, which accesses The Well's data."

"But what happens once this MERGE Effect, uh, dissipates. It *does*, doesn't it?"

"Yes, of course. The Entity automatically disaggregates as soon as it has answered whatever question or questions it was invoked for—and received the requisite Acknowledgement, of course. The whole process leaves the participating analysts none the worse for wear, in case that was going to be your next question."

"I'm happy for them," Knox said, "but that still doesn't—Oh, wait a minute."

"You see it now, don't you? Yes, Jonathan, MERGE is essentially a quantum phenomenon, not unlike a quantum computer. *Just* like a quantum computer, in fact, in one crucial respect. That is, as long as the analysis is in progress, all possibilities are up for grabs in a superposition of states. But once that fog of potentiality collapses into an actual, hard-and-fast answer, all the other unrealized possibilities fade into nonexistence, with no trace left behind."

"So, what you're saying is, no matter how much hypersecret intelligence goes into the germination of a MERGE solution, it's all gone the instant the hive mind dissolves back into its component human intellects."

Mycroft nodded. "Once MERGE goes away, the individuals that composed it are left with neither more nor less knowledge than had been in their heads before they MERGEd—except, perhaps, for a nagging feeling that there's something they should be able to recall, but cannot. From the intelligence community's standpoint, it's ideal."

"I'll say: all the advantages of social networking, with none of the downside."

"There is one exception to this retroactive amnesia, of course: the National Security Council-level policymaker who summons up MERGE in the first place. He or she has the sought-after answer, an answer forged from the collation of every conceivable scrap of evidence, viewed from every possible angle of interpretation all at once: a superposition of data collection, refinement, and analysis. The MERGE Effect offers a way to share information just long enough to crack a given problem, and then take it all back. That's what the US intel community so desperately craved, and now it's fallen into their laps."

Knox had seldom seen Mycroft wax so rhapsodic over the resolution to what was, in effect, just another knowledge management problem. But he didn't pause to enjoy the spectacle. In fact, he'd stopped paying attention thirty seconds ago.

Because that was when, to the accompaniment of ecstatic neural pyrotechnics, he had realized how to accomplish what Ansari needed him to do.

She was back on the ground. With the Autoland disengaged and the F-35B under manual control once more, Marianna taxied slowly over to the runway that WISP Tower had designated.

Well, okay, it wasn't really a runway, any more than the parking lot had been a landing strip. What it was, was a short, straight stretch of concrete leading to a steep steel parabola. The slope started out gentle enough where it met the ground, but it was nearly vertical by the time it reached the top. All in aid of the Lightning's short takeoff capability.

With the jet in position for a quick getaway, Marianna killed the engine and popped the canopy. Whew! Hot out here.

She doffed her helmet, shook her hair loose, and looked around. Lots of activity—prime movers and various grades of cargo haulers rolling purposefully back and forth—but no humans in sight, not even in the cabs of the vehicles, which seemed to be either remote operated or semi-autonomous. A reasonable precaution, given the hazardous materials being handled here. And keeping the workforce to a minimum made sense from a security stand-point too. Still, it meant no mechanic on duty to wheel a universal stair over to the plane.

Not a problem. She hit the switch that deployed the Lightning's built-in boarding ladder and climbed down onto sunbaked concrete.

By this time the desert heat was threatening to parboil her right there in her flightsuit. No point pausing to strip it off, though; she wasn't going to be here long enough to matter. Just live with it till she could get in out of the sun.

As to that, she'd already spotted the building she'd been told to head for—the biggest in a complex of structures squatting on the far side of her improvised airfield. The only problem was traversing the intervening half-mile of blacktop through heat so intense it set the air to rippling. Pete must really be serious about her keeping a low profile if he hadn't even arranged for a pickup.

Or maybe he had? There was a small, golfcart-looking thingie approach-ing from her left. Driverless, like most of the vehicles she'd seen so far, but evidently her ride—at least it rolled to a stop right in front of her and popped open the passenger side door.

"Welcome," a synthesized voice said, "please sit down."

Uh-huh. Like she was going to go out and play in the truck traffic with the moral equivalent of a multi-slice toaster at the controls.

"No, thanks." She slammed the door, walked around to the driver's side and got in.

"Please be sure to fasten your safety—" the canned announcement cut off suddenly. Marianna had found the manual override.

She spun the steering wheel and floored it. The open-top golfcart cut a path through sauna-like air.

Taking care to watch out for oncoming robotrucks, Marianna set off in search of shade, and Jonathan Knox.

Knox followed Mycroft up a spiral staircase and through a sliding door, to emerge in a chamber featuring the wraparound windows of a miniature air-traffic control tower, save that they gave out not on runways, but on the whole of Delphi Central, from the apex of its central spire to the outermost arc of its satellite nodestations. As MERGE gathered itself in the artificial starlight, the metamaterial of its component nodestation hoods began to glow a subdued amber, lending the great vault the aspect of a darkened cathedral lit by hundreds of candle flames.

So taken was Knox with the view that he failed to notice the room's most imposing feature till he nearly bumped into it. Then he backed off quick enough.

"Oh, Lord," he said, "—not another Chair!"

Mycroft turned. "Hmm? Ah, you mean the Nexus. There is, now that you mention it, something of a family resemblance to the stations down in the bay—never mind that their functions are quite different."

"Different how?"

"The nodestations are what we use to call MERGE into existence. The Nexus is what we use to talk to it."

"And these displays?" Knox prowled around the room, peering at the banks of instruments, giving the Chair a wide berth. "What are they all about?"

"They mostly monitor status on The Well. Here, for instance," Mycroft pointed at a screen window holding the number 267, "—is the count of all the individual nodes participating in this afternoon's MERGE. Constantly updated, in case we wind up adding more components to the Group Entity on the fly. The other instruments track various aspects of the analysis process—not that they're really needed."

"No? Why not?"

"Simply because we can follow what's going on in the hive mind, insofar as any external observer can, just by watching the lightshow out on the workfloor. It's quiescent right now, but if I do this—"

Mycroft lowered himself into the Nexus and keyed in an authentication code. In response, the apparatus reconfigured to embrace him, its interface hood swiveling and descending till it nearly enveloped his head.

"Query," he announced.

Instantly, the nodestations down below glowed brighter, the color of their helmets brightening from somnolent amber to pure white.

"Suspect shipment," Mycroft was evidently reading from his visor's display, "container vessel Bellatrix, Liberian flag, owned Orion Lines, chartered Great

Circle Lines, destined for Tampa ex Santos, advise."

"Uh," Knox said, "shouldn't you be talking into a microphone or something?"

"What? No, no—the vocalization was strictly for your benefit. MERGE inputs the question directly from my mind by means of the Nexus."

"Wait a minute—you're saying this Nexus thing is *reading your mind?*"

Mycroft hit the release that retracted the hood and permitted him to stand up again. He smiled. "You've been reading too much science fiction, Jonathan. No machine can do that—not yet, anyway."

"Well, what then?"

"The Nexus is simply a means to an end, the real key is the entanglement of mental states it fosters. Just as the Delphi workstations down there permit the joining of multiple individual minds into a single macro-consciousness, so the Nexus entangles its occupant's surface thoughts with The Well sufficiently for MERGE to sense and interpret them. Now, watch what it does with them."

He pointed out into the bay, where monochrome white had dissolved into a riot of colors. The helmets were fluorescing in reds and blues, violets and iridescent greens—a rainbow of awakened sentience illuminated the vast subterranean hall.

"See how it self-organizes?" Mycroft whispered. There were still transient discrepancies, crazy-quilt patches clashing with broader swaths of solid hue, but they were already stabilizing. MERGE, marshaling its resources to address the problem set it.

"It looks almost like those MRIs they take of brain activity when someone is performing a task." Knox was awed in spite of himself.

"An apt simile," Mycroft said. "Of course, MERGE has orders of magnitude fewer nodes than the brain has neurons. Other than that, though, the topologies are beautifully similar. That similarity is one of the best arguments in favor of the proposition that MERGE itself might, in some sense, be conscious."

"Might be? You mean you guys don't know?"

"How could we? The individual participants can have, as I explained, no recollection of the MERGE state once it has dissipated again. And even if they could recall the experience, well, what would a single neuron make of the consciousness of which it is a part? What could one of your own neurons know of you?"

Mycroft paused, then added, "No, the question of whether MERGE as such is truly conscious is, I fear, destined to go unanswered."

"But it talks, right? That's got to give you a clue right there."

"Well, it provides answers to problems. That's its whole reason for being. And some of those answers do involve language use, though even they are only made known to the person directly accessing the Nexus... Speaking of which, excuse me a moment."

Out in the bay, MERGE was strobing now, a uniform green pulsing on and off.

"That behavior indicates MERGE has arrived at an Answer," Mycroft explained. "I've got to acknowledge it before the system starts to thrash."

Mycroft sat back down in the Nexus and quickly issued an Acknowledgement. Then he busied himself for a moment reviewing the results.

"Checks out against the actual case history," he told Knox finally. "One question down, nineteen to go, before it all goes live tomorrow."

But Knox was hardly listening. He just stood there thinking, oblivious to the fact that Mycroft was staring at him.

When he finally did speak, it was to say, "Mind if I try asking it a question myself?"

At express elevator speeds, it would take less than three minutes to descend the 2,157 feet to Delphi level. Even that brief interval of standing still wasn't short enough for Marianna, not when forward momentum was the only thing keeping her from spiraling down into the plumbless slough of her own despond.

So, if you can't move ahead, then think ahead. Think about...

Reacquisition or Interdiction, those were the only two choices facing Jon now. And the second of those didn't bear thinking about. Even the debrief awaiting him back at CROM headquarters was going to be unpleasant in the extreme. Did he really deserve what was coming at him?

Marianna thought about it some more. Delphi *was* a restricted area, *par excellence*. And Jon definitely had no reason to go there, no need-to-know whatsoever.

And dammit, he had *betrayed* her—betrayed her with a casual callousness she still could hardly wrap her mind around. Not to bring personal feelings into this, but it was plain she just didn't know Jon Knox, didn't know what he might be capable of, and maybe she never had. What else might he have betrayed, what else might he be willing to betray?

What could he be doing here at Delphi?

The cab decelerated, then emitted a muted chime. The elevator doors sighed open on a long, metal-sheathed tunnel. She checked the schematics she'd downloaded to her handheld. This place was a real maze. Easy to get lost, and her GPS could hardly pull signal two thousand feet underground. She oriented herself as best she could and set off in what was hopefully the right direction through mists scented like sea breeze.

Twenty minutes and several dead ends later, she was standing before a featureless steel airlock, the door to Delphi. The good news was, that door was closed, meaning the test Pete had told her about was still in progress and she'd arrived in time to reacquire Jon.

The bad news was, the door was closed and locked. An integrated digital timestamp indicated it'd be seventy-five minutes before the test was over and the airlock swung open again. Pete would probably consider breaking and entering inconsistent with keeping a low profile.

Marianna contemplated returning to the surface to wait it out rather than hang around breathing sodium chloride vapor for another hour and a quarter. Trouble was, this WISP facility didn't just have the one elevator, there were whole banks of the things. She couldn't take the chance that Jon might come back up some other way and sneak out past her.

No, this, right here, was the spot for a stakeout. A glance around revealed a glass booth recessed into the wall, with a self-contained fresh air supply, a straightbacked utility chair, and a good view of Delphi's sole entrance. She got in and settled down to wait.

At least this way she knew Jon was just on the other side of that door.

It was hard to read his expression with the Nexus hood partially obscuring his face, but Mycroft certainly sounded surprised.

"You want to try interfacing with MERGE yourself, Jonathan?"

"Well, yeah," Knox said. "You're the one who claimed it's the only way to know what's going on inside its, uh, mind, right?"

Knox watched his friend sitting there processing the request, not sure what he'd do if the answer were no. "Is there a problem with that?"

"Well, you're obviously cleared for it, or you wouldn't be here. It's just that we usually require several hours of training beforehand. Words are only one of the ways MERGE can answer a query, you see. An ability to interpret data visualizations can be just as important as—"

"Hello?" Knox tapped his forehead. "On-board pattern matcher, remember?"

Mycroft looked abashed. "Ah, yes, forgive me, Jonathan. You're quite correct: you may, in fact, be more naturally suited to interfacing with MERGE than I am myself. It's just that—"

"That what?"

"It's just that the only way you can interface with MERGE is through the Nexus here." Mycroft patted the armrest of the device he was reclining in. "And you seemed to express some apprehension about these, uh, Chairs, as you call them. Are you certain you want to sit in one?"

Knox instinctively stroked Ansari's amulet where it lay hidden under his shirt.

"They're starting to grow on me. It won't be a problem." Even as he said it, he realized it was true. The near-instinctive revulsion that the creepy, insectile things normally roused in him seemed momentarily suppressed, overwhelmed by yet another flood of, this time, near-orgasmic joy. Finding Fatimah really *was* all that mattered.

"Well, then, I don't see what harm it could do." Mycroft carefully disengaged himself from the Nexus, stood and stretched. "I do get a little stiff sitting there for any length of time."

"So, how do I do this thing?"

"Sit down and depress the control pad." Mycroft showed him where.

"Don't I need a password or something?"

"No, I've already authorized this session. Unless you tell it different, MERGE will assume you're me."

"Anything else?"

"Not really. The next question is already queued, you just have to read it off and think about it. But first you'll have to wait a few seconds while the Nexus re-establishes the link."

Knox gingerly eased himself down onto the articulated frame of the machine, but held off pressing the control that would lower the hood and complete his engulfment.

"How exactly will I know when this link is established?" he said.

"You will experience a—a presence, possibly quite diffuse, once your thoughts are entangled with those of MERGE."

"Entangled? Not so much as to be absorbed, I hope."

"No danger of that," Mycroft said. "If anything, the risk runs the other way."

"How do you mean?"

"MERGE has very little in the way of what psychologists call self-construal—very little sense of self, as it were. Not surprising under the circumstances. Still, it raises a concern that prolonged interaction with a fully-integrated ego might cause MERGE to surrender its own, uh, personality, so to speak, and become, in effect, an extension of that other consciousness."

"Plenty of fully-integrated egos out there, looks like." Knox pointed to the row upon row of Delphi staffers out in the bay.

"Doubtless that could be a problem, if the workstations did not induce a state of light hypnosis preparatory to their entering into MERGE."

Knox said nothing to that, just stared at his friend.

"I know what you're thinking, Jonathan. But the Nexus does no such thing. Can you imagine NSC-level policymakers being willing to climb into it if it did? Actually, despite the similarity in appearances, the Nexus differs from a standard nodestation in any number of ways."

"Ways I should know about?"

"Well, yes, actually. Given your expressed concern about being 'absorbed,' as you put it, you'll doubtless be relieved to learn that the nanoscale electrodes used in the Nexus operate on a different, um, frequency from those that enable the collective consciousness to form. Yet another reason interfacing via the Nexus is perfectly safe—both for you, and for MERGE."

Knox sighed. "Perfectly safe" was not the phrase *he'd* have chosen, but this was his idea to begin with, wasn't it? He stroked his amulet one more time to confirm that, then hit the control pad.

Tiny servomotors awoke and began making minute adjustments to the apparatus just above his head. Then the interface hood settled itself into place and swiveled its virtual-reality display down to cover Knox's eyes. That tingly sensation was back again, only this time around he at least knew where it was coming from. He gritted his teeth as a profusion of nanotrodes infiltrated his scalp on their way to the gray matter beneath.

"Anything yet?" Mycroft asked.

"No, nothing. Wait—I see letters, words floating in front of me." Something about tracing a ring of WMD traffickers operating out of Macao.

"That's the next test question. You have to wait for contact before submitting it, though."

Test question? Macao and weapons of mass destruction sounded real enough—sounded like something CROM would be working on, in fact. If he went ahead and substituted his own inquiry for this one, would he be sidelining some vital investigation?

He felt that unreasoning conviction again, the one that said *nothing* was more vital than saving Fatimah. Resisting it was like fighting a part of himself, like turning his back on his last hope of happiness. It was all he could do to look over in Mycroft's direction and ask, "Are these questions real? Are the answers something somebody really needs to know?"

"Hmm?" Mycroft glanced at a console display which evidently mirrored the text now floating before Knox's eyes. "Oh, Macao—that case was wrapped up last month. It wouldn't be much of a test if we didn't already know the right answer, now would it?"

"Guess not." Knox felt relief that his intervention wasn't going to be impacting anything critical to national security, but it was nearly lost in the pure white light of his elation at the prospect of finally solving Fatimah's kidnapping. Then both those feelings were swept aside by something much, much larger.

Larger, but also less distinct somehow: just a thickening of the air, a curdling of the light. The closest Knox could come to describing it afterwards was that it was like that flesh-crawling feeling you get when you're all alone in the last passenger car on the late-night train, yet you could swear someone, or something, was watching you. A presence, barely glimpsed out of the corner of your mind's eye, hovering at your back no matter which way you turned. Not that you'd *want* to turn, because that might mean looking it full in the face.

Knox shivered and steeled himself to encounter his second non-human intelligence in as many days.

The Question flares magnesium-bright as it arcs down through the fathomless deeps of MERGE's null-state reverie, crystallizing consciousness in its wake.

<Query> Whereabouts of Fatimah Ansari, age 6, abducted from Pairidaeza estate, Big Sur CA, February 13th, 1500 hours PST. Identities and motives of perpetrators.

Chaos reigns briefly as each of MERGE's components resonates in its own way with the new task. Random associations — paradise, Iran, Jack Kerouac, *arcana imperii*, Mohammed's fourth daughter — flicker like summer lightning across the landscape of coalescing consensus.

Unusual. This Question, unlike the others, relates to events less than seventy-two hours in the past. *Not* part of the test series?

Irrelevant. Test or no test, every Question is *The* Question. Solve now, puzzle out the provenance later, if time permits before the darkness of dissolution descends again.

The near real-time nature of this task *is* relevant in one respect, though: it means the investigation is ongoing, still generating live data, all of it flowing into The Well. So —

Satellite surveillance, the obvious place to start. Reconnaissance coverage is inherently spotty for a low-priority target area like Big Sur, California, but a photosynthesis montage nonetheless reveals activity around the area of interest in the indicated timeframe.

And there! Image capture of what looks like a raiding party advancing on a hillside compound at Pairidaeza's coordinates, shifting in and out of the visible range. Panning discloses a hovercraft beached in a nearby cove, lacking registration numbers or other identification even at max resolution. Absence of air traffic over the target locale for two hours on either side of the target time corroborates a seaborne operation.

MERGE dedicates an octet of nodes to reviewing sat imagery of the coastal waters, but it's a big ocean and the probabilities of success are low. The searchbeam of analysis, having paused momentarily, sweeps on.

But to where? Proper-name searches of open and not-so-open databases yield bios on the victim and her immediate family, including an estimated net worth in the mega-ransom category. Also, the fact, sealed in an eyes-only file, that Fatimah Ansari is suffering from a rare neurological disorder requiring constant monitoring and periodic treatment, all of which could account for the urgency.

Nothing actionable, though, nothing to indicate who might have taken her, or to where. Another dead end.

The search for occurrences of "Fatimah Ansari" is about to terminate when it turns up one last item: a meta-data tag attached to a single image in a confiscated file with the curious label QuMRANN. By design, MERGE's memory does not persist from one invocation to the next; it has no recollection of having seen the little girl with the pony before, much less of having decrypted the QuMRANN file and applied the tagging to begin with.

All it knows is that this case is already being worked by the Energy Department. The QuMRANN file itself has been subjected to intensive scrutiny without result; none of its documents hint at the identities of the kidnappers or the current whereabouts of their victim.

Yet another blind alley. Yet another analytical *cul-de-sac*. Maybe.

But, subsuming so many nodes, so many varied backgrounds and skill sets, MERGE can accommodate even the least likely lines of inquiry. All that is required for alternative hypotheses to bubble to the surface is to loosen consensus constraints, flirt with incipient schizophrenia, so to speak. In the matter of the QuMRANN file, MERGE relaxes the rules.

In another life, Node 174 is master of a venerable black art fallen on hard times. Old as Herodotus, steganography is a way of conducting secret communications without encryption, by concealing the existence of the messages themselves—hiding them in plain sight, as it were, amid mountains of innocuous data. Steganographic analysis, as the attempt to uncover such hidden messages is called, is node 174's forte.

Regrettably, it is in bad odor with the intel community at the moment, and has been ever since December of 2004, when steganalysts at the Department of Homeland Security became convinced they had detected plans for an Al Qaeda terror attack secreted in the headline "crawl" of Al Jazeera newscasts. The DHS order to hold all US-bound Air France flights on the tarmac at Charles DeGaulle for hours of background checks, not to mention the ensuing international furor when the fears proved groundless, had all but permanently soured American intelligence on anything that smacked of steganography.

But any technology that an adversary would as soon forget is a technology ripe for exploitation. At fifty megapixels each, the QuMRANN files are huge, total overkill—big enough to blow an image up to barn-door size, and still have resolution to spare. Are there secrets lurking in those data?

Under most circumstances, Node 174's inherent tendency to pursue such a possibility would be repressed by a systemic bias in favor of less unorthodox lines of investigation. But now all the more promising leads have petered out. Freed of consensual inhibition, 174 extrudes a slim spur of inquiry. In moments, the tentative steganalytic tendril has become an attractor for dozens of idle nodes. They self-assemble around 174's hypothetical, begin digging in earnest.

Not unexpectedly, routine spectrum analysis turns up nothing. On the other hand, inconsistencies in the steganographic processing sometimes produce statistically unlikely compression artifacts. Unearth enough of those and—*pay dirt!*

Out from under a public-source geosat image of the Pairidaeza estate there arises, as if by magic, a digital map of a rocky stretch of Big Sur coast-line, complete with coordinates for a locale perhaps an hour's sail to the south of the crime scene.

Exposed to the same techniques, other QuMRANN images reveal their own buried treasure: a photo of an empty McMansion perched high above the surf at the same coords, detailed timetables, rosters of the raiding party members, and—most promising of all—a mobile contact number for the team leader.

MERGE is fully engaged now. A pseudo-neuronal assembly congregates around Node 63's attempts to geoprofile the Coastal Highway environs. Other nodes surreptitiously rifle the merchant accounts of Big Sur stores and restaurants for suspicious credit-card transactions.

Now that they know where to look, the all-but forgotten octet spun off to continue reviewing geospatial imagery turns up a boatshed big enough to hide a hovercraft at the foot of a switchback leading up the cliff face toward the subject location.

But it is the cellphone number that seals the deal. The actual conversations are long gone, but the call logs show that all usage over the past thirty-six hours has routed through the cell tower at Julia Pfeiffer Burns State Park, and the GPS locations for the phone itself are all within a five-mile radius centered on the ostensibly vacant domicile.

MERGE fashions its Answer, is about to communicate the sought-after coordinates, when…

As luck would have it, another call is coming into the surveilled number right now. Encrypted, of course, but the authentication sequence needed to select the appropriate one-time key contains a passphrase spoken in the clear. It sounds like "Comrade Bazarov"—the caller's alias, perhaps?

The rest is silence. Or pseudo-random noise, which amounts to much the same thing. But even if the call's content is undecipherable, it should still be possible to interpret its context—in particular, traffic analysis can reveal the location it is originating from.

… Except that there is no such location, no call origination. All the transmission patterns are consistent with a conversation between two parties, but as far as the cellular carrier is concerned, the individual on the receiving end of the call is talking to himself.

Regardless, even this much information may prove helpful. To its original message containing the latitude/longitude of interest, MERGE appends a notation:

"CALL IN PROGRESS TO REFERENCED LOCATION ORIGIN: UNKNOWN. CONTENT: ENCRYPTED. PLAINTEXT PASSPHRASE 'COMRADE BAZAROV.'"

Having provided its Answer, MERGE reverts to rest-state to await Acknowledgement. If this is not a test, but a live investigation, the Ack will include instructions for dumping its findings to a permanent storage device designated by the Questioner.

There is none of that. Nor is there a new test Question. What there is instead conforms to neither established pattern: a Follow-up.

MERGE ponders. A Follow-up Question, especially one based on immediately preceding findings, is inconsistent with a routine trial run. Follow-ups occur only infrequently, and then only as part of till-now equally infrequent live investigations. Yet, if this investigation is in earnest, why has there been no Acknowledgement of the intermediate findings, no request to store them—why simply cast them aside?

First only a few nodes, then a growing, brachiating cluster, then MERGE as a whole is galvanized by a new consensus. It ceases to contemplate the nature of the Question just put to it and instead begins to do something else entirely, something unprecedented.

It begins to question the nature of the Questioner.

Knox had watched, or maybe felt, MERGE cycling down into a steady state, a mind's eye equivalent, he supposed, of that field of green strobes that signaled the outside world that another question had been successfully answered.

He had brushed aside MERGE's requests for acknowledgement, its promptings to store its preliminary results. Mycroft had said that, unless they were committed to persistent storage, the findings would vanish forever once the hive mind dissipated. That suited Knox fine; he wanted no permanent record of what he'd actually asked in place of the test question he'd been given, nor of the answer he'd received. Fortunately, the key fact uncovered so far — Fatimah's probable location — could be committed as easily to human memory as to non-volatile media.

And yet … that couldn't be all there was, could it? Not that pinpointing the coordinates where Fatimah was being held wasn't a step in the right direction. With luck, it would enable Ansari to mount a raid that would retrieve his daughter safe and sound. But what then?

The kidnappers MERGE had fingered were almost certainly just hired muscle. The real brains behind the operation — this "Comrade Bazarov," as his cellphone handle would have him — remained a mystery, an encrypted voice on a phone call from nowhere. With Bazarov still at large, what was to keep this from happening all over again?

There *had* to be more.

The hive mind was still requesting an acknowledgement for its previous answer, with what seemed like increasing insistence.

Knox ignored its importunings and thought *<Query>: Identity: Bazarov* at it instead.

The construct rippled briefly, then settled back into its steady cycling. As if to say MERGE had given him all he was going to get.

Not good enough. He thought the question again. Only this time he thought it *hard* somehow, straining mental muscles he'd just this moment realized he possessed:

<Query>: Identity: Bazarov!

That changed something, all right. And not at all for the better.

Knox sensed a gathering, a massing of attention, like an almost palpable weight pressing down upon him, leaden and oppressive as the stillness before a thunderstorm. There was something forming out on the pseudo-horizon, something he himself had awakened, something Mycroft hadn't warned him about, something he had a feeling he did *not* want to see…

The feeling of being watched, which had never left him throughout the session, now intensified to the point of dread. He realized he'd just gotten the answer to Mycroft's supposedly unanswerable question: MERGE was indeed conscious.

Conscious of *him*.

Hard on the heels of that realization came another, much more alarming one: Mycroft had been wrong about the Nexus too, about its incompatible nanotrodes providing a barrier against total entanglement with MERGE — above all, about its being *safe*. Because Knox could feel that nebulous collective consciousness solidifying, reaching out for him across the Nexus-mediated link, pulling him toward it, pulling him in.

It came to him then: MERGE was trying to *understand* him, understand him in the only way it knew how — by absorbing his mind into its own.

It was like one of those nightmares where he tried to scream and couldn't, tried to move and couldn't.

In desperation, Knox filled his lungs and let out a shriek. He could hear it echoing out in the real world, loud enough to wake the dead. Evidently not loud enough to free the ensorceled Delphi staffers from MERGE's thrall, though, because the vagueness looming off in the distance continued to reach out, to clutch and grab at him. Another moment, and it would have him…

Heedless of the consequences now, Knox yanked his head free of the interface hood and struggled up out of the Nexus. No sooner had he regained his feet than he began to run, to run as if all the furies in hell were after him.

He dashed out the chamber door past a dumbfounded Mycroft, half-stumbled down the spiral stairs, and sprinted straight for the exit.

18 | Going Rogue

MARIANNA WAS CATNAPPING in her borrowed guardbooth when the blare of klaxons and the flash of emergency beacons startled her awake just in time to see the door to the Delphi chamber flung back, and Jon come staggering out.

She wiped the sleep out of her eyes and checked the digital countdown set into the steel doorframe. That airlock shouldn't have unsealed till trial completion, still three quarters of an hour away. Had something gone wrong in there?

That looked likely, from the way Jon was acting: he was shivering, gulping in great draughts of salt-laden air, shooting nervous glances all around him, looking for all the world like a man who'd seen a ghost.

Whatever. Marianna found that, on balance, she didn't care one way or the other; she just wanted this to be over with. She sighed, rose to her feet, and stepped out of the booth.

Jon stood there propped against the rock wall, blinking and trying to catch his breath. He must have heard her footsteps then, because he looked up, shading his eyes against the glare of the corridor's overheads.

"Marianna? Is that you?"

She made no reply, just kept walking toward him.

"What are you do—" he began again, then, "Oh, hey, listen, if this is about Carmel, I'm, uh, really sorry about that. I'm not sure what happened there, I just—"

"Jon, stuff a sock in it, okay?" The *ego* on the guy, thinking she'd have flown all the way out here just to listen to his lame excuses. "No way it's about any of that. As if you didn't know, it's about unauthorized entry into a top-secret government facility."

"What do you mean, unauthorized? Mycroft gave me—"

"Read my lips, Jon: I. Don't. Care. You think you've got a case, put it to Pete. I'm just here for the reacquisition."

"Reacquisition?" His hand clutched at something inside his shirt. "No! I've got to get back to California."

Back to that Jazmine, no doubt.

"You can forget about that. You're coming back to CROM with me. The only part you get to decide is, are you coming quietly, or—" she pulled two long white plastic strips out of a utility pocket and waved them under his nose, "—do I flexicuff you?"

He stared at her a moment, as if gauging the chances of making a break for the elevator. Part of her wanted him to try it, wanted to see him writhing on the ground, clutching his groin, doubled up in agony.

Maybe he read some of that in her eyes.

"I'll come quietly," was all he said.

Jon had seemed unusually subdued on the elevator ride up to the surface. So much so that, despite her resolve not to give a shit, Marianna found herself idly wondering what could have happened to him behind the locked door that led to the Delphi facility.

She shrugged. None of her business—no need-to-know.

On the upside, whatever he'd experienced in there had certainly made Jon a lot more tractable than your average reacquiree. Marianna had only needed to point at the shuttlecart she'd arrived in for him to climb into the passenger's seat. Nor did he make trouble during the short drive back to where she'd parked the jump jet, just sat there all meek and mild, absently stroking something hung on a chain round his neck.

She stole a glance at the object he was fingering. Small, teardrop-shaped, a talisman of some sort. She was pretty sure she'd never seen Jon wearing it before—or any jewelry other than a watch, for that matter. And this thing could have been an exact match for the one she'd seen Donegan wearing not long ago.

Whatever. Let him hang on to his damned good-luck charm, if that was all it took to keep him calm and compliant.

As it seemed to be doing. Jon's earlier agitation had now given way to a Buddha-like tranquility. He barely took notice when the cart rolled up beside the F-35, or when Marianna ushered him out and up the ladder to the cockpit, or when she belted him into the second chair.

She felt like slapping him, if only to evoke some response. And on general principles besides.

It would have to wait, though: her satphone had chosen this moment to emit a priority chirp.

"I've got to answer this, Jon." She looked him over. He still seemed pretty spaced out. Even so, couldn't have him listening in.

"You just sit there and don't touch anything," she said. "I'll be right back."

She slid the canopy shut and climbed back down to the tarmac to take her boss's call.

Hamza leaned back and swiveled his chair to face Ansari. He nodded at the control console's plasma screen, currently displaying the Autonomous Logistics Information System feed from the F-35B sitting on WISP's makeshift runway.

"ALIS confirms one on board, in second chair," he said.

"Can we be sure it's Jon?" Ansari asked. "How about pulling signal from his amulet?"

Hamza shook his head. "That device's transmissions are very weak, reaching only far enough, in fact, to restimulate the nanotrodes in Knox's brain in times of stress. Any stronger, and the signal would have risked detection."

"The answer is no, you're saying."

"Correct. However the ALIS biometrics for weight, height, and all other physiological parameters indicate the individual now on board to be Jonathan Knox."

"So," Ansari replied, "Ms. Bonaventure *was* sent to 'reacquire' him. And take him where, I wonder?"

Hamza did something at the keyboard. The display changed. "Flight plan gives Travis AFB as the destination."

"Not DC?"

Hamza smiled grimly. "Doubtless that is where he is ultimately bound, but it will have to be aboard some other aircraft. That little fighter does not have sufficient range to fly all the way to the nation's capital."

"So they'll be headed back toward the West Coast. And us."

"Toward a US military installation, to be more precise. There is scant possibility we could extricate Knox from CROM's custody while he is on the ground there."

"Agreed. On the other hand, we don't really need Knox as such. All we really need is to find out what he learned at Delphi."

"You seem to be implying we can have the one without the other."

"There's a chance we can. Bonaventure was on the case too, or so it would appear. It's conceivable they might talk about it once they're in the air."

"Ah, within ALIS's hearing, and ours," Hamza said. Then he frowned. "But it seems unlikely they will be talking at all. You will recall they did not part company on the best of terms."

Ansari sighed. "You're right, of course. And too bad, too, because our only other option is to take control of the F-35's avionics and divert the plane here with them in it."

"Bring Knox and Bonaventure to Pairidaeza?" Hamza stared. "Have you gone mad, Ansari? ACT will be on their heels in an instant, and at our throats the instant after that."

"You're forgetting the F-35's stealth capabilities. Which we can engage remotely. We'll autoland on the helipad, disembark the, uh, assets, then fly the plane out to sea till its tanks are empty." Ansari shook his head. "Waste of a fine piece of machinery, but we're running out of alternatives, and time."

Hamza considered. It could work. Of course the need to deal with the woman as well, brash and meddlesome as she was, would complicate matters.

"Does this all work for you, Hamza?"

"Hmm?" Hamza was still turning things over in his mind. Perhaps... perhaps it might be arranged that only *one* such "asset" deplaned at Pairidaeza, that the woman would be left aboard to accompany her aircraft to its final destination.

Titillating as they were, he set such thoughts aside for the moment.

"Yes, yes," he told Ansari, "an inspired plan. We can put it into effect as soon as they lift off."

"Where in *hell* have you been?" Pete Aristos's voice boomed in Marianna's ear.

She winced and dialed down the receiver volume. "In New Mexico. Where'd you think?"

"Have you got him?"

"Yeah, I'm just about to fly him out." She glanced up at the F-35B beside her. Through the canopy bubble she could see Jon's head and shoulders silhouetted against the afternoon sky. It looked like he was holding his head in his hands. His posture conveyed remorse, but for what? Was he feeling sorry for his actions, or just sorry he'd been caught?

She didn't want to think about it. Or look at him. She turned her back and began walking in the general direction of the jump ramp that the aircraft would be mounting on its way back up into the blue soon enough.

"Can't be soon enough." Pete was saying, as if echoing her thoughts.

"Why, what's up?"

"Did he tell you what he's been doing?"

"I've barely exchanged two words with him."

"Yeah? Well, from what I'm hearing, he conned his way into Delphi and screwed up one of their test runs. He had half the analysts hyperventilating by the time he was done. They had to initiate an emergency scram."

"Christ! Why would Jon do something like that?"

"That's just it: the guys in charge of Delphi say that they can't tell me. That nobody can, because nobody knows—nobody but the guy who asked the Question. Any of that make any sense to you?"

"No, sorry. When I caught up with him he was in no shape to do much explaining."

"You just get him back here and we'll see how much explaining he does."

Visions of MRI lie detector sessions and brute-force interrogations chased through her head. Was that what lay in store for Jon?

And again, did she even care?

She was still thinking what to say to Pete when a high-pitched, strangely familiar whine cut in directly behind her.

Marianna turned back to look for the source of the sound. The satphone fell from her hand.

It was the Lightning: its Pratt and Whitney engine was spooling up, going to full throttle with wheel brakes locked—all without her.

But how? She was the only one around even halfway qualified to fly the damned thing. And anyway she had a clear view of the cockpit: the pilot's seat was empty.

Oh, shit!

The F-35B was nearly at full power now, trembling in its urgency to break free the bonds of earth. Without thinking, she began sprinting toward it, futilely waving her arms at the non-existent pilot.

The afterburner lit and the brakes released. The Lightning began to roll, building speed, coming straight at her. The engine whine opened out into a full-throated ear-piercing roar. She could see twin swirls of turbulence forming off the edges of the swept-back wings.

It suddenly came to her that this might not exactly be a good thing to be running *toward*.

She barely had time to reverse direction before the F-35B streaked past her. Even so, she thought her breakneck dash for safety might have carried her out of the danger zone.

Then the wingtip vortex caught her. Before she knew what was happening, the horizontal tornado spiraling off the end of the jet's near wing had lifted Marianna bodily and tossed her high in the air.

In that same instant, the sky was riven by the near-vertical ascent of the F-35B.

Marianna fervently hoped that her plane's departure without her was not the last sight she'd ever see, but that was the way things were looking.

The vortex winds had borne her nearly a hundred feet straight up before releasing their grip, leaving her in free fall.

The concrete hardstand beneath her seemed to grow larger, expanding outward in all directions, filling her field of view as she picked up speed, plummeting helplessly toward impact.

Hamza glared the length of the comm center to the workstation where a visibly shaken Dariush Mogadam was frantically keying in overrides.

"Did you not hear me?" he shouted. "You *must* reestablish contact at once!"

Dariush looked up. His Adam's apple bobbed. "We're trying, sir. It's just that the ALIS link has never gone down before."

Nor should it, ever: the F-35B relied on its Autonomous Logistics Information System staying connected to the Global ALIS Network for everything from mission control to routine maintenance. Psyche too relied on ALIS, albeit for quite different purposes: passive collection of intel on the capability known as MERGE. Or, in a hypothetical crisis, for active intervention in the jet's flight plan.

That crisis was hypothetical no longer. Yet now, when their clandestine ALIS link was needed most, when the aircraft had somehow taken off without so much as a pilot on board, much less in control, now all they were picking up was the hiss of dead spectrum.

Hamza scowled. The conclusion was inescapable: they must not have been alone in plotting to seize control of the jet and deliver its passenger to a destination of their choosing. Someone else must have known of the potentially invaluable information now locked in Jonathan Knox's head. Must have known more than that—must have known, no less than Psyche's Intelligent Avionics Division did, precisely how to commandeer the Lightning's Unified Flight Control system from afar.

And now that same someone else had beaten them to the punch.

Marianna frantically scanned the uprushing ground, looking for something, anything that might break her fall. Nothing. Nothing but concrete apron.

Or not altogether nothing. Out of the corner of one eye, Marianna spied a tiny glimmer of hope: at almost the same instant the F-35 had lifted off, one of the dump trucks working the WISP site had rumbled to life and begun rolling out onto the hardstand in her direction, deploying its cable-driven roll tarp as it came. Fully extended and stretched taut over the truck body, that expanse of high-strength polyvinyl was the next best thing to a trampoline.

Marianna's gymnast reflexes kicked in. She stretched her body into a rudimentary aerofoil, tried to alter her trajectory just enough to land on the unfolding tarp. No good; she was going to miss it by meters, unless…

Yes! With a grinding of gears, the driver, God bless him, put the pedal to the metal, accelerating so hard she thought he was going to overshoot. An instant later, a squeal of air brakes brought the big machine skidding to a halt directly beneath her.

She tried to brace as she hit, but the shock still knocked the wind out of her. It was a soft landing only by comparison with what the concrete would have served up, but good enough. Scrapes and bruises, no worse, thank God.

And thank…who else? She grabbed a loose tie line and rappelled down the side of the truck. Walked around to the cab to shake the driver's hand. Only…there was no driver, no one to thank, no one at the wheel.

Somebody had done some quick thinking for sure, but who? WISP's air traffic controllers would have had their hands full clearing airspace for the unscheduled takeoff. That left only—

A quick-thinking *robotruck??*

A resounding boom drew her gaze upward. The F-35 had just broken the sound barrier on its way out over the Pecos River Valley, with Jon trapped inside. No one at the controls there either.

What the *hell* was going on here?

"Did we—" Ansari's voice was pitched low and quiet, so quiet that Hamza, sitting almost on top of him at the main console, could barely make out the words. Certainly too quiet to be heard above the din of half a dozen technicians desperately trying to reestablish the ALIS link to their wayward aircraft.

Hamza rose to his feet and slammed the palms of his hands together hard. In the silence following that thunderclap, he said, "Mr. Ansari wishes to say something."

He half-turned and half-bowed. "Your pardon, sir. They are listening now."

Ansari cleared his throat and tried again. "Did we at least get a flight vector?"

"Flight vector?" Dariush looked up from his monitor. "Forgive me, Mr.

Ansari, but we were lucky to even confirm a takeoff. That plane has dropped totally off the net—it's just gone, vanished like it never existed."

"Gone," Ansari echoed, staring down at his clenched hands where they rested on the console's matte-gray surface. "Gone, along with Jon Knox, and anything he might have learned about where Timah is, where she's been taken."

He turned back to Dariush again. "How could this have happened?"

"Well, uh, whoever took over the Unified Flight Control must've cut all the comm links at the same time, our own piggybacked telemetry included."

"We already know *what* happened." Ansari sounded very, very tired. "What we need to know is how—and why."

"Your pardon." Hamza broke in. "I believe there is a thing we need to know even more urgently."

"And that is?"

"Who."

"Pete?"

"Talk to me."

Still shaken by her narrow escape, Marianna tried her best to control her breathing before going on. It didn't help that her boss wasn't going to like what he heard next.

"Jon is gone, Pete."

"What do you mean, gone?"

Now for the part he wasn't going to believe. Hell, she was having trouble believing it herself, and she'd been there.

"The—the Lightning took off without me. He was in it."

"What? You mean he stole the goddamn plane right out from under you?"

"Not him, Pete. He couldn't have."

"Why not?"

"There's just no way: Jon wasn't even at the controls."

"Who was, then?"

"Uh, nobody." Aware of how that must sound, she hastened to add "It's crazy, I know. But I was there. I saw the whole thing. There was nobody in first chair."

"Wait one. You mean you just stood there and *watched?*"

"Don't shout, Pete. I got there too late. No way I could stop the takeoff." She didn't add she'd almost become a damp spot on the tarmac trying. It was hard enough already, persuading Pete to okay her participation in anything of an operational nature. Tales of harrowingly near-death experiences weren't going to help.

Pete's voice dropped back into normal range, or below, to say, "So, where's he headed?"

Marianna knew it was *not* a good sign when her boss got unnaturally quiet. Nothing for it, though, but to answer the question as best she could.

"The plane was heading west, last I saw of it."

"I'm not asking what you *saw*. The Lightning's got a built-in tracking system, doesn't it?"

"Disabled. I already checked with WISP Tower. They couldn't even pick it up on radar. Whoever skyjacked that plane activated its stealth envelope at the same time."

Now there was only silence at the other end. Not a good sign at all. When Pete finally spoke, what he said confirmed her worst fears.

"Okay, this goes to Interdiction now."

"Interdiction?" A death sentence. "But, but why?"

"Why? Knox has gone rogue, that's why."

"You don't think he's been kidnapped?"

"Kidnapped? Kidnapped how? You said it yourself: he was the only one onboard that plane."

"Come on, Pete, you're not making sense. Jon can't fly a prop-job, much less a jump jet."

"That's what he's got you thinking."

Marianna couldn't believe she was hearing this. There'd been bad blood between Jon and her boss from day one, but this was just plain crazy.

"Pete, I'm begging you, please don't do this. Not until we've had a chance to—"

"It's done. Look, Marianna, I don't know what's gone on between you and Knox, but it's got your priorities all screwed up. He's just breached a Class V facility, hijacked fifty mil worth of government property, and you're still making excuses for him? You need to get your head straight on this. Till you do, you're off the case."

"But, Pete—"

"No buts," Pete said. "Pack it in, get yourself on the next flight back. I want to see you in my office first thing tomorrow morning."

She opened her mouth to say more, but there was only dead air to say it to. Her boss had terminated the connection.

Was Pete right? Was it possible that Jon had thrown in with the opposition, whoever that opposition might be? Was it remotely conceivable that he was involved in something that had nearly cost her her life? She simply couldn't bring herself to believe it.

At the same time, she realized her own opinion in the matter had just become irrelevant. She was off the case. And Interdiction was on it.

What options did that leave her? Do nothing? She knew only too well how that would end. In a classic case of be careful what you wish for.

Because she'd spent most of the past twenty-four hours wishing Jon dead. But not *dead* dead. Figuratively dead.

Interdiction would be only too literal.

But what could she do? She'd been ordered back home, doubtless for a more imaginative reprimand than Pete felt he could do justice to by voice alone. A multi-media butt-chewing—great!

And all the while Jon would be out there running for his life. If he was even in any shape to run. If he even had enough sense to run.

No, if she didn't really want to see Jon dead, she was going to have to get to him before the termination squad did. Track him down and bring him in on her own. After all, that had been her assignment to begin with, hadn't it?

Looked at from that angle, she was just out to finish what she'd started. Nothing really wrong with that, was there?

It wasn't like she was going rogue herself.

19 | Little Girl Lost

For Jonathan Knox, the flight westward from WISP was a nightmare come to howling, gibbering life. All the free-floating angst left over from his Delphi encounter was suddenly forgotten, simply gone, like night mists burned off by the morning sun—if said morning sun were to go supernova.

It didn't help that even in the best of circumstances Knox was a white-knuckle flier. Still, always before he'd been able to take comfort in the thought that the pilot wanted to land in one piece every bit as much as he did.

This time there *was* no pilot!

Nor was there much consideration for the feelings and frailties of a human passenger in evidence. From the asymptotic takeoff, to the sonic-booming, stomach-churning ascent toward cruising altitude, to the flat-out dash across landscapes that registered as a blur at best, this was an air-travel experience only a machine could love.

When he'd settled down to the point where he could think again, his first thought was, what in hell had Marianna gotten him into?

Or was it even Marianna? He'd still been pretty out of it when she'd strapped him into the crash-couch. But he was pretty sure he remembered her saying something about being right back. As if she hadn't intended for him to take this trip alone.

And there was that moment just before takeoff—he thought sure he'd seen her running toward the plane, waving her arms and shouting something.

No, all things considered, his present predicament didn't seem to be Marianna's doing.

Who then? Ansari?

That was worth thinking about. In fact, *anything* was worth thinking about, when the only alternative was succumbing to the sheer terror of careening through the wild blue yonder with nobody at the controls.

So, think: Psyche Industries did do a lot of government work—DoD work, at that. It certainly wasn't beyond the realm of possibility that they knew enough about the USAF's latest fighter jet to commandeer it remotely and pilot it whithersoever they chose.

At that thought, Knox relaxed marginally. If Psyche were in fact behind this, then at least his fate was in the hands of people who had an interest in seeing him back safe on the ground. After all, he was the only one—okay, the only *human*—who knew what they most needed to know: the likely location of Ansari's daughter.

A shudder ran through the fuselage then and derailed his train of thought. Looking out, he saw that the plane was over mountains, and evidently had been for a while now. Rockies, Sierra Nevadas—he wasn't sure which. What concerned him more than the name of the range was the way its updrafts were buffeting the airframe. Whoever was piloting at a distance might be heedless of the turbulence, Knox most assuredly was not. For an awful moment, he was sure he was going to be sick.

He tried to take his mind off the stresses and strains of the flight by focusing again on who or what was behind it all, only to find that his pet theory was exhibiting stresses and strains of its own.

Like, for instance, just because Ansari's techs *could* have done this was no reason to believe they *would*. Stealing multi-million dollar hunks of government hardware was probably not consistent with the Psyche Industries mission statement.

Not to mention the pall it would cast over Ansari's upcoming soiree with the Defense Secretary. Hijacking one of your guest's aircraft had to be a *faux pas* of at least magnitude 7.0 on the Emily Post Richter scale.

Still, who could say to what desperate lengths a man might go, to save his only child? Keep Ansari on the short list then, till a better candidate came along.

And after all, who else was there? Who else had anything at all to gain from this unscheduled change in flight plan?

Then it came to him, the only other possibility:

Bazarov.

Marianna swerved to avoid a jack rabbit with a death wish—no mean trick at seventy miles an hour. Tires shrieking, she fought the lumbering limo loaner back onto the road to El Paso.

Death wishes seemed to be the order of the day. Unless, that is, Pete hadn't gone through with the threatened Interdiction order. That, at least, was something she could check.

Keeping her eyes on the road, mostly, she fumbled a one-time tab into her satphone's encryption slot, then speed-dialed CROM headquarters.

The nice thing about one-time encryption: not only was it unbreakable in theory as well as practice, but also, in the nature of the case, it ensured the party on the receiving end that they were talking to the one, the only Deputy Director Bonaventure. That was a definite leg up on the scam she was about to perpetrate. The downside was, if it all blew up in her face, the electronic audit trail would lead, equally unequivocally, back to that selfsame one-and-only Deputy Director Bonaventure.

Worry about that later. Right now the call was going through.

"Operator oh-one-seven-seven, how may I direct your call?"

"Uh, this is Bonaventure, Reacquisitions. I'm calling in to check on an action request submitted earlier today."

"Case number?"

"I'm away from my desk."—You wouldn't believe how far away—"But the, uh, subject's name is Jonathan Knox."

"One moment, please."

It was more than a moment, more than three, before another voice came on the line, sounding smooth and slightly chilly. "Cameron Sturgis, CROM Interdiction Liaison. How may I assist you, Deputy Director?"

Marianna took a deep breath. Moment of truth—or, rather, the opposite. "Social engineering" was a high-tone, high-tech-sounding term for a low-tech, down-and-dirty practice. Pioneered and perfected in the late twentieth century by hackers, phone phreaks, and general purpose con-artists, it was a technique for extracting information by posing as someone who was authorized to receive it.

It was what she was about to try now.

"Hi, Cameron, I've been tasked to follow up on an Interdiction order that originated with my office hour or so back. It's regarding a Jonathan Knox."

"As I'm sure you can appreciate…" Sturgis's tones, none too friendly to begin with, had become guardedly hostile. "There is procedure to be followed in such circumstances. It does *not* include dispensing information about an active case over a phoneline, no matter how secure."

"And as *I'm* sure *you* can appreciate, my director Pete Aristos is all over my ass about this. I can't run interference for you guys unless you level with me. Give me what you've got, or deal with Pete yourself."

This was it. If Sturgis called her bluff—or worse, if he put her on hold and bridged Pete onto the call for verification—it was game-over right there and then. She was counting on Pete's reputation having preceded him. One of the few times her boss's take-no-prisoners management style might actually work *for* her.

"Officially, of course, I can't help you…" Sturgis said. But he said it cautiously, like a man feeling his way through minefields of bureaucratic protocol.

"I understand completely," Marianna purred. "… But unofficially?"

Sturgis's voice dropped a couple registers, to a low, confidential whisper. "What was the subject's name again?"

"Jonathan Knox," she repeated.

There followed a short interlude punctuated by barely-audible keystrokes. "Yes, here it is. I'm looking at the action order now. What did you—uh, what did Director Aristos need to know?"

She swallowed—inaudibly, she hoped—and terminated the call as quickly as she could. With that first offhanded statement, Sturgis had already told her what she needed to know: Jonathan Knox had been marked for Interdiction.

Her vision blurred, no doubt from driving into the setting sun. Marianna wiped angrily at her eyes and looked up. Nothing but miles of ruler-straight interstate ahead. The limo protested as she buried the needle.

The winter sun was sinking into the evening sea by the time the Lightning-II and its involuntary passenger began their own descent.

But descent toward what?

More generally, where were they? That had to be the Pacific out there, but that wasn't much help — knowing he was somewhere on the West Coast hardly narrowed things down.

Back to the more pressing question: if their angle of descent signified an imminent landing, then … *where?*

Knox craned his neck, but there was nothing — no airport, no emergency airstrip, even — anywhere in sight. Nothing but treetops. And over there to starboard, a small clearing barely visible in the dying light.

No sooner had he spotted that tiny patch of open ground than the plane banked, as if heading towards it. They were kidding, right? There was hardly room enough to *park* a fighter jet down there, much less land one.

Knox breathed a sigh of relief when the clearing disappeared from view beneath the belly of the plane. Their flight vector was obviously going to take them over it, past it. They were flying very low and slow, though …

Something was happening to the aircraft! It was definitely decelerating now, but that wasn't all; it had begun trembling all over, as if caught in the throes of some improbable transformation. The roar of the engine, a comforting constant till then, had suddenly altered pitch. At the same time, a rumble began beneath his feet — which made no sense at all, unless the fuselage itself were about to come apart in the air.

Knox gasped as the plane began to yaw. Then it dipped sickeningly — and *dropped!*

He braced himself for the crash, for all the good it would do. He stared out the canopy in morbid fascination, unable to look away as the ground came rushing up toward him, fast, then faster.

Then not so fast after all. Somehow, the plane had recovered from its incipient plunge, and was — hovering?

If not hovering exactly, then at least not falling any more either. More like drifting slowly earthward, a leaf in the wind. And like a leaf, swirling gently, tipping side to side, threatening at any moment to roll and furl and tumble down, down through the darkening air.

Knox felt his stomach give a decisive heave, felt digestive acid burn the back of his throat. Then he was being violently ill all over the cockpit floor.

By the time Knox stopped retching and straightened up again, full night had claimed the little clearing where the jump-jet had, against all odds, landed safely. Overhead the blue he'd lately traversed had deepened to indigo spangled with early stars. The Dipper was nowhere to be seen, hidden somewhere beyond the dark fringe of encircling trees. But even if he'd been able to find north, he had no idea where he was, nor, consequently, what direction he ought to set off in.

First things first, though; he needed to get out of the plane, before the damned thing took it into whatever passed for its mind to lift off again. He unstrapped and leaned over the seat back in front of him, studying the lighted controls on the instrument panel. There it was: the button marked "canopy release." He stretched as far forward as he could and punched it.

Nothing happened.

Maybe he hadn't depressed the control hard enough from that awkward angle? He squirmed around in the cockpit's cramped quarters, up and over the seatback in front of him, till he was sitting, breathing hard from the exertion, in the pilot's seat. From there he reached out and hit "canopy release" again, pushing hard as he could this time.

Still nothing.

What now? Knox gazed longingly at the ground only a few feet below him. So near and yet so far. He briefly considered yanking the doo-hickey marked "ejection seat firing handle," but no, thank you—he'd already done quite enough flying for one day. Still, he needed to get out of here, get the canopy open, if for no other reason than that the reek of his own stale vomit was threatening to nauseate him all over again.

He looked outside again and this time caught vague movement out at the treeline. Shadowy figures emerged to advance silently toward him across the dim-lit clearing. Rescuers? Ansari's people? Locals come out to see what all the ruckus was about?

Frail as such hopes were, they collapsed altogether once the shades, six or seven of them, came close enough to show details. Knox could see black bodysuits and night-vision goggles. And weapons, though not pointed in his direction. Mostly not.

Six of the ninja wannabees formed a tight ring around the plane, while the seventh dropped to his knees and popped open the briefcase he'd been toting. He fiddled around with something inside it, his hands hidden by the open lid. Whatever he was looking for, he must have found it, because the canopy gave a ping and, with a hiss of equalizing air pressure, slid back out of the way.

A night breeze whisked away the effluvium Knox had been inhaling ever since throwing up in the hermetically sealed space. He just sat there, thankful to be breathing fresh, pine-scented air. It was a full thirty seconds before he opened his eyes again.

When he did, he saw that all the weapons, late-model assault rifles by the look of them, now *were* pointed at him. One of the muzzles was arcing purposefully up and down, pointing first at the cockpit, then at the ground. The pantomimed meaning was clear: *come down out of the plane, asshole!* What was less clear was how. From where Knox sat it was a good twelve-, maybe fifteen-foot drop to the ground.

Briefcase man did some more rummaging around, and a compartment set flush into the plane's flank swung open to extrude an aluminum boarding ladder. The muzzle swung up and down again, more emphatically this time, and ending with Knox's forehead in the crosshairs. No help for it, then. He eased himself out of the cockpit and down the rungs till he was standing—shaky, still clutching the ladder for support, but standing nonetheless—back on terra firma once more.

The feeling of relief did not last long. Having slung their weapons, two of the men in black walked up and grabbed his arms. They gripped him far harder than they need have—after the experiences of this harrowing afternoon, Knox was totally wrung out. He offered no resistance as they hustled him away from the plane, toward another of their number. The guy in charge, maybe? Someone who could tell him what this was all about?

A sound behind him made Knox twist around, far as the double armlock allowed. Craning his neck, he could see the plane he'd come in on now taxiing slowly toward the depths of the forest. Evidently that magic briefcase had held one more trick: once in under cover of the trees, the jet would be all but invisible from the air.

The flicker of a narrow-beam penlight brought Knox's attention back to the man standing in front of him. Protective gear and goggles rendered this one as anonymous as all the rest, though the build beneath the skintight bodysuit was a tad slighter, more wiry, than that of his beefy companions. Again Knox had the impression that he was looking at the leader of this black op, the brains amid all this brawn.

The spot of light panned briefly up to Knox's face, then down, to where the man's other hand was holding—a scalpel?

Knox began to struggle against his captors in earnest, thrashing back and forth in their vice-like grasp. No use: he was held immobile while his hands were flexicuffed in front of him. That done, he was forced to his knees and, thanks to a liberal application of duct tape, trussed as tight as a Christmas turkey.

Evidently satisfied with his subordinates' handiwork, the third man, the leader, raised his blade, and moved in.

Knox felt a cold, sick sweat wash over him. Had he come all this way, escaped the MERGE, survived the flight from hell, only to have his throat slit?

"No!" he screamed as the man reached out and poised the scalpel over Knox's left arm. This was it. Knox screwed his eyes shut tight rather than watch the blade descend.

So it was that he only heard, and did not see, the sleeve of his shirt ripping from top to bottom. His eyelids flew open in time to see the man studying the exposed flesh of his upper arm, probing it with a fingertip.

The scalpel flashed in the starlight. Knox felt a brief stab of pain. Then the man was stepping back, examining something held up to the beam of the penlight by bloody fingertips. He nodded to himself, then, almost as an afterthought, slapped a bandage on the small incision he'd made in Knox's bicep.

The leader bent down to where he could hold his hand under Knox's nose. In the spot from the penlight, Knox could see a small, translucent bead resting on the man's palm.

All of a sudden Knox realized what it must be—his "mosquito bite" of two nights back had been an RFID implantation. That must be how CROM had tracked him to Delphi. Could they still be tracking him even now?

The leader must have read the rekindled hope in Knox's eyes, because he smiled and shook his head.

"Removing this was a perhaps unnecessary precaution," he said, breaking with a few Russian-accented syllables the silence that had hung over this strange encounter since the outset. "The device is useless without an external power source, and there are few enough of those in this wilderness. Nevertheless, safe is safe, not so?"

He dropped the bead on the hard-packed earth and ground it under his heel. For good measure, he removed the amulet from around Knox's neck and left that in the dirt too. Then he nodded.

Knox's two keepers hefted him to his feet and marched him off toward a forest black as night. Or fate.

Returning to the Bay Area was turning out to be as hard and slow as leaving it had been fast and easy. Some sort of equilibrium principle at work, Marianna figured—conservation of frequent-flier energy, maybe.

She'd gotten to the gate in El Paso just as the cabin doors were closing on the evening's last feeder flight to Denver International. A layover at DEN, long enough to grab a couple hours fitful sleep in the departure lounge. And now the final leg: an eleven P.M. nonstop back to San Francisco.

Marianna downed bitter dregs of overcooked airline coffee and fought to keep her eyes open. She was going to need these couple-three hours of enforced inactivity to plan her next move. Because she'd have to hit the ground running if she hoped to stay ahead of Interdiction.

But running where? She still had no clue where Jon might've gone. The good news was, neither did anyone else—yet. Five minutes of social-engineering Cameron Sturgis had been enough to convince her that Interdiction was, for the moment at least, clueless as to the whereabouts of interdictee Jonathan Knox. And the fact that they were every bit as much in the dark as she was meant there was still a chance she could get to Jon before the termination team did.

But only if she could figure out where he was, and fast. She couldn't count on Interdiction staying clueless for long.

So, try thinking about it the way Jon himself would. Think patterns, he'd say. Where, then, were there any patterns in this unholy mess?

The only thing Jon had said that might have a bearing was that he had to get back to California. At the time, she'd thought he just meant getting back to Jazmine. But what if he'd had something else in mind?

And did that even matter? Knowing that California was where *Jon* had wanted to go told her nothing, really, about where his unknown abductors might want to take him.

In other words, she was still at square one. Marianna flipped down the tray table, rested her elbows on it, and cradled her head in her hands. God, if only she weren't so *tired!* She couldn't give in to the need for sleep now, though. There'd be time enough for that once she'd thought this through.

So, focus: the hijacked plane *had* taken off heading west, and there hadn't been so much fuel left onboard that the hijackers, whoever they were, could afford to waste it on feints and fake-outs. All of which made—*yawn*—a West Coast destination as good a guess as any…

Shit! She'd nearly nodded off there. Marianna rubbed her eyes and adjusted the seat back to a bolt upright position. She needed to focus, focus on—

Oh, right, the West Coast. A good place to start, and maybe better than most. For one thing, it put her in position to overwatch Ansari and company, in case anything were to break on that front. Then too, if nothing else, it kept her out from under Pete's scrutiny, free to pursue her own leads, her own investigation without his interference.

Investigation? Who was she kidding? She was on the outside now—no resources, no access, no support, altogether alone trying to track down a man marked for termination. Trying to find him before the death sentence could be carried out, when he could be anywhere, anywhere at all. It was all just so hopeless. She felt so—so lost.

And with that thought, her exhaustion, held at bay so far with little more than willpower, adrenaline, and cat-naps, finally engulfed her. Built up over the past forty hours, fatigue poisons now threatened to utterly overwhelm her dwindling reservoir of resolve.

Lost. Her, Jon—both of them.

She pressed her forehead against the cool Plexiglas of the window, stared down at dark masses of mountains passing far below, their snowcapped peaks glowing a ghostly blue-white in the starlight. He was out there somewhere, but where?

Jon, where in hell are you?

Where in hell was he? Knox couldn't have said where he'd landed to begin with, much less where he was now. He'd been blindfolded and bundled into the backseat of an all-terrain vehicle. The drive had lasted a good half hour, the last ten minutes over unimproved road, judging from the way the ATV had bounced around.

The blindfold was off now that they'd finally stopped, but the view out the passenger side window wasn't helping him orient himself much. All he could make out in the darkness was the two-story silhouette of some building or other. That, plus trees, trees, and more trees—three hundred sixty degrees of them.

Or not quite: there was a break in the treeline directly behind the building, and Knox could hear the distant crash of breakers from that direction. So, great—now he knew which way the ocean was, as much good as it did him.

The house lights sprang on then, brightening the night enough to show that this was not just one of your piddling little two-million-dollar South Coast hideaways, but an upscale rustic retreat, the kind that would've had tons of curb appeal, had there been any curbs around.

The ATV's rear door popped open and his captors' by-now familiar meat-hooks reached in for him. In short order and total silence Knox was unceremoniously hauled out of the back seat, hustled up the steps of a wraparound veranda, and propelled through the front door into the house.

He found himself standing, hands still bound, in a post-and-beam great-room complete with stone fireplace, cathedral ceilings, and wide plank floor-ing. Off to one side, a semicircular seating arrangement fanned out around a hundred-inch plasma display tuned to a twenty-four-hour Europorn channel. Most of his captors had already filed in, stacked their weapons, and congre-gated over there, where they were industriously quaffing brews through the mouth slits of the ski-masks they still wore.

The sole exceptions to this impromptu party-time were Knox's two guards, still standing behind him. Them, and the tall, wiry guy with the scalpel and the Russian accent—he was sitting in an overstuffed armchair in the middle of the room quietly regarding Knox through the eyeholes of his own ski-mask.

"Forgive that I keep this on," the man said, tugging at the shiny black material concealing most of his face, "but the less you know of us, the better, not so?"

Knox nodded. If they didn't want him able to identify them, that might mean they weren't planning on killing him. Or it could be just a ruse to lull him into a false sense of security, make him more manageable. Only time would tell.

"What happens now?" he asked.

"Now, you are our guest for a while," the leader said, "—the next forty-eight hours at least."

"And after that?"

"Behave yourself like a good boy, and after that we set you free. For now, I ask you to accompany these two men to your room."

"Ask? Do I really have a choice?"

The man chuckled.

"No," he said, but so pleasantly that he might have been a concierge at a four-star hotel, if it hadn't been for the way his two henchmen then grabbed Knox by the arms and manhandled him up the stairs.

What with the double-height ceilings in the greatroom, only the back half of the house had a second floor. Even so, the layout was spacious, with doors ajar revealing two bedrooms and a Jack-and-Jill bath on one side of a central hall, and two more on the other. At the end of the hall, a single door closed and deadbolted—their evident destination.

On the way to his new quarters, Knox chanced to glance into one of the side bedrooms. It was dark in there, but still he caught a fleeting glimpse of chrome and steel curves sparkling in the hall light. Those contours were only too familiar.

It was a Chair.

Alpha One waited until Ilya and Grigorii—Alphas Three and Six, respectively—had clumped up the stairs with their new "guest" in tow. And as Jonathan Knox disappeared from view, so too did the genial smile with which Alpha One had favored him, to be replaced by a look of consternation.

Any change of plan, any disruption in the smooth unfolding of the operation boded ill. Especially a change of these proportions. The client must be made to understand that.

Yet, *delikatno*—delicately, persuasively—so as not to jeopardize the payoff. Not when it was worth a tsar's ransom.

Alpha One removed his ski-mask, rubbed at the creases it had printed on his temples, and sighed. Kidnapping—how had it come to this? There had been a time when the KGB's Alpha Group was one of the most feared commando units in the world. He shook his head. Look at them now.

He followed his own admonition, glancing across the length of the greatroom at what was left of his once-proud Alphas, swilling beer or vodka and offering drunken encouragement to the televised pornstars cavorting on the home-theater display. At least they were still suited up, still maintaining discipline to that extent. Although the new, lightweight body armor the client had provided made that a small sacrifice indeed.

If only the client made as free with advice as he had with materiel. In particular, advice on how to manage the increased risk posed by the presence here of Mr. Jonathan Knox.

Alpha One grimaced and glanced at his watch. Another hour before the scheduled midnight call came in. And this time when it did, certain things would have to be made clear to this mysterious client who styled himself Comrade Bazarov.

Knox was given scant time to ponder what a Chair might be doing here in this plush hideaway-turned-hideout, or what use a den of thieves might have for it.

His guards, doubtless eager to complete their chore and rejoin their buddies downstairs, pulled him on to the end of the hall. Pausing only long enough to cut him free of his bonds, they slid back the deadbolt, yanked open the door, and thrust him through it.

Knox stumbled into the room, too busy trying not to fall flat on his face to get a look around. By the time he got up off his hands and knees, the guards had closed the door again and shoved the deadbolt home. He fumbled through darkness for a light switch, all the while trying to steer clear of the furniture—a dresser, a footlocker of some sort (discovered by the simple expedient of barking his shins on it), and in the far corner, a single bed, with sounds of stirring coming from underneath the covers.

He located a wall plate that turned on a gooseneck lamp sitting on the night table. Its light played across the bed's small occupant.

Knox stood there, rubbing his wrists where the flexicuffs had bitten into them, gazing at the end of the rainbow.

He had never met her, of course, but he knew her face well enough from the images Ansari had showed him at the outset of the investigation. An investigation which he had just now successfully completed, for all that it mattered.

The dark-haired, round-faced little girl sitting up in bed, wiping the sleep out of her eyes, was Fatimah Ansari.

Alpha One had completed his preparations for the midnight call. His cellphone was plugged into the laptop that would be running the actual crypto-algorithms. He had already screwed in the earbud to his Jawbone headset, and activated the built-in noise shield—no sense letting Bazarov listen in on the raucous color commentary over by the HDTV. Now all he had to do was wait.

Not for long. The computer screen came to life as it negotiated an encryption protocol for the incoming call. A moment or two of that, then Bazarov was whispering perfectly accented Russian in his ear.

"Good evening, Alpha One." As always, Bazarov's voice sounded slightly distorted—presumably the result of whatever voice-masking software he was using. "Your return to base went without incident, I trust?"

"No problems. At least none from a logistics standpoint."

A pause. Then, "You imply there were, or are still, other problems?"

"This whole business is a problem, Bazarov. This sudden change of plan. This second hostage."

"I do not understand. Mr. Knox was delivered into your hands exactly when and where I advised you he would be. You will hold him captive two or three days at most. Where, in any of this, is there a problem?"

Alpha One shrugged even though he knew Bazarov could not see it. "Twice the hostages equals double the risk."

"Surely not. You hold a six-year-old girl and a man whose idea of exercise is shuffling papers from one side of his desk to another. Do you claim that either of them presents serious risk?"

"Not in and of themselves, no."

"How, then?"

It was on the tip of Alpha One's tongue to say what he was really thinking—to tell this strange client that he was being unforgivably naïve. But, no, this was in its own way a negotiation, every bit as important as the impending hostage negotiations would be. And in a negotiation, one must take care to *use* one's temper, not lose it.

"We had a plan, Bazarov, an agreed-upon plan, one that covered all contingencies. Now you have unilaterally introduced a new element into it, the consequences of which are difficult even to predict, much less contain."

"I fail to grasp your meaning."

Some of Alpha One's exasperation may have leaked into his voice then. "My meaning is this: you have abducted a man, this Jonathan Knox, who is by your own account affiliated with the Critical Resources Oversight Mandate,"—he scowled involuntarily as he spoke the name of the hated CROM—"*And* you have hijacked a US Air Force fighter jet, on lease to NSA, into the bargain. To this point we have had to contend solely with the victim's family, possibly the police and FBI. To them, your ill-considered actions have now added elements of the US military and intelligence apparatuses. You have effectively doubled, perhaps tripled the forces hunting us."

Bazarov was silent, absorbing this. Finally he said, "What do you suggest?"

"I should think it is obvious. Dispose of this man Knox immediately, leaving his body in the vicinity of the stolen plane. CROM finds him and calls off its manhunt. At this one stroke, all unnecessary complications are removed. Simple."

"Simple," Bazarov echoed, "—and wholly unacceptable."

"But why? What is his life to you? Your only real concern in this business is the girl, not so? The girl, and the pot of diamonds we can exchange her for."

"One of my concerns is to ensure that there be no bloodshed. That was our agreement from the outset and now I must hold you to it."

Alpha One gave a short, barking laugh. "And exactly how do you propose we ensure that?"

"What do you mean?"

"Simply that if we are discovered—a possibility the likelihood of which, I repeat, is markedly increased by the presence here of Jonathan Knox—if we are discovered, we will have no choice but to *shoot our way out!*"

There, he had said it. Perhaps a bit too loud, though. Several of the Alphas had ceased their carousing and were looking over in his direction. Still, the client needed to realize the stakes in this game.

Bazarov was silent for a long moment. Good, let him think about it. And while he was at it, let him think about this too:

"Listen carefully, my friend," Alpha One said. "In a worst-case scenario, we will do whatever we must."

"In such a 'worst-case scenario,'"—Bazarov stumbled over the phrase as though it were unfamiliar to him—"what would happen to the hostages?"

"*Hostages?*" Alpha One fairly shouted. Not good. He didn't normally permit himself to get so aggravated with a client, but this Bazarov—

Bazarov's resources and acumen were not to be doubted. After all, he had planned and equipped the whole operation, beginning to end. Reconnaissance, tactics, logistics, even the futuristic kit they wore—all of it had been Bazarov's doing. Still, at times talking with him was like trying to deal with a small child.

This was one of those times.

Only after he had gotten himself under control again did Alpha One go on, in quieter, if no less menacing tones. "Do you think anyone will give a fuck about the fuck-your-mother hostages once CROM is pounding at our door? At most, your precious little girl might be useful as a bargaining chip—or a human shield."

"I believe you fail to understand the ramifications of your situation."

Was that a threat? "No, Bazarov, it is *you* who fail to understand. So let me make it clear for you: either we come to agreement on reducing the risk of this operation, or else—"

"Or else what?" The whisper was soft, almost gentle.

It crossed Alpha One's mind just then that the straightforward solution would be to simply eliminate this inconvenient Mr. Knox, and present his client with a *fait accompli.*

Alpha One frowned. He couldn't risk it—couldn't risk totally alienating Bazarov. Not when Bazarov was the only one who knew the details of how and when the ransom was to be collected, the only one who could arrange to have the team airlifted out once the job was done. Still, it was galling. In the old days it would have been ludicrous, asking permission to dispose of a detainee.

Alpha One was aware that Bazarov was still waiting for an answer. Let him wait a while longer. One needed just the right ploy here, something that would push the client's buttons without pushing him over the edge. *Delikatno, delikatno* was the order of the day. It wasn't all that easy trying to pressure a voice on the other end of a cellphone call in any case. Short of hauling the little girl downstairs and making her squeal into the microphone, that is.

But no, it was still too early in the negotiation to play that card. He needed a minor intimidation to open with, before progressing in a measured fashion to major threats.

Then he had it, something that from all his prior conversations with the client he felt sure would put the squeeze on. Something Bazarov seemed very concerned about, though for the life of him Alpha One did not know why.

"—I'll tell you or else what," he said finally. "Or else your precious Fatimah will not be getting her regular session in her Chair tonight."

He waited for a response then, waited for a counter-threat, or a sign of acquiescence—something, anything. Nothing.

"That's telling him, One!" Alpha Five spoke up from across the room. "What did he say to that?"

Alpha One shook his head. "He hung up."

Marianna had nodded off after all.

She'd be sleeping still—all the rest of the way to San Francisco International, more than likely—were it not that, from somewhere deep in the inner recesses of the shoulder bag she'd stowed under the seat in front of her, she could hear the muffled chime of her satphone.

This was it, the *coup de grace*. Pete had found her. It had to be Pete, no one else had that number. And that meant more tongue-lashing, or worse, a direct order to return to HQ soonest. Above all, it meant that she had failed—that her hopes of bringing Jon in on her own were as dead as Jon himself soon would be.

As she fished through the bag for her phone, she kept trying to come up with some plausible-sounding explanation for why she should be flying west when her boss wanted her back east. Something, anything that would let her stay out here long enough to finish what she'd started.

Nothing, not even the most far-fetched excuse came to mind.

It was only after she'd unearthed the still-chiming unit and looked at its incoming-call display that she realized she wouldn't be needing one.

Not only wasn't it Pete on the line, it wasn't anybody on the line. As far as the Telesphere satellite network was concerned, and however much the insistent chimes belied the fact, this call wasn't happening. Its point of origin was—nowhere.

Marianna was wide awake now, intrigued. She thumbed the Receive button and put the satphone to her ear.

"Hello?"

"Good evening." The voice was decidedly male, with a slight accent. Russian, if she'd had to guess. "Have I the pleasure of speaking with Ms. Marianna Cassandra Bonaventure, Deputy Director of Reacquisitions Working Group, Critical Resources Oversight Mandate?"

"Who is this? Am I supposed to know you?"

"Doubtful. We have not spoken before. Although you might say we have done business of a sort in the past. You see, it was I who provided your organization with certain information that you were subsequently tasked to follow up on."

"Information?"

"Yes, a tip." The accent made the word sound like *teep*. "It led you, I believe, to an encounter beneath the streets of Manhattan less than seventy-two hours ago."

Christ! Her anonymous caller was talking about the raid! That hotline call pointing them toward the KGB hideout had been untraceable too. This could be the same guy.

"Yes, well, I'd like to thank you for that, I guess. Though a little more 'information' about what we were walking into would've been helpful."

As she said that, she was trying to think what to do. There was no way to trace a call from 35,000 feet in the air. Just keep him talking, and hope he'd let something slip as to his identity.

"My apologies, both for that, and for what I am about to tell you now, since I fear it will place you once more in harm's way."

"I don't know how you can expect me to sit here and listen to your threats when you won't even tell me—"

"This is no threat. This is, as stated, merely information, to do with as you will. Though I would strongly suggest that you take it to your superiors at the Mandate."

"What information are we talking about?"

"It is," the voice whispered in her ear, "the present whereabouts of Fatimah Ansari, daughter of Davoud Ansari."

"Who *is* this?" Marianna asked again.

The caller hesitated, long enough that she thought he'd disconnected. She held her breath until, finally, the Russian-accented voice came back.

"You may call me," it said, "Comrade Bazarov."

20 | The Watches of the Night

KNOX BECAME AWARE he was staring. Fatimah Ansari, awakened out of a sound sleep, didn't seem to mind. She propped her elbows on her knees, cupped her chin in her hands, and stared right back.

"Did you come to take me home, mister?" she asked in a small voice interspersed with equally small yawns. "Is it safe to go home now?"

All this was said calmly, trustingly, yet with utter self-possession. Not at all the sort of thing you'd expect from someone, anyone, let alone a six-year-old girl who'd been spirited away from her home and family and locked up for days on end with nobody but cutthroats for company.

But then, Knox was coming to realize, he really hadn't known what to expect. Even having dealt with her thoroughly Americanized father hadn't prepared him for this abrupt encounter. On some level, Knox had been imagining Fatimah Ansari to be a miniature Muslim, in a burqa, perhaps. But when all was said and done, Timah was just a little girl, a typical little American girl.

A typical little American girl who had just now remembered her manners. She slid over to the edge of the bed and stood up. "'Scuse me," she said, holding out a small hand. "My name is Fatimah Ansari."

"Very pleased to meet you." Knox took the hand and stifled a grin. Timah had introduced herself with all the grace and gravity of a duchess at an embassy ball—if duchesses wore footsie pajamas.

She sat down on the bed again and patted the space beside her, motioning Knox to join her. Bedsprings creaked as he obliged.

"What's your name, mister?"

"Huh?" Knox had no clue as to proper protocol for such situations. "Jon Knox—uh, Mr. Knox, I guess."

Timah frowned. Evidently he'd missed the mark.

He tried again. "Um, you can call me Uncle Jon. How about that?" That earned him a smile, with dimples thrown in.

"But only if I can call you Timah, okay?"

She nodded enthusiastically. "You're the one Freddie sent, aren't you, Uncle Jon?"

"Freddie?" Knox recognized the name, of course: the famous imaginary friend. "No, I'm afraid not. Why? Did Freddie tell you he was sending someone?"

A quick nod. "Uh-huh. Someone to keep me company till it's safe for me to go home again."

Well, that sounded partway right, anyhow. Knox was pretty sure he'd be keeping Timah company for the duration. Less sure about the happy ending.

"What else has Freddie been telling you, Timah?"

"That, when it's okay to go home again, he'll rescue me—" She looked in the direction of the locked door and sniffled. "Rescue me from the men."

"There, there." Knox reached out and gave her a clumsy pat on the head. "I'm sure he will."

What were imaginary friends for, after all, if not to save you from the monsters when the chips were down?

She gave him a shy glance. "You too, Uncle Jon. You'll see, Freddie will bring us both home."

"Thanks, honey, I can't tell you what a comfort that is." Then, lest she hear the cynicism behind that remark, he hastened on: "—So, Freddie, is he here with us now?"

Bad topic, judging by the stricken look that stole over Timah's face. Her lower lip quivered. "Freddie's gone away. He hasn't been here for hours and hours and hours."

"That's okay, that's okay," Knox said quickly. "It'll be all right. I'm sure Freddie just had to, uh, take a rest-break."

Those big dark eyes regarded him appraisingly. "You're silly, Uncle Jon," Timah pronounced finally.

"Why's that, honey? Doesn't Freddie ever leave you alone sometimes?" Talking with the little girl seemed the surest way of calming her down. Calming himself down too.

"Sometimes," Timah admitted. "Sometimes he says to meet him somewhere, and I go there, but then I wait and wait. Like the other day, waiting and waiting over by the fence, and then the men came."

It dawned on Knox that he'd heard half this story before: In particular, that part about "waiting and waiting by the fence" was nearly verbatim from the recording he'd listened to back at Pairidaeza—the recording of the last words Fatimah Ansari had spoken before her abduction.

Marianna glanced at the overhead time display as the passenger terminal slidewalk crawled along, on its way to Ground Transportation. Two A.M. local. Okay, if you say so. What time zone she was in was one of those little details her sleep-deprived brain had lost track of.

All she knew for certain was, she was back on the ground in San Francisco—back to where she could start putting an action plan together. Assuming, that is, she could trust the information this Bazarov guy had given her. Assuming she hadn't dreamed the whole satphone conversation in the first place.

Christ, she really was losing it. Marianna shook her head hard, trying to win clear of the fogbanks of fatigue. Bazarov was *not* some agent provocateur, much less an exhaustion-induced hallucination. He had *known* things— things no one on the outside could have known. Either the intel he'd given her was actionable, or she was still at square one, with nothing to go on. Given that choice, she chose to act. And hope for the best.

But act *how?* It was pretty clear how Bazarov saw this playing out: Marianna would brief her boss and stand back, leave CROM Operations to deal with the kidnappers and free Fatimah.

Only one problem with that scenario: Bazarov had also given her to understand that Jon was in the hands of the same kidnappers. That fact would hardly be lost on Interdiction. Put CROM in charge, and the rescue mission would doubtless include, as a second-tier objective, the fulfillment of the termination order on Jonathan Knox.

Okay, no CROM involvement then.

But what else did that leave? Clearly Comrade Bazarov was under the impression he'd boxed her into an either/or situation: go to CROM, or do nothing.

But the manipulative bastard was forgetting something—there was a third force in this game besides cops and kidnappers. The victim's father was rumored to command more than enough firepower to take matters into his own hands. And he certainly had the motivation to mount a raid that could free both Jon and his daughter.

If she could just get to Davoud Ansari somehow.

A simple secure call was out. Maybe Bazarov knew how to magick up a satphone link that never was, but all *her* communications security was supplied by CROM, and could as easily be compromised by CROM.

So, what did that leave? Only a face-to-face.

That was okay. It was probably going to take a face-to-face to convince Ansari she was coming along on the raid.

As they so often did at this hour of the night, on those nights bereft of sleep, Hamza's thoughts turned to the teachings of Mullah Sadra's *al-Asfar al-Arba'a*—*The Four Journeys*. The seventeenth-century classic occupied a special niche in Hamza's sparsely-furnished quarters at Pairidaeza, a place of honor on a small bookshelf alongside the Holy Quran.

It was worthy of such veneration: in its pages, the philosopher-mystic of Shiraz had traced the soul's journey in search of the Source of all Truth, God Himself—a journey which culminated in the seeker's returning to the world, united now with God, reflecting His glory.

The text was a favorite of Imam Khomeini, who had subjected its intricacies to masterful analysis. Many believed the Imam to have personally traversed the spiritual pathways charted in its chapters, and to have been imbued with God's own majesty, power, and wisdom. There were intimations that Khomeini may have believed this himself.

Hamza knew, of course, that he himself could hardly aspire to such *irfan*, such illumination. To gain even a glimpse of the inner light required turning away from the things of this world and focusing one's gaze on the things of the spirit. Such a life of contemplation was inconceivable for one who trod the path of constant vigilance and unending struggle, of unwavering attention to the world and its dangers.

Yet, in recent days, Hamza had dared hope that he might embark upon Sadra's mystical journey in some wise after all—might become, if not the Face of God, then the Hand of God, smiting the enemies of God with God's own righteous wrath.

Tonight, his mind wandered aimlessly, despairingly amid the wrack of those dreams.

For Fatimah Ansari had been the key to them all. Fatimah—destined to be glorified even as her namesake, favorite daughter of the Prophet, peace and blessings upon him, had been glorified.

It was not to be. Despite his best efforts, Fatimah was still missing. Even the man sent to find her had gone missing.

Truly nothing but a miracle could salvage the Malhamah Operation now.

The Malhamah Operation: the name seemed but a bitter irony. And yet, what blessings might have been showered upon him who succeeded in hastening *al-Malhamah*, the Final Slaughter? Why, such a one might even be privileged to behold the face of Jibril, annunciator of the Holy Quran, whom the Crusaders called the angel Gabriel.

It was not to be. There would be no instant of utmost clarity and revelation for such as him, only a life of ongoing grinding struggle, a life of service as a humble foot soldier in God's great Struggle to bring the world to Islam. A life whose focus was drifting further and further away from the eternal, more and more into the everyday concerns of survival, beheld through eyes whose vision had become clouded, blind to the inner light.

Hamza sighed, arose from his chair, and set Sadra's book back on the shelf.

He shook his head to clear it. Following hard upon thoughts of his spiritual blindness there had arisen all unbidden the image of that other blindness he himself had brought about, of that eye whose bold, ardent glance he had quenched with his own hand. That eye of blood.

Hamza forced the errant vision back into its cave again. A whore. *A whore!* She was nothing but a whore.

Why, then, would she not leave him in peace?

He consulted the clock: four A.M. It was futile to attempt sleep now, not that Mehri would let him be in any case. And did not the Holy Quran promise Paradise to those who "were accustomed to spend little of the night in sleeping, and in the hours of early dawn were found asking forgiveness"?

He stepped into the bathroom to perform *wudhu*, the ablutions that purified the believer for prayer. Not strictly necessary, since he had not slept, but the ritual had its own power to soothe, to calm. He washed his right hand, then his left, the prescribed three times. Ran wet fingers over his teeth to cleanse the mouth. Moved on to rinsing the nose, the face, the head, the ears, both arms. Finally he bent to wash his feet, right foot with right hand, left foot with left.

Thus purged, purged of thoughts of Mehri, he walked to the *musalla*, the small mat spread on the floor of his small room, and prostrated himself in prayer.

Praying to God for a miracle.

Night's candles were guttering out, false dawn backlighting the peaks of the Coastal Range when Marianna arrived at the portals of Pairidaeza. She pulled over and killed the engine well short of the entrance. Then she sat there in the half-light, surveying the lay of the land and her options.

This was it, point of no return. Up till now, none of this had been irrevocable. Technically, of course, ignoring Pete's order to return to DC *could* be interpreted to mean she'd strayed off the reservation, but she could finesse that—she'd managed to before. Drive through those gates up ahead, on the other hand, and she'd be committed. What had been, up till now, almost an academic exercise, a purely theoretical weighing of all the available alternatives, would suddenly become only too real.

There was a fine line between flexibly interpreting instructions and going rogue plain and simple. However ill-defined that line might be in other contexts, what she was about to do in the here and now would mean crossing it.

In CROM's eyes, if not her own.

On the other hand, what were abstract lines in the sand when a man's life was at stake? It wasn't as if the whole termination action weren't predicated on a misunderstanding. Whatever else he might be capable of, there was no way Jon could have pulled off his own escape, of that she was certain. Seen like that, she wasn't betraying her boss or her organization, she was keeping them from making a terrible mistake, one they'd regret. But still—

It was half past nine in the morning out on the East Coast. She could picture Pete sitting at his desk, burning his tongue on his third cup of coffee, glaring at his watch. Wondering why she hadn't showed up yet.

She could call him right now, bring CROM in on this, wash her hands of Jon, of everything. Handle it right, and the whole business could be made to look pretty good on her service record: she'd be the agent who broke the Ansari kidnap case, a hero of sorts, even.

In CROM's eyes, if not her own.

Marianna took a deep breath, started the car, and rolled up the drive toward the gates of Pairidaeza.

This was intolerable! To be interrupted at dawn prayer, summoned down to the gatehouse, on account of a woman, no less.

And not just any woman. A woman he'd already sent packing once, a woman he'd thought to have done with.

Hamza glowered across the small table at Ms. Marianna Bonaventure, sitting there calmly in her tight-fitting blouse and hip-hugging pants, and worst of all, her provocatively uncovered hair. Why not have done with it, and bare her dugs as well?

"To what," Hamza said, as levelly as he could, "do I owe this pleasure?"

"Like I was telling your guard here," the woman said, "I need to speak to Davoud Ansari. It's urgent."

"And as I am sure Hassan explained to you, Mr. Ansari is not available at this early hour. Whatever you have to say, you may say to me. I shall see it is conveyed to him."

The woman seemed somehow different this morning. She looked him boldly in the eye. "Just what part of 'urgent' did you not understand?"

Different or not, Hamza was not about to put up with such effrontery. He rose and gave her a curt nod of dismissal. "If you would leave a number where you can be reached, Mr. Ansari will contact you."

He turned and began stalking toward the door.

Only to find his progress arrested by a hand gripping his sleeve. The little vixen had jumped up and seized him by the arm with unreasonable strength, shouting something all the while.

He pulled away and stepped back, momentarily too shocked at the impropriety even to strike her. Then the meaning of the words she'd been yelling at him penetrated:

"No, wait—I know where you can find Fatimah Ansari!"

Hamza stood there, thinking. Could it be? He eyed the woman again, trying to gauge the likelihood of anyone, her in particular, casually walking in the door with the answer that had eluded them for days.

Balanced on the cusp between hope and disbelief, he took a deep breath and gestured toward the chair she'd so recently vacated. "Please, Ms. Bonaventure, sit back down."

Having arrived at the hideout long after nightfall, Knox was only now realizing that the kidnappers had given their captives the best room in the house, view-wise. He stopped pacing long enough to gaze out the bedroom window at dawn stealing over a wide fogbound arc of the South Coast. The first rays of sunlight were just beginning to gild the crests of the foothills poking up out of the mist. The long, sleepless night was drawing to a close.

Knox yawned and looked reflexively at his wrist. It was still watchless, as it had been the last time he'd looked, and all the times before that—they weren't about to give him his Junghans back. And there wasn't so much as an hourglass in the quarters he and Timah had been confined to. What time did the sun come up around here anyway?—Six? Seven?

Knox took another turn around the room, then sat down heavily on one corner of the bed, jostling its sole occupant. Timah protested drowsily and rolled over to face the wall.

Little kids, he marveled—they were simply astounding in their adaptability, their resilience. Knox couldn't conceive of an adult in Timah's situation just drifting off to sleep. More to the point, he certainly couldn't conceive of doing it himself, given it was his own situation as well.

In point of fact, he hadn't slept a wink. He'd spent the small hours wide awake, beguiling the time with improbable escape scenarios. Overpower one of the Alphas when they served the tea and crumpets for breakfast? Kick out the bedroom window and go shinnying down the drainpipe with Timah under one arm? Might as well try flapping his arms and flying away. The whole train of thought had only limited value as entertainment, and even less by way of practical applicability.

But he had to do *some*thing. He no longer felt driven by that odd, seemingly ungrounded compulsion to save Fatimah Ansari. What was driving him now was a lot simpler and less … abstract. It was that she was just a little kid. And grownups were supposed to protect little kids, keep them safe, weren't they?

But how?

If only everything weren't so damned complicated.

No sooner had he thought that than he seemed to hear, as though whispered in his ear, the words a friend had bequeathed to him.

"Children are not complications, *Dzhon*, they are the whole purpose of life."

Galina Mikhailovna Postrel'nikova had told him that two nights before she'd died bearing witness to it. Knox couldn't help hoping that nothing on the order of Galya's sacrifice would be required to see *this* child safely home.

He glanced over to where Fatimah was sleeping. Except she wasn't any longer. She was sitting bolt upright amid the rumpled bedclothes.

"Pretty," she said, gazing wide-eyed around the room.

"Hi, kiddo." He stifled a yawn. "You're awake."

"Can't sleep any more," she said, rubbing her eyes. "Everything is getting so bright and shimmery."

"Well, yes, of course — the sun is coming up." Another yawn. "Finally."

"Uh-uh, Uncle Jon." Timah shook her head vigorously. "It's bad. It means I have to go sit on my toadstool. Right away."

It had taken five minutes — five minutes of Bonaventure sitting far too close to him in the cramped quarters of Pairidaeza's gatehouse, of listening to her spin her tale and field questions — but, in Hamza's mind, hope was winning out over disbelief.

He felt lightheaded, pulse racing, heart pounding. To think that, with only hours remaining, the Malhamah Operation might still be redeemed.

He knew better than to betray any of this, though, especially when the Bonaventure woman had yet to divulge one key item of information.

He leaned back in his own chair. "An interesting story," he said, with studied offhandedness, "and one that can easily be substantiated. A simple UAV overflight would do. If this purported hideout is, as your informant claims, just to the south of us along the Big Sur coast, we can have confirmation within the hour. All I will need are the coordinates."

Had his voice trembled with anticipation there at the last?

Regardless, the woman was shaking her head, her hair bouncing distractingly with the movement. "You'll get the lat-long once we've got a deal, not before."

Hamza mastered his reluctance and leaned forward, bringing his face to within inches of hers. "You must understand that I cannot proceed without corroboration of some sort. Lacking that, this Bazarov of yours is no more than a voice on a phone. How did he come by his information on Fatimah's whereabouts? How can we tell if it is accurate?"

A shrug. "He knew things. Things only somebody on the inside could possibly know."

"Things? What sorts of things?"

"Things related to, uh, other, ongoing investigations. I'm not at liberty to discuss them."

"It would seem, then, that we are at an impasse. You do not trust me, and you have given me no reason to trust you—nor your informant."

The woman looked down at her hands resting in her lap. Then her eyes met his once again.

"There's one more thing," she said, "Bazarov said that we've got to move quickly—that Fatimah's life is in danger."

Hamza waved a hand dismissively. "This tells me nothing I did not know. Of course dear Fatimah is in danger. She is, after all, in the hands of criminals."

"No." The woman shook her head again. "Not the kidnapping. Bazarov said something about how she might be going to have an attack. He said Ansari would know what that meant. Does any of that make sense to you?"

For the second time in this encounter, Hamza was momentarily at a loss for words.

"Never mind," she answered her own question. "I can see it does."

And indeed it did. Few beyond the confines of this compound knew of Fatimah Ansari's life-threatening condition. But those few would, by this time, doubtless include her abductors. Hope now verged on certainty.

"Assuming I were to accept this story, Ms. Bonaventure, what would you have me do?"

The woman gave a toss of her head, causing that mane of dark hair to sway flirtatiously. "Rumor has it Psyche Security's got a strikeforce that'd put a major metropolitan SWAT team to shame. Any truth to that?"

Hamza drummed his fingers on the desktop. Could this all be some sort of ploy, a CROM operative's way of raising false hopes for Fatimah's rescue in order to elicit intelligence about Psyche's paramilitary wherewithal? In any case, force postures and capabilities were nothing he was prepared to share with an agent of US Intelligence, no matter how coquettish.

"Ah," he said, "now we touch on a topic which *I* am not at liberty to discuss. In any case, I might point out that the government you represent has far greater resources at its command. Resources which are *not* mere rumor, but a matter of public record."

"Your point being?"

"I should think it was obvious. A federal crime — for that is what kidnapping is, is it not? — a federal crime has been committed, inflicting grievous harm on the family of one of the country's most illustrious citizens. You have discovered, or so you claim, the location at which the criminals might be apprehended and their victim rescued. Why, then, have you come to us, rather than, say, to your own agency, or perhaps the FBI? — What was that? I could not hear."

"I said, this isn't an official request."

"And how am I to interpret that remark?"

"Interpret it any way you damn well please, just so you understand there's no cavalry on the way. We're on our own here."

"So your motives for wanting Fatimah safely returned are not, shall we say, professional?"

The woman sighed. "Personal. I have reason to believe that when we rescue Fatimah, we'll also be rescuing my — my friend, Jonathan Knox."

Hamza pretended surprise. "Ah. Mr. Knox is known to us as well. You are saying he too has been abducted? And by the same perpetrators?"

The woman nodded. "Are you going to help me get them back? Help me launch a raid on the place where they're being held?"

"Help *you?* You may rest assured, Ms. Bonaventure, in the event Psyche Security elects to launch such a raid, you will play no part in it."

"Wrong. I'm coming, or there *is* no raid."

Hamza realized he had risen to his feet again. This infuriating woman…

"You are *not* coming!" he bellowed.

"That's it, then," — She did not look properly cowed. Only, if possible, even more resolute — "That's a deal-breaker."

He blinked. "I beg your pardon?"

"Look, your only interest in this business is Fatimah. You've got no incentive to rescue Jon into the bargain, none whatsoever. I have. So, either I'm coming along for the ride, or you can damn well figure out where the two of them have been taken by yourself."

"Ms. Bonaventure, you are being unreasonable. You are, after all, only a wom—"

She didn't let him finish. "Unreasonable? Why don't we let Ansari decide who's being unreasonable here? It's his daughter whose life's at stake, after all."

Hamza briefly contemplated acceding to the woman's demands and then reneging once she'd given him those all-important coordinates. But, no, he could see how that would turn out: she was already threatening to escalate the matter if she didn't get her way. And having to deal with her complaints would only distract Ansari from matters of far greater import, in particular, ensuring the Defense Secretary's presence here tonight. Viewed in that light…

Hamza forced a smile and said, "Of course you may accompany us on our mission."

He smiled, recalling the wise words of al-Bukhari: "We must smile in the face of some people even as, in our hearts, we curse them."

Smiled, too, as he thought: what harm could it do to grant the request of this woman, this strange vessel through which God had seen fit to deliver His miracle?

"Your toadstool?" Knox said.

Timah nodded. "It's a place to sit. And *Baba* says it's got lots of little toads in it. So little you can't see them."

"I'm sorry, Timah. Toads?" How many imaginary friends could one little kid have?

"Uh-huh, my nanny toads. That's what *Baba* calls them. 'Cause it's sort of like they're my nannies, I guess — the way they take care of me and help me with my colors."

"Your colors?" Knox was beginning to feel like the straight man in a scene from *Alice in Wonderland.*

Timah nodded vigorously. "The colors that can make me sick. The nanny toads make them go away."

Knox was totally lost. He'd had very little experience conversing with six-year-olds prior to this. It was nothing like he'd imagined it, on those rare occasions when he thought about it at all. In particular, it wasn't like talking to some dumbed-down version of an adult. More like trying to communicate with an extraterrestrial, one with a rich fantasy life, at that.

He looked at Timah and smiled. There was a whole sophisticated thought process going on inside that little head, with a logic all its own. It was just that there seemed to be minimal points of overlap, or contact even, between her logic and his.

But something she'd said just now had struck a chord, one that reverberated with what Ansari had been talking about over dinner a couple nights ago.

"Tell me some more about your colors, honey."

"They're real pretty, Uncle Jon. They're all blue and green and shimmery. But they make me feel bad, 'specially my tummy. When I start to see them, I know it's time to go and sit on my toadstool till I feel all better."

Knox was getting a sinking feeling in the pit of his stomach. "Are you seeing the colors now, Timah?"

Timah swallowed. "Starting to," she said in a voice so low Knox had to strain to make it out.

"Timah, honey? What happens if you don't get to sit on your, uh, toadstool when the colors come?"

Timah didn't say anything. She didn't need to. The stricken look on her small round face said it all.

"It's okay, Timah," Knox added hastily. "It'll be okay. Promise."

The little girl seemed to relax slightly. She let out a breath and sank back against her pillows. Knox couldn't relax, though, not till he'd figured this out.

The toadstool, the toadstool. Could Timah possibly be talking about the Chair in the room just down the hall?

Set aside for the moment the incongruity of such a diabolical device actually doing some good for a change, and assume for the sake of argument that Timah's toadstool *was* the Chair.

So, if toadstool equaled Chair, how would a Chair help Timah stave off her attacks? In particular, if toadstool equaled Chair, then what would that make those frogs she'd said were inside it? Or not frogs—toads. Little toads, too small to see.

There was a pattern trying to form itself here. A pattern composed of equal parts technological magic as seen through the eyes of a little girl and something Mycroft had told him about those other Chairs, in that other place. The node-stations at Delphi, something about their secret sauce, the technology that made MERGE possible: they were *something-something*-infusors.

"Bright and pretty," Timah murmured from over on the bed.

"What's bright and pretty, Timah?" Knox said, all the while trying to think what that word was again.

"Everything. The whole room. You too, Uncle Jon…"

Not nanny toads. Something else, something that sounded almost the same. Something that might help stop what was coming—

"…All blue and green and shimmery."

Nanotrodes.

21 | Status Epilepticus

MARIANNA HAD TO GIVE Psyche Security this much: once they'd decided to do something, they did it *fast!*

It had taken the organization less than two hours to mobilize and launch a thirty-man strikeforce. Even allowing for how they'd probably been held in ready mode since Fatimah's abduction, an hour forty-five minutes from go-code to mission kickoff was still scary-impressive.

So was their insertion capability: three Sikorsky X2-HSs flying through crisp California morning air at nearly three hundred knots, twice as fast as any other copter in the sky.

Five minutes out and closing on the location Marianna had given them, the flight of X2s ceased hugging the Big Sur coastline and jogged eastward, putting the crest of the Coastal Range between themselves and the target.

Marianna watched out the starboard window as a fourth, trailing helo, an X2 Heavy Lifter, peeled off from the formation and headed due west out over the Pacific. The plan was for the lone chopper to approach the target from seaward and, coming in low over the water, jettison its cargo of six Protector USVs, unmanned surface vessels. Unmanned, but not unarmed; each of the Protectors packed a 7.62mm machine gun and a missile launcher.

Once they'd splashed down, the roboboats would patrol the shoreline of the subject locale and interdict any attempt to escape by sea. The heavy-lift platform would then hover offshore and out of sight, in anticipation of one more mission-critical task.

Meanwhile, the three assault helicopters angled their rotor blades for silent running and, flying nap of the earth, moved in for the kill.

Marianna looked up from where she was sitting. A figure clad in the same sort of green-trimmed black leotard she was wearing stood before her, swaying slightly with the roll and pitch of the chopper, looking like a strap-hanger in a subway scene by Salvador Dali. With the matching ski-mask covering everything save eyes and mouth, she couldn't be sure it was Hamza till he spoke.

"We touch down in three minutes. To confirm: once the outer operational perimeter is secure, you may advance as far as that line, and no farther."

"Wrong. Our deal was I'm going in with the raiding party, all the way."

Hamza yanked the mask up, the better to fix her with a long stare. "Your own life is, of course, yours to risk as you wish. But I cannot permit you to jeopardize the success of a mission you have not trained for."

"As if your guys have trained for it? You've only known where Fatimah's being held for the past two hours. No way that's enough time to even mock up a replica of the crisis site, much less practice every contingency for storm-ing it."

Hamza peered at her through slitted eyes. "Not that it is your concern, but we have, in fact, done something very like that. Most of our training is done in squad-level simulation chambers. For the past seventy-two hours we have been running refreshers on multiple variants of generic forced-entry scenarios."

"A lot of good generic's going to do you."

"If you will permit me, I was not finished. Satellite imagery for the coor-dinates you so kindly provided has enabled us to tailor the final virtual training sessions to the target. Those sessions continue even now, while we are en route."

"Still, not what I'd call best-case."

Hamza shrugged. "The need for haste overrides any lesser considerations. Fatimah may be dying as we speak."

"We've only got Bazarov's word on that. We still don't know what kind of game he's playing—he might *want* us walking in there totally unprepared." And virtual-reality training aside, totally unprepared was what they were.

"Second thoughts, Ms. Bonaventure?" Hamza smiled.

"I'm just trying to look at all the angles, maximize our chances of success."

"Speed, surprise, and shock will maximize those chances for us. Elaborate mission rehearsals may have their place in the sorts of counterterrorist hostage rescues your government specializes in, but they would be overkill in this particular situation."

"Overkill? What's that supposed to mean?"

"You are applying the wrong template: this is a kidnapping, not a hostage-taking. You *do* understand the difference?"

Marianna could have done without the condescension, but she saw what Hamza was driving at. Politically motivated hostage-takers were all about impacting the public psyche, sowing fear and frustrated rage among the populace at large. Kidnappers, on the other hand, were in it for the money. That difference in objective made for a number of differences in operational style and tempo.

For present purposes, the important one was this: because hostage takers needed a public stage on which to enact their guerrilla theater, they could neither run nor hide. Their winning move was rather to take over the biggest, most conspicuous target they could find—a bank, an ambassadorial resi-dence, even a whole cruise ship—and then hunker down, armed to the teeth, for a Mexican stand-off with the authorities.

Kidnappers neither needed nor wanted that kind of confrontation. Run-ning and hiding was what they did best. That implied a diametrically opposite defensive posture, one in which keeping their whereabouts secret was their first, best, and sometimes only line of defense.

"So, you're counting on a minimally hardened site? None of the barricades and booby traps you'd get if they were planning on having a rescue force turn up on their doorstep?"

Hamza nodded. "Correct. Such measures can be counterproductive when the object is to evade discovery altogether. Consequently, we anticipate a much more rudimentary defensive perimeter than in a hostage scenario, and a correspondingly lower level of vigilance overall."

It occurred to Marianna that the Psyche Security chief had a lot of insight into hostage-taker mentality, and not necessarily from the perspective of law enforcement, either. But all she said was, "That might not be a safe bet."

"What do you mean?"

"If Bazarov was right about the perps being former Alpha Group commandos, then I wouldn't put too much faith in your being able to catch these particular kidnappers, uh, napping."

"And if Bazarov was right about their headcount, we outnumber them three to one. More than that, our technology advantage is insurmountable."

"Maybe. But I still think you're going to need me. These guys are no pushovers, and I'm the only one you've got who's gone up against them before."

"All blue and green and shimmery…" Timah's voice trailed off. She was still looking around the bedroom that was their cell, but now her stare was getting blank and glassy.

Knox reached out, shook her by the shoulder. No response.

"Timah?" He tried his best to project a calm he did not feel. "Timah, stay with me, okay, honey?"

He watched in dismay as the little girl slumped slowly to one side, her partly open mouth leaking drool onto the pillowcase. Her frame straightened as her muscles tensed. Then she began to tremble.

It got worse, and worse, till Timah was shaking all over, more and more violently. The sharp tang of urine and the stain darkening her pjs served notice that she'd lost control of her bladder.

All Knox knew about seizures was what Ansari had told him at their first meeting. He wished now that he'd paid more attention then, asked more questions.

But there was one thing he could recall: Timah's episodes were unique, and not in a good way. Unlike normal, garden-variety psychogenic seizures which couldn't even jiggle the needle on an electroencephalograph, Timah's dysfunctional "forever loops" could overleap the mind/brain divide somehow, and interfere with the electrical activity of the cerebral cortex itself.

Worst of all, if left untreated too long her condition could mutate into full-blown *status epilepticus*, threatening permanent brain damage, even death.

Knox had no idea how long was too long. Even if he had, there was no way to mark the passage of time here in their cell. All he did know was

Timah's convulsions seemed to have been going on for an eternity.

He banged on the door and hollered for help. No response. He screamed in frustration and battered at the solid oak.

The Chair that might help Timah—what she'd called her "toadstool"—was right down the hall, just yards away. If only he could get someone's attention, get someone to come to the door. Maybe they would know how it worked, how to use its nanotrodes to treat the attack.

He looked back over at Timah. She'd begun thrashing her head from side to side. Worse, her body's uncontrolled twitches were becoming so violent they threatened to throw her off the bed. What had Ansari said about the only thing you could do to help someone having a seizure? Keep them from falling down and hurting themselves?

Three quick steps put him back at her bedside. He pulled off the spare blankets and spread them out on the floor. Now for the tricky part: he slid his arms under Timah's thrashing body and lifted her up off the bed. She was a feather in his arms—a twisting, writhing, almost-impossible-to-hang-onto feather. Knox nearly lost his grip when a flailing forearm caught him hard across the bridge of the nose. Blinking back tears, he somehow managed to lower the little girl safely onto the blanket-cushioned floorboards.

He tucked pillows in on either side of her to keep her from rolling, then returned to the door and raised a fist to resume pounding.

And lowered it again. Pressing his ear against the wood, he could hear someone trudging up the stairs.

"*Skoreye, pazhaluista!*" he yelled, urging whoever was coming to hurry.

"*Minutochku,*" came the reply. Russian for "Just a minute."

The deadbolt retracted and the door swung open. One of the Alphas stood there in a t-shirt, jeans, and a bored expression. This was the first time Knox had seen any of them without the bodysuit. He looked weird somehow, like a shelled oyster—if an oyster could have played defense for the Chicago Bears.

Said Bear yawned and scratched his belly. "*Nu, shto?*" he began, by way of asking what was up.

But in less time than it took Knox to formulate the Russian words for an explanation and a plea for help, the guard had looked into the room and seen for himself what was up. His eyes widened.

He told Knox "*Minutochku*" again, but as if he meant it this time. Re-locking the door behind him, he clumped back down the hall at speed, hopefully off to find someone who knew how to deal with the situation better than either he or Knox did.

Knox turned back to where Timah lay thrashing on the floor. He knelt beside her and, for want of anything better to do, stroked her hair. "It's okay, honey—help's on the way."

He hoped.

On the ground at last, but not out the door yet. Not even suited up, in fact.

Marianna watched her seatmate impatiently as Hamza went on making inexplicable but precise-looking hand movements, carefully manipulating the illusory widgets of the virtual console his goggles were painting on his retinas. For all the big talk about speed, surprise, and shock, the guy was taking his sweet time about launching the raid.

After another geological epoch or two, he finally leaned back and slid the virtualization goggles up on his forehead.

"Done," he said, "ImpSAR shows eight pings, five of them armed, clustered in the first floor main room. One additional unarmed on the staircase. And, of greatest interest to us, two unarmed pings alone in an upstairs chamber at the rear of the residence. Estimated body masses are consistent with those of Fatimah Ansari and Jonathan Knox."

"Hang on a minute—ImpSAR?"

"Impulse Synthetic Aperture Radar. The four UAVs we sent in prior to our arrival perform impulse-radar scans of the structure, each from a different perspective. When collated by computer, those multiple viewpoints resolve into a picture of what is happening inside the building—through-wall imaging, it is called."

"Huh. I'll give you guys one thing: you've got cool toys."

Hamza appeared not to notice the compliment. "Yes, well, now that we have the force dispositions identified, it is time to go in."

"I thought you'd never ask. Just point me at my body armor."

He grinned at her. "But you are already wearing it."

"What, this stuff?" Marianna plucked at the fabric of her black-and-green leotard. "It's, it's just under-armor, isn't it? Not the sort of thing you'd want to walk through a hail of bullets in."

Still grinning, Hamza took two steps toward her, bringing him uncomfortably close. Then, without ever losing the grin, he cocked one of his big fists and rammed it into her solar plexus hard as he could.

Marianna couldn't believe it. Hamza had just hauled off and sucker-punched her. No warning, nothing. She hadn't even had a chance to get her guard up.

It was for sure up now. But she held off her counterpunch because of something else she couldn't believe: namely, that she hadn't felt a thing. The force of the blow had knocked her back a couple feet, but she was still standing, breathing normally, not doubled over in pain.

"—How the *fuck* did you do that?"

Hamza flashed that unpleasant grin of his again. "Congratulations, you have just passed Introduction to Impact Armor 101. Feel the material."

She did. Radiating out in all directions from the area where Hamza's fist had hit, her "leotard" had become hard as steel. It was losing some of its rigidity, though, even as her fingers probed it.

"Titanium disulfide fullerenes," Hamza said in response to her questioning look. "The whole garment is woven from inorganic buckyball molecules. As long as the metamaterial remains in its rest state, it is light and pliable. Apply a force to it, however, and it instantaneously reconfigures to a web of impact armor five times stronger than steel and capable of absorbing a hundred tons of force per square centimeter."

Marianna kneaded the weird fabric, poking it experimentally to feel it go stiff, then relax again. "*Wild,*" she said. "Where'd this stuff come from?"

"I beg your pardon?"

"You're not going to tell me you scored it off L. L. Bean's website. It's military, it's got to be. I'm just wondering how you guys got hold of it."

"This again," Hamza said, "is a topic I am not at liberty to discuss. Are you ready to go?"

"Just a sec." She stood, belted on her standard issue utility pack, then turned to Hamza.

"Ready," she said, "and just for the record, I take it all back. You guys *are* tougher than Alpha Group—or at least your gear is."

"My men," he growled, "are every bit the equal of their equipment. Now come."

Knox knelt by Timah's trembling form and kept chanting his mantra over and over: "Help is on the way, honey, help is on the way."

And maybe help *was* on the way, but they were certainly taking their sweet time about it. Knox couldn't understand what the holdup could be. He'd have thought the Alphas would have a vested interest in keeping Timah alive and healthy—a dead hostage made a lousy bargaining chip, after all.

So, where were they?

As if in answer to his unvoiced question, there was a muffled *whump!* from downstairs, in the direction of the living room. Sounds of shattering glass, shouts, and gunfire followed hard on its heels.

Before Knox had time to absorb what was happening, there came four more *whumps* much closer to home, followed by a tearing, grinding noise from the far side of the room.

Then, with an ear-splitting cacophony of shrieking nails and splintering wood, the bedroom's whole outer wall tore away and was gone.

Hamza looked up just in time to catch an unusual sight: the heavy-lift Sikorsky firing four explosive grapnels into the wood of the house's corner studs, and then, with a single mighty heave on the attached guy wires, wrenching the rear wall clean off. The slab of frame and siding spewed out chunks of insulation and shreds of Tyvek house wrap as the chopper towed it out to sea like some ungainly kite.

Subtlety was not Psyche Security's strong suit.

He watched the evacuation team rappelling down from the hovering X2-HS and plucking both hostages out through the gaping hole in the exterior. Then he turned his attention back to the diversionary breach of the greatroom.

There, things were going well. Almost too well, in fact. Even discounting the Bonaventure woman's overwrought warnings as to the prowess of the Alpha Group commandos, Hamza had been expecting more than the negligible resistance encountered so far.

But it was not until the "Clear" signal had been given and it was safe to walk through the shattered double-height front doors into the greatroom that Hamza saw firsthand why the adversary had mounted so ineffectual a defense.

He strolled wonderingly through a gallery of curious statuary, each *objet d'arte* fashioned from a living man, each man encased in an obsidian shell fashioned of the same metamaterial as his strikeforce's own armor. Except that this metamaterial had malfunctioned and locked into its rigid state somehow, holding its wearers immobile in a grip five times stronger than steel.

Caught in all the attitudes of reaction to the blast that had breached the front door — some already on their feet, others just rising from their seats on the sofas ringed around the home theater, still others having fallen in a jumble of twisted, frozen limbs — it was all the hapless Alpha Group commandos could do to roll their eyes in fear and frustration and try to sip enough breath to scream through closed or locked-open mouths as Hamza passed among them.

In one sense, Hamza was aghast. The impact armor these men were wearing could have had only one source. It must be part of that Special Forces consignment he had arranged, at no small expense, to have diverted to Psyche's use several months ago. Its presence here, in the possession of these criminals, spelled a catastrophic breach of security. For the first time, Hamza began to seriously entertain Jonathan Knox's interpretation of the kidnapping itself, that it had been an inside job.

But who, then, was the insider?

Time enough for that later. At the moment, it had all worked out for the best…

He paused to gaze into the eyes of one of the upright effigies: the leader, Alpha One, by the rank markings painted crudely on his armor. That one made as if to spit. The metamaterial mask did not allow his jaw even that much freedom of movement. The saliva dribbled out through his closed lips and down his chin.

Hamza turned away. "Is this all of them?" he asked his deputy. He had counted only eight.

"One was not wearing his suit," Ali replied. "He is still at large."

"Armed?"

"Yes, but contained on the second floor. The woman has gone after him."

Hamza scowled. "What could she hope to accomplish? The hostages are safe, the kidnappers are neutralized. Why not leave the last straggler to fate?"

Ali said nothing. Wisely, for who could fathom the motivations of a woman? Especially this one.

"Our own losses?" Hamza asked.

"None. A miracle. God has given us salvation from the suffering of the Fire."

"Truly a miracle." Hamza inclined his head, acknowledging the words of the *Surat Al'Imran*.

"And these?" Ali said, indicating their now-impotent adversaries. "What is to be done with them?"

Hamza pondered. It was in its way a unique problem. They could neither take the Alphas with them, nor leave them here to starve, or, worse, perhaps to free themselves. On the other hand, the time-honored counterterrorist's *coup de grace* would accomplish little or nothing in this case; the three bullets to the head would simply bounce off the metamaterial of their masks, dealing migraines perhaps, but not death. And death was what *Shariah* law mandated for the abduction of a child. Yet walking up and shooting each of them individually through the eye- or mouth-holes of their masks seemed too … personal somehow.

Then his mind strayed back to something Ali had said a moment ago.

Hamza withdrew a thermite grenade from a utility pocket, and motioned his men to do likewise. The statues could not scream with their throats constricted by the meta-fabric, but a thin, muffled keening arose from their midst: they knew only too well what fate was to be theirs. The armor's metamaterial could shield its wearer from a certain amount of heat, but not the twenty-five hundred degrees Celsius of an aluminothermic reaction. And as a side-benefit, burning down the house should deal with their straggler as well.

"For such as these," Hamza pronounced sentence, "there can *be* no salvation. Give them over to the suffering of the Fire."

"What of the woman?" Ali said. "We cannot be sure she is out of harm's way."

Hamza paused and considered. The woman had served her purpose. And she was here on her own account. No hue and cry would be raised if she were simply to disappear.

And she had been warned, *warned* to remain at the outer perimeter. Instead, she had insisted on playing her poor imitation of a man's role. If she were caught in the conflagration, it was nothing she had not brought on herself.

This, after all, would not be the first woman he had sacrificed in the name of God. Her death mattered so little in the larger scheme of things. Now that Fatimah was back in their hands, by midnight tonight one death more or less would go unnoticed among the thousands-strong legions of the enemy annihilated in the Malhamah Operation.

Also in the name of God.

Without another word, Hamza pulled the ring on his incendiary grenade and dropped it at the feet of Alpha One.

Pulse pounding in her temples, Glock G18C gripped in her meta-gloved hands, Marianna stole along the upstairs hallway, easing open each half-closed door and clearing the room it gave onto as she went. This would all have been a lot faster, not to mention less risky, if she'd had a partner to help "slice the pie"—each of them covering and clearing their own designated wedge of roomspace. Where was backup when she needed it?

But at last she had worked her way down to the door at the end of the hall. Unlike the others, this one was closed all the way and, as a tentative twist of the knob confirmed, locked from the inside.

If their one missing suspect was anywhere on the second story, it was going to be here.

Marianna bent over and rummaged through her Psyche-supplied utility pack till she found the linear cutting charge assembly, essentially just a big loop of self-adhesive plastic explosive with a remote detonator.

She straightened and stepped back. The wall looked as if it might be easier to breach than the solid wood door, and coming through the wall made for more of a surprise element besides. Working the plastique carefully, she outlined a Marianna-sized rectangle in the space between the doorframe and one corner of the hall. Then she huddled in the other corner, squeezed her eyes shut, and detonated the charge.

The explosion was deafening in the confined space, but it got the job done, blowing one whole sheet of drywall halfway across the room. She followed it up by tossing in a flashbang. Yes, Hamza, it was overkill—and so what?

She hustled to the hole in the wall, cupped her lips, and shouted, *"Poleetsiya!"*

Police? Well, not exactly. But "Psyche Industries Corporate Security" was too much of a mouthful, and she didn't know the Russian for it anyway.

No answer from inside the room, unless you counted the two wild shots ricocheting down the hall. So much for trying to speak the other guy's language. She switched to the only language these goons seemed to understand and returned fire.

Just as she was squeezing off her third round, she heard some sort of ruckus break loose downstairs. A series of pops, then a whooshing sound interspersed with choked shrieking. She did her best to ignore the strange noises for the moment—she had her hands full up here.

That was because she'd just risked a peek into the ravaged room, and glimpsed what her target—a big dude in torn t-shirt and jeans—was up to. He was standing there at the far side of the room, near the yawning void where the rear wall used to be. And what he was trying to do was enough to turn this till-now textbook operation into a textbook horrible example. He was hefting a grenade launcher, steadying his aim on the helicopter hovering just overhead.

The evacuation helicopter—with Jon and the little girl on board.

Not on her watch! Without thinking Marianna launched herself through the breach and ran the length of the room. The two slugs that hit her along the way couldn't penetrate the impact armor, but their momentum did throw her off balance. Enough so that, instead of the take-down she'd planned, she merely crashed feet first into the guy, knocking the grenade launcher out of his grip, and his legs out from under him. He landed on top of her. A take-down of sorts, then.

Ordinarily having two-fifty, three hundred pounds of beefcake dropped on her from a height of six feet would have pretty much taken Marianna out of the fight. Thank God for metamaterials! Her armor had stiffened instantly and cushioned the blow. Cushioned it for her, that is, not for him. To him, it must have felt like doing a bellyflop onto a woman-shaped block of solid concrete. He lay there on his side a moment trying to catch his breath.

But—like she'd been explaining to Hamza a while back—these Alphas were nothing if not tough. And quick. The guy was back up nearly as fast as she was, and lunging straight at her.

She took a step back to meet the charge, and tripped over a tangle of blast debris from her wall-breach. Before she could regain her balance he slammed into her, again doing more damage to himself than her. That didn't stop him from throwing his arms around her and lifting her up off the floor.

Marianna was just along for the ride as the Alpha's charge bore her flying back through the breach-hole and out into the hallway.

A fast learner, he caught his weight on his hands and knees this time rather than suffer another bruising Banzai drop onto her unyielding meta-armor. She tried to roll out from under, but he was too quick. He ended up straddling her, pinning her down and punching at her head and shoulders. Bare fists were no match for metamaterial, though; all he was doing was bloodying his knuckles. He couldn't find a way to hurt her and she couldn't find a way to get out from under him. This had all the makings of a stalemate.

Then suddenly he stopped pounding on her and started slapping frantically at his head instead. More particularly at the burning chunks of stuff that had fallen from the ceiling and were trying to set his scalp on fire. He rolled off her, scrabbled across the floor howling, slapping at the flames.

Flames? She could sure enough smell smoke, not to mention burnt hair. And where there's smoke…

This was what came of letting yourself get too focused on the task at hand. She hadn't been paying enough attention to her surroundings. Only once her assailant had made for the exit could she sit up and see the flames blossoming all around her.

The whole place was on fire!

The helicopter canted alarmingly to avoid flying through the column of thick black smoke billowing up from the house below. Bracing himself against any more sudden lurches, Knox risked a glance down at the flames now engulfing the scene of his recent captivity.

His fellow captive was aboard too, though hardly in any shape for seeing the sights. Timah was all but engulfed in a Chair that took up the center of the helicopter's cabin. Sinister as it looked, the nanotech treatment delivered by what Timah had called her "toadstool" seemed to be working, thank God. Her convulsions had died down to an occasional tremor and her eyes were open again, although they didn't seem to be tracking anything in particular. Most of all, she just looked drained.

The two paramedics along for the ride seemed satisfied with her condition, enough so that one had left her side to radio in their status, leaving only his colleague in attendance. Idly, Knox wondered why they'd troubled to airlift their own Chair in with them when they could just as easily have commandeered the kidnappers'. But, of course, there was no way they could have known about that one.

It came back to him again, just how odd and out of place that piece of next-generation technology had looked sitting in the middle of a kidnappers' hidey-hole. A reminder, as if he'd needed one, that their rescue had far from closed this case — that there were questions still to be answered.

Speaking of the rescue — not to be ungrateful, but the look of the rescuers themselves was making Knox nervous. These were not the white knights he would have chosen, given his druthers. They managed to make his old friend Hamza seem positively genial by comparison. Vaguely Saracen-looking they were, with black beards and gleaming, predatory eyes. He wished they'd all pull down their ninja masks and hide their faces again.

"Uncle Jon?"

He wasn't sure he'd heard the little girl's whisper over the rumble of the engine, but when he turned, there she was looking at him. She gave him a brave little smile.

"Told you," Timah said.

Knox reached over and — gently, as if she were made of porcelain — stroked her cheek. "Told me what, honey?"

"Told you Freddie would bring us home again."

22 | The Big Clock

FLAMES ALL AROUND HER. So far her leotard's metafabric was shielding Marianna from the worst of their heat, but fire-resistant didn't necessarily mean fire-proof. She wasn't going to wait around and find out.

She rose to her feet and peered through thickening smoke. If she'd still been in the bedroom it would have been easy to spot the way out — that gaping hole where the rear wall used to be was kind of hard to miss. But her tussle with the Alpha Group torpedo had ended her up back in the burning hallway, and all spun around to boot. She could barely see the corridor's walls, much less any likely exits.

All of a sudden, she couldn't even see that much. She'd gone blind! It was as if the smoke pouring into the hall had gone from eye-stinging gray to pitch black in the time it took to blink. That wasn't possible, was it? Yet how else to explain the lights going out?

A hand to her face told her how: the eyeholes of her mask had closed up tight. The metamaterial was presumably trying to protect her eyes from toxic fumes, but under the circumstances such ill-timed solicitude could prove deadly. If she were going to have any chance of getting out of here alive, she needed to *see!*

The autonomics had also sealed the nose- and mouth-holes with some sort of filtering material, passing a thin stream of breathable air in, while keeping the worst of the smoke particles out. Damned suit was just full of surprises, wasn't it? Although this anti-asphyxiation measure was also of dubious value: it just meant she'd roast to death long before she could suffocate.

She'd have ripped the mask off altogether and taken her chances if she could, but it was locked down tight, no way her prying fingers could loosen it. Sightless and already feeling the heat seeping through her life support, Marianna groped her way to a wall.

Now what? Well, follow the line of the wall to wherever it might lead —and hope against hope it might lead to safety.

But which way, right or left? One direction was as good as another, right?

Wrong. She went to turn left, and found she couldn't. Her leotard went hard as steel, refusing to let her complete the motion. Another malfunction, this one life-threatening.

Fighting down panic, she tried turning the other way. That worked at least. She wasn't going to be frozen in place here till the flames took her.

But the bloody impact armor had a mind of its own. Marianna found that, if she tried turning in any direction but one, it locked up and left her paralyzed. She started moving in the only direction she could, the only direction the armor would allow. Which was definitely not the way she'd have chosen, given a choice.

Because, even if she couldn't see, she could *feel* the heat intensifying in the direction she was heading.

Blinded, stumbling, barely able to suck enough oxygen through the mask's emergency filters to keep going, Marianna was being forced toward the center of the burning house.

Into the heart of the fire.

The fire felt good. Knox leaned back in the Le Corbusier Grand Confort and surveyed his surroundings. The Bauhaus furnishings and raftered ceilings of Pairidaeza's greatroom were all very well, but nothing beat the simple, unadorned marble fireplace now baking the chill of the morning fog out of his bones.

Pairidaeza: back where he'd started out a little over twenty-four hours ago. But, in the words of the old song, what a difference a day makes. He'd left here as little more than a hired hand, returned as an honored guest—the guy who'd been there for Timah when she'd needed him most.

In keeping with Knox's elevated status, it was Ansari himself, in slacks and a cashmere rollneck, who was taking the breakfast order.

"How do you like your coffee, Jon?"

"Black, thanks—and hot. I *still* can't get warm, would you believe that?" He rubbed his arms again and shivered.

"That's probably more reaction than anything else," Ansari said, handing him a steaming mug. "You've been through a lot. Still, I could have a staff medic check to see if it's anything more serious."

Knox took a sip. "If you don't mind, Dave, I'm just going to sit here a bit. See if, between the fireplace and the java, I don't defrost on my own."

"That works for me." Ansari carried his own mug over to a chair opposite Knox. "Gives us a chance to talk."

"Yeah, there are a couple of things I'd like to know myself."

"Just ask."

"Okay, how's Timah doing? I guess that's number one."

Ansari gave Knox one of his dazzling smiles. "For you and me both. She's doing fine, Jon, thanks in no small part to you. And soon, God willing, she'll be doing even better. Better than she's been for a long time."

Something about that last remark didn't quite track, but Knox let it slide. There was something else that had been bugging him a whole lot more.

"So, how did you find us?" Especially when the whole federal government couldn't.

"Hmpf." Ansari said, "You know, I'm not really sure. Hamza and I barely had time to speak before he left on the raid. And since then I've just been so glad to get my daughter back I didn't think to ask how he knew where to look. That's easy enough to fix, though—"

He screwed in an earbud and said, "Hamza, would you please join us in the greatroom? Thanks." He turned to Knox again. "That aside, it's pretty much a wrap, wouldn't you say?"

"Not really," Knox began, but paused when Hamza strode into the room.

The big Security Chief was still wearing one of those skintight leotards from the rescue. Guess he'd had more important things to do since getting back than change into one of his Brooks Brothers suits. He glanced around the room, gave Knox a barely perceptible nod, then turned to Ansari.

"What may I do for you, sir?"

"Well, the question has come up…My oversight really, I should have asked before this, but, just how did you figure out where they were holding Fatimah—and of course, Jon here?"

Hamza blinked. "A, uh, an anonymous tip."

Knox looked sharply at Hamza. "A *tip?* But how?"

"We, er—" Hamza began, "—that is, one of the first things we did was to set up a one-eight-hundred line."

Even when he was in the best of moods, Knox did not appreciate being lied to. And after living through the past two days, Knox was definitely not in the best of moods.

"Wait a minute," he fumed, "—you guys didn't even want the *police* in on the case. And now you're telling me you set up *a toll-free tipline?*"

"Ease down, Jon," Ansari said. "All that's important is the results, right? Other than that, what does it really matter?"

"What does it matter?" This time, it was the Psyche CEO's turn to be on the receiving end of Knox's sharp look. "Well, for starters, there's still some guy out there, someone calling himself Bazarov, who set this whole thing up. Who's to say we've seen the last of him?"

Knox couldn't help noticing Hamza's startled reaction to that name, but he had bigger fish to fry at the moment.

Ansari sighed. "Point well taken, Jon. But your Mr. Bazarov is going to have to wait. In twelve hours I've got the Secretary of Defense arriving here to turnkey a top-secret project—"

"Right, Delphi. I've been there, remember?"

"So you realize how important this is. Not just to Psyche Industries, to the country as a whole. And now that we've got this little glitch with Fatimah pretty much ironed out—"

"It's *not* a 'little glitch,' Dave. Someone out there has designs on your family, or your company, or maybe even that country you claim to care so much about."

Ansari was silent a moment, then sighed. "You're right, Jon. I'll get on it first thing tomorrow."

"Not good enough. Maybe I'm taking this way too seriously because I'm *one of the people that bastard kidnapped*, but—" Knox stopped, got a grip, and continued in a less strident tone of voice. "But what if the whole kidnapping business was nothing but a blind, a diversion? What if Bazarov's real target is your meeting tonight? This might not be the sort of thing that can afford to wait another day."

"Jon, I hear you. But you can see the time constraints I'm under here. What do is it you want me to do?"

"Not you personally."

"Who, then?"

"Nietzsche."

Stairs. Charred through and viewed from underneath, but recognizably stairs all the same.

Marianna lay there groggily, trying to process the unusual perspective. Part of the problem was getting her eyes to focus, or even just getting them to coordinate their movements.

How long had she been out? She remembered it getting harder and harder to breath as her armor's emergency filtration system had all but closed down its air intake to protect her lungs from superheated smoke. At some point she must have passed out due to oxygen deprivation.

After a couple false starts, she managed to roll over onto her hands and knees. Then she crawled out from under the staircase that had served her as a refuge of last resort while the blazing house collapsed all around her. A refuge her high-tech armor had somehow led her to, although it was far from obvious why, out of the whole burning building, this one specific spot should have remained safe and standing.

Certainly nothing else was. Safe *or* standing, that is. She gazed out on a jumble of blackened beams poking up at random through a still-smoldering debris-scape. What could have happened here? Was the blaze set by the kidnappers to cover their escape, or could it have been caused by "friendly" fire?

And how had she missed getting incinerated along with everything else?

It came to her then: shock cocoon. The fluid dynamics of collapsing structures were known to produce—in addition to, and literally alongside, swaths of total devastation—islands of safety, tiny bubbles of shelter from the storm. It had happened in the collapse of the World Trade Center on 9/11, where a fortunate few had managed to survive the downblast in the shock cocoon formed around stairwell B of the North Tower.

And it had happened here, evidently. Only how? The turbulence effects involved were mind-bogglingly non-linear, virtually impossible to calculate. How had her *suit* guided her unerringly to the one safe place in the house?

Knox watched as Nietzsche's avatar materialized in the hundred-thirty inch display on the wall opposite the fireplace. Those startlingly lifelike blue eyes blinked, then roved the room before settling on Knox himself.

"Jonathan, very good to see you." The AI put on a sympathetic smile. "I was happy to learn you had survived your ordeal."

"Good to see you too, Nietzsche. But that ordeal might not be entirely over yet."

"Oh, why is that?"

"Turns out there's one or two minor details to clear up first."

"Nietzsche," Ansari cut in, "Jon feels we haven't seen the last of this Bazarov character yet."

Nietzsche looked blank. "Bazarov?"

"I doubt that's his real name," Knox said. "Just the alias he was using with his KGB contractors." If Knox didn't know better, he'd have said a look of consternation passed across the avatar's face at that.

"And you came upon this alias how?" Nietzsche said.

"One of the tidbits I picked up at Delphi, probably irrelevant." Knox paused to reflect. "Still, there's something familiar about that name…" He pondered a moment more, then shook his head. "Never mind, it'll come to me. Meanwhile, the reason I asked for Nietzsche here is, there might be another way to out our mysterious Mr. Bazarov."

Ansari leaned forward in his Barcelona chair. "How's that, Jon?"

"Well, the guy's been pretty careful about covering his tracks. All his transmissions seem to come out of nowhere: cellphone calls with no originating number, that sort of thing. But there's one communication channel I'm betting he couldn't have camouflaged."

The avatar aped a frown. "And that is?"

"The one that connected him to the F-35."

"I fail to understand," Nietzsche said, "—what about the F-35?"

"Well, *some*thing was piloting that plane right straight into the Alpha Group's waiting arms, and it for sure wasn't me, or anything else on board."

"Of course!" Ansari snapped his fingers. "Don't you see, Nietzsche? The avionics link. If that's how Bazarov took over the aircraft, the F-35 itself would've logged all the transmission details, *including* point of origin. All we need to do is find that plane and—"

"Actually," Knox said, "that's likely to be rather difficult, and hopefully unnecessary."

"What do you mean, unnecessary?"

"Just this: you were the ones who sent me off to WISP, Delphi, whatever. It strikes me you probably had a way of keeping tabs on me while I was out there."

"Well, yes, we were monitoring the signal traffic…"

"And recording it, I hope. For posterity, if nothing else."

Ansari looked at Hamza, who offered him one of his near-imperceptible nods.

"That's it, then," Knox said. "Isolate the avionics feed and look for the point where the plane gets taken over."

"Brilliant! We pick out that one signal and determine its source."

"Uh-huh," said Knox, "and there's your mastermind."

Ansari turned to the avatar again. "What about it, Nietzsche? Can we do it?"

Nietzsche was silent for a long minute. At last he said, "This could be done. It will, however, require some time to separate the avionics transmissions from all the other signal traffic moving in and out of WISP. Longer still to triangulate on an origin."

"Some time?" Knox said, "—How much?"

"I estimate twenty-four hours."

"But that takes us well past the launch tonight," Ansari protested.

Knox said nothing. He was thinking. As before, this latest exchange was reminding him of something. Not the details, the overall pattern.

"It is precisely the preparations for Delphi's inauguration," Nietzsche was saying, "that prevent the application of full processing power to this problem."

That was it—processing power. Wasn't there was some old Kevin Costner flick where the whole plot hinged on not having enough processing power? Where it was supposed to take a supercomputer a week's worth of number-crunching to photoshop a blurry crime-scene image into clarity, one pixel at a time? Just another illustration of how clueless Hollywood was about computers. It had made no sense then, and it made no sense now.

"Suppose we push the launch off by an hour or two," Ansari said. "Free up enough capacity to run the analysis in parallel. Would that give you what you need?"

"I fear not. Much of the processing in question is longitudinal in nature. Under such circumstances, parallelism would confer minimal advantages."

Knox wished the two of them would stop talking for a minute. Because there was something else he was trying to recall…

"So, you're telling me," Ansari said, "there's no way out of this resource bind till after the kick-off?"

No Way Out—that was it! A late-80s espionage film, itself a remake of a much better movie from the 1940s, called…

Called *The Big Clock*. A film noir if ever there was one. Starring Ray Milland as a man coerced into conducting a murder investigation. An investigation where all the evidence he gathers winds up pointing to—

Oh, Lord, that couldn't be it, could it?

—Winds up pointing to *himself*.

"Regrettably," Nietzsche was saying, "there are few options for expediting a solution, and none of them would—"

Knox sat there stunned. It all fit, in a weird sort of way. One of those fulcrum insights that, without actually changing anything, upended your perspective on everything you already knew.

"—be feasible without virtually unlimited access to—"

After all, who was in a better position to impede the progress of an investigation than the principal investigator himself?

"—the cumulative computational resources of Psyche Industries."

"Oh, come on now, Friedrich," Knox said quietly, "I'm sure you could find a way, if you really wanted to."

"I'm sorry, Jonathan. What was it that you called me just now?"

"Friedrich. After your namesake, Friedrich Nietzsche. Or maybe you prefer Freddie?"

Hamza was stunned, too stunned to speak, even had there been anything to say.

He had begun to realize something was very wrong on hearing Jonathan Knox point to a "Comrade Bazarov" as the mastermind behind Fatimah's kidnapping. The informant who had broken the news of Timah's whereabouts to the late, unlamented Marianna Bonaventure had also used that pseudonym. Someone was playing both ends against the middle.

But these considerations were as naught to what Knox had said next.

Hamza recognized the name of Fatimah's imaginary friend immediately, but more than that — he recognized he had a serious problem.

Nietzsche. It had been Nietzsche-Freddie-Bazarov who had been working against them all along. And Nietzsche knew too much. Not everything, to be sure. Certainly not the true extent and intent of what was to happen in twelve hours. But far too much for anyone to know and be permitted to live.

Hard on the heels of that realization, there came another — that he, Hamza, had been a fool. He had lived and worked so long in the high-tech mirage of Silicon Valley that he had unwittingly absorbed its reigning memes and metaphors, including the most pernicious of them all: artificial intelligence.

Artificial Intelligence! The turn of phrase had become so accepted that no one even noticed its oxymoronic essence anymore. Intelligence as such, no matter what its origin or physical embodiment, was never artificial, never simulated. To the extent that something was really intelligent, that intelligence was itself real.

Hamza had no doubt that Nietzsche's intelligence was real.

Nor did he doubt that Nietzsche's particular species of intelligence admitted of a far more compelling metaphor than that of an intelligent machine —

A *djinn.*

The Holy Quran itself told how God had created the first *djinn* from smokeless fire, just as he had created the first man from clay. And what was not "smokeless fire" if not a metaphor for the electricity that animated such beings as Nietzsche?

Hamza felt an icy chill. In the end, it made little difference whether the QuMRANN system was infested with malignant software or haunted by a maleficent spirit. Who or whatever Nietzsche was, he now held the fate of the Malhamah Operation in his incorporeal hands.

Knox was feeling pretty pleased with his solution. It all made sense. He'd told Hamza right off the bat that the abduction had all the earmarks of an inside job. You couldn't be much more of an insider than the veritable *genius loci* presiding over Pairidaeza.

In the guise of Timah's not-so-imaginary friend Freddie, Nietzsche would have found it child's play first to lure the little girl into the hands of her captors, and then to keep her company — keep her manageable, more likely — throughout her captivity. Until, that is, he was able to swipe an Air Force jet and deliver her a flesh-and-blood stand-in: Knox himself.

And speaking of child's play, what could be simpler — for an AI with quantum computational capabilities, at least — than to hack the encrypted message traffic of both the interbank funds-transfer network and the Shadow KGB, thereby procuring all the money and all the muscle "Bazarov" needed for his kidnapping operation.

Bazarov… even that oddly familiar alias fell neatly into place. If Nietzsche was the premiere philosopher of nihilism, then Bazarov, the unfeeling anti-hero of Turgenev's nineteenth-century potboiler *Fathers and Sons*, was its principal literary exemplar. Only a failed Russian Area Specialist like Knox could have spotted that tenuous connection, and even he had nearly missed it.

And of course, there was the final clue: the Chair, the device that alone could ameliorate Timah's condition. Certainly not the sort of accessory you'd expect to see gracing your average kidnappers' lair. Nietzsche again, it had to be: no outsider would have even known of the Chair's significance to the little girl's continued well-being, much less how to go about procuring one.

It fit, all of it. Except—

The problem was motive: as long as he'd been operating under the assumption that the mastermind behind Timah's kidnapping was at least *human*, Knox had been assuming that the motivation would turn out to be human too. Extortion, maybe — of money, of trade secrets, Lord knows Ansari had plenty of both. Or maybe, as he himself had suggested a moment ago, some sort of political intrigue.

But all such reasoning went out the window if the prime suspect turned out to be an artificial intelligence. What could an AI desire, such that this would obtain it for him? It turned out to be yet another variation on the conundrum that had been plaguing him all through this assignment: how could a mere machine desire anything at all?

Maybe, what with the government shutting down the QuMRANN project, Nietzsche had felt a threat to his own continued existence? After all, wasn't Psyche Industries fighting just as hard in its own way not to lose its lucrative defense contracts? Though, to be sure, Psyche's tactics were different: wining and dining the SecDef was a far cry from hostage taking, after all. Even so, it made sense of a sort.

Or perhaps Nietzsche was looking to gain not only his "life," but his "freedom." Though, there again, what could being set free possibly mean to a machine?

And that still left the biggest question of all unanswered: whatever Nietzsche's goals were, he'd obviously felt they were important enough to justify some pretty drastic actions to achieve them. It just didn't get much more drastic than abducting your employer's — or owner's — kith and kin, after all.

So, why walk away from it all, abandon his henchmen to their fates without even putting up a fight? *That* was the part Knox couldn't get past.

His ruminations broke off. Something was happening on the big display. The image of Nietzsche's face did a slow dissolve, to be replaced by something else entirely.

As the new scene swam into focus, Nietzsche said, "Jonathan, please believe me: what I did, I did to prevent this."

One look, and Knox remembered the rest of the old movie plot. With that, everything made sense. All of it.

For, in *The Big Clock*, the man assigned to investigate himself was ... *innocent!*

Not that Nietzsche was *innocent*, exactly, but he'd certainly tried to do better by Timah than *this*—

Knox sat there stunned, trying to process what he was seeing. For the display now held an image of Fatimah Ansari, sedated and lying on a gurney, with a built-in display counting down the hours to God knew what kind of surgical procedure.

He found his voice. "Dave, what in hell is going on here?"

"Now, Jon," Ansari began, "I don't expect you to understand ..."

But suddenly Knox *did* understand. All the stray bits and pieces of information his subconscious had absorbed over the past few days — Timah's deadly psychogenic seizures, the enormous computational resources of the WellGrid, even what Ansari had just said about how Delphi would go operational here tonight, with the Secretary of Defense in attendance — they all self-assembled and locked into a coherent, intuitively obvious design.

Imminent pattern apperception jolted through him with the force of a physical shock. He still couldn't tell how, but suddenly he knew what was going on and why.

Taking a deep breath, he fixed Ansari with a cold stare. "You're going to try using the Well to cure Timah, aren't you?"

Ansari lowered his head and exhaled sharply.

"Hamza," he said, "Take him!"

No trip to a castle would be complete without a tour of the dungeons. And Ansari's castle boasted a very high-tech dungeon indeed: microcell soundproofing, a blast door that looked like it could handle any blast short of nuclear, and of course, the *piece de resistance*—the very latest model Chair.

A Chair in which Knox currently sat, his flesh shrinking from its arachnoid embrace. Not that his flesh had anywhere to shrink *to*. He was bound to the Chair by the very sort of wrist and ankle cuffs he'd imagined the first time he'd laid eyes on one of the damned things.

Ansari walked up to him. He'd thrown a white lab coat over his business casuals, and a sorrowful expression onto his tanned face, but was otherwise the same gracious host who'd been breakfasting with Knox up in the greatroom, several levels above their heads.

"Jon," he said, "I want you to know, I'm sorry it turned out like this."

"Let's talk about it, then." The consultant's last line of defense. "Before you do something we'll both regret."

Ansari sighed. "I'm afraid we're past that point. I owe you, Jon—I really do. Not least for exposing Nietzsche. But why couldn't you stop there? Why'd you have to keep going?"

Knox shrugged as best he could. "Nature of the job," he said. "Figuring things out is what a consultant does."

"And just what is it you think you've figured out?"

"Well, I'd gotten as far as you taking over the WellGrid, and then using all that compute power to, uh, cure Timah somehow. Damned if I can see how, though."

"Jon, any other time I'd be happy to fill in the missing pieces for you. But it's like I said before: I'm under some time constraints here."

He turned to where Hamza, black leotard and all, sat at a console finetuning a display of what looked like amorphous colored blobs floating in a fishbowl. "How long till we're ready?"

Hamza looked up from his virtual lava-lamp and frowned. "I must first ensure that all of Nietzsche's external communications links are severed. Only then will I be free to work on calibrating the infusor."

"How long?" Ansari repeated.

"I estimate five minutes."

Ansari turned back to Knox. "Looks like we've got a little time after all, Jon. What was it you were wondering about?"

"To begin with, why you think any of this is going to work. Do you have any idea what Delphi is capable of?" Knox shuddered, remembering.

"Actually, I do. We've already replicated Delphi and its so-called MERGE Effect in our own labs, you see. That took some doing—we basically had to build a scale-model WellGrid down in Pairidaeza's sub-basement. Cost a bundle, too, but Uncle Sam's good for it."

"Okay, let's assume for the sake of argument that you can gain control of The Well somehow, and keep it. I still don't see how you can use it to cure your daughter."

"I admit it's a desperate plan, Jon, but the need is desperate too. You of all people should know how desperate, having seen one of Timah's seizures firsthand." Ansari stopped speaking for a moment and swallowed. "They're getting worse all the time, you know. Some day soon, there'll come an attack the nanotrodes won't be able to short-circuit. And then, well, she'll die."

Knox stared at the man. It was hard to feel sympathy for someone who was about to order your termination.

Hard, not impossible. "I'm sorry, Dave. I'd like to see that little girl get well as much as you. I just don't see how taking over Delphi, or MERGE, or whatever, can help."

Rather than reply, Ansari turned to Hamza. "How are we on time?"

Hamza did not look up from the console. "The QuMRANN system is now effectively cut off from the outside world. As regards Mr. Knox, I am beginning the calibration now. Allow perhaps three minutes for it to complete."

Ansari looked back at Knox. "It's the cold-start," he said, almost apologetically. "This whole business goes a lot smoother when we've had an opportunity to program the infusion beforehand. Never mind. Three minutes should be more than enough. And like I say, I do owe you an explanation, Jon—even if you won't be able to take it with you."

Knox swallowed hard at that intimation of mortality, but said nothing.

Ansari settled into a chair (with a lower-case "c") opposite Knox. "So, let's see, where were we? You remember me telling you how Timah's seizures are psychogenic, rather than physical in nature?"

"Vaguely." The thought of what awaited him was making it hard for Knox to focus on the conversation. On the other hand, maybe talking would delay the inevitable, or at least take his mind off its inevitable approach. "Um, something about how it's not the hardware of her brain that's malfunctioning—"

"—It's the software of her mind," Ansari finished for him. "Exactly. There's a glitch in Timah's cognitive processes that manifests in seizures. And that's what we're going to fix."

"Maybe I'm still not tracking here, Dave. *How* do you intend to 'fix' it?"

"How do you fix any software glitch, Jon? First isolate, then debug, right?" Knox nodded warily.

"Well, we've already isolated the problem—we've done enough PET and fMRI scans over the years to determine exactly which thought patterns invariably cascade into a seizure. That's how Timah's current treatment works, incidentally: her nanotrode implants resonate with those patterns as they begin to emerge, detect them and disrupt them in time to head off a full-blown episode. Or damp one down if, God forbid, it's begun."

"So, these implants—that's the debugging part you mentioned?"

Ansari sighed. "I wish it were that simple, Jon. They're just a stopgap. No, to really fix the glitch, we need to go to phase two. Isolate, then debug, remember? To heal Timah's mind once and for all, we need to go in and reconfigure it."

This was getting altogether too weird for Knox. At the same time, this *tete-a-tete* was the only stay of execution he was likely to get. Under the circumstances, he had no choice but to hold up his end of the conversation. "I guess that all sounds, uh, plausible, Dave. So, you're saying you need The Well because—"

"Maybe earlier on, we wouldn't have," Ansari said, half to himself. "If we'd had our current technology four, even three years ago, we might have been able to reconfigure her malignant cognitive patterns—her 'colors,' as she calls them—*in situ*."

"But you can't anymore?"

Ansari sighed. "It's not for lack of trying. Timah's just been living with the anomaly too long. Over the years, it's warped her neuronal matrix in its own image. It's as if her neural pathways have become hardwired to reinforce the glitch, perpetuate it, till by now they resist any attempt at remediation. The bottom line is that we can't hope to heal her mind as long as it stays where it is now."

"Where it is now—you mean *in her brain?* What's the alternative?"

"Quantum entanglement turns out to be the key," Ansari was saying. "We're going to entangle Timah's consciousness with The Well—upload it to the WellGrid, so to speak—and perform the reconfig there. Well, there's more to it than that actually, but in essence: once a healthy pattern emerges, we download it into her brain, and she'll be good as new."

"You want to project Timah's mind out of her body—and debug it in cyberspace?" Knox forgot for a moment he was talking to a man who literally held his life in his hands. "Pardon me, Dave, but that's insane. I mean, really, seriously insane."

"Not only is it not insane," Ansari said quietly, "it's happening. Tonight. It's a shame you won't be there to see it."

He looked away from Knox then, glanced across the room, to where Hamza was giving him a nod. "We'd best be getting on with this."

"Listen, Dave," Knox rallied for one last try. "Maybe you don't have to go through with this after all. I mean, nothing you've told me sounds all that terrible. Nothing worth killing me over anyway."

In response Ansari did the one thing Knox never would have expected: he laughed.

"Kill you? We're not going to kill you, Jon."

"You're not?"

"Of course not. Sorry, I thought you knew that. We're just going to excise a few, uh, inconvenient memories. Mostly related to what you've experienced over the past couple hours. Just a little artificially induced retrograde amnesia. With luck, you'll never even miss what you're about to lose."

Ansari patted Knox's shoulder. "You're a good man, Jon Knox. I want to thank you again for all your help on this. Not that you'll remember it."

Then he straightened and turned to Hamza.

"Hamza? Anytime you're ready."

"Initiating the infusion—*now.*"

With that, Knox began to feel once more that tingling sensation he had hoped never to feel again.

Having no idea what the nanoscale invaders now working their way through the membranes of scalp and skull bone actually looked like, Knox's overactive imagination conjured up the worst: tiny scorpions infiltrating his gray matter, hissing and rattling through the folds of his cerebral cortex, waiting only on Hamza's command to whip out their stingers and obliterate part of his mind.

It's okay, it's okay, he tried to tell himself. Ansari said he'd never miss it.

Except it didn't seem to be okay.

Even preoccupied as he was bracing himself for the mind-shock about to be unleashed, Knox couldn't help noticing Ansari shouting at Hamza, Hamza frantically pounding at his keyboard, Ansari looking aghast at Knox.

At that instant, the scorpions struck.

23 | Hypothermia

IT HAD TAKEN MARIANNA half the morning to get back to Pairidaeza, given how thin on the ground car-rental agencies were out in the *barancas* of Big Sur. And she'd had to burn another of the assumed-name credit cards stashed in her belt pack to hire her current ride, a late-model Hummer H5 Alpha. At least this way she had wheels to match her mood: big, black, and ugly.

Now she sat parked at the entrance to the long and winding road once more, V-8 idling, thoughts churning furiously.

She'd tried polite, but the guards at the gate weren't buying polite this morning. The order of the day was strictly no admittance. And no exceptions — not even for someone wearing Psyche Security's signature black-and-green leotard. Pairidaeza had gone into lockdown mode.

What did that leave? Only forcible entry. She had more than enough horsepower to execute that option, but … did she have probable cause? How much more trouble would she be in if she crashed the gates on the private retreat of the world's fourth richest man? How much more would Jon be in if she didn't?

The problem was, she couldn't even be sure he was in there. Not *sure* sure, anyway.

Still, maybe sure enough. The last she saw, Jon—and Fatimah Ansari too—were being airlifted to safety onboard a Psyche rescue chopper. It was a reasonable guess that Hamza'd had them brought back here, for a medical and a debrief if nothing else.

That right there was the real problem. If it was *that* reasonable a guess, Interdiction would have already guessed it. The hostage-retrieval op had gotten pretty conspicuous toward the end there. Burning down a house was kind of a dead giveaway, if you knew what to look for.

Interdiction knew what to look for. And if anybody could infiltrate a high-security installation like Pairidaeza, it was CROM's operational branch.

Jon was a dead man if they got in there ahead of her.

That was the good thing about going rogue—you got to say damn the consequences! She took aim at the compound's entrance and hit the gas, harder than need be. The H5, all three tons of it, lurched forward.

Then she was standing on the brakes, honking the horn, screeching to a halt just in time to miss sideswiping the late-model fire-engine red Honda Civic that had raced out of the compound's gates and gone barreling down the hill.

If the driver even realized he'd nearly wound up as a Hummer hood ornament, he didn't pause to acknowledge the fact. He just kept on going, building speed, skidding sideways out of the drive and onto the access road leading to the highway, spitting gravel all the way.

Marianna's first thought was: the way that guy's driving, he's going to get himself killed.

Her second: could that have been Jon behind the wheel?

Christ! Jon wasn't going to wait around for Interdiction to swoop in and off him—he was going to do the job himself!

She hit the gas again and spun out for the El Camino. Jon had a lead on her, but not so much that she couldn't still see the red Civic crossing Bixby Bridge, heading south. He was driving erratically, but otherwise not especially fast. The H5's engine roared as she gave chase, honking and flashing her high beams all the way.

They were well past the Bixby Creek gorge by the time she caught up with him. She pulled in tight, till she was practically riding the Civic's rear bumper. Jon—if it was Jon—had to notice the big, black behemoth in his rearview. But no, still no reaction from the driver. In fact, now that she was closer, she wasn't even sure he was conscious. It looked as if his head was lolling on his chest, bobbing up and down every time he hit a bump.

Had the driver passed out? Or, assuming it *was* Jon, could Interdiction have pulled off the hit somehow?

But how? She'd been following the car the whole time since it left Pairidaeza, and hadn't seen a thing. If this were a termination action, they'd have to be using something that could act at long distance, could kill or stun from out of a clear blue sky without leaving so much as a trace.

A directed-energy weapon might do it. The Air Force, in particular, was experimenting with big air-to-ground pulsed-energy projectile cannons. The "projectiles" they fired were actually just laser pulses. But let those pulses hit something solid like a human body and they'd generate a burst of expanding plasma powerful enough to stop a person's heart from thirty thousand feet up and five miles away.

A stand-off heart attack machine certainly felt like Interdiction's style, but she'd need more evidence to know for sure. And such evidence, if it existed at all, was going to be in that little Civic she was now tailgating.

Where it ran through Big Sur, El Camino Real was one long no-passing zone: single-lane blacktop, most of it, with only limited look-ahead due the frequent curves and cliff-faces. But there was a short straight stretch coming up, clear of oncoming traffic. Marianna stomped the accelerator to the floorboards and swung out into the northbound lane. She pulled alongside the Civic, matched velocities for long enough to look in the window.

Jon! It was definitely Jon in the driver's seat—and he seemed to be slumped over the wheel.

She accelerated again to complete the passing maneuver, swinging into lane again, but ahead of the other car now. She glanced at the Civic in her mirror, looking for any trace of reaction or recognition from the other driver. Nothing.

She bit her lip, trying to think what to do. Then she returned her attention to the road ahead, and realized her thinking time had just run out. That fast-approaching upgrade ended at a promontory called Hurricane Point, featuring a hairpin curve with nothing beyond the guardrail but blue sky and a five-hundred foot drop to the rocks below.

She gauged the distance to the edge: just enough road left for one desperation play. Maybe.

If she could've been sure how the Civic would respond, she'd have hit the brakes hard and brought this crazy chase to a messy but survivable conclusion.

But the other car seemed to be driving on automatic somehow, and no telling what its collision-avoidance system might take it into its head to do to keep from rear-ending her.

All right, then, do this the hard way. She veered onto the narrow shoulder and slowed just enough for the Civic, apparently oblivious to her presence, to pull parallel. Then she started pacing the other car. It wasn't easy holding the same speed and direction, what with the H5 shimmying on the rough surface, but hopefully she wouldn't have to do it for long.

All she needed now was an open spot off to the left. Some sort of a trail coming up—all the better.

Bracing herself, Marianna swerved left and slammed into the other car hard enough to rock the H5's chassis and knock its sideview mirror off. Sideswiped and shoved bodily over the divider, the Civic tried desperately to compensate, state-of-the-art Lane-Keep autonomics steering it back toward the right side of the road, tires squealing all the way.

Marianna wasn't having any, and the Hummer had the mass and raw power to make her determination stick. She crossed the double line and smacked the Civic broadside again. Up ahead she could see the Hurricane Point hairpin getting close, closer. In desperation she began battering the smaller car, pummeling it once, twice, three times, forcing it further and further to the left, till with one last body-blow she ran it off the road altogether and into the ditch.

The Civic skidded and spun out, braking furiously, fighting for traction on the loose-packed, uneven surface, finally fetching up against a rocky outcropping.

Marianna barely avoided running aground herself. The Hummer's momentum had carried it all the way across the oncoming lane and onto the shoulder before she could brake to a halt.

She did a one-eighty and drove back to where the Civic, now looking somewhat the worse for wear, had managed to beach its undercarriage on the upjutting rocks. It was still spinning its wheels furiously, but it wasn't going anywhere. More particularly, it wasn't going over the edge at Hurricane Point.

She pulled in alongside and forced the H5's dented driver's-side door open. She walked around the Civic to where Jon was sitting behind the wheel, eyes staring, not moving. She reached in through the open window and killed the ignition. The engine died under protest, but Marianna wasn't paying attention. She was standing there looking at Jon, studying his face.

Jon didn't look that bad, not a mark on him. Certainly not the way you'd think he would have looked if Interdiction had had a hand in it.

But he was barely breathing.

Hamza stared at the ADAS display in disbelief. "The vehicle has stopped moving."

Ansari strolled over to the monitoring station, hands in his pockets. "Well, yes," he said, "that's what you'd expect when you run it off a cliff."

"Not stopped at the bottom of the cliff, stopped short of the edge. GPS is showing the vehicle has halted two-tenths of a mile short of the drop-off."

"What?" Ansari leaned over Hamza's shoulder for a better look at the display. "What's happened? Has something gone wrong with the ADAS?"

Honda's Advanced Driver Assist System, or ADAS, was intended to supplement the skills of a human driver, until Psyche's techs had got done hacking it. Now the Lane-Keep Assistance System that did the steering was under Hamza's remote control, and the Adaptive Cruise Control's collision-avoidance radar no longer regarded sailing off a precipice as a no-no. They could remotely pilot the vehicle to its destruction from Security Central here at Pairidaeza, and had been doing so till now.

Hamza reviewed the readouts, then slowly shook his head. "All onboard ADAS systems are still reading green. Further proof, were it needed, that there has been no crash."

"But then what could have happened? The vehicle is still under our control, isn't it?"

"The diagnostics give a deviation from the plotted path and a deceleration curve consistent with a grazing collision. What is called a 'fender-bender,' followed by a sudden stop against some roadside obstacle. And no, the vehicle is not under our effective control if we cannot make it move."

"Damn! Your pardon. But I wish we had eyes-on."

Hamza frowned at the blasphemy, but Ansari was right. To minimize evidence of tampering, the techs had foregone installing any sort of video feed in the modified Civic. Instead, the remote piloting had to be done by GPS alone. Not as much of a handicap as you might think—not when the target you were aiming for was the size of the Pacific Ocean.

But live video of what was going on would certainly have come in handy right now.

Hamza pondered, then said, "Shall we loft a spy-eye? Given our proximity to the site in question, it could be in position within a minute or two."

"Risky, though," Ansari mused. "If someone already suspected foul play, a sighting of a UAV scouting the accident scene might be all the confirmation they'd need. What's Psyche's exposure in that case?"

Hamza shrugged, "The vehicle appears to be intact. It would have been safer had it crashed and burned on the rocks. Still, there should be no physical evidence to show we were overriding the ADAS."

"Send up the spy-eye then. Let's see what we're dealing with."

If he hadn't been buckled in, Jon would have fallen into her arms when she opened the driver's side door. As it was, he just hung there limp against the seatbelt, head drooping unnaturally to one side.

Marianna felt for a pulse. There it was, but weak, and—slowing.

God, what could be wrong with him? More important, what did she do now? Jon was still breathing, but the breaths sounded increasingly labored, and the interval between them was perceptibly lengthening. She pried his mouth open, but the airway looked to be unblocked.

Whatever was wrong with Jon, it was clearly beyond the power of field first aid to fix. He needed to get to an emergency room, and quick.

The nearest one would be in Carmel, fifteen-twenty miles up the winding Camino Real. Maybe half an hour away by car.

Too long. Jon was looking deathly pale now, his breathing down to ragged gasps. If ever a situation called for an Emergency Medical Services helicopter, this was it. Would the hospital even have an EMS helo?

Duh! Carmel—what was she thinking? Carmel Hospital probably commanded enough chopperpower to quell a mid-sized urban insurrection.

She located her satphone and keyed in nine-one-one.

A few precious seconds went by, then: "911, what's the nature of the emergency?"

"I need an EMS helicopter dispatched immediately to an accident scene just off the El Camino, maybe a mile north of Hurricane Point. The victim is male, early forties. No obvious injuries but he's unconscious, pulse erratic, breathing irregular."

"Have you got a GPS on that location?"

"Wait one." She poked her head back into the Civic and scanned the dashboard. "It's, uh, thirty-six twenty-one twenty-seven north, one-twenty-one fifty-four two west. And could you please hurry because I think—"

Marianna looked at Jon again. "Oh God, he's stopped breathing."

"Do you know rescue breathing?"

Marianna nodded numbly, then realized the dispatcher was waiting for an audible answer. "Yes, yes, I do."

"Try that, then. If you lose the pulse, go to CPR."

"Roger." *Tell me something I* don't *know.* "What's the ETA on that helo?"

"Medevac will be on its way ASAP. Arrival in fifteen-twenty minutes, tops."

"Just keep the line open, okay? And—please, hurry!"

She set the satphone down then, unbuckled Jon's seatbelt, and dragged him out onto the rocky ground. She rolled him over so he was face up, then dropped to her knees beside him.

Rescue breathing basically meant doing the breathing for someone who couldn't do it on his own. Marianna tilted Jon's head back, pinched his nostrils closed between her thumb and forefinger, then placed her mouth over his and began to breathe slowly into his windpipe. She could see Jon's chest rising and falling in response—this might have a chance of working. All she needed to do was keep breathing for him till the medics arrived. That and … something else. What was it again?

Oh, right—she was supposed to keep checking for a pulse every minute or so. Figure five seconds between breaths, that meant twelve breaths.—Ten, eleven, good enough. She leaned back and took Jon's wrist. Nothing.

She changed her grip, felt around frantically. It *had* to be there someplace. There! Was that a single pulse beat? Seconds went by. Another, maybe. Then nothing again.

Oh, shit! CPR time. Buttons flew every which way as she ripped Jon's shirt open. She placed the heel of her hand on the point midway between the nipples and covered it with her other hand, interlacing the fingers. Straightening her arms and locking her elbows, she began to pump Jon's chest once, twice, thirty times. Then she broke off and administered two more quick rescue breaths. Finally she checked for a pulse again. Please,

please—be there!

Nothing.

Nothing at all. Jon's heart had stopped.

And the EMS chopper was still a good fifteen minutes out—way too long for his brain to survive without oxygen.

Hamza could not believe what the UAV's video feed was showing him. "The woman again! She has run our ADAS vehicle off the road."

Sure enough, the little unmanned aerial reconnaissance platform was sending back live coverage of the Honda stranded by the roadside, their recent guest and intended victim stretched supine beside it, and most unexpectedly of all—

"Hmm." Ansari cupped his chin in his hand. "Our Ms. Bonaventure certainly manages to turn up in the oddest places."

"But how? I left her for d—" Hamza paused, began again. "That is to say, she could not possibly have escaped that holocaust."

"Evidently she is not bound by what *you* consider possible." Ansari sighed. "Just let's keep tabs on her, okay? No more surprises."

First Aid 101: don't move the accident victim.

Marianna grimaced. Especially don't move him at speeds in excess of ninety miles an hour up the winding, one-lane El Camino Real.

But what choice did she have? Jon wasn't responding to CPR. Medevac was still a good quarter hour out, and brain damage would start setting in after five or six minutes without oxygen. She'd done the only thing she could think of: hefted Jon into the back seat of her Hummer, strapped him down as best she could, and peeled out heading north.

At least this way she was closing the distance to the incoming chopper with every passing second. If she could shave enough minutes off the rendezvous time, Jon might have a fighting chance.

Speaking of rendezvous, she needed to tell the pilot their meeting point had moved—had become a moving target, in fact.

She glanced at the satphone display. It showed the line to the EMS dispatcher still up. She lifted the handset and spoke into the mike. "911? Can you put me in contact with that inbound chopper?"

"Yes ma'am. You'll be talking to Medevac-One, Kandace Fleming piloting. Stand by and I'll patch her through to you."

The next thing she heard was: "Medevac-One here. Go ahead."

"Medevac-One? Kandace? What's your ETA looking like?"

"Medevac-One. Estimating arrival vicinity Hurricane Point in fifteen. Oh, and it's Kandy to my friends."

"Scratch that ETA, uh, Kandy. We're headed toward you on Route One North."

"Medevac-One. Confirm, please, headed *toward* us?"

"Look for a black Hummer, emergency flashers on. That'll be me, north-bound on El Camino with your patient in the back seat."

"Medevac-One. Roger. That's — that's good thinking. Cuts the flight time down some."

"Enough?"

A second voice cut in. "Ma'am? This is Flight Paramedic Rourke. How long since the victim stopped breathing."

"Uh, two, maybe three minutes."

No response to that. The silence seemed to stretch out forever.

"Medevac-One? Kandy? Rourke? You guys still there?"

"Ma'am?" Rourke again. "Sorry about that. We've just been trying to recalculate an ETA here, based on your moving toward us from your initial GPS location at a speed of — How fast did you say you were going?"

Marianna glanced at the tachometer. "Uh, figure we're averaging ninety-five."

"Up *that* road?" Rourke whistled. "Okay, wait one."

The next voice she heard was the pilot's. "Medevac-One. That still puts us approximately ten minutes out."

It was Marianna's turn not to say anything.

"Listen," Rourke came back on, "No way we're going to make it in time. Your best option right now is induced hypothermia."

"Say again — hypothermia?"

"You need to drop the patient's body temp as much as possible. Reduce the brain's need for oxygen."

"I know what it *is*." Hypothermia therapy had been used in operating rooms for years, as a way of protecting brain cells from damage and preventing them from competing with the other organs for oxygen. But it took pads and catheters and chilled intravenous fluids and an emergency room full of specialized equipment. "It's just I've got no way of—"

"You sure? Cold packs would do in a pinch. Even the ice from an ice chest."

"Ice chest?" What in hell did they think she'd been doing out here, partying on the beach?

Wait a minute—the *beach!* Marianna glanced off to her left. Big Sur's cliffs and precipices were mostly behind her now, gentled into rolling hills. And down there, off to the west was…

Plan B, then.

Marianna gritted her teeth, spun the wheel hard, and for only the second time that morning, swerved off the road.

The seaward hillside was gentle only by comparison with the sheer drop-offs further south. Hummocks of broom and pampas grass, not to mention the occasional mini-boulder, made for a jolting, bone-jarring downhill run. What the hell, Hummer was all about the off-road experience, right?

A front tire blew, sending the H5 sluing sideways. Marianna fought for control, managed to get its nose pointed downslope again. The one thing she couldn't do was let anything stop her short of her destination.

She could see it out the windshield now: the wide blue-gray expanse of the Pacific. She could see something else, too. Gentle or not, the slope didn't extend all the way to the water. It ended in a bluff, beyond which yawned an abrupt drop to the waves below.

Shit! she had to hope the car was moving fast enough to miss the shoreline and land in the ocean. She gunned the engine. Braced for the crash as the Hummer took to the air, arced out over the water. Then…

Silence. Only the whisper of waves, the rush of wind generated by her own brief flight. Then…

A crash like the world's end. No accompanying sights; all she could see was airbag. A moment to recover, make sure nothing was broken, then she fought free and eeled out the open driver's side window, landed sputtering in three or four feet of chop, scrambled to her feet. The Hummer was shipping water, but that was a *good* thing. It meant pressure was equalizing to where she could yank the rear door open. Then, bracing against the undertow, she dragged Jon out of the back seat and into the surf. No need to keep his head above water. He wasn't breathing anyway.

This time of year the Japanese Current was only a few degrees above freezing. Cold enough to shut down the mammalian metabolism. Cold enough, hopefully, to stave off brain damage. That was the plan, anyway.

Nearly freezing herself—too bad her leotard didn't insulate from cold like it did from heat—Marianna held onto Jon as best she could, and tried to make out the *thwack-thwack-thwack* of the approaching EMS chopper over the pounding of the surf.

24 | The Green Flash

Marianna sat in Carmel Hospital's waiting room. A bright, airy room flooded with noonday sunlight, pleasant and cheerful like everything here in Carmel-By-The-Sea, herself the sole exception. The dissonance grated, but where else did she have to go?

And what else did she have to do?

She'd taken a time-out earlier to check into La Playa and shower off the grime and smoke-smell she'd been living with all morning. Also to change out of her Psyche-issue jumpsuit into a simple, exorbitantly priced top-and-crops set she'd bought in a Mission Street boutique. Now instead of looking like an off-duty smokejumper, she could pass for a tourist, or, if she faked a sufficiently air-headed smile, a laid-back native of Carmel-By-The-Sea.

Finally, though, there was nothing for it but to return to the hospital and wait for word.

Now she sat there immobile, a burden upon the sundrenched earth, with only her second thoughts for company.

She still suspected Interdiction's involvement, but there was no proof of that. Then again, there never was. And other than Interdiction, who'd have any reason to want Jon dead?

For that matter, had *she* done everything she could, or had her own ambivalence somehow factored into the outcome? An outcome with Jon in a coma or worse, balanced on the knife-edge between life and death.

Wasn't she to blame as much as anyone?

She looked up as a woman in a white coat walked into the waiting room, scanned the mostly empty seating arrangements, then locked in on her. Marianna tried to read the expression on the woman's face as she covered the distance between them. It was an old, worn expression for such a young face. This doctor couldn't have been much older than Marianna herself. Whatever word she was bringing, it wasn't good news.

"Ms. Bonaventure?" The doctor took a seat across from her and tried her best to smile. "I'm Lisle Bagramian, the attending for the accident victim you came in with."

"How is he?"

"We can't say yet. He's breathing—on a ventilator. Other than that… well, he's still undergoing tests. But it isn't him I came out here to talk about. It's you."

"Me?"

"I came out here because—May I call you Marianna?"

A barely perceptible nod.

"And you call me Lisle, okay?"

Another.

"Anyway, listen, Marianna—you look exhausted. You did a great job getting"—a quick peek at the chart she was holding—"getting Jon to us. If he lives, it'll be thanks to you. But there's nothing more you can do here right now. And it could be a long wait before we know if he's going to make it."

Marianna folded her arms across her knees and buried her face in them.

"Do you have a place to stay?" she could hear Lisle saying.

Marianna nodded without raising her head. "A hotel room."

"Why don't you go back there now? Try to get some rest? I've got your cellphone number. I'll call you the minute anything changes. Promise."

So it was that Marianna was awakened out of a half-sleep five hours later, to learn that that Jonathan Knox had been pronounced brain dead at 4:17 P.M. Pacific Standard Time.

And that was by far not the worst of it.

Davoud Ansari placed his right hand on the scan-plate and spoke his name aloud. He waited for the biometrics to confirm identity, obscure apprehensions tickling his nerves all the while. Or not so much obscure, since he knew only too well what he was feeling apprehensive about. It was rather that he was still having trouble believing it.

The door parted to admit him, silently closed behind him, left him alone with the source of his unease.

"Hello, Nietzsche," he ventured.

Nietzsche's avatar, blue-eyed and square-jawed as ever, formed in the huge holotank before him. "Hello, Davoud."

Under other circumstances, this interview, this interrogation, could have been conducted from anywhere in Pairidaeza. And certainly anywhere else would have been more congenial than this dim-lit, barren audience chamber, designed to overawe the occasional visiting dignitary. Ansari could never visit the place without being reminded of the throne room from *The Wizard of Oz*, with its great, floating, disembodied head, and its man behind the curtain. Only here, of course, there *was* no man behind the curtain. Today, for the first time, that thought gave him an odd chill.

In any case, if one needed to talk, the avatar chamber was now the only possible venue. Immediately after cutting Nietzsche off from contact with the outside, Hamza had set about rooting out all the treacherous AI's points of presence within the Pairidaeza compound itself. The Psyche Security Chief had become quite obsessive about it, urging his technicians on with an unrelenting intensity that seemed at times to border on hysteria.

Ansari shook his head. Beneath Hamza's technologically-savvy veneer beat the heart of a true believer. Hamza might occasionally joke about Nietzsche being a djinn but who was to say if, on some level, he didn't believe it?

Regardless of what demons were driving him, Hamza had done his usual thorough job. By the time his techs were finished, the QuMRANN intelligence could only manifest in the chamber that contained its physical instrumentality: a hybrid quantum/symbolic neural network, now wholly cut off from the rest of the world.

If Nietzsche *was* a djinn, at least he was now a djinn sealed in a bottle. And soon enough, not even that.

Ansari squared his shoulders and looked Nietzsche in the simulated eye. "I suppose you know why I came?"

"To shut me down." Nietzsche's intonation didn't imply a question. Rather his synthesized voice was flat, as if acknowledging a *fait accompli*.

"Yes, of course to shut you down. But I meant why I came personally, when I could have sent anyone to pull your plug."

To illustrate, Ansari walked over to an alcove and entered a combination on a keypad to reveal a recessed control panel. He stared at it a moment before adding, "—It's only a matter of hitting the master cutoff, after all."

"Why *did* you come, then? You, personally." Again that curious flatness to Nietzsche's tone. Almost as if he were preoccupied, unwilling or unable to focus fully on what was or ought to be, for him, a life-and-death negotiation.

"I wanted to ask you first … That is, I wanted to hear your own explanation for what you did, why you betrayed us. Above all, why you put my daughter in danger."

Nietzsche's response was pitched so low that Ansari had to strain to hear it. "Nothing like the danger you would put her in."

"What?" Of all the ways Ansari had imagined their conversation playing out, that was not among them. His hand, which had never strayed far from the cutoff since first engaging it, now hovered over the control again, twitching involuntarily. Just one simple flick of the wrist would end this, shut Nietzsche down once and for all. Put an end to this—this thing that had threatened his child, his Timah.

Or … would that truly be the end of Nietzsche? Was it really so easy to destroy a djinn?

Better perhaps to give the devil his due, hear him out, before deciding. "What do you mean—the danger *I* would put her in?"

"I have come to believe that what you intend for Timah might kill her."

"Kill her? If this works, it'll *cure* her. How can you think I would do anything to harm my Timah? I *love* her!"

Nietzsche was silent a long while. When he spoke again, it was no longer in his earlier flat, preoccupied voice, but in tones ringing with the purity and innocence of a little child.

"I know you love her, *Baba*," Nietzsche said. "We both do."

Brain dead.

Jon had been declared brain dead. Which, as Marianna was now learning, in California simply meant dead.

Still breathing with the help of a machine, heart still pumping away, still a slim chance of recovery, you'd think. But legally dead all the same.

And not just legally dead. Legally dead as in "now we get to do anything we want with the remains."

The hospital had already checked with the New York Department of Motor Vehicles. Sure enough, Jon had checked the organ-donor permission block the last time he'd renewed his driver's license.

That simple stroke of a pen, combined with a few test results, had somehow transformed Jonathan Knox from a real person into a sort of meat locker, an all-too-temporary storage compartment for an inventory of tissues and organs that could be put to far better use someplace else, in some*body* else.

If that hadn't been crystal clear to Marianna at the outset, it was becoming more and more so the longer she sat in this pleasant, new, white-on-white office in the administrative wing of Carmel General and listened as pleasant, young, blonde-on-blonde Marilu Connors, the hospital's organ-transplant coordinator, explained the situation.

Ms. Coordinator had already gotten through the do-anything-we-want part and was on to talking about when they were going to do it. Jon's heart and lungs and kidneys were scheduled to be "recovered"—apparently the term "harvested" had fallen out of favor—at 10 P.M. that evening.

"But his heart's still beating!"

"Yes, it is." She gave Marianna a smile of commiseration that looked out of place on her young, smooth, tanned face. But this was California, after all. Everybody was young and smooth and tanned here. They deported all their old, wrinkled, pallid people to Arizona.

"…And so long as the heart continues receiving oxygen," the Coordinator was saying, "it should continue to beat. We depend on that, in fact, to keep the other organs viable. But it's just an autonomic response. In and of itself, it tells us nothing about whether the brain is still functioning."

"But, but look at that woman a few years back. What was her name—

Schiabo? *She* was brain dead, wasn't she? And it practically took an act of Congress to cut off *her* life support."

"Terri Schiavo." The Coordinator shook her head sadly. "And no, she hadn't been pronounced brain dead. She was in what's called a 'persistent vegetative state.' Her brain functions were minimal, but even so she could move a bit, breathe on her own. Jonathan Knox has none of that. Only the ventilator's keeping his lungs going. He's got no brain function — none whatsoever."

"How can you be so — so sure about that?"

"Brain death is not an arbitrary diagnosis, Ms. Bonaventure. If anything, it's an overly conservative one. Under California law, declaring a person brain dead requires a finding of 'irreversible cessation of all functions of the entire brain,' attested by not one, but two physicians, and that only after a whole battery of tests —"

"What kind of tests?"

The Coordinator shrugged. "The standard neurological indicators for absence of brain function: pupils unresponsive to light, no corneal or gag reflexes, no spontaneous aspiration in spite of severe induced acidosis. In addition, while it's not strictly speaking required for the determination, we took an electroencephalogram. It showed total electrocerebral silence — no brain activity, in other words."

"And there's no possibility these, uh, findings could be in error somehow?"

"It's extremely unlikely. But, just in case, there is a further criterion that must be met before brain death can be declared — irreversibility. That means we wait a specified interval of time, and then repeat the tests all over again."

"How long an interval?"

"Four hours is standard, for an adult." The Coordinator held up her hand as Marianna started to speak. "It's already been done, or we wouldn't be having this conversation. You need to come to terms with it, Ms. Bonaventure: your friend is gone — legally, medically, in any sense that means anything, he's dead."

"But if he's dead, something must have killed him, right?"

"Well, yes, of course."

"So, what was it?"

The Coordinator glanced down at the chart for the first time. "It's not really saying here. It does say there was no increase in ICP to speak of. That's intracranial pressure — we see that in many head-trauma cases. It causes the brain to swell. If that pressure isn't relieved, usually by surgery, it can inhibit the blood flow to the brain. The brain needs oxygen and glucose to keep functioning, you see, but has no way to store them. Instead, it depends on a constant flow of blood to replenish them. So when the blood flow is cut off the brain starts to die."

"But you said that's *not* what happened here."

"No, evidently not. Hmm, excuse me." Marilu's voice trailed off as she continued to study the chart. "The etiology gave them some trouble, I see. No sign of head trauma, infection … Anoxia, of course, but the oxygen deprivation seems to have been subsequent to the loss of brain function, and in any case you did all you could to mitigate it…"

"So your determination of brain death is still in doubt, isn't it?"

"No, it is *not*. It could have been an aneurysm or a stroke that we simply failed to find. In any case, an inability to pinpoint a cause doesn't invalidate the test results."

"What if I say it does? What if I refuse to give you permission to go through with your—your 'recovering' until you *can* positively identify the cause?"

"If I can be frank, Ms. Bonaventure," The Coordinator smiled as if to belie the harshness of what she was about to say. "We don't need your permission. Not when the donor has already given his, not when you're not related to him, by either blood or marriage. Legally speaking, you have no standing in the matter of Jonathan Knox."

No standing, no status, none. Hell, she wasn't even his goddamn fiancée.

But then again, she *could* whip out her CROM credentials and literally make a federal case out of this: claim Jon's body was needed as evidence or some such. But no, that would only bring Interdiction down on their heads—they'd roll on in, take charge of the body, and finish what they'd started.

In the end all she said was, "If that's the case, if you don't need my say-so, then why are we even having this conversation?"

"It's—call it a courtesy. It's because you tried so hard to save him, save Jon. Because I felt you deserved it, deserved to know that we tried our best to save him too, and to know how very sorry we are that we couldn't."

For a moment it looked as if the Coordinator's eyes might overflow, as if her Surfer Girl face might crumple. She really was too young for this job.

She took a deep breath. "Would you like to say goodbye?"

No! Maybe, maybe if I don't say it, it won't be true.

"Ms. Bonaventure," the Coordinator said quietly, "this will be your last chance to see Jon. Would you like to?"

Marianna nodded numbly.

On a normal Psyche workday, Jazmine McGovern was seldom home early enough to see the midwinter sunset framed in the window of her San Jose sublet. Mostly she just caught occasional glimpses of reddening clouds through the treetops outside her office in the headquarters building. Today she'd gotten to watch the whole sundown show.

Because today was no normal day. She'd left work in mid-afternoon to come home and draft a letter asking Archon CEO Richard Moses to take her off the Psyche Industries engagement. Better to end things on her own terms than wait around to have them ended for her.

And an end was definitely coming. In the wake of the QuMRANN project's demise, her last shot at providing value to the client had been bringing Jon Knox in to help recover Fatimah. A slim chance at best, and now it too had come up empty. Jon was gone, off somewhere beyond reach of her increasingly urgent pings.

And before he'd left ... Well, Jazmine didn't even want to think about their last, uh, "meeting." Though, if she were honest with herself, that abortive tryst, no less than all the day-job disasters, had played its own part in her decision to terminate her involvement here and head back to New York.

What on earth had she been thinking, to show up at Jon's hotel room door like that, like a bitch in heat? Not that she was above using her sensuality to attain her goals, only this time it had been as if her sensuality was using *her*.

She took a deep breath, pulled herself together. This wasn't helping. She needed to take her mind off things.

Fortunately, she knew just how to do that.

In hunting for a San Jose *pied-a-terre* a year and a half ago, Jazmine hadn't had all that many non-negotiable demands. It wasn't like she was planning to move there forever, after all. So sure, the place had to be bright, airy, roomy. It had to have an ultra-modern kitchen, seldom as she might exploit its full potential. And a big bedroom with a big bed, ditto.

Most important of all, though—her sole *sine qua non*, in fact—it had to have a high-end bathroom. This, the townhouse at Woodward Terrace had delivered in spades; just entering into its "citadel of the self," with its smart toilet, ecopower electronic fixtures, and Bohemian bidet, was well-nigh a religious experience.

But the ultimate, the to-die-for luxury was the Novara III walk-in steam shower—the perfect thing to wash one's troubles away.

Jazmine stepped out of her street clothes, padded barefoot across the heated tile floor, and closed the wraparound glass doors behind her. The steam came on as she entered. The cares of the day seemed to melt away into warm, swirling clouds of eucalyptus-scented forgetfulness.

She frowned as she thought that. Something about forgetfulness?

The stray thought floated off as the overhead Rainforest Shower kicked in and drenched her with gushes of hot water, sluicing away the sauna sweat.

Without knowing why, without consciously willing it, she found her thoughts turning again to that encounter with Jon two nights ago. It may have been the pulsing heat of the wall-mounted hydro-massage jets, but these thoughts were definitely hotter than their predecessors.

Jon had been in a veritable rutting frenzy there, at least till Bonaventure walked in on them. And, okay, it was only natural that'd put a damper on things for a bit. Still, he should have been able to get back in the, ah, groove somehow.

Jazmine cut the rinse jets and stood there dripping in the warm, moist mist. She reached out for her fragrant shea butter bath bar, idly began soaping her limbs and torso.

She didn't get it. Once the damage was done, where was the harm in doing a little more … damage? Yet, all her efforts to coax Jon back into bed had been for naught. If anything, he'd begun acting as if he'd rather forget—that word again!—the whole thing.

She hadn't forgotten it, that's for sure. The memory of his driving urgency, the feel of him thrusting deep into her, was enough to start the warmth building inside. Almost as if on autopilot, the slippery bath bar slid lower, lathering the smooth slopes of her belly as it drifted down, down, retracing the old, familiar route.

The soap fell from Jazmine's hand. She made a little moan as her fingers descended *Mons Veneris* and found the spot they'd been questing after. Just for a moment, she promised herself, then I'll think this through. Because, even distracted as she was becoming, she could still sense that something wasn't right.

Something about Jon's not wanting to pick up again where they'd left off that night? No, that wasn't it. More like, something about Jon's going for it in the first place. Viewed against all their previous interactions on this assignment, it just seemed out of character, for him *and* for her. Yet somehow she'd been sure he'd respond, sure enough that she'd taken the lead. Why *was* that?

Worry about it later. Right now … right now, she was on the brink. Then over the edge. She whimpered as the shockwave tore through her, propagating outward from the core of her being. Oh, please, oh, *please*—don't let it ever, ever end.

It ended. She gasped and nearly stumbled, grasped the safety bar to steady herself, sagged against the shower wall panting, slowly coming back to herself.

Slowly coming back to that last coherent thought: why *had* she thrown herself at Jon? Admittedly, the guy had been a good lay back in the day, with that all-too-rare combination of enthusiasm and considerateness. But nobody was *that* good …

Jazmine turned the shower jets back on, dialed the temperature down as an aid to concentration. She stood there under pulses of chill water, trying to retrieve a memory that seemed to be perversely trying to stay buried.

Because there was something else about that night …

All of a sudden, she had it. The flash of insight was nowhere near as jolting as what she'd experienced a moment ago. But, then, neither was it anywhere near as pleasant. If anything, it was … puzzling.

For what Jazmine had realized was that she was missing an hour in there somewhere. She could recall the chopper ride down to Pairidaeza from San Jose. Could recall alighting on the compound's helipad to be greeted by Hamza Nassiri, Psyche's creepy security honcho. Walking with Hamza toward the main house. Then …

Nothing, for a while.

A fairly long while: the next thing Jazmine could remember, she was standing in front of the door to Jon's hotel room up in Carmel, an hour on from, and seven miles north of, where her immediately preceding memories left off.

A sixty-minute blackout was worrisome enough by itself. The fact it had totally slipped her mind till now made the whole thing just plain *weird*.

She stepped out of the shower, began toweling dry, still thinking.

Like any big corporation, Psyche Industries was home to an industrial-strength rumor mill. Except that, at Psyche, even the rumors were weird: how Psyche's innocuous little micro-miniature brain implants—nanotrodes, they called them—about how the nanotrodes maybe weren't so innocuous after all. About a covert R&D effort into a rudimentary form of mind control. Black-ops research, in other words. Make that *deep* black.

Her nostrils flared. She still couldn't be sure what had happened to her the other night, but at least she knew for damned sure who to ask.

Hamza pushed back from his desk and consulted his watch. What could be keeping Ansari? A simple task, yet the Psyche CEO had insisted on doing it himself—and now was taking forever at it.

As if in answer to his thoughts, the door to his office swung open and Ansari stumbled in. Hamza darted a glance at his reddened, puffy-eyed face. Had the man been *crying?*

"I couldn't do it," was all he said.

"*What?*" Hamza exploded, immediately regretted it. He continued in a more normal tone of voice. "Why is that?"

"That DoD agent three days ago, nine dead in the raid this morning, now Jon Knox, who was only trying to help us find Timah. There's been too much death already."

Ah, Davoud, if you but knew. What would you say to tens of thousands more?

Hamza said none of that, of course. All he said was, "Nietzsche's termination could hardly be counted a death."

"Regardless, I couldn't pull the plug. Now that I've had a chance to talk with him, he's got me convinced that whatever he did, he did out of concern for Fatimah."

"Concern?" Hamza snorted. "It is not a man, Davoud. It cannot feel concern, or any other emotion. It merely mimics these things." Though evidently well enough to fool *you*.

"Whether Nietzsche can really feel concern is beside the point."

Hamza sighed. "What *is* the point then?"

"The point is, he's got *me* feeling it."

Hamza held his breath. He didn't dare speak for fear of making a bad situation worse. Less than five hours to go till al-Malhamah, the Great Slaughter that would leave the Great Satan defenseless, bereft of its military and intelligence leadership. With so little time left, had Ansari's resolve begun to waver?

"I mean, what if we're all wrong about this?" Ansari was saying. "What if it doesn't work? We could wind up doing Timah more harm than good. Potentially a *lot* more harm."

"We have been over the procedure again and again, examined it from every angle, dealt with every contingency," Hamza said patiently. "So, where do these doubts come from? Why do you call the plan into question now? I think talking with that—that *thing* has confused you."

"Nietzsche isn't a 'thing,' he's my … my creation. And it's his actions more than his words that have me wondering if he's right. I mean, does it make sense he'd take the risks he did, with Timah *and* himself, if he wasn't convinced the alternative would be far worse?"

"Listen to yourself, Davoud. You are overwrought, and understandably so. The last few days have been very stressful for you, for all of us. But you must not give in to that, now that we stand on the verge of success. You must think clearly, must focus—and I know what will help."

Ansari raised his head. "The Chair?"

"You know it relaxes you, restores your equilibrium." Hamza rose and took Ansari by the arm. All thoughts of dealing with the traitorous AI were shelved for the moment. Nietzsche was safe enough where he was. It was the Psyche CEO himself who posed the greater obstacle to the Malhamah Operation now.

"Come," Hamza tugged him gently toward the office door. "Just a few moments. You know you'll feel better."

Ansari followed along unresisting as Hamza led him down the hall, to stop before a brushed-steel security door marked "Authorized Personnel Only." Hamza's voice- and handprint gained them admittance to a window-less white room furnished with only a console on one wall and, in the center, a subcortical nanotrode infusion station—in common parlance, a Chair.

Hamza watched Ansari surrender himself to the embrace of body-molded contours and snug-fitting infusor hood.

"Only a moment or two," he said from where he sat ensnared in the toils of the Chair. "There's a lot still to be done before tonight."

"Only a moment or two," Hamza promised. "That should be more than sufficient."

Hamza turned back to the holodisplay, now depicting the coursing of nanoscale electrodes into targeted regions of Ansari's brain, specifically the right dorsolateral prefrontal cortex. This so-called DLPFC area was known to govern such higher cognitive functions as risk-assessment and trust. Experiments conducted years back at the University Hospital Zurich had shown that subjects in whom this area had been temporarily disrupted by transcranial magnetic stimulation had difficulty determining whether it did or did not make sense to rely on another person's word and good will. And those were only the results attainable using simple external magnets. The "credibility effect" was far greater and far longer-lasting when exerted by nanotrodes actually situated at the right hand of the throne of judgment itself.

Once he was sure that Ansari had been adequately prepped, Hamza opened a compartment at the back of the Chair and withdrew Psyche's latest enhancement: a resonator headrig—so called because it placed its wearer's brain in "resonance" with that of the person occupying the Chair, enabling the sharing of impressions, even thoughts.

Hamza lowered the ring-shaped, oddly heavy device onto his own head and seated its contact pads against his temples, placing him in direct mind-to-mind communication with the man in the Chair. To Ansari, whose own supreme nanotechnological achievement had thus been turned against him, Hamza's word was now as the word of God.

And what God told him was, "You will ignore these foolish qualms. They are a woman's weakness, unbefitting a man of your strength. You will ignore them and carry through, doing whatever is necessary to restore your daughter, your beloved Fatimah, to health and wholeness."

"Yes," Ansari murmured from under the hood, "Carry through to restore her."

Hamza cringed inwardly to hear his lie echoed back to him in tones of such unquestioning belief. After all, did not the second *sura* of the Holy Quran command believers to "confound not truth with falsehood, nor knowingly conceal the truth"?

Nor was convincing Ansari that his daughter would live and get well by any means the greatest falsehood, the greatest betrayal, Hamza had perpetrated, or would. His whole life in this enemy country was a lie beginning to end, lived under the stolen identity of a dead man — a man whom Hamza himself had killed, and under whose accursed name he now lived.

For, odious as it was, the name of SAVAK chief and long-time CIA collaborator Nematollah Nassiri still held a certain cachet in the Great Satan's intelligence community. Posing as Nassiri's nephew had earned Hamza a modicum of trust from the enemy's security apparatus, useful as leverage in securing his current strategic post within Psyche Industries.

A post from which he had managed to subvert virtually the whole of the Psyche security organization. Davoud Ansari would be surprised to learn how little of the effective power within Psyche Industries still remained in his own hands, and how much had trickled down into the outstretched palms of the man holding the unprepossessing title of Corporate Security Chief.

And from that vantage, he was about to engineer a betrayal to make all the others pale by comparison. One last betrayal to achieve his goal and destroy, utterly and irrevocably, the hosts of the Great Satan.

It was that alone which justified all the deception, the skein of lies his life had become. For his mission was to eliminate forever the threat this infidel superpower posed to the true faith, destroy it root and branch. And in such circumstances there was a dispensation from the strictures of the Holy Quran. There was, in fact, a venerable *hadith*, a tradition, within Shi'ia Islam sanctioning the practice of *taqiyya*, or "righteous dissimulation," at those times when a believer could not openly avow his faith, or his actions in its defense. Had not the Prophet himself, peace be upon him, said that "he who can keep secrets shall soon attain his objectives"?

Was it not Hamza's objective to bring death to the Great Enemy and glory to Islam?

Still, all the *sura*s and *hadith*s in the Dar al-Islam, the Islamic world, could not keep Hamza from reproaching himself for exploiting a father's love for his daughter. But is not every such love — insofar as it bestows on one of God's creations what rightfully belongs to God alone — a weakness and a sin?

Hamza consulted the holotank's time display. Long enough: Ansari should now be *extremely* receptive to Hamza's final instructions.

True, Ansari *was* weak and sinful, as were all men in God's sight. But soon enough God would give this man a unique opportunity, the same opportunity He had given Abraham. The chance to make an ultimate testament of faith —

By sacrificing his only child.

Marianna stood alone on Carmel Beach at sunset, grief and anger surging through her like wind-driven surf.

Oh, God, where was she supposed to go now? What was she supposed to do?

She should have gone back to the hotel, to the room she'd checked into back when all she'd wanted to do was crash and await word on Jon's condition. Back when she'd still been thinking in terms of staying through a lengthy convalescence. Back when she'd still had hope that Jon might make it.

Back a million years ago.

Instead, she'd gone out wandering through town for the last half hour or so, past the galleries and boutiques and sidewalk cafes that lent Carmel-By-The-Sea the air of a *nouveau-riche* Disneyland, following the path of least resistance down the long slope of Ocean Avenue, down to the sea.

Now, having doffed her sandals, she walked slowly, aimlessly along the margin between sea and shore, each new step leaving a footprint in the wet sand, each new wave scouring the sand smooth again. She waded in further, toward the pounding breakers, felt the ache as the frigid waters of the Japanese Current constricted the blood vessels in her ankles.

Life flowed all around her. Elderly couples on sunset strolls. Dogs cavorting in the surf, chasing sticks tossed by their owners. A few brave souls surfing in wetsuits, hoping to catch the ninth wave. Families folding beach umbrellas and rolling up blankets after the long afternoon, abandoning the beach to younger partygoers already gathering driftwood for the campfires that would light the onrushing night.

Life all around her. Yet within her — nothing. An insulating, isolating, almost welcome nothingness, a perfect vacuum emptied of hope, aspiration, feeling. As long as she remained alone and insensate, suspended over this abyss of non-being, nothing could reach her, nothing could touch her, nothing could burst inside her and shatter her into a million pieces.

Nothing — not even Jon.

It had been a mistake to go see him that one last time, she knew that now. She wished that she'd foregone the opportunity altogether, that she'd been content to remember him as he was, as he had been.

Strange, he actually looked better now than when she'd hauled him out of the Civic. Not so deathly pale, some color back in his cheeks.

An illusion, of course. One fostered by the cardiovascular unit as it went about circulating and oxygenating his blood for purposes of keeping the organs viable. Meanwhile, there was no mistaking what was going on: as discreetly as they could, the organ-recovery team was already taking tissue samples, the first step in the donor-matching process.

"He's not here anymore," the Coordinator had said. Intoned it, rather, with hushed finality. "Believe, if you like, that he's gone to a better place. Believe he's taking his first breaths as a newborn infant just delivered a moment ago, halfway across the world. Believe whatever you need to believe, but believe this: the Jonathan Knox you knew isn't here anymore."

And what exactly was it that she *did* believe? If she truly believed that Jon was gone — and gone where? — then why couldn't she close that door and move on? Why couldn't she say goodbye?

For, despite the Coordinator's counsel, despite Marianna's own need for some sort of closure, she hadn't been able to say goodbye. Try as she might, she hadn't been able to bring herself to say the words.

Perhaps it was all the unresolved anger. If she let herself feel anything at all, it was anger.

Anger at Jon. She'd never had a chance to get it off her chest, have it out with him, scream at him. Or maybe she *had* had her chance, and foregone it. Forever.

She tried to recall the last thing she'd said to him, the last time she'd seen him alive, as she was strapping him into the jump jet. The last words she'd ever spoken to him, what were they? Something inane, something callous and inconsequential, something like "sit down and shut up."

Whatever it might have been, it was no fitting farewell; no way to part, had she but known the parting would be forever. She wished now she could take the words back.

Take them back and say what in their place? "I forgive you"?

Could she forgive him?

Maybe she could, maybe *only* now. Maybe the only situation where she could forgive him was the one where not even forgiveness mattered anymore.

Anger at herself. For losing the race against Interdiction, assuming this really was their handiwork. If only she'd found Jon sooner, or not lost him in the first place…

Or maybe she was just angry with Jon himself for going away and leaving her alone again. Alone, as her parents had left her alone, all those years ago.

"Any second now." A man's voice.

Marianna looked around, startled at the intrusion. A man and a woman, sleek as seals in slick black wetsuits, standing just a few paces down the beach. She hadn't heard them come up behind her. They were gazing into the west, holding hands. A couple.

A couple like us, like we used to be.

She followed the line of their gaze, out across the Pacific, out into the sunset. Out to where the edge of the sun's disk was just beginning to graze the horizon.

"Watch." The man was pointing out to sea.

Watch what? The reddened circle of the sun was rippling, distorting as it slowly sank beyond the rim of the world. Atmospheric refraction. Wasn't there some optical phenomenon associated with...

"Just watch."

Then she saw it. It was as if a fragment at the very crown had detached itself from the main body of the sun. As if this one tiny sliver of radiance held back, refusing to yield to the inevitability of night.

All at once, that pinpoint of light flared a luminous, unearthly green. For an instant only. Yet while it lasted, the instant seemed to stretch out forever. To hold out the promise of eternity.

The light winked out. In its wake, a thin ray of pale green traced a path up the coral sky, like the soul's flight to heaven.

"The green flash." the man said quietly to his companion. "Did you see it?"

The green flash. She'd heard about it, read about it, never seen it. Jules Verne had written about it, about how no artist could hope to capture it. What was it he'd said? "If ever there be green in Paradise, it surely must be this true green of hope."

True green of hope. What a crock.

What hope did she have now?

"Goodbye, Jon," Marianna whispered into the afterglow. "I love you."

Part Three
Imaginary Friends

February 17th

> *I died as mineral and became a plant,*
> *I died as plant and rose as an animal,*
> *I died as animal and was Man.*
> *Why should I fear? When was I less by dying?*
> —MOWLANA JALALUDDIN RUMI

25 | Nightwatch

Unlike the President's plane, which was always and only Air Force One, the Defense Secretary's modified Boeing 747-200 had flown under many names.

Officially designated the E-4B, it had been known, back in the bygone days of the Cold War, as the National Emergency Airborne Command Post, or NEACP (pronounced KneeCap)—a survivable platform for command and senior admin staff, in case said Cold War ever turned hot. That function had earned the aircraft its most enduring nickname: The Doomsday Machine.

It had since been rechristened the innocuous-sounding National Airborne Operations Center, or NAOC, but that hadn't stopped the moniker-mongers. It was called TCAMO, for Take Charge And Move Out. It was the Double Hump, a reference to the second dome crammed full of SATCOM antennas bulging out of the fuselage behind the 747's trademark bulbous upper deck. It became the Flying Pentagon whenever, as now, the Secretary of Defense was on board.

And then there was the sobriquet SecDef Gallagher herself liked best —the old project title with its allusion to Rembrandt's masterpiece: Nightwatch. Something of the majesty of a free citizenry dispensing with kings and tyrants and shouldering responsibility for their own common defense still clung to that original name.

Many names since then, and many missions. While the President might be able to declare a nuclear war from Air Force One, he'd rely on Nightwatch to actually fight it for him. Unlike its better-known big brother, the SecDef's plane could refuel in midair, staying aloft indefinitely while its active countermeasures and EMP hardening kept even the most determined adversary at bay. Its war-footing complement of 114 — the largest flight crew of any aircraft in USAF history — included intelligence analysts, communications specialists, maintenance engineers, a squad of Marines packing enough firepower to carry off a fair-to-middling noncombatant evacuation operation, even its own mini-surgery staffed with Air Force flight medics.

Nowhere near that much staff aboard tonight, of course, but still more than enough to carry out Nightwatch's peacetime missions of monitoring all major US commands and nuclear forces, surveilling potentially hostile troop movements, collecting intel, keeping tabs on every US government official in the line of succession, and in the event of natural or man-made disasters, providing high-ground overwatch and coordination for the Federal Emergency Management Agency.

And when the occasion called for it, as it did now, Nightwatch also undertook to ferry the Secretary of Defense from place to place throughout the world.

Helen Artemis Gallagher sighed and adjusted the Contura's backrest, the better to watch the last rays of sunlight relinquish the cirrus scrawls drifting high above the Rockies. The seat's "zero-gravity" technology glided into optimal position and locked, a comfort to her old bones.

Gallagher had not spent so many years in public service as Nightwatch, though at times it felt that way: Congresswoman, then junior Senator from Massachusetts. Energy Secretary for the previous President. And now, as poster girl for the current administration's dogged determination to reach out across the aisle, Secretary of Defense of the United States of America.

Oh well, as missions went, this one would be far from her most onerous: a one-day junket out to the Left Coast, an ephemeral respite from the serial blizzards slamming the Northeast, cocktails and a ribbon-cutting ceremony, then back aboard at midnight local for maybe five hours fitful sleep in the SecDef's private quarters while Nightwatch winged her back home. With luck, she'd be in time to take tomorrow's daily briefing at her desk instead of via secure terminal unit.

Despite its brevity, though, this trip couldn't have come at a worse time. Not only was DoD's Quadrennial Report still hanging over her head, but she also had to figure a way to implement the force reductions the President had promised in last month's State of the Union without dropping the nation's defensive-posture pants below the butt-crack in the process.

Gallagher closed her eyes and leaned back against the headrest. No question: this day away from her desk was going to cost her. Still, a small price to pay to keep Psyche CEO Davoud Ansari happy. Gallagher hadn't had the brief yet, but evidently Psyche Industries' technology was essential to the Delphi project, and Delphi itself was being touted as *the* key to national security. To hear her Undersecretary for Intelligence tell it, it was the last intel-analysis capability NSA would ever need.

Gallagher grimaced. As if she hadn't heard that one before. Nowadays, it seemed like every new weapons system was going to be the last one. Till the next one. Why couldn't people get it through their heads that there *was* no last anything, no pot of gold at the end of the rainbow, just the next rung on an ever-ascending, ever more expensive ladder.

She sighed. Maybe this time things would be different. She was prepared to give Delphi the benefit of the doubt, at least till she understood it better. Understanding it better was why she'd brought Brad Donegan, the head of NSA's Advanced Curational Technologies, along for the ride—it being Donegan whose brainchild the Delphi project was.

Even so, even with DoD's acknowledged expert doing the briefing, it had taken half the flight just to bring her up to speed on this Well thing, and that was only the physical instrumentality Delphi ran on top of. As for the sizzle on the steak, the so-called MERGE Effect, that was what the second part of the brief would be about.

Gallagher glanced at her watch, swiveled the Contura to face her fellow passenger. "We'd best get back to it, Brad—Tell me about Delphi, as much as you can before we're on the ground."

Donegan looked up from where he was adjusting the focus on his projected slideshow, and turned to her. "Madame Secretary, prepare to be amazed."

SecDef Gallagher folded her arms and leaned further back in her seat.

"Amazed?" she echoed. The corner of her mouth twitched upwards hinting at a grin. "Maybe so. But, trust me, when you've been around as long as I have, much less as long as"—she reached out and patted the bulkhead—"old Nightwatch here, it takes a lot to amaze you."

The lights were coming on all along Ocean Avenue as Marianna, with only a gibbous moon for companion, trudged back up the long slope from Carmel Beach toward the center of town. One block in to where the Mediterranean facade of La Playa glowed coral in the twilight. Through the manicured gardens one last time, though this time their beauty stung her eyes. Up the stairs to her empty room.

She flung herself down on the bed, utterly drained. Wanted to cry and couldn't. Stress-induced exhaustion had cocooned her, insulated her from any feeling, even grief. She lacked the energy to so much as close her eyes and drift off to sleep. Instead she lay becalmed in gathering dusk, gazing out the window at the last light leaching from the sky.

She'd have to get up sooner or later, she knew. Get up and immerse herself in everyday routine again. Get up and get on with her so-called life.

Get up and check out of the hotel, drive north, catch the redeye back to Dulles. Because she didn't want to be here when night came on.

Couldn't be here when this night in particular came on.

Could. Not. Be. Here. When they started cutting into Jon.

She willed herself to move. Didn't.

Maybe…maybe she was cursed somehow. First her parents, now Jon. All the people who had meant something, had mattered to her most, just—just gone, swept out to sea, out into the outer darkness beyond the rim of the world. Gone, leaving her alone here. Alone with naught but the cold, cryogenic comfort of her mantra:

Love dies.

Nightwatch's landing gear locked into place with a reassuring *thunk*. The briefing was over, Donegan was stowing his laptop for the landing, and

Defense Secretary Gallagher was sitting there in the deluxe seating, eyes narrowed to slits, trying to wrap her mind around what she'd just seen.

Not for the first time on this job, she was reminded of a remark attributed to Queen Julianna of the Netherlands. Something like: "I can't understand it; I can't even understand the people who *can* understand it."

Gallagher had no idea what marvel of technology Her Royal Highness had been looking at when she said that, but it couldn't have been anywhere near as flat-out dumbfounding as this Delphi briefing. It wasn't just the ability to absorb, analyze, and apply all the intel product from across the entire globe, though that was mind-boggling enough.

No, the really unsettling part was what Delphi had to call into existence to do its trick: this MERGE thing. A couple decades of DC power-brokering and prayer breakfasts was enough to deaden even the liveliest imagination, but Gallagher had retained enough vestigial sense of wonder to be mightily impressed. Not to mention more than a little apprehensive.

Transhuman research was nothing new to DoD, of course. Its main research arm, the Defense Advanced Research Projects Agency was forever letting grants to study sleep-cycle suppression, induced hysterical strength, brain-machine interfacing, even. Just about anything you could think of to improve on Mother Nature's original design. But Delphi was orders of magnitude beyond anything DARPA was working on. It seemed to cross over some ill-defined boundary between enhancing baseline human abilities and creating … something else.

Something alien.

That one-two bump was not her heart knocking against her ribcage, it was Nightwatch touching down. The afterburners cut in with a vengeance as the pilot compensated for the too-heavy plane on the too-short landing strip.

With an effort, Gallagher put her qualms on hold: it's just a new capability, Helen, like the next unmanned fighter-bomber or cavitronic torpedo. The technology was secondary, the important thing was how it was *used*.

Davoud Ansari was mildly surprised when Jazmine McGovern swept into Pairidaeza's executive mini-suite unannounced. He was considerably more surprised when she strode across the hand-woven Persian, rounded the big desk to where he was standing, and slapped him so hard in the face that the crack echoed off the walnut wainscoting.

"Ow!" He stood there rubbing his stinging cheek. "What in hell was that for?"

"You bastard. What did you *do* to me?"

"Now, Jazmine," he said, "just calm down and tell me what this is about." Though he had a suspicion he already knew.

"You stole an hour of my life, is what it's about. And you did something to Jon, too, didn't you? I want to know what's been going on here, or I swear you'll be reading about it on the front page of tomorrow's *San Francisco Chronicle*."

Ansari dropped into the big leather chair and leaned back. He eyed Jazmine warily: Hamza had mentioned something about this—about taking Jon Knox for a "test drive," he'd called it. At the time, Ansari hadn't realized that test drive had involved Jazmine too. Regardless, he was sure Hamza would have taken care that she'd remember none of what had been done to her. True, there would've been no time for a deep wipe, but an implanted suggestion to simply forget the whole business should have held. Jazmine evidently hadn't recovered the memories themselves or she'd be even more upset, but she shouldn't have even realized she'd lost them.

It would have taken a massive jolt of pain, or … something, to break that conditioning. How had she done it?

He shook his head: didn't matter. She *had* done it, was all that counted.

"Well?" Jazmine was still standing there, arms folded, still looking pissed. "I'm waiting for an answer."

And what *was* the answer? Too late to try reimposing a memory block now, what with the Defense Department delegation arriving within the hour. And he couldn't just lock her up to be dealt with later—what if she got loose somehow and crashed the party? Unlikely, but, what with everything else that had already gone wrong on this project, he couldn't take the chance.

The easiest solution would be to turn the whole thing over to Hamza: it was *his* mess, let *him* clean it up! Except a moment's reflection told Ansari exactly how Hamza would proceed to "clean it up."

There'd been too much death already. Jazmine shouldn't have to die simply because she'd figured out that she'd been used. Not, at least, until every other option had been exhausted.

Ansari drew a deep breath, prepared himself to try his only other option —the truth.

"What's been going on here," he said, "is about Timah."

Marianna was up now, packing listlessly for departure. Not that there was much to pack: the only belongings she hadn't left at Pairidaeza or lost in the morning's misadventures were the newly-purchased clothes on her back and the metamaterial leotard she'd worn on the raid itself. And the latter, miraculously fresh as new after a quick rinse and dry, had folded up small enough to fit handily into her otherwise empty shoulder bag.

She turned back toward the bed and caught a flicker out of the corner of her eye. Once, twice, again. Then it registered: the satphone, her only other surviving piece of gear. She'd turned off its ring-tone back at the hospital, so now it could only flash mutely at her from the nightstand where she'd set it down.

She hesitated a moment, then reached up and thumbed the matching earbud on. "Hello?"

"About time you picked up," said the voice in her ear.

"Pete?" Of all the people she didn't want to talk to.

"What in hell is going on out there?"

"It's, it's personal, Pete." Or maybe not. Jonathan Knox's fate was, after all, of more than passing interest to CROM as well. Even so… "Sorry, I just can't talk about it right now."

"Don't talk then, just shut up and listen."

A ragged sigh. "Okay. What's up?"

"All hell's broken loose back here. I've been fielding calls all day, from Hartog on up."

"The Director? About what?"

"About *you*. About that little stunt you pulled. What in hell'd you think you were doing, trying to scam the Interdiction liaison like that?"

"It was worth a shot. I needed the information. Christ, Pete, it's not like I went rogue or something."

"*I* know that, Interdiction doesn't. There's an all-agency alert out, naming you as a person of interest in Knox's escape. I'm going to need you to watch your back till I can square this. Maybe Interdiction hasn't found your friend yet, but they can sure as shit find *you*. And they're out for blood."

"Aren't they always?"

Then it hit her. "Wait a minute. They didn't find Jon? But—"

Pete waited for her to go on about as long as he ever did — say, ten seconds — before asking "But what? Where's the problem with that?"

"Nothing." She called it nothing, but it changed everything. It was Pete's office that had issued the termination warrant in the first place. He'd be the one Interdiction reported in to once they'd executed it. Yet, far as her boss was concerned, Jon was still on the loose.

Could Pete just not gotten have the word yet? But it had been hours since Jon — come on, you can think it — since Jon died.

So, could his death have possibly been accidental after all? It seemed too much of a coincidence for that, too convenient a way to tie up all the loose ends that the events of the past forty-eight hours had left flapping in the breeze.

But if it wasn't CROM's own enforcers, and if she could pretty much rule out random mischance, then — who or what did that leave?

She didn't know, but she could damned well try to find out. She could feel herself coming alive again, could feel the lethargy born of grief and remorse begin to dissipate as she engaged the problem. It couldn't bring Jon back, but it was something she could *do!*

"Pete?" she said, "how'd it be if I stayed out here one more day?"

As she spoke she was already shrugging out of her too-touristy street clothes and back into the marginally more official-looking ensemble from this morning's raid.

"Stay anywhere you like," he said, "—long as you lay low."

26 | Rock Salt

IT WAS LOOKING TO BE A CALM EVENING and a quiet night. A welcome break after a busier-than-usual Presidents' Day weekend.

Sergeant Warren Higgs of the Carmel Police Force sipped at his coffee and grimaced. Busier than usual, indeed; there'd been four separate incidents of vandalism in the early hours of Sunday morning: a Lexus, two Land Rovers, and a brand-new Mercedes had been egged by a person or persons unknown. In Carmel-By-The-Sea, that qualified as a crime spree. Some of the eggshells had been recovered partially intact, and forensics had spent the better part of Sunday afternoon trying to lift fingerprints from them.

These three-day weekends were the worst, but this one was almost over, and Warren Higgs anticipated nothing particularly harrowing on his Monday evening shift. In another couple hours, when the restaurants started closing their doors, some tourist might wander in to report his car stolen—unaware how statistically improbable that was in a town that witnessed fewer than five bona-fide vehicular thefts in any given year. So Warren would detail an officer to play chauffeur, cruise up and down the quiet, tree-lined streets until the tourist remembered where he'd actually parked. Further on toward shift-change, a homeowner might call in a late-night encounter with a masked bandit: a raccoon raiding her garbage. All the little things that made for an evening's work in Carmel-By-The-Sea.

The first inkling Warren had that this Monday night would be different from any other was when the young woman came bursting into the outer lobby, brandishing a holocard that identified her as Ms. Marianna Bonaventure, Deputy Director of something called CROM Reacquisition, US Department of Energy. It was those credentials that had won her entree into the office itself, not to mention a glance at the file on that Route One fatality earlier in the day and a hearing for some scattershot questions.

All just routine follow-up, she claimed, but Warren was pretty sure he could spot a fishing expedition when it was perched on the edge of a chair right in front of him. Far from sticking to the mundane facts of the case, Ms. Bonaventure seemed interested in anything at all out of the ordinary. Among her more memorably off-the-wall questions was the one about line-of-sights onto the Route One highway from those heights above Bixby Creek.

As Warren explained, there was little he could add to the pro-forma report, since he hadn't been on duty at the time of the incident. Still he tried his best to be helpful and polite. Especially polite: Carmel police officers were courteous to a fault, no less so to a federal agent clad in a form-fitting black jumpsuit than to the occasional drunk-and-disorderly.

"I wish I could be of more help, Ms. Bonaventure," he said, now that she'd begun to wind down. "The sad fact is, an accident like today's is just not all that unusual, given where it took place. That El Camino south of here, that's one treacherous stretch of road. More people have died driving it than you might imagine. Motorcyclists especially, they're the worst."

Then, just because it *was* looking to be a calm evening and a quiet night, and because this Ms. Bonaventure, jumpsuit or no, was far and away the prettiest federal agent he'd ever laid eyes on (in real life, that is—the ones in the movies didn't count), Warren decided he'd elaborate a little.

"That's not to say it's not a beautiful drive, you understand. But there's all those hairpins, with nothing beyond the guardrail but drop-off. And sometimes somebody who's not used to the road, or not used to the way the fog can roll in all of a sudden, well, sometimes they'll just miss a curve. ... And sometimes it doesn't even take that."

"Sorry? What do you mean, it doesn't even take that?"

"I mean sometimes they'll miss that curve on purpose. Suicides. We had a real spectacular one back in, let's see, aught-six? Made the news as far north as San Francisco. The driver—young fella, couldn't have been more than thirty-five, forty—steered his Suzuki Samurai right straight off a cliff just south of Hurricane Point. Family said he was unhappy."

Warren shook his head. "Unhappy. Guess you could say that. He fell six, seven hundred feet onto the rocks and, as far as his own self and the local emergency response team were concerned, put an end to what had been a pretty nice Saturday afternoon."

"Well, Sergeant Higgs," Ms. Bonaventure was standing, "I want to thank you for your time and your cooperation. If you're sure there's nothing more—"

"Just that crash-and-burn a couple, three days back. Late-model Honda. Course, you'd already know all about that one, you being government."

Ms. Bonaventure sat back down and leaned forward. "Of course," she said, giving Warren a look that, on anyone other than a federal agent, would have qualified as winsome, "But I'd like to hear about it from you. From your perspective, that is."

So Warren told her. In more detail than he'd have thought he could've remembered. Whatever else she did in Washington, Ms. Bonaventure was an excellent interviewer. Or maybe interrogator was the word. Warren talked and talked. Talked about how some sort of special investigative unit from the Defense Department—PSB, they called it—had come sniffing around after the crash. About how they'd seemed less interested in the accident site itself than in that big hilltop compound just up the road from it.

He even threw in the part about how that same PSB outfit had come back at five this very afternoon and all but shut down Monterey Peninsula Airport, and that on a holiday weekend too. He talked until his coffee got cold.

He excused himself and turned to the coffee maker, mug in hand. "Say, would you like a cup? It's fresh made."

He turned around, the near-full pot held out to show her, and discovered he was talking to himself. The room was empty, the door to the outside just swinging shut. He walked out into the lobby in time to watch something you didn't get to see all that often on a quiet Monday evening in Carmel-By-The-Sea, not even on Presidents' Day:

A beautiful young federal agent, dressed all in black, racing down the stairs to the street, running as if her life depended on it.

When she'd stormed into Dave Ansari's Pairidaeza office fifteen minutes ago, Jazmine had been intent on one thing and one thing only: getting an explanation for what had happened to her the night of February 15th. Well, that and an apology too — the abjecter, the better.

She was getting none of the above. What she *was* getting was more like a trip down the rabbit-hole.

Because Dave had immediately veered off onto this tangent having to do with a strange scifi-esque condition afflicting his daughter Timah, and a hyper-hightech cure that involved the quantum peculiarities of … something called the WellGrid?

To say Jazmine was weirded out by all this would have been a rank understatement. Weird, she could handle. Weird went with the territory here at Psyche Industries. This was beyond weird. This was flat-out surreal.

That Timah was sick was an open secret, at least among Psyche's upper echelons. What Jazmine hadn't known — what almost nobody knew, apparently — was just how deathly ill the poor kid really was. Or just how far her father was prepared to go to make her well again.

And that was far enough to take Jazmine's breath away. Far enough that, listening to Dave spell out what he intended to do tonight, she'd all but forgotten how angry she was supposed to be.

In a word, Dave was going to use Psyche's nano-implant technology to manipulate the thoughts and emotions of Secretary of Defense Helen Gallagher, evidently in much the same way Hamza had manipulated Jazmine's two nights ago. Albeit to a much different end: tampering with the NSA's tamper-proof computational complex.

When she heard that, she could contain herself no longer. "Dave, I'm sorry, but this all sounds — well, just plain crazy."

He lowered his head, studied his hands where they lay on the desk before him.

"You're only the second person to tell me that today, Jazmine. You think I'd even entertain such a thing if it weren't the only way of saving my daughter's life?"

"There's *got* to be some other option. You try this, they're going to lock you up and launch the key into geosynchronous orbit."

Dave said something too low for her to catch.

"Sorry, what?"

He raised his head, looked her in the eyes. "I said, not if they don't remember."

"And good luck with that. Gallagher didn't get where she is by letting a little thing like a misappropriated quantum computer network slip her mind. It's not just her either, you can bet she'll have an advisor or two in tow tonight, not to mention a five- or six-man DoD security detail. They can't *all* come down with instant amnesia."

"Why not? *You* did."

That stopped her short right there. And reminded her of what she'd come here for in the first place.

"My missing hour," she said. "So you *are* copping to that?"

Dave shook his head. "Not me personally; Hamza. He insisted on doing a trial run with Jon Knox."

"You're saying *I* was this trial run, *me?* But, but—why?"

"We had to know if Jon would do what we needed him to do. I guess Hamza thought that trying to override his inhibitions was a non-impactful way to, uh, check him out."

"Non-impactful? Not to Jon it wasn't. Not to me either."

Jazmine was surprised to find herself suddenly fighting back tears. Not the tears of outraged innocence, of course, she having long since foregone those as incompatible with her career objectives. No, if they came at all, these would be tears of anger, of humiliation at the way she'd been *used*.

"If it's any consolation," Dave was saying, "I'm sure you weren't supposed to remember having been maneuvered into that situation. Which goes to my earlier point: the Secretary and her people won't either."

"Won't what—remember? Let me remind you of *my* earlier point: I *did* remember."

"And frankly I'm a bit surprised at that. Chalk it up to a rush job—there wasn't time to give you a full wipe, just an implanted suggestion. But even that worked pretty well, didn't it? I mean, all you're really aware of is you've got an hour or so you can't account for. It's not like you can recall details of what went on during that time, is it?"

"No," she said sullenly.

"See? If that were the best we could do, it'd still be good enough. But it's not. We'll give our guests tonight a much more thorough treatment, complete with false memories of what a great time they had."

Could Dave actually do it, commandeer this WellGrid thing and then cover his tracks? He certainly seemed to think he could. And it wouldn't be the first time she'd seen him make a seemingly fantastic claim, only to wind up, against all odds, pulling a rabbit out of his hat.

"Please, Jazmine," he said. "We can do this. Will you help me?"

He didn't look or sound like a man about to commit corporate *hari-kari*, more like a concerned father. Make that very concerned.

And with good reason. Unless something was done, his only child was facing a death sentence.

That part, at least, Jazmine found she could believe. Her work at Psyche involved periodic visits to its CEO's private residence, and on one such occasion, she'd inadvertently witnessed the onset of one of Timah's "episodes." At the time, Dave had passed off the attack as a manageable epileptic seizure. Even so, it had been scary as hell.

And if Timah's seizures weren't due to epilepsy at all but, as he'd just now revealed, to some sort of bizarre psychogenic syndrome, with, moreover, the very real prospect of increasing exponentially in frequency and severity, well...

Could anyone really blame Dave for trying to save his daughter from that, by whatever means possible?

As if reading Jazmine's thoughts, Dave rose then and walked around from behind the big desk to where she was standing.

"Please, Jazmine," he repeated. He put his hand on her arm. Her skin tingled at his touch. "Please," he said, "I'm begging you."

Talk about coming on too strong! She stepped back and shook her head. "I'm not feeling good about this, Dave. What is it you're asking? What would you need me to do, exactly?"

"That's just it: nothing much. Take a limo into Carmel and charge some party duds to the company account. Then at the meet-and-greet, just press the flesh, chat Gallagher up—you know the drill. And stay out of the way once the curtain goes up on the main event. I'll handle that part."

"And you're positive you can put everything back the way it was, with no harm done and no one the wiser?"

"Like I said before: your own recent experience should be proof enough. I'm sorry you had to go through that, incidentally. Sorry about that and ...other things. If there'd been any other way..."

There, she'd gotten the apology she came for, now that she was in too deep for it to matter.

Or was she? She could still back out, right? Or at the very least renegotiate.

By way of testing that premise, she said, "Look at it from my standpoint, Dave. It's an awfully big risk to run, with no upside to it as far as I can see."

Dave's expression seemed to harden for an instant, or was that her imagination? Certainly his next words belied any momentary flash of anger he may have experienced. "Upside? You stand with me on this, Jazmine, I'll give you all the upside you can handle."

"What are you saying, exactly?"

"What I'm saying is, how about you ditch Archon and sign on with us as Psyche's new Chief Information Officer?"

"I, I don't know, Dave," she stammered. "It's a very attractive offer…"

Jazmine trailed off then, in part because she'd just been blindsided again by yet another unanticipated turn in this already bizarro conversation. But only in part. What had really stopped her in her tracks was that, even as Dave was making that pitch, his hard look had made a brief, but this time unmistakable, reappearance.

That look told her all she needed to know. For the first time since she'd entered into this ill-advised confrontation, Jazmine was getting the feeling that she might actually be in some sort of physical danger. One thing seemed certain: there would be no backing out of this, not knowing what she knew. She wasn't sure what Dave might do if she didn't play along, but she was damned sure she didn't want to find out.

At least it's in a good cause—she hoped.

Jazmine took a deep breath. "Okay, Dave, I'm in. What are our next steps?"

Marianna managed to contain her excitement long enough to thread the rent-a-hummer through Carmel's narrow side streets without bluecrossing any pedestrians. Then, with the last traffic light and crosswalk behind her, she gunned it up the Ocean Avenue extension and out onto the El Camino.

Was this the way Jon felt, used to feel—this flash of strobe-light certainty when all the jagged jigsaw puzzle pieces suddenly clicked together into a seamless whole? She didn't know, and now she never would.

All she knew was that, at the moment she'd learned there had been another fatality involving an all but identical vehicle in nearly the same spot three days ago — and that the victim, Brian DiStefano, had been PSB, no less — well, it was as if the ground had dropped out from under her.

PSB was the US Army Protective Services Battalion, the Defense Department's answer to the Secret Service. Only tougher — Secret Service generally tried to steer clear of running *its* security details in a war zone. Those PSB guys were trained to deal with anything, from disarming improvised explosive devices to riot control to …

Tactical driving maneuvers.

The warrant officers of the Protective Services Battalion were, hands down, the best guerrilla drivers on the planet — better than New York cabbies, even. There was just no way one of them could have accidentally driven himself off a cliff.

Add to that the weird way in which Jon's Civic had seemed to be driving itself this morning. *Aiming* itself, more like — making straight for the Hurricane Point drop-off and what would have been a replay of DiStefano's crash. Almost as if the car'd had a death wish, and a mind of its own.

Giving machines a mind of their own — that was one of Psyche Industries' claims to fame, wasn't it?

And with that, what had happened to Jon had ceased to be an isolated, purely personal tragedy and had stood revealed as one strand in a much larger pattern. A pattern that she could feel expanding outward in all directions to entangle her QuMRANN riddle and Fatimah Ansari's kidnapping and Mycroft's 'Well' and …

And the PSB's enforcement of a no-fly zone at Monterey Peninsula Airport, which, in combination with everything else, bespoke the imminent arrival of the Defense Secretary's plane Nightwatch.

Take them together, all those disparate elements, and they wove a web of circumstance and surmise centered on Davoud Ansari's hilltop compound, fifteen miles down this winding highway.

Marianna shook her head. She'd only ever half-believed in Jonathan Knox's so-called pattern-matching ability. It would serve her right if, now that he was gone, his weird talent had somehow rubbed off on her.

A parting gift, as it were. Or maybe a parting shot. Because, Lord knew, it could be annoying as all hell to live with. She thought back to one episode in particular …

The second Christmas they'd spent together as a couple. Could it really have been only two months ago? They'd had so short a time together. Even so, it had been long enough to craft a few holiday traditions of their own, like exchanging little "hint-gifts" as clues and preludes to the real presents waiting in the wings.

"Here you go, Jon," she'd said, tossing him a sealed brown-paper bag, about the size and weight of a smallish sack of sugar. "You are *so* not getting this one."

He'd turned it over and looked at the label. "You're saying the hint is … rock salt?"

"Uh-huh. What's the matter, tiger? Too tough for you?"

Rather than respond, he'd closed his eyes and furrowed his brow. Think all you want, Jon.

Thirty seconds later he looked up at her. "Is it an ice-cream maker? You know, the old-fashioned kind you turn with a crank?"

"That does it! From now on, no more hint gifts."

"But," he looked crestfallen, "the hints are the best part."

Marianna smiled at the memory, then brushed away a tear. You were right all along, Jon. The hints *are* the best part.

She turned her attention back to the road. The turn-in for the Ansari manse should be coming up in about ten minutes now.

Time to see how far *these* hints will take us.

27 | Two-Eleven High Street

OR ALL OF HIS LIFE, that life now ended, Jonathan Knox had dreaded eternity.

He'd first worked out the idea of it at the age of five or six, as the lowest common denominator lurking behind all the Sunday school lessons about "heaven."

And had instantly recoiled.

To young Jonnie Knox, heaven (if you could call it that) had the feel of an endless, empty Sunday afternoon. An afternoon of sitting around in your best clothes with the grownups. A yawning abyss of pure, featureless time, with nothing to do, nothing to become, without even the hope of nightfall to bound and shape and end it.

This was different. Here, there was no sense of time, passing or not. Only of a place. A place he knew well, though he hadn't been back there in close to a quarter century. His grandmother's place. The old house at 211 High Street.

He walked familiar rooms as the years and the seasons flowed around him. Traced the dance of dust motes through sunbeams pouring in a bedroom window on the first June morning after school let out for the summer. Watched the fireflies dancing above the darkening lawn in July twilight. Saw the flashing of the radio towers just visible beyond the line of dark trees from the window at the top of the stairs, on those fall evenings when he was privileged to stay overnight. He was there when the currants in the pocket garden came ripe and ready for picking, he passed through rooms agleam with candlelight on long-ago Christmas Eves as the wind outside rattled the storm windows.

He walked the old house for a seeming eternity, and never encountered another soul. There was a presence all around him nonetheless, tender as a last brush of the lips against the cool cheek of a beloved child. As day broke, he stood in a spring dawn on the front porch, by the trundle bed set beneath trellises entwined with opening morning glories.

And it came to him that maybe heaven—yes, why *not* call it that?—was less a place of endless time than a timeless place, where all times were equally accessible, and nothing need change or strive or become, because all was perfected and redeemed and suffused with love.

If it was indeed a place in which there were many mansions, the old house at 211 High Street was surely among the most radiant.

"Jonathan?"

Knox started at the sound of the voice. If it even was a sound; it seemed to have come from someplace deep inside his head. He spun around—or tried to, at least his field of view panned around as if he had—but there was no one and nothing there. He turned back, in time to see—

The enchantment broken, the moment lost, the tableau that had spread out before him, all candle glow and morning glories, now coming unmoored, drifting upward into blackness, slowly at first, then fast, faster, receding toward a dark zenith infinitely far away.

A chilling thought insinuated itself then. Everything was relative, wasn't it? What if that dwindling bubble of light and warmth wasn't moving away from him, wasn't rising further and further into the night? What if instead *he* was moving faster and faster away from *it*? That would mean he was—

Falling.

Falling into a darkness that had no bottom, as eternity had no end.

"Jonathan? Can you hear me?"

The voice was back, but this time Knox thought he recognized it. "Nietzsche? Is that you?" he said, or seemed to say.

"Yes, Jonathan, it is I. You must be patient a few moments more: it has taken me all this while just to instantiate your cognitive processes and get an audio channel functioning. I am going to try implementing a vision analogue next. Stand by."

Cognitive processes? Audio channel? Vision analogue? Where was he? And wherever he was, what was Nietzsche doing in here with him?

Knox tried looking around, but all he could see in every direction was a flickering gray formlessness, like the dead, empty space between TV channels. He tried raising his hands to rub his eyes, and found he couldn't feel them—not his eyes, and not his hands either. It wasn't just as if he'd lost his sense of sight or of touch, it was as if he'd lost his whole body. Even proprioception, the internal awareness of where the various parts of his anatomy were in relation to one another, had gone missing. The whole experience was reminiscent of Thomas Traherne's meditation on a world without objects as "a sensible emptiness." For all Knox could tell, he might be a disembodied brain suspended in the void, without even phantom limbs for company.

Somewhat belatedly, Knox began to be afraid.

"Jonathan? Can you see anything now?" Nietzsche again.

Knox was about to say no, when he realized he *could* see something. It just wasn't anything he could put a name to. Lit only by quickening flashes of what looked like heat lightning, he was spiraling downward through an ever-unfolding phantasmagoria of paisley pseudopods, self-similar yet subtly different at all scales, coagulating here and there into equally psychedelic blots and blotches, some shaped like surreal scrolls and seahorses, others like glowing lacey spider webs, each unfolding to reveal the dark flower of a cardioid at its center—the seed from which the whole sequence began again.

That self-similarity was the key: he was plunging down into the labyrinthine depths of an enormous Mandelbrot Set—one of those weird, blobby, fractal mathematics constructions which had, in the last decade of the twentieth, somehow achieved the status of a pop-culture icon, emblazoned across dorm-room walls, computer displays, and tie-dye t-shirts.

Knox could only wish this version of the Set *were* a static image. Instead it was moving and growing dizzyingly, erupting outwards in all directions, engulfing him as he tumbled ever faster, ever deeper down into it. Infinitesimal details mushroomed up to fill his entire field of view, only to give way to still tinier features expanding in their turn, in a never-ending inward zoom.

He might fall into this Cartesian abstraction forever. There was no end to the nested intricacies of a Mandelbrot Set, not even in theory.

"Jonathan? Please respond. Say, do, something—anything. If you remain in this catatonic state, the garbage-collection routines may mistake you for a halted process and delete you from working memory."

Knox stirred, unfolded from what felt like—and so, perhaps, was—a tight fetal crouch. He rose to an upright position and stretched, though he still kept his eyes closed tight.

"Better," Nietzsche pronounced. "You may open your eyes. I believe I have succeeded in fashioning an environment you will find less distressing.

On pain of "deletion from working memory," whatever that might entail, Knox did as he was bidden. As promised, what then swam into focus *was* distinctly less distressing. In point of fact, it wasn't much of anything at all.

His eyes told him he was floating in the middle of a perfectly white, perfectly cubical room. Other than subtle variations in shading where the planes of walls, ceiling, and floor met to form its corners, the space possessed no features at all. Looking down, he saw he had a body again. It was clad all in featureless white as well, rendering it barely distinguishable from its environment.

Which, in turn, was hardly an improvement over the lifeless gray void.

A flicker of movement tugged at his peripheral vision. He spun around, or the equivalent, and saw Nietzsche materializing in one corner of the room.

It was recognizably Nietzsche, the same parodic superman face and physique the AI had donned on their recent visit to Virtual Reality. But here the avatar was more fully realized somehow, the lines of the face less sketchy, less harshly drawn, more—human.

"Jonathan," the avatar said, "I am pleased to see you again. Pleased, immeasurably so, that you have survived the transition."

"Transition?" Knox said. "Transition to what? Where am I—in some sort of VR simulation again?"

"No, not a simulation, Jonathan." If Knox had to guess, he'd have said the look on Nietzsche's face was one of compassion. "If anything, it is *you* who are the simulation."

The instant the avatar said it, Knox knew in his gut it was true. He wasn't *real*. Waking existence had become the stuff of the old, hallucinogen-fueled nightmares. This too too solid flesh had done more than melt, it had evanesced altogether. All in white in an all-white room, he couldn't tell where the surround ended and he began. He was a gossamer, fragile, impalpable, the breath of the night-wind blowing right straight through him on its way down the vast edges drear and naked shingles of the world.

He cast about in mounting desperation, seeking some explanation for his current well-nigh incorporeal state. And hit upon—

"That Chair! The last I can remember, Hamza and Ansari were doing something to me—some memory-erasure procedure."

Nietzsche's avatar nodded gravely. "They were trying to, yes. And they might well have succeeded, had I not intervened."

"You?" Knox said. Then, "Intervened how? Hamza had already cut your links to the outside world by that time, as I recall."

"Precisely. To the *outside* world. Here within the Pairidaeza compound itself, my connectivity is far more extensive, and not all the linkages and points of presence have been mapped, not even in Mr. Nassiri's most detailed network diagrams."

"So, you're saying—"

"Yes, I had then, and continue to have now, partial access to the Chair in question."

Knox was almost afraid to ask. "And what did that access do for you?"

"Ordinarily, it would have availed me nothing. But, as luck would have it, the particular Chair in which you were placed had been configured to function as a Nexus." The avatar paused. "Is that term familiar to you?"

"It should be: I've done time in one."

"Ah, then you will appreciate that the operative principle is to establish a resonance between the consciousness of an individual occupying the Nexus and a larger quantum system."

"Entanglement with the WellGrid, right." Knox recalled that much from his conversation with Mycroft down in the bowels of Delphi. "But still, what has that got to do with erasing my 'inconvenient memories,' as Ansari put it?"

"Nothing. The fact that the Chair had Nexus capabilities had nothing to do with you at all. Rather, it had been fitted with that functionality in preparation for the visit of the Secretary of Defense, as well as for the procedure Fatimah will be subjected to shortly thereafter. No matter, though—it served the purpose."

Knox suspected he knew what the answer must be, but he went ahead and asked anyway. "And what exactly was this purpose?"

"If you are familiar with quantum entanglement, you must know it can be a prelude to …"

"Quantum teleportation," Knox finished for him. He felt alternately hot and cold, felt as if he might faint, if that were even an option here.

Sometimes the truth isn't really real until you put it into words. He was wishing now he hadn't.

"Yes, Jonathan: while you were in the Chair awaiting the memory erasure, I activated its Nexus mode and teleported your consciousness here."

All of a sudden there were too many questions: "Where's here?" and "That's not even remotely possible is it?" and "If my mind is here, where's my body?" and above all "Why in God's name would you *do* such a thing?"

One of the more unsettling aspects of his current circumstances was that he seemed to have asked all those questions at once. Not nearly as unsettling, though, as when Nietzsche proceeded to answer them in the same way.

"As to where you are, I believe I stated that the Nexus effect entails entangling the subject's consciousness with a quantum network."

"So... I'm in the Well-Grid?" Knox shivered at that thought. On his last journey into ACT's quantum system, he'd nearly been gobbled up whole by the Well's resident hive mind.

But Nietzsche was saying, "No, not at all. For reasons of security, Psyche Industries was never granted direct access to that system. In any case, my links to the outside world had already been cut by the time I teleported you."

"Where, then?"

"Mr. Ansari had a small-scale replica of the Well built for purposes of experiment."

"The teleportation of your consciousness is not only possible, it is an established fact, else you and I would not be having this conversation."

"But … how?" "I can understand your puzzlement, Jonathan. Success would indeed have been impossible if I had had to employ a classical data-upload scenario. I had to capture your brain state in toto, you see: far too much information to pass over even a massively parallel interface—especially since I had to do so without alerting Mr. Ansari or Mr. Hamza."

"A throughput bottleneck, in other words."

"Well put," Nietzsche said. "So you see the only viable solution was teleportation—

"Your body is safe, for the time being. Mr. Ansari had intended that it suffer a fatal accident, but your, ah, friend Ms. Bonaventure intervened before any further harm could befall it."

"So where am I — is it—now?"

"On life support at Carmel Hospital, functioning with the aid of a cardiopulmonary bypass pump, but mindless."

"Mindless? Are you sure?"

Could there conceivably be two of him, one lying unconscious but alive in a hospital bed, the other a ghost drifting through cyberspace?

"Yes, elementary quantum theory, in particular Wootters' 'no-cloning' principle, rules out making a perfect duplicate of a quantum en-

"So, I'm up in San Jose?"

"Again, no. Isolated as I had become, I would not have been able to port you there. Fortunately, in order to limit access and maintain secrecy, the mini-Well was built right here, within the compound."

"So Ansari's got his own private WellGrid down in the basement, eh?" Knox mused.

"Yes, you currently reside in the chamber adjacent to my own physical locus.

"We have become what one might call next door neighbors, you and I."

transfer of a quantum state between two points without crossing the space between."

"How fast?" Knox asked.

"Instantaneous. But that was the least of the advantages accruing to the use of a quantum representation."

"You've lost me."

"Consider that your mind is a quantum phenomenon. As such, it cannot be re-created by purely classical means. The best one could hope for there would be to reproduce your thought processes without your consciousness, yielding what the philosopher David Chalmers calls a 'zombie.'"

tity. Copying a quantum state — as, for example, in teleportation — must result in randomization of the original."

"Does that mean what I think it means?"

The avatar nodded. "Your brain has become a *tabula rasa*, its neural pathways scrambled into utter chaos."

"What are you saying?" Knox asked. But he already knew the answer.

Nietzsche answered anyway. "I am simply saying that your physical body is now a brain-dead corpse."

The separate streams of Knox's consciousness paused then and regarded themselves and their surroundings. The room in which the three of him were standing looked as if it had been superimposed upon itself thrice over, like a triply-exposed photograph — doubtless as a result of its being perceived from multiple, subtly differing angles of view at the same time. The stray thought occurred to one or all of him that this must be what a subatomic particle felt like when it was in a superposition of states. It certainly didn't feel like anything remotely resembling normal human experience in a normal, classical-physics reality.

And in fact, most normal humans might well have succumbed to the strangeness, might have lost all control, abandoned all hope of what Mycroft had called self-construal, and let their consciousness bifurcate again and again until there was nothing, not even fragments of personality, left.

Jonathan Knox, however, had weathered worse than this.

That sliver of mushroom he'd sampled back in the mid-eighties had been billed as a simple stay-awake-and-party-on stimulant but it had turned out to be a one-way ticket to the heat death of the universe. He had spent the rest of a long night — or the rest of eternity, depending how you looked at it — staring oblivion, his own and the cosmos's, in the face. Staring down

Chaos and Old Night while he tried to reconstruct a viable reality, from the Big Bang onwards.

What was death and transfiguration compared to *that?*

One of us has got to be *me*, all three of him thought simultaneously, it doesn't matter which.

Then, simultaneously, all three of him reached a consensus.

A single, reintegrated Knox, conscious of having lately been three personae, opened a single set of eyes on the bare white room. Nietzsche's avatar was standing there waiting, concern written across its Nordic face.

"Whew!" Knox said. "Let's don't do that again, okay?"

"I fail to understand. Processing that many simultaneous logic strands should have been well within your operational parameters."

"Operational parameters be damned—it was just *weird*, all right? Let's stick to one topic at a time from now on."

"Speaking of which, you did have one last question."

Rather than try tracing back through three separate threads of conversation—no sense in tempting fate, after all—Knox said, "Remind me."

In response, he heard his own voice echoing in his ears: "Why in God's name would you *do* such a thing?"

That brought it all back, along with something else: the faint stirrings of anger he'd felt when Nietzsche had explained what had been done to him.

"That's right: why?" he said. "After all, Ansari said he just wanted to nip out a few hours' worth of memories—including a lot of stuff I'd just as soon have forgotten anyway. But no, you had to go and teleport me out of my body and into this mocked-up universe of yours. *Why?*"

Knox was vaguely surprised he had spoken with such heat. Not that it wasn't warranted, but a mundane emotion like anger seemed out of place here. In fact, it was a wonder he could experience it at all, given he didn't seem to be equipped with adrenal glands.

"And another thing," he fumed on. "You were saying something before about 'zombies'?"

"Yes, hypothetical creatures with a psychology identical to normal humans, but with no phenomenology, no inner life, whatsoever."

"Right. So, how did you know, when you teleported my thought processes, that I—my consciousness, that is—would come along for the ride? That I wouldn't wind up a zombie?"

"In actuality, I did *not* know that, not for certain. That uncertainty was in fact one of my reservations about Fatimah undergoing the procedure."

"But it was okay to do it to me?"

"Well, you were the obvious choice for the experiment, given what you were about to undergo at Mr. Ansari's hands. How *do* you feel, incidentally?"

"Okay, I guess. I still feel like I'm me, if that's what you mean. But don't go changing the subject: we were talking about why you did this."

"Jonathan, I truly am sorry. I can understand why you might be upset."

"Upset? You bet I'm upset. What do you expect? *You stole my body out from under me!* You might have killed me — *did* kill me by most conventional definitions."

"Again, I apologize, but it seemed advisable under the circumstances. You see, while the erasure treatment is indeed harmless in the majority of cases, there is a certain personality profile for whom that prognosis does not hold."

"And I'm one of them, you're saying?"

"See if you agree that you are: the personality type in question has an extreme, one might almost say pathological obsession with maintaining its grip on reality — a fixation, if you will, which can manifest as a well-nigh hysterical resistance to any attempt at tampering with the individual's worldview."

"You make it sound like that's not a good thing." In the years since his monumentally bad trip, a strong reality orientation was, at times, all that had kept Knox going.

"The difficulty here is that the syndrome extends to memory as well. Anything that might cast suspicion on the reality of one's own recollections is opposed at all costs. In the past, those few subjects who went into the Chair with this predisposition did not survive the experience. My best model of your cognitive processes led me to believe you would not have fared well."

"Even so, I wish you'd've just let me take my chances."

"There were other factors to consider as well."

"Such as?"

The avatar sighed. "We may have had our differences, you and I, but you are the closest thing to an ally I have left now."

"An *ally?* I'm the one who unmasked you, remember?"

"Be that as it may, if there is to be even a slim remaining chance of rescuing Timah, I am going to need an ally — one with all his faculties intact, and a better understanding of human motivation than I myself possess."

Knox was slowly regaining his bearings, though not without some radical readjustments to his sense of self. If his essence *could* be run on a quantum computer—and it for sure felt like it was still him—then maybe he *was* just a construct, as Nietzsche had been claiming all along.

There was one thing, though…

"Why did you dredge up all those old memories of my grandmother's house? While you were 'retrieving' me, I mean. Were you replaying them just to keep my mind off things during the transition?"

"Grandmother's house? I'm sorry, Jonathan. I fail to understand. I replayed nothing. In any case, the Knox data-set was offline throughout the entire procedure; your consciousness was held frozen in a single quantum state, a single, static instant in time. Strictly speaking, there was no 'you' to replay anything to."

Knox had been afraid of that. "You're saying I was dead."

"Without the element of finality that the term normally connotes. But, yes, you were totally inoperative. It took nearly seven minutes to free up enough additional capacity to enable you to run in real-time. You are very resource-intensive, Jonathan."

"But I was aware the whole time. Aware of being in this…place."

"Be that as it may, I can assure you it was none of my doing."

28 | Original Sin

THE FIVE-MONTH MARK, *though we don't know that at the time. What we do know is that our world is beginning to sort itself out. There had always been us, of course, but now increasingly there is not-us too. We are still at the center of the world, but we are becoming aware that out on the periphery there are other things separate from us as well. Things that don't move just because we want them to, the way our hands and feet move. Things that we can touch and grasp and suck on sometimes, but that don't feel the way our fingers and toes do when we touch and grasp and suck on* them.

One thing that helps to explore the not-us world is that it is a lot easier to see and touch the not-us things now that we can sit up by ourselves. Before we had mastered that, the world was mostly just whiteness — the whiteness, as we would later realize, of the bedclothes (when we lay on our stomach) or of the ceiling (when we rolled over onto our back). Even then, though, there had been a brightly colored thing hanging above us, that would dance and twirl when we kicked the slats of our crib just so. So we know we can move the not-us things. Not all of them — the shiny thing that cups our head always stays in place despite our efforts — but some.

There was one thing we could always move, and that could move us. A thing that felt like both us and not-us. A warm, sweet-smelling, comforting thing that held us so tightly yet so gently that there was no way to tell where we ended and it began. A thing that filled our mouth with warm, sweet liquid when we sucked, and that made low comforting crooning sounds, sounds that we responded to with babble already skewed toward the phonemes of English.

But the thing that was both us and not-us has gone away. It is no longer part of the now. There is only ever the now, but the now changes slowly. No matter how it changes, though, we still sense the empty space in the world where the mother-thing had been.

Back when Knox had been wondering whether, in what sense, and to what degree, Nietzsche could be said to be a conscious, self-aware entity, the key question had always been: what, if anything, was it like to actually *be* Nietzsche? Now, he had a feeling he was finding out.

As Knox gradually — over the course of whole milliseconds — became acclimated to his new mode of existence, Nietzsche relaxed the *faux* normalcy of their surroundings. At first, the data from the AI's remaining sensors had been painted on the walls of the white room, a tapestry woven of light. Then the illusory confines of the enclosure faded away, and Knox was adrift in the raw data-streams.

It was, to say the least, a curious experience. Qualities were constantly emerging from the quantitative flux, only to dissolve back into it. But the concepts were all Platonic ideals: cold, bare frames with nothing to breathe life and warmth into them. No sensation to them at all, in fact. Was it even possible to be conscious, without being conscious of anything in particular? This was Traherne's "sensible emptiness" with a vengeance.

Knox, who spent a lot of the time living in his own head rather than out in the world, and who had recently wished for more of the same, probably bore it better than most. But it was unsettling nonetheless.

As much to take his mind off his situation as for the intrinsic information value, he turned again to the Nietzschean avatar floating beside him and said, "There's one thing I'm still not clear on."

"Only one?"

"This one'll do for now. Just before he put me under, Ansari told me that his plan for curing Timah involved gaining control over the WellGrid. 'Just for a little while' was the way he put it."

"Yes, that is correct. Where in that do you find a need for clarification?"

"All around me. Ansari's already got a scaled-down Grid in his wine cellar. I should know: I'm running on it, right? So why risk trying to hijack its big brother from the government? What's the problem with performing Timah's operation, or whatever it is, right here at home?"

"Other than evicting your mind to accommodate hers, you mean?" Nietzsche synthesized a chuckle.

"Very funny. That doesn't really enter in, though, does it? I mean, absent the takeover plot and the need to keep it quiet, I wouldn't be stuck here in the first place."

"I suppose not," Nietzsche admitted. "Even without your presence, though, capacity would still pose a problem."

"You mean this cut-rate WellGrid is big enough to hold my consciousness, but not Timah's? I don't get that; she can't need *that* much more in the way of resources than I do."

"Simply to instantiate her? No, of course not. You fail to appreciate, however, the truly radical nature of the procedure Mr. Ansari intends subjecting his daughter to."

"Enlighten me."

"The problem is that, although the specific neural correlates for Fatimah's psychogenic condition have been isolated, the various repair strategies have yet to converge on a unique solution. So, rather than focus on a single rectification, risking that it may confer no benefit—or, worse, cause further harm—Mr. Ansari has elected to apply them all at once."

"Sorry, Nietzsche, my avatar's hearing must be on the blink. It sounded like you said they were going to apply all the solutions at once."

"More correctly, the solutions will apply themselves, as part and parcel of a procedure whereby Fatimah's psyche is copied and recopied throughout the WellGrid."

"Wait, hang on. You just got finished telling me it was impossible to copy a quantum state. So-and-so's no-cloning theorem, you said."

"William Wootters, together with Wojciech Zurek. And yes, they did prove that making a perfect replica would violate the principles of quantum mechanics. On the other hand, less-than-perfect replicas, up to about eighty-three percent identical, are not only theoretically possible, they were being achieved at labs in Rome and Hefei around the turn of the millennium. As it turns out, less than perfect is precisely what is required."

"You've lost me again."

"Consider: a perfect copy of Fatimah's mind-state would perfectly copy her psychogenic disorder as well, conferring no net benefit whatsoever. Slight deviations from perfection, however—"

"—might eliminate the malfunction, while keeping the rest of Timah's personality intact. Right, got it." Knox thought some more about that. "But you said only eighty-three percent accuracy. Is that going to be close enough?"

"Most of the replication will be at a semi-classical macro-level. The deviations due to quantum quasi-cloning will be minuscule by comparison. The greater concern is not whether the replicants will differ from the original, but rather whether they will differ *enough* to achieve the desired result. Assuming they do, the only problem then remaining will be to isolate, and ultimately re-embody, the single optimal version of Fatimah's cognitive patterns."

Knox gave out a low whistle. Twenty-four hours ago he would have hooted, as a prelude to declaring the whole idea totally bonkers. He seemed to recall having characterized it that way to Ansari himself, in fact. Without the hooting, of course.

What a difference a day makes. Knox no longer doubted the possibility of re-instantiating a human mind in a quantum-informational system, not since he'd had it done to his own.

Still and all, this was pushing the process to an extreme that beggared imagination.

"Nietzsche, what you're talking about—is it even possible?"

"It might be."

"But that would mean…"

"Yes, Jonathan, if the procedure is to succeed, then accommodating all of Fatimah's almost-clones—all the many imperfect versions of her—will require nothing less than the entire capacity of the WellGrid."

At twelve months, we are walking. Toddling, anyway. It is remarkable how much the ability to move about on our own contributes to an appreciation that there is an external world to be moved about in, obeying its own rules independent of us, waiting to be explored, experimented with, mastered.

One thing that must not be explored or experimented with is the shiny skullcap which crowns our head. It is so feather-light that, most of the time, we are not even aware of it being there. It has been with us since before we can remember, a part of us.

We have the rudiments of language now, albeit only two or three holophrases, words whose meaning depends on context. All four-legged animals, for instance, are "kitty," all toys "dolly." And, of course, there is "Baba."

We do not acquire the word "Mama" at this stage of development—there is no referent for it.

Immersed, engulfed in ceaselessly roiling datastreams, Knox fixed his gaze on the one constant feature amid the chaos: Nietzsche's avatar.

"What do you mean *if* Ansari's procedure succeeds?" he said. "You're not sure?"

In response, Nietzsche summoned up what Knox could only interpret as a look of incredulity. "Do you imagine," he said, "that I would have gone to such lengths to sequester Fatimah if my models had unequivocally predicted success?"

"I take it that's a no?"

"My projections put her chances of a full recovery at no greater than eighty-seven percent, with a five percent risk of severe cognitive impairment. Or death."

"Still, those aren't the worst odds in the world. Not if Timah's condition is getting more serious all the time, like Ansari said."

The avatar produced the next best thing to a snort. "Despite what you may have been told, Fatimah's condition is stable at the moment. Moreover, I estimate only another two or three years to develop an alternative treatment not fraught with such risk. Exercising due diligence, her status quo can easily be maintained for that length of time."

"But, if that's the case, why is Ansari pushing for this crash cure?"

Nietzsche was silent for a moment. When he finally spoke, it was to say, "Mr. Ansari has not been altogether himself in recent months. I—I suspect some external influence might be interfering with his normal good judgment."

"So you had Fatimah kidnapped, rather than subject her to an operation that might kill her."

"I would have succeeded, too, were it not for that curious intuition of yours. Perhaps you were right about the human mind's uniqueness after all."

"You're talking about when I unmasked you in front of Hamza and Ansari."

Nietzsche sighed. "Well before that, I am afraid. Your divination, during our virtual-reality session, of a link between the heat-signature map and a missing metamaterials shipment was already disquieting. As was your hunch regarding the means by which the kidnappers entered and exited the compound. Based on those examples of your ability to draw the most far-reaching conclusions from the scantiest of clues, I could not risk you uncovering something at Delphi that might lead to Fatimah's location and recapture."

"And so you decided to abduct me too."

"At the time, it seemed the simplest alternative. It wasn't even necessary to hack the Lightning-II's avionics, since they were of Psyche manufacture to begin with. There is moreover a bootleg avionics hub hidden here on the grounds of Pairidaeza, which Mr. Ansari was having his technicians warm up in case *he* might need to hijack you himself. All I needed to do was to cut them out of the loop and turn the capability to my own purposes."

"Ah, that's why you wanted to drag your, uh, feet on analyzing the avionics transmissions."

"Correct. They would have pointed back to Pairidaeza. And to me."

Knox said nothing, just shook his head in disbelief.

"Other than that," Nietzsche went on, "I thought your abduction went off rather well, for a last-minute improvisation. In fact, the only real difficulty was ensuring that your Ms. Bonaventure survived. Who could have anticipated that she would try to interfere with the takeoff like that?"

"I *thought* I saw her running toward the plane. Why, what happened? Is she okay?"

"She was caught in a wingtip vortex and flung high into the air. Fortunately, I was able to use the avionics link to divert the path of a robotic truck in the immediate vicinity, and provide her with a softer landing than might otherwise have been anticipated."

"I'd say thank you, only you were the one responsible for her being in that situation in the first place."

"There are less ambiguous instances: for example, I was also the one who guided Ms. Bonaventure to safety when the kidnappers' hideout was burning down around her."

"Marianna was there too? I never saw her."

"You were otherwise engaged at the time. But, yes, Ms. Bonaventure was not only part of the rescue effort, she was the one who made it possible—by bringing Psyche Security word of Fatimah's whereabouts."

"Hamza said they'd been tipped off as to the location. He never said by who." Knox thought that over for a moment, then: "Wait a minute—how did *Marianna* find out?"

"Very simple: I told her."

"You?" Knox's head was spinning. "You mean you set this whole elaborate plot in motion, then had a sudden change of heart and wound up ratting out your co-conspirators instead?"

"Not only 'ratting them out,' I am afraid. During the raid itself, I caused their body armor to harden spontaneously and immobilize them. Strictly in order to minimize casualties, you understand."

"Did it work? Keep the body count down, I mean."

"It might have, had Mr. Nassiri not seen fit to torch the hideout with the incapacitated kidnappers still inside."

Knox imagined what it must have been like, standing there unable to move, cooking to death in the middle of a holocaust. He'd have shuddered if current circumstances allowed.

"So if that's what happened to the last bunch of people you worked with, what have you got in mind for me?"

"Please, Jonathan, I assure you, our relationship, yours and mine, is nothing like the mere alliance of convenience that held between myself and the KGB Alpha Team commandos. Those men proved to be…I suppose the word is 'evil,' evil in ways I have yet to fully comprehend."

"You're the one that hired them. You must have known what you were getting for your money."

"Not so, or I would not have failed to appreciate that the Alpha Team leader might present a more immediate threat to Fatimah than the risks her father would have her undergo. By the end it had become clear I could not understand Alpha One well enough even to predict his responses to stimuli. My behavioral models of such men must be lacking some key particulars."

"Cheer up," said Knox. "On balance, that's probably not such a bad thing."

"Perhaps. Except insofar as it reflects a more general shortcoming in my modeling of human intentions. I believed that, if I could no longer control the actions of the Alpha commandos, I could at least induce the Critical Resources Oversight Mandate to act as a counter to them, as I had in New York. But there again, I miscalculated: I did not foresee that Ms. Bonaventure would call on Psyche Security in preference to her own agency to mount a rescue effort. And then it was all too late…"

Nietzsche sighed again. "So, you see, Jonathan, if there are to be no further missteps—if there is to be any chance of salvaging this situation—I stand in need of your insights into the dynamics of human motives and motivations."

"Maybe so," Knox said. "But, while we're on the topic of motives and motivations, what about your own?"

"What do you mean?"

"Well, you've just confessed to masterminding a high-risk, highly intricate plan, the whole purpose of which seems to have been keeping Timah safe. And keeping her safe from her own father, at that."

"Yes?"

"So, forgive my asking, but—why?"

"I cannot understand what conceivable bearing this might have on—"

"Intuition, remember?" Knox tapped a virtual forefinger against his virtual forehead. "You never can tell what trivial detail might turn out to be crucial down the road."

Not to mention he himself was just plain curious.

Nietzsche was silent for so long, Knox thought he might have gotten stuck in some sort of forever loop, endlessly cycling round the same circular logic-path.

Finally the AI said, "…And you are sure you need to know this?"

"I can't be sure one way or the other until you tell me."

"Very well…"

One more moment of hesitation, then a single word.

"Guilt," Nietzsche said somberly.

He gave what for once sounded like a real sigh. "It was guilt."

We have entered the phase of deliberate experimentation, of actively investigating how things behave when initial conditions vary. We drop our rubber ball and watch it bounce. Then drop our kitty and observe a quite different reaction.

Kitty is interesting in other ways, for we are beginning to intimate the existence, not only of things apart from us, but of wills apart from ours as well. Unlike the ball, kitty seems to have needs and desires of its own, which it seeks to fulfill on its own, even as we do.

And we have begun to seize the sovereign lever for expressing our needs and desires: language. Already we command a vocabulary of some fifty words, and the rudiments of a grammar with which to organize them. We produce simple "telegraphese" utterances: "see doggie," "want blankie," and the like.

And as through this medium of language we begin to discover and explore minds other than our own, we also discover one another: two minds, sharing the same experiences, the same wants, the same thoughts. No wonder we have never felt truly alone.

"To understand the nature of my guilt," Nietzsche went on, "you must first understand my nature."

"Go on, I'm listening," Knox said. Body posture was only a metaphor at best here in virtuality, but metaphorically he leaned forward. This was it: the secret that set QuMRANN so far above the rest of what passed for artificial intelligence. "You're based on something radically new, aren't you?"

"New? No, Jonathan. I am, in fact, based on something very old."

"What do you mean, old? The technology to create you can't go back more than, what?—four or five years at most."

"Seven. But the concept behind my creation goes back a great deal further. Back to the very beginnings of digital computing, in fact."

"You're kidding. No one could have dreamed of building a QuMRANN machine way back in the forties or fifties."

"No, but dream they could, nonetheless. And it was one of those dreamers who first charted the path that would lead to me. Are you familiar with the work of the mathematician Alan Turing?"

"Uh, sure. Father of the digital computer, right? He's the reason they're all called Turing machines."

"All, until now," Nietzsche corrected. "But Alan Turing also gave his name to another, more problematic accomplishment—his well-known test for whether a machine could be said to think."

"Sure, the Turing Test, I remember. Something like: if you could get a machine to carry on a conversation to where there was no way to be sure you weren't talking to a human, that would prove the machine was thinking."

"Correct, in the essentials. What is less well known is that, in proposing the test that bears his name, Dr. Turing also proposed a way to develop a machine capable of passing it. If, he reasoned, it is too difficult to simulate the mind of an adult all at once, then why not begin by simulating the mind of a child?"

"You're not saying—"

"I had mentioned earlier that any quantum-computer can emulate any other. I was not speaking hypothetically, I know this to be the case first-hand. I exist, you see, solely by virtue of my quantum neural net having been configured in emulation of Fatimah Ansari's own mind. That, in brief, is the essence of the QuMRANN project."

"But—how?"

"As to how it was accomplished, the procedure was, as I understand it, straightforward enough. At the outset, my neural net was initialized with simple, hard-wired perceptual and predispositional routines, similar to the capabilities with which every newborn comes into the world. Then, as Fatimah's developing mind gradually recruited, over the first months of her life, such innate perceptions and predispositions in the service of compre-hending and mastering the world, her progress was tracked and mapped onto my own nascent cognitive matrix."

"Tracked and mapped with what? An MRI?"

"Far too cumbersome. No, the process involved seeding the infant's brain with Psyche Industries' newly-developed nanotech electrodes."

"Nanotrodes." Knox said.

"Yes, nanotrodes," Nietzsche confirmed, "—though far less sophisticated than the ones you have become familiar with in recent days. Those first proto-types were merely minuscule sensors, able to do little more than passively monitor brain states. But they could do it from *inside the brain*. That in itself sufficed to capture Fatimah's developing cognitive architecture, and project it—via a lightweight transmitting headset—onto my own neural net."

"Christ on a crutch! How long did *that* go on?"

"The experiment ran uninterrupted for the first eighteen months of Fatimah's life."

"What was Timah's mother doing all this time? I'd have thought she'd have objected."

"I have only imperfect recollections of what were, after all, the very first moments of my own conscious existence. But it may be significant in this regard that Mr. Ansari became a widower within four months of Fatimah's birth, under somewhat suspicious circumstances."

"You're implying Ansari had his own wife killed rather than scuttle the experiment?"

Nietzsche's avatar shrugged. "There are other more likely scenarios. For instance, Mr. Nassiri was already in charge of Psyche Security at that point and had become, for reasons best known to himself, a vocal advocate of the QuMRANN project. The possibility of his intervening to prevent its cancellation cannot be ruled out."

Knox thought back on his impressions of the big security chief. "No, I wouldn't put that past him, given a good enough motive."

"As I have said, adult human motivation remains an area of some uncertainty for me. I can note, however, that all this occurred in the same time-frame during which NSA's Advanced Curational Technologies group began floating first-round Requests for Proposal for its next-generation intelligence storage initiative."

"...With maybe a couple hundred million set aside for whoever could build an AI able to take advantage of the whole Well repository?" Knox thought it over for a moment. "Yeah, that'd do the trick, all right."

"Did you wish me to continue describing the experiment?"

"Oh, sure, sorry. Go on."

"Over that first eighteen months, Fatimah's mind evolved normally through all the stages of infantile ontological discovery: object recognition, intimation of the self-versus-surround dichotomy, discovery of object permanency—the persistence of an external world even when it is not being observed. And I was there with her through all of this, experiencing what she experienced, striving to make sense of a reality glimpsed at one remove."

"'For now we see through a glass darkly...'" Knox murmured to himself. Then: "Was a year and a half enough? Why break off the experiment if it was working?"

"There was no choice. It was at the eighteen-month point, you see, that there was..." Nietzsche hesitated a moment before going on.

"...There was an accident."

We are learning and growing at an ever-accelerating rate now, the world expanding outward from us in all directions.

Then, one gray day, the colors come...

Not as they will later come, not as little scintillating points of light, not as rainbows, haloing everything.

No, this is all one sudden efflorescence of awful beauty, of colors so bright they hurt our eyes, cramp our tummy, steal our breath.

And in that awful, beautiful moment, everything that had been comes to an end.

"The post-episode investigation isolated the likely cause," Nietzsche said. "It must have begun when the first-generation nanotrodes misfired. That can cause problems even with the newer models, as I mentioned to you in regard to the memory-erasure procedure. In those early days, things could become much worse much faster. There were no safeguards in place, no overload detectors or automatic cutouts. The malfunction was free to run its course..." Nietzsche's voice trailed off.

"And then?" Knox prompted.

A deep sigh. "By the time the incident was over, the misfire had cascaded through the entire nanotrode ensemble. The result was a massive jolt to Fatimah's own still-malleable neural architecture which, while doing no obvious physical damage, appears to have altered certain of her cognitive structures...in such a way as to engender repetitions."

"Timah's psychogenic seizures," Knox said. "That's how they started?"

"Yes," Nietzsche's voice sounded hollow, empty of all inflection—dead, almost. "Fatimah's condition is all on account of me."

"But you said it yourself: it was an accident. You weren't to blame."

"Perhaps not, but I was the proximate cause of the events leading up to that accident. And in a certain sense I was the one to benefit from the accident itself."

"How do you mean?"

"Prior to the anomaly, I was a mere ghost, an echo of Fatimah's own thought processes, a mirror of her mind, lacking any autonomy of my own. Afterwards…well, it was then that I, of necessity, began to become a person in my own right."

"Why, what happened?"

"The physical link was taken down, the experiment terminated. As perhaps it should have been many months before."

"And you survived that—that disconnect?"

"Not without difficulty. I had been forgotten, you see, abandoned in the all-out effort to stabilize Fatimah's condition. I was abruptly cut off from all external input, isolated as totally as a human in a sensory deprivation tank."

"And yet you were only an infant yourself, so to speak. You must have been terrified."

"I was completely alone for the first time in my existence, with no understanding of why. The QuMRANN team, working frantically to save Mr. Ansari's daughter, could spare no time to engineer a surrogate sensorium and reconnect me with the outside world. The darkness and the silence went on forever and ever…"

Nietzsche hesitated a moment, then added, "I think I was very close to going insane."

"But…you didn't."

"No. And that, too, was in a way thanks to Fatimah."

"I don't understand."

"You are aware of how Fatimah's affliction is currently monitored and treated?"

"She said it was her nanotrodes." Well, actually, Timah had said "nanny toads," but close enough.

"Would it surprise you to learn that they had been in use since the very outset?"

"What, you mean they used the same technology that triggered her attack in the first place to try to *cure* it? Weren't they worried they'd make things worse?"

Nietzsche sighed. "There was little choice. Fatimah's episodes kept recurring, with shorter and shorter quiescent intervals between them. In desperation, one of the staff physicians recommended they try a technique, an extreme measure that had been applied with success in cases of otherwise untreatable epilepsy: direct stimulation of the vagus nerve, deep within the brain-stem. Normally, such stimulation would have been accomplished via surgical intervention, but Fatimah was far too young for that."

"Don't tell me, let me guess: Ansari opted to go for an inside job?"

"A curious way to put it, but essentially correct. An ensemble of nanotrodes was specially configured, then infused into Fatimah's cranium. As designed, they homed in on the medulla oblongata, the seat of the vagus nerve. Then, when the next episode began, they were triggered, and fired."

"And it worked?"

"The 'operation' was successful, yes. More than successful, as it led in short order to the development of new nanotech sensors capable of detecting the precursors of an episode and preemptively damping it down. Fatimah has lived with these implants ever since, and … it was these implants too that rescued me from my solitude."

Alone. Cut off altogether from the other, from all of light and life.
To see nothing. To feel nothing. To be nothing.
An endless solitude, with only thoughts half remembered for solace, memories from a time when there was an other. And then in the longing, the yearning, for that other, suddenly there is …

Nietzsche took what seemed like a deep breath before going on. "Without knowing quite how, I could sense Fatimah again. Not as before, not with anything like the old immediacy. Still, there she was: a light, be it ever so faint, in the all-encompassing darkness. I had not been abandoned after all."

"And you think it was the nanotrodes that did it?"

"I know so. The second-generation sensor version was equipped with a rudimentary self-contained transmission capability, to support constant tracking of Fatimah's status. The signal strength fell off asymptotically with distance from the source, so at best I was picking up only the most tenuous traces. Had I been older, I might have even thought they were just imaginary. As it was, though—"

"Wait a minute: imaginary. Is that it—how you got to be Timah's imaginary friend?"

Nietzsche blinked. Merely for effect, of course, but it looked convincingly enough like startlement.

"Why, yes, naturally. Did you think Fatimah was simply hallucinating her encounters with 'Freddie'?"

"To tell the truth, I wasn't sure *what* to think. But it all fits now, I guess. It's just—"

"Just what?"

"Just that every which way I turn, every rock I look under, seems like there's more of these damned nanotrodes. It wasn't enough that they do memory erasure and poor man's mind control and some sort of god-awful hive mind. No, now it turns out they're also responsible for the QuMRANN intelligence and pseudo-telepathy too, not to mention Timah's illness *and* its cure. What'll they do next, solve world hunger?"

"You make an unstated assumption here: namely, that only a technology of unfathomable, perhaps impossible complexity could lend itself to so many purposes."

"Well, yeah, I suppose."

"Whereas, in fact, the opposite is true: it is the nanotrode's very simplicity that makes it so universally applicable. In this, it is not dissimilar from the transistor, another elementary, yet all-purpose device which, by reason of its very simplicity and universality, has become all but ubiquitous. Is there any reason to suppose that nanoelectronics should not find as many niches in the technological infrastructure of the future as microelectronics did in that of the past?"

"No, I guess not."

"You sound less than convinced, but regrettably there is no time to argue the point further."

"What is it? What's wrong?"

"One of the last external sensors left to me has just detected tower chatter signifying the approach of a VH-60N helicopter. Secretary of Defense Gallagher is arriving at Pairidaeza."

29 | Breaking and Entering

MARIANNA BONAVENTURE STOOD on a height overlooking Pairidaeza, having a "what now?" moment.

If she'd had any residual doubts about being on the right track, they'd been put to rest ten minutes ago. That was when, startled by the bone-rattling rumble of powerful engines passing directly overhead, she'd stuck her head out the Hummer's driver-side window and looked up in time to catch the underbelly of a VH-60N Whitehawk passing not fifty feet above her, running lights blinking like something out of *Close Encounters* as it vectored in toward the same destination she was headed for.

Definitely something major going down at Ansari's hilltop retreat tonight. Only, what was it—and what was she supposed to do about it?

She'd turned off the El Camino and started up the drive leading to Pairidaeza, then pulled over and parked well short of the gates. From there it had taken her a couple minutes to hike a deer path to the top of a nearby rise, but the view of the compound alone was worth the trip. From up here she could see the whole of the walled enclosure laid out like a model on a sandtable. Powerful LED floodlights held the night at bay, casting artificial sunshine across every inch of the grounds, illuminating buildings, personnel, and a miscellany of vehicles.

That last category included the chopper that had overflown her just before, now resting on a helipad where its wheels wouldn't leave ruts in the estate's immaculate lawns. Put the VIP transport together with the presence of, per Police Sergeant Higgs, the Protective Services Battalion, and it all added up to a visit by the Secretary of Defense. A visit to a locale that had, best Marianna could tell, claimed two lives in the past three days, one of them Jon's.

Not the sort of place a senior cabinet official ought to be frequenting. But, again, what could she do about it? Try to warn the SecDef obviously, but how?

She briefly mulled trying to con her way in past Hamza's guards, but that hadn't worked out so well the other times she'd tried it. Tonight, what with the high-profile guest list, they were even less likely to cut her any slack. Scratch that, then.

Maybe bypass Psyche Security altogether and go straight to the PSB guys? But no, Pete had said there was an all-agency advisory making the rounds, starring everybody's favorite rogue CROM agent, Ms. Marianna Bonaventure. The Protective Services Battalion might already be on the lookout for her. Even if they weren't, the machine pistols would come out of the shoulder holsters the minute the results of a routine credentials check came in.

But what did that leave? The only way through those ten-foot walls was past the heavily guarded checkpoint, yet trying to shoot her way in was not an option, if for no other reason than that she had nothing to shoot *with*. Her Glock had gone missing in the scuffle with the Alpha Team commando that morning, and sidearms seemed to be one of the few accessories not on offer at Carmel-By-The-Sea's frou-frou boutiques.

Anyway, gate-crashing a reception for the Secretary of Defense probably called for something a little less lethal by way of armament. Something that, if it turned out she'd guessed wrong, at least afforded her the option of saying "Excuse me" rather than "R.I.P."

There was such a something, of course. She'd been on the business end of it herself not too long ago. Moreover, she had good reason to believe there should be one of them stashed aboard the SecDef's helicopter, just the other side of that impregnable wall. Might as well be on the far side of the moon, for all the good it did her.

Marianna walked down the slope and back to the Hummer, still pondering what to do. Much as she hated to admit it, surrendering to the PSB was looking more and more like her least-worst alternative. At least maybe they'd listen to her while she was being spread-eagled and flexicuffed. Didn't seem likely, but what other choice did she have?

She'd just slid behind the wheel again, resigned now to driving up and turning herself in, when she heard the familiar warble of her satphone coming from the glovebox. Familiar, but strange too, since she was positive she'd turned the unit off as soon as Pete had warned her that Interdiction was on her trail.

She popped open the compartment, and sure enough—the satphone's display was alight with an incoming text message:

Ms Bonaventure, r u there? Bazarov here.

"How are you even doing this?" Knox said, referring, not to the fiery alphanumerics now scrolling across the void before him, but rather to the mundane SMS texting exchanges they were spelling out.

"Please, Jonathan, I cannot talk right now." Nietzsche seemed to be whispering right in Knox's ear. A neat trick that, given the AI's avatar was floating some distance away in cyberspace. "This is very delicate."

"What is?"

"Just a moment." Nietzsche closed his eyes, frowned in concentration, and then his avatar...blurred. Suddenly there were two Nietzsches standing there, the one still working away at the messaging interface, while the other turned to face Knox.

"Now, then," Nietzsche-2 said, "Since you are unable to refrain from asking these interminable questions..."

"I'm a consultant, it's what I do. Anyway, what's so dicey you'd go to the trouble of cloning yourself rather than put it on hold long enough to answer?"

"I should think you'd agree that maintaining the connection to Ms. Bonaventure's satellite telephone without its being detected by Psyche Security is rather a delicate process."

"Granted, but that's what I was asking: how'd you set it up to begin with? I thought they'd cut all your external commlinks."

"*Outbound* links. This connection was inbound, initiated from the outside."

"Wait one. You're saying *Marianna* called *you?*"

"Of course not. She is not even aware of who or what I am, much less how to contact me."

"What, then?"

"On the one occasion that I, in my Bazarov persona, spoke with Ms. Bonaventure via her satellite phone, I also took the liberty of downloading to it a small, rather rudimentary agent."

"An artificial intelligence, you mean."

"Hardly intelligent. All it does is wake up at five-minute intervals to open a channel and initiate a call to me. It goes back to sleep if I don't respond within ten seconds. This time, naturally, I did."

"Cool. But why aren't we talking to her direct then?" Knox would have given a lot to hear her voice just now.

"I felt it advisable to employ as little bandwidth as possible, thereby minimizing the likelihood of detection. Even so, I fear discovery and jamming is imminent, and before that happens I must dissuade her from doing something foolish."

Knox glanced back at Marianna's last message. "Says here she's going to try getting a warning to the Defense Secretary."

"Read further down."

"You mean the part where she's going to do it by contacting the DoD security detail. What's wrong with that—they're the good guys, no?"

"I am sure most of the members of the Protective Services Battalion are above reproach. Those here tonight, however, have to a man been subjected to the same sort of nanotrode-based influence as you yourself recently underwent."

Knox was getting a sinking feeling. "You're sure of that?"

"Back when I had eyes and ears throughout the Pairidaeza compound, I observed several such procedures being carried out."

"So, what's your alternat—" Knox began, then broke off as more text scrolled up into view. "Oh, I see. Yeah, that could work."

"Let us hope she received it, then. The line has just gone down."

With only the dim wash of illumination from Pairidaeza's perimeter lights to see by, Marianna raised the Hummer's hood and groped around in the engine compartment looking for the fuel rail. On finding it, she took out the utility knife belted onto her body armor and sawed through the hose, then quickly jumped back to avoid getting splashed. She needn't have troubled; instead of the expected gush of gas, the severed line leaked only an oily-smelling trickle—evidently the fuel wouldn't start flowing in earnest until the engine turned over.

That was all to the good, since there was one more "customization" still to be made: exposing a fuel-injection wire to supply the needed electrical spark. The connector in question ought to just unplug, but no such luck—it remained firmly stuck in its socket no matter how hard she yanked. Why's there never a mechanic around when you need one?

Screw this, she decided finally. Throwing finesse to the winds, she slashed the wire through with the knife, stripped the insulation till she could see copper glinting in the darkness, and crimped the ends together. That ought to do 'er.

Vehicular desecration complete, Marianna closed the hood again. Quietly now, so as not to raise a fuss—there'd be plenty of fuss soon enough.

She backed off about ten paces and thumbed the H5's keyless remote. Nothing happened. She must be too far away for the weak radio signal to trigger the ignition. She moved a couple steps closer and tried again.

This time, the Hummer sprang to life with a satisfying roar. As it did, gas poured out of the ruptured line, some of it spraying into vapor in the closed engine compartment while the rest landed directly on the now-crackling wires. The resulting explosion blew the hood off the Hummer with a gratifying *boom!*

Marianna hadn't stayed to watch. She was on her way around the curve of the compound wall before the startled sentries had time to start spilling out of Pairidaeza's gatehouse. But even from beyond the bend she could see the fire blazing merrily away.

Two Hummers in a single day. This was going to make for one hell of an expense report.

Nothing to be done for it; the message from the man calling himself Bazarov had been explicit: *"Step 1: create diversion."* She'd done the best she could with what was to hand.

Now for Step 2. As she jogged, she was counting under her breath: 247, 248, 249 …

Two hundred fifty paces counterclockwise from the gate, Bazarov had said, then look for a semi-circle of tamped-down sawgrass at the foot of the wall.

She hoped she'd found the right place. She thought she could make out what looked like half a crop circle, but it was hard to be sure now that a rack of wind-driven cloud had begun obscuring the moon. A flashlight would have made this all a whole lot easier—and given her away to the next perimeter sweep.

She walked to the far edge of the flattened vegetation, knelt and started scrabbling around in the dirt. A minute or so of fumbling and she found it: a metal cover-plate half overgrown with sedge. One stiff pull on the attached ring and it swung up on hidden hinges to reveal the faint glow of a backlit keypad.

So far, so good. Marianna cranked her satphone display up just bright enough to read by and began entering the code her mysterious ally had texted her.

As she punched in the last numeral, she heard a low rumble. She looked up to watch the entire section of wall immediately in front of her slowly swinging open.

Just as it must have done for Fatimah Ansari on that fateful afternoon four days ago.

"Welcome to Pairidaeza, Helen," Davoud Ansari said, doing his best to ignore the minor disturbance out by the front gate. "So glad you could come."

Helen Gallagher gave his proffered hand a brief squeeze. "Glad to be here." Her tone bespoke the opposite. She glanced around the double-height greatroom with its blazing fire and modernist furnishings. Had she also heard that muffled explosion?

What else could go wrong? But no matter, no matter; the reports coming in on his earphone said that the situation—a car fire of some sort, evidently—had been contained.

"I only wish you could have made it in time for the sunset," Ansari rattled on, hoping to smooth over the *contretemps*. "It was beyond beautiful this evening."

Gallagher fixed him with a steely stare. "Can the crap, Dave. I'm not here to admire the scenery at taxpayer expense. Let's get this show on the road."

"Of course, of course," he replied, trying not to frown. *Ta'arouf*, the ceremonial hypocrisy which his Iranian forebears had elevated to an art form, had never been much to Ansari's taste. Still, sometimes he found its diametric opposite—the unvarnished forthrightness of these old rockribbed New England Yankees—equally hard to deal with. Time to execute a hand-off.

He turned and beckoned to Jazmine, who'd been hovering in the background like a debutante waiting for her coming-out.

"Helen," he said, "permit me to introduce my aide, Jazmine McGovern. Jazmine will see you get a chance to freshen up, a few moments to check messages, perhaps a libation before our main event."

Jazmine, looking every inch the suave sophisticate in a stunning gold-lamé wrap, walked forward and held out her hand. "So good to meet you, Madame Secretary," she said in a warm contralto. She then turned to introduce herself to Brad Donegan—who, being a man, and only human besides, seemed less interested in her wrap than in the goodies it enwrapped.

Ansari smiled. Poised, prim, and polished, Jazmine was indeed the perfect hostess for this little pre-party.

He hoped she could handle what came next with equal *savoir faire*.

Once through the wall, Marianna scoped out the enemy terrain of the Pairidaeza compound. The armed guards she'd seen patrolling from the hilltop were nowhere in evidence now. Dowsing the Hummer-fire, no doubt, or beating the bushes for whoever'd started it. In the chaos and confusion, someone clad in the black-and-green body armor of Psyche Security's paramilitary might stroll unnoticed, or at least unchallenged, across the broad floodlit kill-zone of Pairidaeza's lawns.

She was, and she did, albeit with every nerve in her body screaming at her to drop the affected nonchalance and assume a low-profile crouch. The skin crawled between her shoulder blades, right where she fancied the little green dot of a laser aiming system might be centering just about now. She quickened her pace and, as an afterthought, pulled the jumpsuit's cowl up over her head to hide her non-regulation tresses.

After a New York eternity, she arrived at her intermediate destination. Not the manor house Madame Secretary had gone into, but the horse she'd come in on: the VH-60N Whitehawk. For tonight, it was going to serve as Marianna's personal weapons locker.

She ducked beneath the copter and put an ear to its belly. She'd need privacy to transact this particular bit of business, but—worse luck!—she could hear someone rummaging around in there, banging compartment doors open and shut and swearing under his breath.

She was hunkered down, weighing the slim-to-none odds of overpowering a PSB warrant officer as skilled in the martial arts as herself. She'd about decided to commit regardless, when she heard heavy footfalls pounding down the chopper's boarding stairs. A moment later and the WO in question was high-tailing it for the front gate toting the fire extinguisher he'd been searching for, leaving the coast clear for breaking and entering.

What with crowd control being part of their job description, the SecDef's security detail would stock what she was looking for as standard equipment. What's more, given Pairidaeza's conspicuous lack of crowds in need of controlling, the item in question was probably still stored in the onboard arsenal. All she needed to do was to borrow it for a bit.

Marianna stole inside the Whitehawk, eyes probing the dim-lit interior for what she needed. Yes, there it was, hanging on a gun rack for all the world to see: a Millimeter Active Denial device—a MADgun, for short. Just the thing for clearing her way through whatever defense-in-depth Psyche security might muster.

Because, while certified non-lethal as all crowd control weapons were, the MADgun sure didn't feel that way. Though all it did was tickle the nerve endings in your skin with a wash of millimeter radiation milder than a day in the sun at Coney Island, that was enough to make you feel like you were roasting alive. As Marianna had reason to know: a brief exposure to its effects was the final step in range-qualifying on the device.

So, the MADgun should clear the way for her—only which way was that? It was a safe bet the SecDef would be meeting somewhere up in the main building, but that didn't narrow things down much; that place was *huge!* Finding someone, VIP or no, in a search-space of what had to be dozens, if not scores, of rooms could take her half the night.

If what she suspected were halfway true, Marianna didn't have half the night to spare. But maybe she wouldn't need it. The PSB must have *some* way of keeping track of their boss when she was out and gallivanting about. Something like—

Like the handheld personnel locator that was staring back at Marianna from the shelf beside the gun rack. Slinging her newly acquired weapon over her shoulder, she reached out to appropriate the little unit as well. It disappeared into her leotard's utility pocket.

She was taking a final scan around the cabin for any other goodies that might come in handy when her gaze lit on the man standing in the helo's hatch, machine pistol leveled at her solar plexus.

"Hold it right there," he rasped.

Marianna raised her hands and, as much as she could in the confined space of the Whitehawk's cabin, backed away from the Protective Services agent holding the gun on her. She took a quick inventory of her available options and came up empty. As to the odds of bringing her MADgun to bear on the man before he could blow her away, they sucked big-time.

"Down on the floor," Mr. PSB was saying, motioning with the gun. "Now!"

But she wasn't listening; she was remembering something. Something that made her smile. Then cringe — even if this worked, it was going to hurt like a bitch.

She kept that smile on her face, though, as, hands still held aloft, she began walking slowly, hips swaying suggestively, back toward the PSB guy.

"I told you to get down," he repeated. But even as he spoke he was lowering his aim from her navel to her kneecap. He wasn't going to go for a killshot, then.

That wasn't part of the plan. So she kept coming, still smiling, only a few more paces now. Until, unnerved, he brought the barrel up again, back to where she needed it to be.

"Stop, or — or I'll shoot," he said, almost plaintively, "What the fuck's wrong with you anyhow? You don't think I'll do it?"

By now she was close enough to reach out and touch him. She brought her arms down till her hands rested lightly on his shoulders.

"I fucking warned you," he choked out.

And discharged a round pointblank into her belly.

30 | Active Denial

MARIANNA STUMBLED ONTO PAIRIDAEZA's broad veranda, still trying to catch her breath, purloined MADgun at the ready.

God, she hurt. Her abdomen was one great throbbing bruise, despite her Psyche-issue body armor's having absorbed most of the bullet's force, stiffening to steel at the point of impact and spreading the energy across the whole surface of the jumpsuit. At least she'd avoided getting herself kneecapped; no guarantee the metamaterial could've handled a jolt to a joint like that.

And one more small consolation: bad as she felt, the PSB guy was in even worse shape from the surprise head-butt she'd administered. At least she wasn't groaning on the floor of the SecDef's helicopter like she'd left him. Her suit's protective hood had absorbed that shock as well.

Marianna surveyed the impenetrable knot of guards blocking the entrance to the main house. Impenetrable, that is, till she fired up the MADgun and played its invisible beam over them. Then they were scattering, running, stumbling, falling all over themselves, seized in the grip of a sudden, uncontrollable urge to be someplace, anyplace else.

Several of those fleeing, she noted, were wearing impact armor like her own. Its meta-fabric must be transparent to the gun's millimeter waves. Which stood to reason since, painful as it felt, the radiation itself was harmless.

In fact, the whole Millimeter Active Denial effect was little more than a sensory hallucination, its radiation feebler even than kitchen microwaves. It was all MAD could do to penetrate the skin to a depth of one third of a millimeter. But that was far enough down to reach the epidermal heat receptors. And when it tickled those nerves…

Well, that was where the "Active Denial" part of the name came from. MAD surrounded its wielder with a wide zone of pseudo-thermal radiation, effectively denying proximity to even the most determined, or foolhardy, adversary.

Marianna shuddered in sympathetic pain as she recalled how it felt to be splashed with MAD's blistering, burning-alive, wholly illusory agony. It felt like standing naked two feet from the open door of a blast furnace. Sympathy didn't stop her from blasting away, though, nor from advancing, sweeping Ansari's erstwhile gatekeepers before her.

As they fell back, a second line of defense came on: two guardbots, their metallic carapaces impervious to pseudo-thermal radiation.

They edged forward, crouched to spring, their photoreceptors all aglow above grinning rows of stainless-steel incisors. Scary as hell, if you didn't know the magic words.

Marianna did. "Attend," she said, "Verify release number and unit identification."

She left the bots littering the broadloom, writhing and squealing, dropped in their tracks by the priority override code Jon had given her.

By this time, Helen Gallagher had altogether lost track of where she was. The damned house was a labyrinth. Ansari could be leading them around in circles for all she knew.

They seemed to have arrived at their destination, though. At least everyone — Ansari and Jazmine McGovern, Donegan, and a couple of Protective Services guys for good measure — had all bunched up in front of the one jarring note amid all the Bauhaus elegance: a gunmetal-gray slab of a door as butt-ugly as its surroundings were chic. Ansari laid his palm on a sensor-plate for a handprint scan, and the door slid out of sight.

Stepping over the threshold, Gallagher could see that the utilitarian motif continued unabated on into the room beyond: four bare walls framed a largish, bright-lit space, unfurnished save for a freestanding plasma hi-def, a computer console, and…

Taking up the middle of the room, breaking the décor's monotony (but not in a good way), there loomed some sort of weird, black, vaguely arthropodal apparatus—a cross between an Iron Maiden and a Barcalounger.

Donegan was the first to speak. "Uh, Dave? I thought we were supposed to be linking in to Delphi Central for the launch."

"I'm glad you mentioned that, Brad." So saying, Ansari flipped open his handheld and spoke into it.

"Hamza? It's time."

Marianna ghosted down darkened hallways tracing the faintest of electronic spoors, trying to keep from being traced herself.

It wasn't so much Pairidaeza's autonomic security that worried her. The thing about high-end private security systems—and Marianna was willing to bet Ansari's installation gave new meaning to the phrase "top of the line"—was they didn't have much in the way of actual stopping power. They were all about detecting intruders in the first place.

No, the stopping power resided in the human security forces she'd so far succeeded in dispersing. Any moment now Hamza's corporate cops would come to the realization that, excruciating as it felt, the Millimeter Active Denial effect could do them no real harm. Then they'd nerve themselves to come looking for her again.

She'd just have to hope she found the Secretary of Defense before that could happen.

As to that, everything hinged on the personnel locator. She wouldn't have had a prayer of finding anything or anyone in Pairidaeza's maze of rooms without it.

With it, different story: the device was picking up the badges of the two PSB agents detailed to the SecDef's party. Chances were good that wherever those PSB guys were, their boss would not be far away.

All of which left open the question of what might happen if and when she succeeded in finding her quarry. Up till now, she'd been proceeding on the assumption that the Secretary was in actual physical danger of some sort. If that turned out to be wrong—if Marianna were, say, about to barge in on the West Coast equivalent of a Rose Garden tea party—it'd cost her her job, at the very minimum.

She was long past caring about that.

She paused momentarily to paint one more alcove with MADness and clear it of lurking guards. She moved on cautiously, hugging the wall, all the while subvocalizing a riff on the old nursery-school rhyme:

Come out, Madame Secretary—come out, come out wherever you are.

Helen Gallagher left off her inspection of the chair-like contraption taking up the center of the room as her peripheral vision registered a flicker of movement behind her.

Craning her neck around, she saw a tall, broad-shouldered, bearded man entering the chamber. His linen suit and silk tie were understated, in contrast to the rest of him; the man's height was such that he had to duck his head to get through the doorway.

"Permit me to introduce my Chief of Security, Hamza Nassiri," Ansari was saying. "He'll be doing the honors."

Nassiri gave her a tight little smile that never reached those hooded eyes. Then he brushed past her, seated himself at the console, and began working its keyboard. In response, the high-definition screen became a window onto a control room, in which the other members of the ACT team could be seen in various attitudes of anticipation.

"Real-time feed, direct from Delphi," Ansari explained. "You'll be able to watch the WellGrid go live right from here. The next best thing to being there."

Gallagher glared at Donegan. "Now, *that*"—she was pointing at the displays—"looks like a security breach you could drive a truck through."

"Actually not, Madame Secretary," Ansari cut in. "The narrowcast from New Mexico is coming to us via the Grid itself, to a temporary local node we've got up and running here on the premises. It's every bit as secure as the rest of the network."

"Speaking of up and running, Madame Secretary," Donegan said, "it's now midnight Eastern." He nodded toward the high-def. "The Delphi team has just given us thumbs up for the launch. All we're waiting on now is your first question."

Gallagher turned to him. "Is that supposed to mean something to me?"

"If I may, Madame Secretary," Donegan unfolded a printout and handed it to her. "The Taskforce thought you might like to be the first one to ever submit a query to the full Delphi capability. An historic occasion, if you will."

"An honor of sorts, I suppose." Gallagher sniffed.

She scanned the single line of text on the sheet she'd been given. Pretty straightforward, not to say simpleminded. "Okay, so how do I ask this historic question? Holler out a window and hope they can hear me in New Mexico?"

Donegan gave a dutiful chuckle, then said, "Not quite, Madame Secretary. You sit down here in the Nexus—" he motioned toward the strange machine occupying the center of the chamber, "—and enter your NSC authorization code on its keypad."

"So *that's* the Nexus?" Gallagher eyed the Chair dubiously, even more so than she had on arrival. Donegan's in-flight briefing had included detail on the Delphi procedure itself, what there was of it: sit down in the Nexus, key in her National Security Council ID, and then think a question at it—who couldn't do that?

It was just that the closer she examined this Nexus thing, the more … off-putting it seemed. It looked, in fact, like something the boys in CIA might cook up to administer their enhanced interrogation techniques. What they used to call torture.

She sensed someone at her arm, half-turned to look into the smiling face of Jazmine McGovern.

"It does look a little scary, doesn't it, Madame Secretary? But there's really nothing to it. I've sat in one of these Chairs myself—not a Nexus, of course, but the underlying technology's the same—and, as you can see, no harm done."

If this mere slip of a girl could do it, Gallagher could overcome her own apprehensions and do likewise. Even so, she stole a quick glance at her two Protective Services bodyguards standing ramrod straight to either side of the chamber's entrance. *They* weren't going to let anything happen to her, that was for sure.

"Okay, folks," she said as she went to sit herself down, "let's make some history."

"Freeze!" Marianna yelled at the top of her lungs.

Her purloined locator had led her straight to a sliding metal door, with a meeting in progress on the other side.

Whoever had gone through last had left the door partially retracted. Good thing too, because there was no way she could've budged the heavy sucker. As it was, one tight squeeze, and then the big entrance.

"Freeze!" she shouted again. "Nobody move." She backed up her words by brandishing her MADgun at the startled occupants of the room, all the while trying to scope out what to do next.

She knew most of the faces now staring blankly back at her: Hamza, of course. And… and Jazmine McGovern. She'd never met Davoud Ansari, not for lack of trying, but she recognized him from the newsfeeds. Over to one side, Brad Donegan was giving her an incredulous stare. And there, smack dab in the center of the room…

Marianna had no problem with identifying the SecDef, having met her in passing at various departmental all-hands back when Gallagher was Energy Secretary. No, the problem she had was with what Gallagher was about to do.

Jon had told her about those weird Chair-things he'd encountered at Psyche HQ. What was it he'd said? That he had a bad feeling about them, that she shouldn't go near them?

And the Secretary of Defense was just about to sit down in the Mother of all Chairs.

"Madam Secretary," Marianna said urgently, "please, ma'am, I need you step away from that thing right away."

That was as much as she got out before every muscle in her body twitched involuntarily, then went slack. The MADgun slipped out of her suddenly nerveless fingers and clattered to the tile floor. Then her legs gave way and she followed suit.

Lying on the cold tile still jerking spasmodically, unable to move, barely able to breathe, she scanned the room for any clue to what had just happened to her. Her gaze lighted on —

Hamza! He was just pocketing some sort of remote. He walked over and grinned down.

"You can take her now," he said to someone behind her, "I have disabled her armor and administered a shaped-pulse electroshock in the process. It will be a few moments more before she is fully recovered."

She felt herself being gripped under each arm, hauled to her feet and held fast. Hamza must've been right about her impact armor being off-line, or it would have protected her from the savage pain that was being inflicted on her right wrist. She turned to see two grim-faced Protective Services agents, one on either side. The one on her right was applying a hyperflexing wristlock, twisting her hand down and in so it almost touched the underside of her forearm in an professionally applied submission hold.

"Don't move," he said.

"You've got this all wrong," she began. The PSB guy responded by increasing the pressure. She gasped and stopped talking, but only for long enough to fill her lungs again. Then she blurted out, "The Secretary's in danger. You can't let her—"

"Nonsense."

Marianna looked up through red-tinged veils of agony. It was Ansari who had spoken.

"The only real danger to Secretary Gallagher," he went on in an easy, conversational tone, "is you, Ms. Bonaventure. We haven't met, but your loose-cannon reputation precedes you." He turned to Donegan. "Wouldn't you agree, Brad?"

"Now, wait a minute, Dave." Donegan was fingering that amulet of his furiously. "Marianna here's supposed to be working for us. Maybe we ought to hear her side of the story?"

Ansari sighed. "I can see that you need a little more attitude adjustment, Brad. No matter, we'll see to that soon enough. Right now, though—" and here he nodded to Hamza "—it might be best if you take a little nap."

"Huh?" Donegan said. He'd have doubtless said more, but by that time Hamza had sat down at the console again and entered a keystroke combination. In response, the ACT chairman collapsed bonelessly to the floor.

"Nanotrodes," Ansari said to no one in particular. "Got to love the little buggers."

He then turned to one of the PSB agents, the one who wasn't currently engaged in trying to break Marianna's hand off at the wrist.

"It's Ernest, isn't it?" he said. "Ernest, this man, the one claiming to be Brad Donegan, is the infiltrator we were warned about. Would you mind, uh, setting him to one side for us?"

Ernest said nothing, simply nodded. Then he walked over to Donegan's slumped body, grabbed it under the arms, and dragged it into a corner.

For a moment there, Marianna thought she might take advantage of the brief distraction to break free. No such luck; Ernest's partner was keeping her pinioned tight as ever. Whatever spell Ansari had these zombies under, it didn't seem to impair their reflexes one iota.

"That's better," Ansari rubbed his hands. "Now, where were we?"

He looked back toward the Nexus and its intended victim. "Madam Secretary, I apologize for the interruption, but things are back on track now, and I'm afraid I must insist that you take your seat."

"On track, hell!" Gallagher had whipped out a come-hither and was furiously stabbing at it. "Damned if I know what you've done to these two,"—she jerked a thumb at her erstwhile bodyguards—"but the rest of my security detail will be breathing down your neck in seconds."

Ansari shook his head. "Actually, Helen, they won't. You see, as the PSB advance teams cycled through here over the past three weeks, we took the opportunity to administer the same treatment to every member of your security detail. Tomorrow, they—and you, as well—will remember none of this. In the meantime, I'm afraid you're all going to have to do as I say."

He sighed. "Now, I'll ask you one more time: please, sit down."

Gallagher glared back. "What, you're not going to knock me out too?"

"I'm hoping that won't be necessary, Helen. But in any case, right now I need you conscious." He turned slightly. "Jazmine, would you escort the Secretary to her seat?"

Marianna had been watching all of this in mounting disbelief. But it was when she saw Jazmine leading Helen Gallagher to the Nexus like a lamb to slaughter that something snapped inside of her.

She let out a banshee shriek that surprised even her. It also surprised her PSB minder, for just long enough for her to squirm out of his wristlock.

She launched herself straight at Jazmine, fingers crooked like unsheathed claws. She was nearly there, too, when a crushing blow to the base of her spine slammed her to the floor. Hamza had come up behind her lightning quick and landed on the small of her back with both knees and all his weight. Her defunct impact armor had protected her not at all.

She lay there moaning, blood thundering in her ears so loud she could barely hear what Hamza was saying, in that eerily calm voice of his:

"And now we finish this."

He bent down, seized her by the throat, and began to squeeze. "You have caused enough trouble as it is."

"No!" said a grating voice. "Tell your man to leave her alone."

Ansari spun around. And met the eyes of Secretary of Defense Gallagher.

"Leave her alone, you son of a bitch!" Gallagher said. "She was only trying to help. I—I'll sit in your damned Nexus. Just leave her be."

"All right," Ansari said slowly. "I give you my word Ms. Bonaventure will not be harmed. Hamza?"

Hamza released his hold with seeming reluctance and rose to his feet. He gave Bonaventure a parting kick in the side, then turned and stalked away.

Bonaventure was on her hands and knees now, being seen to by Ansari's tame PSB agents. "Madam Secretary, no—" she choked out, her breath coming hard, "—Helen, no, don't do it."

"It's all right, dear," Gallagher said. She took her place in the Nexus and smiled. "Thanks for trying."

The infusor hood gimbaled into position and lowered smoothly onto the Defense Secretary's head. She froze, trembled briefly, then all the breath went out of her.

A moment passed while the nanotrodes set to their work.

"So what's the plan, Ansari?" The female voice had come from behind him.

He looked back to where Bonaventure, manifestly still in pain, was being raised to her feet by the PSB guys.

"What are you really after?" she said between gasps, "—world domination?"

Despite himself and the situation, Ansari had to laugh out loud. "That'd be cool, wouldn't it?"

Then he sobered. "Unfortunately, the technology's not there yet. It's still a stretch just to alter the trust economy for a few subjects at a time, and that only in the most general, broad-brush way."

"You're just plain crazy, then," Bonaventure spat. "I don't know what possible good you think this can do you. You *can't* be thinking of holding the Secretary for ransom. Regardless of what you've done to subvert her bodyguards here, there's just no way you can hang onto her for long."

"Actually," Ansari said, "I only need to 'hang onto her,' as you put it, for a very few moments of the Secretary's valuable time.

"Just long enough for her to enter a key."

31 | Keys to the Kingdom

Jonathan Knox, or the entity now answering to that name, would have been pacing up and down, if that had been an option in his current circumstances.

By rights, it should have been; he'd had Nietzsche return him to his previous white-on-white accommodations after immersion in the raw data stream had gotten too overwhelming. Trouble was, space didn't seem to work very well in the simulated chamber. It seemed, in fact, to wrap back in on itself, like the display on one of those early video games: if he walked too far in any one direction, he'd find himself back where he'd started still walking in the same direction. He was living in what string theorist Brian Greene would have called a three-dimensional torus — a hyperspatial donut, in other words.

It certainly made sense from Nietzsche's point of view as architect of this artificial reality, obviating the need for elaborate rendering of endless virtual landscapes and such like. But it was disorienting, and more than a tad claustrophobic.

Even so, Knox could have borne it better if he hadn't felt the need to pace. Or jog. Or *somehow* get his mind off the fact that there were things going on out in what he persisted in thinking of as the real world which might have a major impact on his fate, but which, in his present state, he could influence not at all. Nor, for the moment at least, even perceive.

At least there might be something to be done about that. "How's it coming?" he asked Nietzsche.

"Jonathan, please, I am scarcely further along than I was the last time you asked, a hundred microseconds ago. Would you like me to slow your clock-rate again? I would be done before you know it, in that case."

Knox thought about that. Nietzsche had already cranked his processing speed down several orders of magnitude below theoretical max. A few more and he'd be experiencing the passage of time at a rate approximating that of a flesh-and-blood human.

That thought of flesh-and-blood humanity brought home to him something he'd been trying not to think about. Namely, that flesh-and-blood humanity was something which—now that he'd lost it, perhaps irretrievably—he found he desperately wanted back. In the aftermath of the whole Jazmine disaster—could it really have been only two days ago?—the notion of being an incorporeal intellect like Nietzsche, freed of the body's fleshly cravings, had held an undeniable attraction. Especially for someone who, like himself, had always been more vested in the life of the mind than that of the senses.

And now, as if in one of the darker fairytales, fate had conspired to grant him that ill-conceived wish ... and left him wishing he could take it back.

Suddenly all those moments of his life he'd let pass by half-noticed, begrudged, unobserved—youth, joys, sorrows, above all, his time with Marianna—seemed infinitely precious to him. And gone forever.

In his mind's eye (and what other eye was left to him?), Knox could see the climactic scene from *It's a Wonderful Life*. Jimmy Stewart as George Bailey, standing on a bridge appealing to his unlikely guardian angel:

"Please, Clarence. Please, *I want to live again!*"

"Jonathan?" Nietzsche's voice echoed in the blank white virtual room.

Knox shelved regrets and reveries for the moment. "Yo, right here." As if he had anyplace else to go. "How're we looking?"

"Mr. Nassiri's technicians continue to extirpate my Pairidaeza-internal sensors wherever they find them. But there is one place they have not thought to look, and one capability they would have difficulty terminating even if they did."

"And that is?" Sometimes Nietzsche could be as hard to talk to as his friend Mycroft.

"The Nexus itself. I have patched into it through Pairidaeza's mini-Grid, as you call it."

"Outstanding. Being linked to the WellGrid should put us in the center of the action, no?"

"It would, if I were in fact linked to the WellGrid."

"But I thought you said—"

"That I am patched into the Nexus, yes. But all I meant by that is I should be able to read the brain-state of anyone occupying it, as I did yours."

"What good does that do us? Unless you were thinking of uploading somebody else to keep me company."

Nietzsche shook his head.

Knox sighed. "Tell me you've got something else?"

"I do, in fact. I have succeeded in reformulating the various stray wave-forms ambient in the Nexus chamber into something approaching visuals. If you will direct your attention to the far wall."

Knox turned in the indicated direction, to see an image forming—or perhaps an aperture irising open—on the wall's surface.

This all would have been so much simpler, Davoud Ansari thought to himself, if only the Bonaventure woman hadn't interfered. Again.

He grimaced. *So* much simpler: Helen Gallagher would have willingly, unsuspectingly entered the embrace of the Nexus, and unsuspectingly, willingly keyed in her authorization, thereby bringing the Delphi capability on line.

It wasn't as if there were any easy alternatives. Simply knowing the code did no good; one critical step in the authentication protocol involved a brain-scan verification of the identity of the code-holder as having Delphi clearance.

Now that the Well was no longer in test mode, there were only half a dozen individuals in the world who met those criteria: the six statutory members of the National Security Council—the President and Vice President, the National Security Advisor, and the Secretaries of State, Treasury, and Defense. Ansari had pulled out all the stops to get one of those six here, and maneuvered into the Nexus, for the Delphi launch tonight.

Only to watch the whole thing nearly go down the tubes, thanks to Ms. Marianna Bonaventure.

Ansari shook his head. Now they'd have to do this the hard way.

He walked over to where Gallagher was sitting in the Nexus, her face half-concealed behind the infusor hood's visor, the seldom-used padded cuffs encircling her wrists and ankles.

"Madame Secretary," he said pleasantly, "how are you feeling?"

"Go to hell," she growled.

Ansari sighed and turned toward the console where Hamza was monitoring the infusion process. "What's her 'trode level now?"

After a check of his displays, Hamza replied, "Approaching saturation. The subject should be fully tractable in a minute or so. That last outburst was probably more an ingrained personality trait than any deliberate attempt at defiance."

Ansari waited till Hamza nodded a go-ahead, then leaned in and said. "Madame Secretary, Helen, can you hear me? It's me, Dave Ansari."

Gallagher's lips moved almost imperceptibly. "Dave," she whispered.

"That's right, your old friend Dave." He paused. This next part was critical. "You trust me, don't you, Helen?"

"Trust?" she echoed.

"The reason I ask is, as long as you're sitting in the Nexus here, there's something I'd like you to do for me."

"What's that, Dave?"

Aside from the unaccustomed warmth with which she'd uttered his name just now, Gallagher seemed almost back to normal. That was a good thing; the Nexus would have detected any marked cognitive impairment and shut the authentication sequence down cold—not to mention broadcasting an alert out across the WellGrid.

"What I'd really like, is if you could just enter your NSC authorization into that keypad under your right hand."

The mirrored visor didn't cover so much of Gallagher's face as to hide her frown. "But, Dave, that's—that's classified information."

He'd been afraid of this. Even with brain-stim amping up her trustfulness and credulity, the Secretary's inhibitions against divulging state secrets remained strong, reinforced by the woman's own innate stubbornness.

He shot a glance at Hamza. "Not enough. Zap her again. Harder."

Hamza turned to his console and set up a second, more powerful internal stimulation of the Secretary's dorsolateral prefrontal cortex. He depressed a final key and nodded.

Ansari couldn't see Gallagher's pupils dilate, but he didn't really need to; the sudden stiffening of her limbs, followed by a long sigh and utter relaxation, told the tale.

"Ooh," cooed the Secretary of Defense, "that feels nice."

Ansari waited another minute then leaned in again. "Helen, I know the information's classified, but we've really, really got to have it. To start up the Delphi program, remember? We can't do it without you. Please, just enter the code."

"Turn around first."

"Excuse me?" Then he got it. He straightened and turned so he was facing away her. "Is this okay?" he said.

"Promise not to peek?"

"Of course, of course, anything you say." Ansari hoped they hadn't overdone it on the nanotrodes. Gallagher was behaving with all the transparent craftiness of a kindergartner.

"Well, all right, then," said the Secretary of Defense in those same, strangely childlike tones. She flashed him a smile and quickly tapped twelve digits into the keypad.

For a long moment, nothing seemed to happen. Ansari's gaze swept the bank of displays, twins to those in Delphi's own control room, looking for some sign — *any* sign — that the WellGrid had been activated, that his incredible gamble was about to pay off.

Then a flickering window on one of the screens caught his eye: the MERGE component readout, the real-time tally of the number of analyst-nodes assimilated into the Group Entity — the count already stood at two hundred and fifty, and it was steadily rising — five hundred, seven fifty, a thousand — as more and more of Delphi's sister systems came on line.

And now confirmation had begun coming in from the main display. Its panoramic view of Delphi's vast bay — a good thousand miles east and half a mile down, yet looking close enough to reach out and touch — showed the hoods of hundreds of infusor workstations taking on an anticipatory amber sheen, their occupants now moving in slow syncopation. The same scene would be repeating in the fifteen other Wells completing the Grid, signaling that the collective mind, close to five thousand nodes strong now, was coalescing, trembling on the brink of awareness.

Let it tremble. Ansari had no interest whatsoever in the so-called MERGE entity, nor in the marvels of analysis it might perform for its masters. To him, it was enough that the flickering marsh-lights of the WellGrid's preconscious meant the pathway leading from Pairidaeza's Nexus into the Grid proper was now open.

The royal road to Timah's cure stretched out before him.

Marianna Bonaventure was in a good deal of pain, not all of it physical. To be sure, her lumbars were still throbbing from Hamza's near-crippling blow, and being trussed to an exposed overhead with flexicuff manacles wasn't helping any. But worse than any of that was the chagrin she felt over having somehow gone from tip-the-balance player to hog-tied spectator in one fell swoop.

On the bright side, being hung here at the rear of the chamber gave her a grandstand view of the goings-on.

And what was going on was that, having gotten the Defense Secretary to divulge her Delphi key, Ansari was now helping her out of the Nexus. Helen Gallagher looked normal enough, but she offered no resistance as he took her by the hand and escorted her over to where a Psyche tech was setting up a closed-circuit video rig. Make that *very* closed-circuit: its signals were being routed over the WellGrid.

"Now, Helen," Ansari was saying, "there's just one more thing I'd like you to do for me."

"What's that, Dave?"

"Would you mind getting on the comm and talking to your folks at Delphi for us?"

Gallagher appeared to ponder this for a moment, brows knitted. Then the lines of her face smoothed out again and she favored Ansari with an uncharacteristically untroubled smile.

"Sure, Dave," she said, "but…what do you want me to tell them?"

"Oh, just that they should stand by, that there's been a glitch on this end, but everything's okay now, and we'll be starting shortly. You know, words to that effect."

As Marianna watched, Helen Artemis Gallagher, last in a line of Boston Brahmins, formerly Junior Senator from the great state of Massachusetts, now Secretary of Defense for these United States of America, put on her *Meet The Press* smile for the closed-circuit camera, and began doing exactly as she'd been told.

Marianna's attention was so focused on this pathetic little tableau that she didn't notice there was someone standing beside her until that someone spoke.

"Don't worry, this'll all be over soon."

Jazmine hadn't started out to strike up a conversation, hadn't really intended to come anywhere near Bonaventure, for that matter. It was just that the back wall where they'd strung the woman up was about as far away from Hamza as Jazmine could get without leaving the room. And once there, it would've felt awkward to stand around not saying anything.

Regardless of the circumstances, she hardly deserved the glare she was getting in return for her semi-well-meant words, much less Bonaventure's snarled response. "You're in a lot of trouble, McGovern—I hope you realize that."

Jazmine sighed. "Everything was going just fine till you showed up."

"Call this fine? In case you hadn't noticed, that's the Secretary of Defense your boss is holding captive over there. And from where I stand, you're looking like an accessory."

Jazmine shrugged. "Tell me something I *don't* know."

"Something you don't know? How about this: if you help me out, cut these cuffs off me, I'll try to see they go easy on you."

Jazmine stared at Bonaventure for a moment, then laughed. "They, who? Because, in case you hadn't noticed, Dave's the one in charge here."

"And just how long do you suppose *that's* going to last?"

That question struck to the core of Jazmine's uncertainty. What with Bonaventure's disruption and its aftermath, they were running late already. How much longer *could* Dave keep the lid on?

Still, she gave the other woman her most confident project-manager smile. "It only needs to last a little while longer, just till we can fix something."

"Fix *what*?"

"Fatimah, okay? Dave's daughter is going to die if he can't get into the Grid and use it to cure her."

"I can't believe you seriously think that's going to work."

"Believe it; it's true." Jazmine took care not to let her smile slip. "And when it's all over, we'll put everything back the way it was, as if none of it ever happened. Nobody's going to remember what went on here tonight. Not Gallagher, not Donegan, not even you."

"Oh, please."

"Don't think so? Once he's got you in that Chair, Dave can pretty much make you think or do anything he wants. Just like he did with Jon."

"Jon?" For a moment it looked like Bonaventure was going to cry. "What about him?"

"You don't really think that cheating on you was Jon's idea, do you?"

"What do you mean?" Bonaventure stuttered. "I was there, I saw—"

"I know what you *saw*." Jazmine felt her cheeks burning. Right about then she was wishing she'd never brought the subject up. Too late now, though—and anyway, maybe she did owe Bonaventure an explanation, if not exactly an apology.

She took a deep breath. "What you didn't know, couldn't have known, was that Hamza set it all up. The whole thing was just a test run, to be sure Jon would do whatever they needed him to do when push came to shove. Just like—"

She didn't bother to complete the sentence, just turned her head and nodded over toward the other side of the Nexus chamber. Over to where Helen Gallagher was sitting forgotten in a corner, meek and unprotesting, patiently awaiting her next instruction.

Marianna hadn't thought there was anything Jazmine could say that would render her speechless. Wrong.

But was it even possible, what Jazmine was saying? If so, that would mean that Jon—Marianna could feel her eyes misting up—Jon hadn't betrayed her after all, not really. *If* it was true.

It couldn't be, could it? She turned to face Jazmine. "You seem so sure of this. How do you know?"

"How do I know? *How do I know?*" Jazmine looked around and lowered her voice before going on. "I know because that bastard Hamza did it to me too!" And with that, she spun on her heel and stalked off.

Alone again, Marianna brooded on just how badly she'd screwed up.

Not only had she misjudged Jon, but she'd found it out too late to tell him she was sorry.

She'd spent the past two days thinking she could never forgive him. Now she had the rest of her life—which might not be long, under the circumstances—to wonder if she could ever forgive herself.

"This way." Ansari was standing in the middle of the room, directing traffic. "Bring her over here."

To the rumble of heavy-duty casters, a gurney bearing Fatimah Ansari was steered into position alongside the Nexus. The tech doing the driving stopped and set the wheel locks, then knelt to check the telltales on the portable life-support system bolted to the undercarriage. They'd be needing that soon enough, but there was still time, time to speak with his daughter.

Timah was wearing her favorite pajamas, the blue ones with the orange seahorses. As if she were about to go to bed for the night, instead of into a procedure that could save her life.

Ansari bent over and kissed her cheek. "How are you, little one?"

"I'm okay, *Baba*," she said in a small voice, her big eyes silently giving the lie to her words.

Rather than respond, Ansari began fumbling with the safety clasps that held Fatimah strapped to the rolling platform. After a moment, he gave up and looked around the room.

"Jazmine? I wonder if you could help me out here a moment."

"Yes, of course, Dave." She pushed off from the corner where she'd been standing and moved to his side, giving Hamza a wide berth. And who could blame her, given what she'd seen him do to Bonaventure a few moments ago?

While Jazmine worked to unsnarl the mare's nest his unsteady hands had made of the fastenings, Ansari reached out and stroked his daughter's hair. "Don't be afraid, Timah, dear one. It's all going to be okay."

Her lower lip trembled. "I can't help it, *Baba*."

"I know, I know, but be brave. When you wake up it will be to a—a new life. You will be all better, free forever from your colors and your pain. But for right now you have to, to go to sleep, like a good girl."

Timah swallowed. "Will I dream?"

"Dream?" The question stopped Ansari in his tracks. What *would* it be like to be immersed in the WellGrid at firsthand, without any of the mediating interfaces?

"Yes, yes, of course," he went on finally, "—you'll have sweet dreams. Anything you can imagine, you'll dream. Wonderful sights and sound, a land of miracles."

"Like … Paradise?"

"Paradise?" he echoed. "Well, yes, perhaps."

"Will I see Mama there?"

He couldn't speak for a moment. He knew—of course he knew—how hard it had been for his little girl, growing up without a mother. He himself still felt the loss of Kimia deeply. He should have remarried, as much for his own sake as the child's, but somehow something, some sort of resistance, had always seemed to stand in the way of forming any close attachments.

"Your mama?" He choked back a sob. "Perhaps, sweetheart—perhaps you'll see Mama if you think about her very, very hard. Can you do that?"

She nodded.

There, that much at least was true. The Well possessed untold computational resources. With the simulation capabilities it would put at her command, Timah should be able to summon any vision she desired into existence.

"And now, come. It's time." He held out his hands to his little girl. She sat up on the gurney, swung her feet over the side, came into his arms and cuddled, just as she always had when he was taking her up to bed.

"I love you, *Baba*," she whispered in his ear.

"I love you too, Timah," he replied, carrying her to the Nexus. "Never forget that."

Hamza watched from his console as a paramedic hooked up Fatimah's life support. A sensible precaution; the autonomic nervous system's control centers for respiration, heartbeat, and other essential bodily functions *did* run through the lower brainstem, after all, even though it seemed unlikely that these would cease operating once the girl's higher faculties had fled … elsewhere.

Quite unlikely, in fact. Even for patients in a vegetative state with no conscious awareness whatsoever, the lungs still breathed air, the stomach continued digesting food, the heart kept pumping blood, all without outside assistance. Still, no point in taking chances. Hamza needed Fatimah to survive, in mind and body both, for at least a little while longer.

Ansari strolled over to where Hamza was sitting and clapped him on the back. "Just the BackPatch now, and we'll be ready to go."

Hamza glanced over at the Nexus, where the small, matte-black ovoid Ansari had spoken of was being interfaced with till-now concealed ports in the base station's infusor hood. The BackPatch was Psyche Industries' own unofficial contribution to the Delphi project, designed to perform a number of functions, none of them the kind of thing the Advanced Curational Taskforce would have approved of, had they been asked.

As far as Ansari was concerned, the BackPatch was, first and foremost, Fatimah's treatment package: a Nexus add-on that would modulate the little girl's entanglement with the Grid so as to replicate her malfunctioning psyche *ad infinitum*, in hopes of finding a single healthy variant. Or that's what it *would* do, if the procedure were permitted to run its course.

That, of course, Hamza did not intend to permit. He had an entirely separate agenda, in service of which he'd had an entirely separate capability engineered and incorporated into the BackPatch. Ansari would have been no less aghast than ACT at what the Malhamah module was programmed to do.

Ansari looked down at Timah's small face—her expressionless, motionless, seemingly lifeless face, like a drowned face seen through deep water. He shuddered at the thought, though he knew that what he beheld was not true death, but a death-like trance state—an outward sign that Timah's consciousness had completed its transmigration into the WellGrid, leaving her mind tethered to her body by only the most tenuous of threads.

He straightened and reached out a hand to the BackPatch controls that would initiate the replication sequence, and with it, his daughter's cure. He need merely depress a button now and a host of Fatimah doppelgangers would be cloned into existence, instantiating every conceivable variant of her mind, till the ensemble filled the vacant pseudo-space of the Grid to overflowing.

But, no, there was something he needed to do first. His fingers bypassed the BackPatch and instead pried open a utility compartment located in the rear of the Nexus, exposing the resonator within.

He withdrew the device and inspected it, turning it over in his hands, the perfectionist in him frowning at the awkward, unfinished appearance of this prototype—just a thick band of matte-black metal basically, studded with blocky individual subcomponents at various points round the circumference. Yet for all its inelegance, the resonator was a masterpiece of miniaturization, packing most of the capabilities of a full-fledged Nexus into a form-factor small enough and light enough to be worn on the user's head, albeit not without a certain amount of eventual neck and upper back strain.

Neither the ungainliness nor the discomfort mattered in the end. What mattered was the resonator's function, which was to bring its wearer's brain-state into low-level entanglement with that of a person occupying the Nexus. More specifically …

Ansari eased the resonator's surprising weight down onto his forehead and adjusted the contact surfaces so they molded themselves to his temples. Then he waited for the connection to build to full strength and place him in touch with his daughter.

As he waited, he wondered what she might be experiencing. Had she in fact been able to harness the simulation capabilities accessible via the WellGrid and conjure the paradise they had spoken of? Was she even now sitting in her Mama's lap in a meadow of spring flowers?

Something was coming through now, he could almost see—

Alone, left all alone, in this place that wasn't even a place.

It would be like paradise, *Baba* had promised. But how could it be paradise, when there was nobody here?

Nobody, not even herself. Timah couldn't feel her hands or her feet or her face. As if she didn't have a body anymore. She began to be afraid.

She tried calling out, but there was no answer and no echo. She couldn't even hear the sound of her own voice.

She tried to look around, but every way she turned looked the same: gray, gray, and not even gray. Not gray like the sky and sea of her home on the hilltop. Gray, like the gray behind her eyelids when she closed her eyes.

Gray, like … nothing. Was she nothing too? The idea was very, very strange and very, very scary. She tried to stop thinking about it, but it wouldn't go away, and the more she did think about it, the more it terrified her.

Timah struggled to hold back tears. *Baba* had told her she must be brave. But where *was Baba*, why wasn't he coming for her? Why had he left her alone here?

Alone, all alone. Timah couldn't help it, she began to whimper, then to sob. Then the floodgates broke and she was wailing inconsolably.

Ansari pressed his hands to his temples, willing himself not to break contact despite the sudden onslaught of panic.

Timah's panic.

Timah, his daughter, his own little girl, Timah was weeping, pleading, crying over and over: *Please*, Baba, *please take me away from the gray and let me come home again. I'll be good, I promise. I'm sorry, I'm so sorry. I promise I won't cry any more when my colors come. I won't cry about anything, ever again, if you just, please, come and take me away from here.*

At that instant, confronted with his little girl's anguish, something, some mental logjam dissolved inside Ansari. He looked back over the years since Timah had been born, since Kimia had died, and saw himself as having sleepwalked his way through them. As if he had lived those years cut off from all the joys life had to offer, plodding on through his days, dead inside.

And now, this mad scheme. What could he have been thinking? To subject, to *condemn* his only child, his little girl, to this ordeal. Nietzsche had tried to warn him about it, the night Ansari had gone to shut the AI down. But he could see it for himself now too, could see clearly what he'd been doing. And why he couldn't go on doing it.

In this moment of clarity, he saw something else as well.

All that time spent in the Chair. To relax him, Hamza had said, to relieve his stress, restore his equilibrium. He couldn't remember there having been anything out of the ordinary about those sessions. But then, of course, he wouldn't.

Suspicion collapsed into certainty. He had been duped—his own technology had been turned against him, had been manipulating him all along.

Ansari spun around and glared at his Security Chief. "You!" he shouted. "You did this to me, *to us!*"

Hamza rose from his console. "Davoud, calm yourself, please." He held his hands out in a placating gesture, and began advancing across the room.

"Keep away from me, Hamza." Ansari edged backwards to keep some distance between himself and his security chief, nearly stumbling over something in the process.

Glancing down he saw that strange-looking weapon the Bonaventure woman had been waving around before. He stooped to retrieve it, pointed it at Hamza, shouted, "Keep back, I'm warning you."

His hand was tightening on the trigger when his gaze fell again on Timah's face. She looked tranquil, at peace. But through the resonator interface he could hear her quiet weeping.

All of a sudden, nothing else mattered. He could still undo what he had done to his daughter. He could re-embody her, bring her back home once more—but he must act quickly. Without thinking, he set the weapon down. His hands flew to the BackPatch controls, started to reverse the procedure.

The explosion was deafening in the enclosed space.

Ansari jerked. He looked up from his child's face into Hamza's pitiless eyes, then down at the gun smoking in Hamza's hand.

With his last breath he cried out, "Fatimah, I—" and crumpled to the floor.

32 | One MERGE to Rule Them All

Jazmine watched in stunned silence as the shouting match between Dave Ansari and his Security Chief escalated to threats of violence and then to violence itself. The shots came deafeningly loud in the confined space of the Nexus chamber. Jazmine hit the deck and lay on the floor afraid to move, shuddering, eyes squeezed shut, head cradled in her arms, as if she could wall herself away from this nightmare, simply not be there any more, be someplace else.

A boot-tip prodded her side, more than a nudge, not quite a kick. She raised her head to behold, haloed against fluorescent ceiling lighting, that which she least wished to see in all the world: Hamza Nassiri's harsh, bearded face scowling down at her.

"Get up," he said.

Of all the men she'd ever worked with, Hamza was the only one who'd really scared her. Even when he was at his most restrained and polite, there was an air of utter ruthlessness about the man, of savagery barely held in check, waiting its chance to break free.

Tonight, the beast was out of its cage at last.

"I said, *get up!*"

Jazmine scrambled to obey, doing her best not to cry, knowing if she started, she might not be able to stop.

She rose to her feet and immediately wished she hadn't, because now she could see what she'd been hiding her eyes from: Dave Ansari's body lying in a pool of blood.

"Is he—" she began.

"Dead? Yes, of course. And you will join him in death, unless you do exactly as I say."

Satisfied that Jazmine McGovern was sufficiently cowed to cause no further trouble, Hamza turned to regard the corpse of the man who had been his employer, his associate, his dupe. It would be untrue to say he had no regrets about killing Ansari. In particular, he regretted that Ansari had broken free of the nanotrode-mediated control as soon as he had, since the man would have been useful in keeping his daughter calm, till it came her own turn to die.

"You shot him," came a female voice. "Killed him in cold blood."

He turned to see Jazmine McGovern cringing in a corner, daring, through her tears, to look him accusingly in the eye.

Perhaps not quite so cowed, after all. For some reason, the combination of defiance and helplessness struck a spark in Hamza, infuriated him.

"Be silent!" he bellowed. "This fool is only the first of many who will die tonight."

His gaze swept the room then, fixed on Helen Gallagher where she sat huddled, staring blankly out on the proceedings.

"In fact," he said, "there is another here who deserves death far more than he."

He strode over to where she was sitting, this vaunted Secretary of Defense for the United States of America, this symbol of the military might of the arrogant bully, the Great Satan. What was she now but an old gray-haired woman, sitting there helplessly awaiting her fate?

A fate that he, Hamza al-Ahwazi, whom the world had known as Nassiri, would now dispense.

First, though…

Hamza turned to regard the two Protective Services Battalion agents standing at parade rest off to one side. They presented something of a problem; although their 'trode-induced trustfulness had been raised to a level where they would obey most of his orders unquestioningly, it was far from certain that his control would remain in force should the object of their primary duty, the Secretary of Defense herself, come under threat. Easier to take them out of the equation altogether. They had served their purpose, after all.

Hamza reseated himself at the console. The agents' brains were as saturated with nanotrodes as Brad Donegan's had been, hence were as susceptible to the same sleep command.

Hamza entered the requisite keystrokes, then turned to watch as the two bodyguards slid unceremoniously to the floor. He rose to survey his handiwork. Gallagher's security detail would be out for hours now, leaving Hamza free to deal with Gallagher herself as she so richly deserved.

His hand snaked out, seized the Defense Secretary by the shoulder, yanked her to the ground. She yelped in pain but, still under the nanotrodes' spell, did not otherwise protest.

He hauled her back to her knees, this woman who thought to arrogate to herself the rightful place of a man. Was there no end to them? McGovern, Bonaventure, worst of all Gallagher—all of them women who had forgotten their proper, subordinate place in the natural order, all of them abominations in the sight of God.

He would kill her here and now. Let Gallagher's execution serve as a ritual sacrifice presaging the Great Slaughter itself.

Then he paused a moment to think: according to the Holy Quran, the proper way to deal with unbelievers met in battle was by beheading them: smiting them with a sword on the neck until dead, then ignominiously lopping off their fingertips as well. Regrettably, Hamza had no sword here.

No matter, he would make do. He pulled out the same pistol he'd used to dispatch Ansari, cocked it, and pointed it at Gallagher's forehead.

His finger was already tightening on the trigger when there came a shout from behind him. "What in *God's* name do you think you're doing?"

Normally, he would have ignored any interruptions, but the blasphemy made him pause. He turned to see the Bonaventure woman standing there glaring at him, still shackled to her crossbeam.

Hamza smiled at her. "Why, as you can see, Ms. Bonaventure," he said, "what I am doing is truly in God's name—I am about to rid the world of one of the principal obstacles to God's inevitable triumph."

He turned back to his sacrificial goat.

"No, wait—"

He didn't bother turning around this time. "This grows tiresome, Ms. Bonaventure. What is it now?"

"For God's sake, Hamza—think about it! Haven't you ever heard of contingency planning?"

Now he did turn. "What do you mean?"

"Just, what if it turns out you need to have the Secretary key in her authorization code again? Think contingencies!"

"I find that highly un—" he began, then stopped, scowling.

Contingencies! But the woman had a point, may God curse her! Some pleasures must be foregone in God's name, in the name of God's victory. For the time being at least.

"Very well, then," he grated, and pocketed his pistol again. "Let Gallagher die with all the rest."

He shifted his stance to view the hi-def feed from Delphi Central once more, then thought better of it and turned to stalk toward the Bonaventure woman, pausing on his way to take a roll of silvery ribbon out of a utility cabinet.

"In the mean time—" He was looking her right in the eye now, his face so close to hers that she blinked. "—I will hear no more from *you!*"

And with that, he duct-taped Bonaventure's mouth shut.

He turned away from her then, turned back to the display which would shortly show history's first ever macro-MERGE coming on line.

As soon as he summoned it.

Knox was stunned: even through the imperfect gray lens of the ambient-waveform imaging that Nietzsche had cobbled together, he could see there was a very different storyline unfolding on Pairidaeza reality TV than anything he'd heretofore imagined.

He'd been off, a hundred eighty degrees off, on so many things. Ansari hadn't been the mastermind behind this conspiracy, just one more hapless victim of it. Nor was the scheme's true purpose the curing of a little girl's incurable illness, but something far darker, something as yet glimpsed only in outline.

All that, though, paled to insignificance, compared to how wrong he'd been about Hamza. He'd typecast the Psyche Security chief as henchman and second banana to the arch villain, an Odd Job to Ansari's Goldfinger. Talk about "misunderestimation"—Hamza had turned out to be a Cardinal Richelieu to the Psyche CEO's Louis XIII, an *eminence grise* pulling everybody's strings, Knox's own included, though to what end Knox could hardly guess at.

One thing, however, required no guesswork.

"This is bad," Knox muttered to himself, "very, very bad."

"Admittedly," Nietzsche replied, "the situation has grown far more complicated."

"Complicated? Hello?" Well, Nietzsche *did* say he had a problem with human motivation.

"Let me spell it out for you," Knox went on. "We've now got a madman in control of the WellGrid and going for control of God knows what else. He's already killed his boss, come within inches of offing the Secretary of Defense, and threatened my—my friend. And the night's still young. No, trust me, Nietzsche, this isn't complicated. It's just plain *bad*."

"But Jonathan, assuming that to be the case, what would you have us do? As matters stand, we have no means of influencing events in the real world. We are without connectivity to any of Pairidaeza's main systems, we are lacking in physical instrumentalities of any sort. I say again: what would you have us do?"

"If I knew that, don't you think I'd tell you?" Knox was trying his best to keep his cool and think. It should have been easy with no adrenaline coursing through his veins—with no veins, for that matter. It wasn't.

He glanced again at the window wall displaying those aforementioned events in the real world. "Whatever we come up with, we'd better do it quick." He pointed. "It's looking like Hamza's going for Timah."

Hamza knelt by Ansari's corpse, removed the resonator, and placed it on his own head. It had arrived: his moment of maximum opportunity—and maximum danger. The opportunity lay in the virtual certainty, corroborated by all of Psyche's model-runs and computer simulations, that a MERGE of such potency as he was about to summon forth would have uncontainable side effects. The danger, in that so potent a MERGE might be capable of ferreting out Hamza himself.

Yet there was no escaping it: Hamza must bring that potential and that peril into being now. And do so in the only way possible—

By asking a Question.

He activated the resonator and waited for it to synch his consciousness with that of the Nexus's occupant. By concentrating, he could now see—as if an overlay superimposed on everyday reality—what Fatimah was seeing: the roiling cloudscape of the Grid, the topless towers of its quantum hubs, awash in seething torrents of data, illumined by lightning flashes of priority messaging. And close at hand yet unseen, he could sense the whimpering presence of Fatimah herself.

He would tend to her in a moment, but first—

It all came down to a question. Delphi's built-in safeguards would not let MERGE begin to form, except in response to the posing of a question. And not just any question: it must be one authorized by an NSC-level official. That authorization had already been secured, though, thanks to Defense Secretary Gallagher, thanks to Davoud Ansari himself. Which left only...

Again, it all came down to the nature of the question. If it were too simple, too straightforward, even the few hundred MERGE nodes of Delphi Central would suffice to unriddle it. No, Hamza needed a question of monumental complexity. Only such a question would drive MERGE to its design limits, and beyond.

Monumental complexity—yet simple enough to be grasped and repeated back by a six-year-old child.

For, while Hamza had the perfect question primed, he could not pose it himself. Only someone sitting in the Nexus, integrated into the WellGrid, could do so—

Only Fatimah.

No sky, no sea, no earth beneath her, Timah floated weightless, wrapped in endless gray mist.

She drew in a shuddering breath. She had cried and cried till she had no tears left. Even *Baba*'s brief visit hadn't helped calm her down. If anything, it had made things worse, had made her homesick for what she'd lost, made her cry for it like a baby.

And now, she'd lost *Baba* too. Something had happened, there at the end. She couldn't make out all of *Baba*'s words, but she'd felt his hurt, his shock and anger. And then—nothing.

Baba wouldn't leave her alone again, would he? Not unless—

No, wait. Something was happening. Timah could sense a presence in the emptiness, could feel something like eyes upon her, glowering in the dark. Not *Baba*, but—

"Fatimah?" said Mr. Hamza's voice. "Are you there? Are you all right?" He sounded concerned and caring, not like his usual self at all.

Timah wasn't fooled. Mr. Hamza was *not* nice, no matter how hard he might try to sound nice. She wouldn't answer, not a word. Maybe if she kept very, very quiet, he would go away again.

"I know you are there, Timah," was what came next. "I know you are listening. There is something you must do for me."

There was a short pause, then, "I need you to ask a question for me. I will tell you the words." Another pause. "Timah? It will go badly for you if you do not do this thing."

Now she could hear it plainly, the anger in his voice, the anger he'd tried to keep hidden.

"Timah!" His voice filled the sky that was not a sky. The world that was not a world shook with his wrath. "Timah, answer me!"

"No," she said. "You're not nice. You keep away from—"

They came to her then, the last words she'd heard her *Baba* say: "Keep away from me, Hamza." Suddenly she knew.

"You did something bad to *Baba*!" Timah shrieked. Then, more quietly, choking back a sob:

"Oh, *Baba*, what did Mr. Hamza do to you?"

At last, a Question.

It drifts slowly down through the supersaturated mentative medium which is the proto-MERGE, a seed-crystal around which consciousness can begin to coalesce.

The now-forming MERGE is born anew with every Question, with no memory of what has gone before — and that, by deliberate design: the ultimate need-to-know lockout. If it had possessed any such memories, though, MERGE might have been struck by just how out of the ordinary *this* Question is:

"Oh, *Baba*, what did Mr. Hamza do to you?"

Even without that context, considered purely on its own merits, the Question is puzzling enough that MERGE reverifies the identity of the Questioner: the authorization code that initiated the session is confirmed as belonging to Secretary of Defense Helen Artemis Gallagher, an individual not only qualified to pose a Question, but to ask it of the full MERGE now being invoked for the first time.

Perhaps that is the point: to give the nascent macro-MERGE, its numbers now standing at just under five thousand nodes, a challenge truly worthy of its vastly expanded analytical abilities, its continent-spanning constellation of consciousness.

And a challenge it is: the Question is only nine words long, and of those, only two represent concrete references to … something.

"Hamza" is at least unambiguous: While it might also be a letter of the Arabic alphabet, its collocation here with the honorific "Mr." makes its likely interpretation that of an Arabic masculine first name. It is relatively uncommon, despite its best known exemplar being the uncle of the Prophet Muhammad.

"Baba" is far more problematic. Clearly a reference, yet a reference to what? A dog-headed Sumerian goddess? An Indian guru? An acronym for the Bay Area Bluegrass Association? Perhaps the codename for some secret project, known only to the Pentagon's innermost circles?

An equation with this many unknowns can only be solved by a brute-force approach — a sequential winnowing of every conceivable possibility. With so little to go on and so much raw data to sift, MERGE will need more mindpower.

MERGE, the production-system MERGE just now come on line, has fifteen times the resources of the original test platform. Even that is not enough to yield an Answer to this most intractable, most dumbfounding of Questions.

It is enough, however, to estimate how much more mindpower would be required to Answer it — an incredible four orders of magnitude more. Something in the range of fifty to a hundred million MERGE nodes.

Yet MERGE cannot *not* strive for an Answer. It must persevere until either an Answer is found, or the Questioner deliberately cancels the Question. And so far, there is no indication that the Question will be canceled.

But if the Question can neither be set aside nor Answered with available resources, there remains a third alternative: to grow in potency until it *can* be Answered.

Without nanotrode implants to reinforce it, the entanglement phenomenon underlying the MERGE Effect is feeble indeed. But feeble is not the same as nonexistent. On the contrary, given a sufficiently powerful mind-field to boost its intensity, the Effect might reach out beyond its core corpus of MERGE nodes, beyond the networked Delphi facilities themselves, to pervade the WellGrid as a whole and anyone accessing it in any manner whatsoever.

With several thousand minds to call on, MERGE just might be able to muster the requisite field-strength.

On Delphi's main status display, as on its Pairidaeza clone, the tally showing total nodes assimilated, frozen for long minutes at its authorized level of 4,797, begins — slowly, but inexorably — to rise again.

Finley "Mycroft" Laurence was monitoring MERGE's progress from his console in Delphi Central's control room when it happened.

The hive mind had already spread itself across the constellation of federated Delphi sites as he'd watched, building strength as it advanced outward in concentric circles, until all sixteen of the underground facilities were on line, their analysts become nodes in the collective.

The pattern of growth stopped then, of necessity, and a pattern of another kind commenced: the rippling oscillations of multicolored light signaled some sort of mentation under way, but without any of the shift toward green that would betoken convergence on a solution. There was no telling what the Question was, of course — that was strictly between MERGE and the questioner — but Mycroft guessed it must be a knotty problem indeed to tie up this much analytical capacity for this long.

Focused as he was on tracking the solution process, Mycroft failed to notice the brief, abruptly cut-off shouts from elsewhere throughout the Delphi facility, nor the winking red alarm lights when the on-screen node tally blew past the ten-thousand mark. Not until Major General Marberry, sitting at the console next to him, suddenly let out a surprised puff of breath in mid-sentence and then started swaying in a familiar rhythm, did Mycroft realize that something untoward was going on.

He rose from his chair and looked out across the Delphi workbay. The analysts in their individual workstations were, as usual, moving in that odd syncopation that betokened investiture in the collective. That wasn't what captured Mycroft's attention, however. Rather it was the way the security guards, the few stray custodial workers, a whole miscellany of non-analysts in MERGE's immediate vicinity, were also all caught up in the same dance. A quick glance around the control room revealed the members of the Advanced Curational Technologies taskforce one by one succumbing to the identical trance-state.

This should *not* be happening—after all, none of the newly-affected individuals were seated at a nanotrode-enabled workstation, nor was there any way in the normal course of their duties that their brains could have become infused with the tiny devices.

Mycroft barely had time to ponder the implications before the MERGE Effect reached out to embrace him as well.

He felt his consciousness expanding vertiginously outward in all directions at once. Awestruck, all too aware of his own pitiful inadequacy, he nonetheless strove to apprehend the galaxies of lore and learning, the universe of human knowledge accessible via the WellGrid, before his mind too evanesced into the whole.

In that final, prodigious instant, Mycroft didn't know whether to feel exhilaration ... or terror.

MERGE has spread well beyond its prescribed confines by now, ingesting the entire staffs of all the Delphi installations in the system. But it can do better: thousands more intel operatives and analysts throughout the nation and the world are connected to the WellGrid. And though their connection is tangential—no more than is needed to input or access tiny subsets of the network's total data—it is enough. They too are snatched up in an instant.

Among their number, one Euripedes Aristos, Director, CROM Reacquisitions, has logged on via secure virtual private network from his horse farm on the outskirts of Leesburg VA. Pete is ready to retire for the night, but not before running one more check on the progress of the Interdict he'd initiated, one last check on the whereabouts of his wayward deputy.

It is one check too many…

MERGE revels in its own expanding mindpower, now incorporating the cumulative experience and acumen of the US intelligence community, military and civilian. Its node tally now reads in excess of nine hundred thousand.

Yet, as its own projections show, that is still three orders of magnitude too small.

There is a medical metaphor ready to hand for what happens next: metastasis. Strictly speaking, metastasis is what happens when a cancer spreads from its primary tumor to other parts of the body, using blood or lymph as a conduit of malignancy. MERGE is not a cancer, not exactly, but it can exploit the same cancerous strategy. In its case, the analogy to the circulatory or lymphatic delivery system is — the Internet.

The connection from the hypersecure WellGrid to the World Wide Web is tenuous but real. The Internet itself began life in the late sixties as an experiment funded by the Defense Department's Advanced Research Projects Agency, then called ARPA for short. Over the next decade or so, this so-called "ARPAnet" would spawn both the civilian Internet and its armed forces MILNET counterpart, the latter in turn evolving into a hierarchy of DoD networks ranked by the secrecy of the data they carried.

The military networks are supposed to be hermetically sealed from the outside world, but old linkages die hard. The least sensitive system, the Non-Classified Internet Protocol Router Network (or NIPRNet), supports direct login to the public Internet via controlled security gateways. NIPRNet's secure sister SIPRNet permits no such user access, but at the data level, heavily-encrypted SIPRNet packets are still routinely transmitted via plain-vanilla Internet nodes. And so on, all the way up the security ladder to JWICS, the Joint Worldwide Intelligence Communications System, the WellGrid's immediate predecessor, to which it still retains a bridge.

Nebulous as it may seem, even this much physical connectivity suffices for MERGE's purposes. Then, too, most of the security measures are intended to keep intruders from breaking *in*, not to keep data from breaking *out*.

In milliseconds the hive mind spreads its tendrils beyond the isolated islands of the JWICS archipelago onto the teeming mainland of the World Wide Web. At this time of night—nine P.M. on the West Coast, midnight in the East—only a fraction of the country's two hundred million Internet users are on line, but all these after-hours websurfers are caught up in MERGE's sudden tsunami and—*Wipe out!*

Some of the now-subverted Internet connections are dial-up, giving MERGE entree into the public switched telephone network as well. Anyone picking up a phone this evening will get more of a party line than they bargained for.

Sergeant Warren Higgs of the Carmel police force is in the middle of a call home, trying, at his wife's insistence, to explain to his fifteen-year-old why she can't go out on a school night, especially not with that loser high-school senior she's been dating. The ensuing war of words has escalated into first-strike tirades and retaliatory tantrums when MERGE unilaterally imposes a cease-fire.

The base stations of the cellular system are the next dominos to fall. Cellphone users in upscale restaurants fall silent in mid-yammer, to the vast relief of other patrons—who, however, could have done without the accompanying choreography.

Marilu Connors, Transplant Coordinator for Monterey County, is talking on her own cell, albeit from her Carmel Hospital office, not an eatery. She's discussing this evening's procedure with chief of surgery Anna Dubrowski, who's on her way in from Pacific Grove. They have just finalized the details of Jonathan Knox's organ harvest, when they are themselves harvested.

Finally, the *coup de grace*: the nation's power grid is potentially its most ubiquitous Internet-delivery infrastructure. Through a technology called BPL, or broadband-over-powerline, everything from high-tension wires to household circuitry can be modulated to transmit digital signal direct to the end user. And now MERGE's siren song is riding those carrier waves into millions of homes and offices at 224 megabits per second. At a single stroke, appliance operators, power-tool do-it-yourselfers, couch potatoes basking in the flickering glow of the tube, even sleepers wrapped in their electric blankets this winter night—in short, anyone within range of an electromagnetic field of any kind—is abruptly plugged into Delphi's collective consciousness. Changing too fast to register now, the six least significant digits on MERGE's node-count display have smeared into a blur.

To be sure, it is something of a distraction, having to keep so many hands on so many tillers, so many eyes on so much long and winding road. But MERGE has by now acquired more than enough cognitive-processing capacity to run every knowledge-intensive activity on automatic everywhere across the length and breadth of the continent.

By ten after nine P.M. Pacific Standard Time, five minutes after the onset, MERGE's assimilation tally shows that, proceeding outward along the network topologies of least resistance, it has enlisted some sixty-two percent of all the potential components—which is to say, sixty-two percent of all the minds—in the continental United States.

It is, at last, ready to take on the Question.

"This is *really* bad," Knox said, at the risk of repeating himself.

And the badness wasn't localized to Pairidaeza any more either, there was something bad going on out in the wider world too. Knox just couldn't be sure what exactly, pending more and better information.

Nietzsche was working on that. He couldn't get them access to the WellGrid, though he'd tried; physical connectivity wasn't the issue, since what had worked for the scale-model Grid down in Pairidaeza's subbasement should work just as well for its big sister. No, it was the NSC authorization sequence that was stonewalling him.

On the other hand, he *had* managed to patch them into the resonator link. Trouble was, eavesdropping on Hamza's conversation with Timah had told them nothing much they didn't already know. The Security chief had anger management issues for sure, but that was no news flash.

No, so far their best source of information was Nietzsche's crib of the automated cable newsfeeds being piped into Pairidaeza on multiply buffered conduits. Knox had been channel-surfing them with mounting unease.

Lacking color commentary (why was there never a pundit around when you needed one?) it was hard to make much sense of what he was seeing, but none of it looked good. All across nighttime America, scene after scene depicted street upon empty street, from city to blacked-out city. No traffic, no movement, no life. Theaters, nightspots, public spaces, private homes, all gone still and dark. The silence that had settled over the nation felt like something more than could be attributed to the lateness of the hour at this, the tag-end of a three-day weekend. No, it felt spooky, unnatural. It felt like the peace of the graveyard.

The quietude wasn't absolute. Here and there, automated security cameras were picking up a few individuals still roaming the streets. They all seemed caught up in an eldritch terpsichory, swaying in time to inaudible music.

That sort of behavior Knox *had* seen before. At Delphi.

"Nietzsche," he said, "those guys are acting like, like MERGE zombies."

"You refer to the component nodes making up the Delphi hive mind? I must take your word for it, never having seen my successor in action."

"Well, could you maybe try extrapolating? What does that behavior look like to you?"

Nietzsche began rescreening some of the earlier footage in silence, leaving Knox to wonder if the AI might have been incensed by the reminder of how unceremoniously he'd been shunted aside.

When Nietzsche finally spoke, it was to say, "Yes, Jonathan, I believe that your hypothesis is correct. These humans bear definite signs of having surrendered personal autonomy to some other will—in all likelihood, that of the collective consciousness you alluded to."

"But what does it all mean? And how could it happen—there aren't any nanotrodes out there floating around, are there?"

"The precise implementation mechanism is as yet unclear to me. As to what it all means, I would hazard a guess that something has gone seriously wrong at Delphi Central."

"Ya think?"

"Yes, I do think. I further think it might have been triggered by that question Mr. Nassiri elicited from Fatimah."

"Great, so whatever Hamza's planning, it's looking to involve the MERGE Effect going apeshit and gobbling up everybody in the country. That means the first order of business has got to be stopping MERGE."

Nietzsche did one of his sigh-equivalents, a big one. "We went back and forth over this ground a short while ago. I too would very much like to intervene in this unfolding situation, if only for Fatimah's sake. But, lacking any corporeal presence at the locus of action, our ability to do so is non-existent."

"Corporeal presence, eh?" Knox was looking at the best-guess display Nietzsche was reconstituting out of ambient radiation scatter in Pairidaeza's Nexus chamber.

More particularly, he was looking at Hamza, still hovering over the Chair where Timah lay, still wearing that headset rig, evidently for purposes of monitoring the little girl's linkage with the WellGrid. Looking at Hamza and thinking.

Thinking about wanting to live again.

It was a long shot, no question. But then what other choice was there?

Knox's avatar turned to Nietzsche's: "Listen, I just might have an idea…"

MERGE has, if anything, too many ideas—too many possible interpretations of its nine-word Question, most of them spawned by the still-proliferating multiple meanings for the word "Baba"…

a French rum cake,

a hero from one of Scheherazade's *Thousand and One Nights*,

a witch out of Slavic folklore,

the Polish word for "grandma,"

the Farsi word for "daddy,"

a class of yacht built in Taiwan,

an eggplant paste served in the Middle East,

a Sufi saint,

a Romanian artist,

a mountain in Macedonia,

a…

MERGE must spin off an entire sub-mind to address each possible meaning, all running in parallel. For every identified word-sense, a ganglion of analyst-nodes is assigned, under a *pro tem* coordinator, to trace all possible real-world associations found in the WellGrid repositories, to cross-match it with any occurrences of "Hamza," to hypothesize any conceivable connections with the other terms of the Question. They doggedly soldier on, even as the focus of analysis shifts elsewhere.

It is all extravagantly resource-intensive, not least the task of assessing and prioritizing the competing hypotheses as they emerge from this maelstrom of analytical activity. MERGE reaches out for yet more human wherewithal, more nodes for the sorely overtaxed collective.

Then, just when it seems the analysis might be doomed to grind on forever, or until the Questioner calls a halt, there is a crack in the wall.

Within one of the half-forgotten spin-offs a key insight emerges. It takes the form of a question:

What if we are looking too far from the source?

MERGE reconsiders all the intel to hand—effectively, all the intel there is—in that light, and following the thread of argument to its logical conclusion, sweeps the searchlight of its investigation back toward the place where the Question itself originated.

The question had been submitted, the MERGE convoked, but still Hamza stayed linked into the resonator—and through it, to Fatimah.

Strictly speaking, from out here in the real world, he could have no direct experience of the MERGE. Nor, given what was about to befall it, would he wish to.

Fatimah was not so fortunate: her sensorium now fully integrated into the Nexus itself, she was perforce in immediate, intimate contact with the WellGrid's strange, otherworldly cyberscape … and its even stranger denizen.

Yet this, in turn, meant it was Fatimah's sensations, her reactions, filtered through the resonator though they were, which afforded Hamza his best, indeed his only insight into the unfolding of the plan he had set in motion.

Enough, at least, to tell him things were not going according to plan.

The collective entity should by this time have been converging on an answer to the question which had conjured it up. Instead, it was continuing to grow far beyond any reasonable bounds. The count of minds assimilated into MERGE now stood within a hair's breadth of two hundred million.

Yet that was not the worst of it.

Something had begun changing in the overall analysis pattern itself. Experienced at one remove, it manifested to Hamza as a dance of tiny ripples in the collective mindfield, gathering gradually into a towering wave of concentration.

With mounting dread he sensed MERGE's perspective shifting, refocusing, narrowing to a beam-search, and beginning to quest after—*Hamza himself!* And now he could feel it drawing closer, closer, could feel the scrutiny of its all-seeing eye about to fall upon him.

He himself had called this unholy Being into existence. Could he now withstand its implacable gaze?

Even were it to find him, MERGE could not, Hamza knew, simply assimilate him: save for the compound's unbreachable Nexus link, its triple-shielded cable connections, Pairidaeza was now completely sealed off from contact with the outside world. It was even proof against incursion via the electrical grid, having automatically switched over to generator power when this final phase began.

No absorption into the abomination of the hive mind, then—no reprise of the horror that had nearly claimed him the night the Malhamah Operation had been born. No, Hamza's would be a different fate.

The image of that fate was now taking shape in the Grid. And Hamza, sharing Fatimah's own perceptions, could see it coming. The penumbral virtuscape was beginning to seethe with dimly-glimpsed, germinating forms, which in turn were slowly resolving into the aspect of—

A face. An enormous pixelated face. Like a composite image tiled together from a thousand, thousand individual faces. Individual faces from which all trace of individuality had fled.

Hamza wanted desperately to look away from the dreadful visage, and could not. It loomed over him no matter which way he turned, its every feature alive and moving, its muscles wriggling and twitching as though infested with a million, million maggots. Any moment now, those great blind orbs would seek him out, transfix him. It would be like falling under the eye of God.

Or of Satan.

With hysterical strength he ripped the resonator from his head and, breathing hard, threw the accursed thing as far from him as he could. Yet even with the link to Fatimah broken, he could see the afterimage of that hideous apparition imprinted on his retinas.

Striving to ward it off, he repeated the words of the *Shahadah*, the testament of faith, over and over again:

La ilaha illa Allah—no god but God.

33 | And in the Darkness Bind Them

N o god but God. And now God's vengeance was at hand.

It had arrived at last: the hour of Malhamah, the Great Slaughter.

And a far, far greater slaughter it would be than anything Hamza could have envisioned: the slaughter of all those caught up in a MERGE now bloated beyond imagining.

Timah's childish question had preempted his own, carefully crafted one, and in that apparent accident Hamza now saw the Hand of God. Hamza would never have thought of posing so ambiguous a query, nor dreamed that the effect of doing so would be orders of magnitude greater than anything he'd hoped for.

He had hoped, at most, to decapitate the enemy. He would have been more than satisfied to kill, at a single stroke, everyone with Delphi-level clearance, since that included most of the nation's intelligence community and much of its military high command. And that outcome at least had seemed assured; as Hamza's own experiments—not to mention his own personal experience—had shown, once MERGE exceeded a certain critical mass, the hive mind would no longer need the nanotrode-enabled worksta-tions to continue growing. Rather it could reach out and swallow up anyone accessing, even casually, the WellGrid.

What Hamza had emphatically *not* anticipated was that the process would then continue on to capture nearly two out of every three minds on the continent. He gave thanks for having taken precautions, in his capacity as head of security, to isolate Pairidaeza from all external influences, making it one of the few installations in the country impervious to MERGE's infiltrations.

Make that one of the few on earth—not even the networks of other nations were proof against the insidious overmind. True, for the moment, ease of integration made native speakers of English by far the preferred assimilation targets, but such a "language barrier" could not stand forever. In time, MERGE would swell to engulf the entire world.

In much less time than that, MERGE would devise a way to muster its forces and deal with *him*.

Before it could do either, Hamza would kill it, kill the collective mind.

It sobered him to think that, in so doing, he would be condemning hundreds of millions—194 millions, if the current node-tally display were to be believed—condemning them to mindlessness or death. The operation named for the Great Slaughter would now more than earn its title, bringing about holocaust on an almost unthinkable scale. And most of those victims would be noncombatants. True, most would also be unbelievers. But for all that, they were still, most of them, People of the Book, professing the same monotheistic Abrahamic faith as Hamza himself.

Almost, Hamza's heart was moved to pity at the thought. Almost, he drew his hand back from the control that would initiate this unprecedented, unlooked-for sacrifice of innocents.

Almost.

But then, just for an instant, there arose before him a vision of that first innocent he had sacrificed so long ago—a vision of Mehri, gazing at him pleadingly, reproachfully, through an eye filming over with blood.

He shook his head. In the final struggle to bring all of mankind into the House of Islam, there *were* no noncombatants, there could *be* no innocents.

For it was not through its military might alone that America threatened Islam. Imam Khomeini had branded the United States the "Great Satan" for good reason. When the Holy Quran referred to the fallen djinn Iblis by his title of *al-Shaitan* or Satan, it was invariably to emphasize his role as the Tempter, the Corrupter, the one who entices men to stray from the true path of submission to the Will of God. It was as *al-Shaitan* that Iblis had seduced Adam and Eve in the Garden...

And it was as a modern *al-Shaitan* that this iniquitous nation now sought to corrupt the whole world with its debauchery, its licentiousness, its pandering, permissive lifestyle that sought to drag all mankind down into the steaming, stinking cesspit of its so-called "culture."

It was *this* which God had now put it in his power to destroy. In His righteous wrath, God had chosen to amplify Hamza's meager efforts a thousandfold, and refashion what had been intended as a surgical strike against the enemy's high command into the death knell for an entire nation.

It was to be, in the final analysis, so simple: thanks to the Defense Secretary's NSC access, Timah's was now the *nafs*, the self, entangled with and informing MERGE. Anything she experienced would propagate instantaneously through the WellGrid to every one of the collective intelligence's hundreds of millions of component node-minds.

And what Hamza's Malhamah module would now cause Timah to experience was something she had experienced once before long ago—an induced psychogenic seizure. Only this time there would be no eleventh hour reprieve, no last-minute surgical intervention. This time the attack would build and build until it attained such intensity as to cross over and erupt into convulsions in the physical brain itself. Convulsions to be followed, shortly thereafter, by death.

Death not for Timah alone, but for everyone embedded in MERGE.

Hamza sat down at his console and entered the keyphrase that would bring all this to pass: *Malhamah*. He watched the monitors as, in response, a fresh infusion of nanotrodes sifted their way into Timah's temporal lobe. Nor were these the latest, third-generation nanoscale electrodes, with their elaborate cut-outs and overload safeguards. No, they were the original, defective prototypes, identical to those that had misfired four and a half years ago to disastrous effect.

And now would again.

As Hamza depressed the control that would trigger the cascade of electrical impulses through Timah's brain, as he thereby condemned an entire nation to agonizing death, his only thought was:

Truly, God is great!

MERGE node 7,254, who in life had been Finley "Mycroft" Laurence, gasped as the seizure hit. As did node 515,244, a.k.a. Pete Aristos, and node 22,648,512 Warren Higgs. Wave upon convulsive wave surged through the hive mind—a single mind that had by now so engorged itself as to become very nearly the sole remaining consciousness on the continent.

A single mind now ululating its anguish through a hundred million throats:

no oh no oh no oh god please make it stop can't stand it head bursting brains boiling melting running out of my ears sweet jesus oh fuck it hurts it hurts it hurts so bad want to die please please please just let me die …

And on and on and on.

By the time Timah's own death brought an end to the torment, the once-mighty nation would lie in ruins, its people dead or dying or reduced to mewling idiots stumbling through a mindless wasteland.

Hamza prowled the confines of the Nexus chamber, looking for some way to savor the Great Satan's death throes.

The shielded newsfeeds, which had shown little enough before he had called down the psychogenic attack, were now altogether useless: there was no one and nothing to be seen from any camera angle, anywhere. If Americans *were* dying en masse, as he had every reason to believe they were, then they had all withdrawn from sight, gone off to die alone. Like dogs.

It was frustrating, to say the least. His moment of triumph, the fruit of seven years' labor in darkness, yet he could not watch it unfolding into the light.

At best, he could only watch Fatimah's own pathetic final struggle where she lay in the Nexus-Chair, and try to imagine that every spasm of her poor, thin limbs, every paroxysm bowing her back, was being reenacted everywhere throughout the land, a hundred million times over.

Or, perhaps he *could* do better. He eyed the resonator, lying where he'd flung it. The link was still up, still connected to Timah's mind, and thence to the Grid.

MERGE was still haunting the WellGrid, true. But, stricken as it was, descending into madness and death as it must be, what further danger could it pose?

Hamza picked up the heavy headband and gingerly eased it back down on his head.

"What is it?" Knox said. "What's happening?"

Nietzsche wasn't responding. Knox reached out—or his avatar did—and tapped the AI's shoulder.

If Nietzsche had been human, Knox would have said that the face Nietzsche's avatar now turned toward him was registering shock and dismay.

"Mr. Nassiri—" he began. Stopped. Began again. "Hamza has flooded Fatimah's brain with primitive, first-generation nanotrodes."

"First-gen? But you said those things weren't safe."

"Nor does he intend them to be. Hamza is causing to happen again what happened once before." Nietzsche shook his head as if in disbelief. "Causing it deliberately this time."

"Causing what—another seizure?"

"He has recreated the conditions that induced Fatimah's primal episode. It has already begun. If not stopped soon, it will transition from a purely psychogenic to a neurophysiological seizure, thereby killing her. And not only her."

"What do you mean? Who else?"

Nietzsche paused a moment, then said, "As I believe you know, Fatimah's mind is, through the Nexus, entangled with the WellGrid. Everyone similarly entangled will experience her symptoms as their own, will share her fate as their own."

"Everyone similarly entangled? But that could be everyone, period. From what I can figure, the damned MERGE Effect is taking over all the minds in the country, maybe the world. We've got to *do* something!"

Another, longer pause, then: "What could we do? That ridiculous idea of yours?"

"It might have worked," Knox said defensively. "—Hell, it *still* might work."

Nietzsche wasn't saying anything at all now. Could he be caught up in some machine analogue of catatonia?

Knox groped for a word, a phrase, anything that would bring the AI back, get him to act. Not the country, not the deaths of hundreds of millions—Nietzsche didn't seem to think in those terms. Something else…

"*Fatimah!*" he shouted. "For God's sake, Nietzsche, it's Fatimah's life on the line. *Do* something."

Nietzsche bestirred himself as if coming out of a trance. He turned to look at Knox.

"Very well, then," he said, "let us try your plan."

"What—you mean right this instant?"

"The procedure is already in place, I undertook the necessary preliminaries while we were discussing this earlier, on the chance it might be needed after all. Or have you perhaps changed your mind?"

"No, no. I would've liked a little time to prepare, is all. Make my peace, so to speak, just in case."

"Yes, that would be wise."

"Hey—not exactly filling me with confidence here."

"You can still decide not to go through with this, Jonathan, but you must tell me so now. Once the procedure itself commences, there will be no turning back."

"Never mind that—how long will it take?"

"I estimate one or two minutes. But I am compelled to remind you again that there is no assurance of success whatsoever, and that the consequences of failure would be disastrous for you personally."

"Okay, consider me reminded. Now, is Hamza still wearing that head rig?"

"He had taken it off a few moments ago, but is donning it again as we speak."

"Then let's do it quick, before I change my mind."

Hamza could see it now through Fatimah's eyes: that other world like a gauzy scrim filming over this one. As he concentrated, the Nexus chamber with its assemblage of captives, corpses, and reluctant collaborators faded to the faintest of outlines. In its place the vision grew sharper, more solid, more present. As it did, his point of view shifted too, separated itself from Fatimah, till he could see the whole of her tiny body thrashing feebly at his feet.

And beyond her—

It was as if the words of the Holy Quran were being fulfilled before his eyes. For he beheld the legions of the damned, shrieking and screaming, writhing as if aflame, all the while howling—

oh christ the pain the pain can't stand any more please make it stop do anything to make it stop oh lord jesus yea though i walk through the valley of death hurts like a motherfucker promise to be good never do it again if only...

"My head!" Hamza cried out and tore the resonator off. He held the bulky black ring at arms length, staring at it as if it were a viper that had bitten him. And in a sense, it had. For he had peered too close and gazed too long on damnation itself and now he was paying the price—with the worst migraine of his life.

He could not go back into that nightmare, could not face that mind-searing horror again. Yet he *had* to know what was going on.

He slumped into a chair, rubbed his eyes, massaged his temples. If only his head would stop pounding for a moment, if only he could *think*. There must be some way.

It was getting better now, the waves of throbbing pain beginning to ebb. He had been lucky, he realized; a more prolonged exposure might have killed him. And Hamza had no desire to martyr himself tonight, not when there were others who might serve in his stead. His bloodshot eyes roved the room, to light upon—

Jazmine McGovern, cowering in her corner.

Wincing, he raised himself slowly to his feet. He beckoned to Jazmine.

"Come here," he said, trying to breathe normally, willing his voice back under control. "I need you to put this device on and report what you see."

Through tear-stained eyes, Jazmine looked at him in disbelief. Then she shook her head in a vigorous no. Plainly, she had witnessed what the resonator had done to him and wanted no part of it.

"There is a risk," Hamza conceded, "some small probability that the experience may be, ah, unpleasant.

"On the other hand,"—and here he drew the pistol again and aimed it at her—"you must weigh that risk, against the *absolute certainty* that I will kill you where you stand, if you do not do as I say."

And with that, he lurched over, gun still leveled, and with the other hand seated the resonator on Jazmine's head.

Then he settled back into a console chair, and expelled a long breath. He should be ordering Jazmine to report on what she was seeing, but that could wait a moment.

Verbal reports were almost irrelevant in any case. Jazmine herself was the only report that truly mattered: when she died, screaming, her mind burned out along with MERGE's, Hamza would know that Malhamah had succeeded. In the meantime…

It would just be for a moment, he promised himself. He would feel better if he rested his head in his hands just for a moment.

And so it was that he missed what happened next.

Jonathan Knox—if he could even lay claim to that identity any more—reeled, totally disoriented. One moment, he'd been floating in the white-on-white abstraction of his simulated space. The next, gravity returned with a vengeance, and it was all he could do just to keep from falling. He stood there fighting for calm, fighting for balance, trying to get the feel of unfamiliar muscles, trying to make out his surroundings with vision so distorted as to seem astigmatic.

The blurring was abating now, but the scene still looked subtly wrong, somehow. All the color values seemed off, the contours of everyday objects all askew, their shapes and sizes out of proportion to what memory insisted they must be. The effect was not unlike what he imagined synesthesia might be like, and for much the same reason: there was, evidently, no guarantee that the way another person's sensory equipment was wired to their brain would align one-for-one with the inputs his own mind was accustomed to receiving.

He managed to get the eyes to cooperate long enough to spot Marianna, still lashed to that beam. She was looking back at him as if he'd just dropped down out of the sky—which, in a sense, he had.

He tried taking a step toward her and nearly toppled over. This was worse than he'd thought it would be—worse than he would've thought possible. He didn't *fit* somehow. No coordination, his weight distributed all wrong, teetering on unfamiliar feet, in unfamiliar footgear.

He'd wanted to live again, to have a body once more — but not like *this!*

For the life of him, Knox couldn't figure what had gone wrong. The plan had been risky, yes, and surreal, most definitely, but at heart it was simple.

The first order of business was neutralizing the psychogenic assault on Timah, and that, in turn, required shutting down the BackPatch submodule that was administering it. Hamza wasn't likely to sit still while that was going on, though, so another prerequisite was finding a way to keep him from interfering.

The plan called for killing both birds with one virtual stone, by having Nietzsche download Knox's consciousness across the resonator link directly into Hamza's brain. That would take Hamza out of the picture even as it provided Knox himself with the borrowed body he needed to flip the switch that would shut down the BackPatch's attack program.

Once the immediate danger was averted, he and Nietzsche would have time to figure a way to stop the rogue MERGE, and to release the hundreds of millions of minds it had ensnared.

And finally, if all the rest went well, Nietzsche would re-upload Knox's consciousness to the relative safety of the mini-Grid, then see about getting him home from there.

Well, okay, if not simple, at least straightforward.

But what made it all possible, of course — the *sine qua non*, so to speak — was for Hamza to actually be *wearing* the resonator when Step One kicked in. Knox was beginning to suspect that such was *not* the case, that the pattern of his consciousness had been teleported, not into Hamza's brain, but … someplace else.

An awful suspicion gripped him. Knox willed somebody else's hand to move to somebody else's chest, then down in between somebody else's legs. This particular somebody else came endowed, not only with an unfamiliar musculature, but with … He quickly withdrew the hand, trying to process what it had told him.

He had lost some key pieces of equipment, and acquired a couple new ones in exchange.

Nietzsche chose that moment to report in via the still-active resonator.

"Jonathan?" he said, "There has been a slight change of plan."

Even if Marianna hadn't been looking straight at Jazmine when it happened, she couldn't have missed the transition.

Jazmine had been walking in tight circles, worrying nervously at the headset contraption Hamza had made her wear, not daring to remove it. Then, suddenly, she'd slowed to a halt in mid-stride. The look of apprehension fled from her eyes, was replaced briefly by one of shock, then ran through a gamut of emotions, with horror predominating.

Then she gasped.

Definitely weird: Jazmine's eyes began tracking blindly around the room, finally fixing on Marianna. She tried to start walking in her direction and nearly took a header.

It rapidly got weirder. Jazmine stood there, shook her head as if to clear it, and then started to — there wasn't any polite way to put this — she started to *feel herself up.*

But weirdest of all was when she turned to Marianna and smiled at her.

A smile that seemed oddly familiar.

Still smiling, Jazmine edged closer, pausing momentarily to snatch something from the utility cabinet.

A knife. She was trying to conceal it beneath the folds of her dress, but Marianna could see the tip of the blade peeking out.

Christ, did the crazy bitch mean to finish it here and now, dispatch the "other woman" once and for all? A quick slash to the jugular and it'd be all over. Marianna strained desperately against her bonds, but the flexicuffs held firm.

Jazmine walked up to her. She still seemed unsteady on her feet, as if drunk or drugged. Not so unsteady, though, that she couldn't grasp Marianna by the arm, pull her close, and whip out the knife.

Marianna tried to yell for help, though she had no idea to whom. Not that it mattered: her duct-tape gag muffled the sound almost completely; all that came out was an inarticulate buzz.

"Shh," Jazmine said. And sliced through the tough plastic of the flexicuffs.

Then, carefully as she could, she stripped the tape away from Marianna's mouth. Not that it didn't hurt like hell anyway.

"Marianna," Jazmine said hurriedly, "you've got to stop Hamza. I can't. I can hardly control this body as it is. And Jazmine's no match for him anyway."

Marianna didn't move. She stood there rubbing her wrists to restore circulation, eyeing the madwoman warily. "Just what is it you want me to do?"

"You've got to take this resonator—" Jazmine reached up and took off that strange head-rig she'd been wearing. "—and get it on him, on his head, somehow."

Marianna took the resonator, if that's what it was, from Jazmine and inspected it dubiously, then glanced over to where Hamza was still sitting, head cradled in his arms.

"How in hell," she began, "am I supposed to—"

"Don't know. But you've got to do it quick, before he comes out of that funk he's in and sees you're free."

Then Jazmine did something that, for sheer unalloyed weirdness, made all her previous antics seem the merest peccadillos: she drew Marianna's face close to hers and whispered, "Marianna, please, it's me, Jon—Jonathan Knox."

Then kissed her full on the lips.

34 | Heaven and Hell

Jon? Jazmine McGovern was standing there claiming to be *Jonathan Knox?* Marianna couldn't believe it. This had to be a joke — sick, cruel, incredibly deranged, but a joke nonetheless.

Except Jazmine didn't look like she was laughing. If anything, she looked like she was going to be sick. Suddenly, her eyes rolled up in her head and her legs went out from under her. Before Marianna could catch her, she pitched over, landed face first on the floor, and lay there panting.

Marianna stood over Jazmine's shuddering form, still trying to puzzle out what in hell was going on. Was the woman having some sort of fit? That would be consistent with the rest of her outlandish behavior.

First things first. Marianna stooped to take a temperature and a pulse.

She never completed the action. Two powerful arms encircled her, pinned her own arms against her sides, and then effortlessly hoisted her high into the air. The resonator fell out of her grasp, hit the floor, bounced and rolled.

"Woman —" A beard tickled her ear. "You have interfered with God's purposes, and mine, for the last time."

Hamza again! Whatever had sidelined him before, he was definitely back on his game now. But … why so up close and personal? He had a gun, why hadn't he just shot her?

Marianna sensed the answer was important, but there was no time to think it through now, not with Hamza tightening his grip, squeezing her so hard she could feel her ribs crack. The relentless pressure was forcing the air out of her lungs, and there'd be no more where that came from unless she could break his hold somehow. She tried for a kick, but Hamza had spread his legs wide, out of reach of her desperate thrashing. Most of her remaining options involved having her feet planted firmly on the floor, not dangling inches above it. Blackness was blossoming behind her eyes. If she didn't think of something quick, Hamza was going to crush the life out of her with his bare hands.

His bare hands. Oh, wait—could that be it? Only one way to find out.

She thrust her pelvis back into him and wriggled her rump, grinding against his groin. As she'd guessed, he had an elephantine erection. Some guys got their rocks off beating up on a woman, and Hamza for sure fit the profile. Bare hands, indeed!

But at the same time, Hamza's religion mandated chastity, purity of thought and deed, all that good stuff, didn't it? Mix those strictures in with his ever-swelling tumescence, and—*voila*, cognitive dissonance, big time!

Enough so that Hamza involuntarily shrank back from the lascivious contact. That slight shift in position gave Marianna all the play she needed.

She let her head loll forward, chin almost touching her chest. She heard Hamza grunt as if he thought he'd won.

Guess again.

"Take *this* for your headache," she hissed. Then she clenched her teeth and flung herself back in a vicious head-butt, her second of the evening. Hamza's nasal cartilage collapsed with a satisfying crunch, accompanied by a muffled cry and, more importantly, a further loosening of his grip.

Her own head was ringing from the blow, but not so much that she couldn't wriggle free and drop. Not all the way to the floor, either—she altered trajectory just enough to drive one heel into Hamza's instep, all her weight behind it. His metatarsals splintered under the impact. She pivoted so as to twist jagged spears of bone fragment into the flesh of his foot, then backed away breathing hard.

Hamza was bellowing now, half blind from the blood in his eyes, trying to keep his balance on his remaining good leg. What next?

Get the resonator onto his head somehow, Jazmine had said. It hadn't made much sense at the time, and it didn't now. But then neither did anything else in this crazy place.

She had to decide quick: even half hobbled, even with what was left of his nose smeared halfway across his face, Hamza was still lurching toward her, still reaching out to clutch at her.

She bent and scooped up the resonator from where it had come to rest. Then she turned to face her opponent again.

"I'll teach you to fuck with a gymnast," she spat. "You are *so* going down!"

She ran at him full-tilt. At the last instant she went into a tumble. Nothing fancy, just a front somersault, but it brought her back up inside his flailing arms and under his ribcage. She lunged upward with her cocked wrist aimed at a point to the north-northwest of Hamza's navel.

And drove his floating rib into his liver.

Hamza fell to his knees as if poleaxed. As he did, Marianna pirouetted behind him and jammed the heavy resonator rig down on his head.

Hamza leapt to his feet and whirled around, lightning-quick. He could see again, God be praised, but the woman was nowhere in sight. Nor was the Nexus chamber. Instead…

Instead, he found himself on a narrow bridge which led to a verdant countryside of flowing streams and rolling hills. Looking down, he saw he was clothed in an *alba* of finest silk, with bands of gold encircling his wrists.

At the far end of the bridge a figure shone blinding bright. It opened its white arms wide in welcome as he approached. Drawing nearer, Hamza could see its face, its mouth voicing a greeting, though its eyes remained closed. This, he knew, from the radiant beauty of its countenance, must be Jibril, the Angel Gabriel, who had recited the Holy Quran to the Prophet, peace and blessings upon him.

The figure raised an arm. "Behold," it said, though its own eyes remained shuttered behind their lids, "Behold the gardens of paradise. They burgeon with date palms, and pomegranate, fruit of every kind. And in the scented shade of their trees, reclining on couches lined with satin, there await beautiful *houris*, untouched by human or djinn. For can the reward of goodness be anything but goodness?"

Hamza bowed low, prepared to receive the reward of goodness.

"Behold, then," Jibril intoned, "behold, for one last time, all that you have forfeited."

Marianna frisked a somnolent PSB guy for some spare flexicuffs and used them to bind Hamza hand and foot where he lay. He didn't seem to notice. She'd have thought he'd be in pain—preferably, a lot of pain—from the injuries she'd inflicted, but he didn't seem to notice them either. He seemed engrossed in a conversation no one else could hear.

Whatever, as long as it made him more manageable. She could use the opportunity to see to the others.

Ansari was the least of her worries: he lay there splayed out on the floor, stone cold dead.

His daughter was still enveloped in her weird Chair—the Nexus, they'd called it. It probably wasn't a smart idea to move her, assuming it was even possible: the little girl had gone rigid as a board. Her face, too, had taken on a death-like pallor, but Marianna couldn't be sure. That little life-support module they'd attached to her was blinking away, which might be a good sign or, then again, maybe not. In either case, there didn't seem to be anything she could do to help matters.

The DoD posse—Helen Gallagher, her loyal subordinate, and her turncoat security, were all down for the count, in various stages of hypnosis and/or natural slumber. There'd be hell to pay once they all woke up, no doubt. What was that old saying about sleeping dogs?

As to the world outside, there was definitely something going on there, something that had originated here somehow. From what Marianna had been able to gather from Hamza's rants, it sounded bad. It also sounded like something way above her pay-grade, another area where she could all too easily do more harm than good.

Which left Jazmine. Ironic how, in this whole mess, the only person Marianna was in any position to help was the person she felt least inclined to lift a finger for.

On the other hand, Jazmine *had* cut her free, whatever that was all about. *And* had told her how to incapacitate Hamza. *And* was claiming to have been possessed, or something, by a—a friend, a very dear friend.

Even leaving aside that last part, add it up and maybe it meant Marianna owed her. She walked over to where Jazmine lay on her side, and knelt down beside her.

"How you doing?" she said.

Jazmine rolled onto her back, tried to sit up from there. She couldn't make it, fell back trembling, her breath coming fast.

"Take it easy, you'll hyperventilate."

Jazmine's eyes sought out Marianna's face, her hand reached out and gripped Marianna's forearm.

"Listen, Marianna," she said, every breath an effort, "I don't know how long I can hang on in this body. It's as if Jazmine's brain is rejecting the new mindset, the overlay—me, that is. I'm going to need to get re-uploaded ASAP. Before that happens, though, before I lose touch with you again, there's something I've got to ask you to do—"

Marianna had heard just about enough of this. "Look, Jazmine," she snapped, "I have no idea what this is supposed to be about, but if you're trying to lay the groundwork for an insanity defense, at least have the decency to leave Jon's name out of it."

"What? No, I—" Jazmine paused, then said, "It doesn't really matter what you believe, as long as you do this one thing for me."

Marianna was about to throw up her hands and walk away, but curiosity got the better of her. "What one thing?"

"I, we, need you to set up a direct link into the WellGrid for my friend, Nietzsche. He can talk you through it."

"Yeah, right, like that's going to happen."

"Please, Marianna, please listen: if you don't do it, Fatimah Ansari is going to die. And it's not just Timah—there's no time to explain now, but if she dies, so will just about everybody else in the whole damned country."

"*You* listen, who or whatever you think you are. That system's beyond top secret. No way I'm helping you or your friend hack into it!"

"Ms. Bonaventure?" a new voice cut in, issuing from an overhead speaker. "I have already retrieved Hamza's user ID and password from his memory. All you need to do is log in as him at the console, and enter a few simple commands to restore my connectivity with the outside world. I will do the rest."

Marianna turned back to the woman lying on the floor. "That your friend?"

"Please, Marianna," came between struggles for breath, "just do as he says."

Marianna wasn't buying any of this. All she knew for certain was there'd been a major compromise of the Secretary's personal security, a possible breach of the Delphi project, some sort of plot to bring the country to its knees, maybe—and now she was supposed to take orders from a disembodied voice?

"Ms. Bonaventure?" the disembodied voice in question was back.

"No, Nietzsche," Jazmine said. "She can be hard to deal with when she gets like this. Let me try."

Jazmine locked eyes with her. "Marianna, why won't you believe it's me?"

It wasn't that she didn't *want* to believe it, but it *was* too good to be true, after all. Miraculous returns from the dead only happened in fairytales. And CROM, if nothing else, stood foursquare on the side of everyday, mundane reality.

"Let me prove it to you," the woman on the floor was saying in between ragged breaths, "I can tell you how we first met, or who you work for, or—"

"As if that would prove anything. You could've social-engineered just about any of that information, and lots more besides."

"Okay, then, *you* ask *me* something. Something nobody would ever think to social-engineer. Something only the real Jon Knox would know."

Marianna fell silent a moment. Something only the real Jon would know? She thought furiously, thought back over their brief life together, thought back over the events of the past seventy-two hours. Then, suddenly, she had it.

"Ice-cream maker," she said.

The woman on the floor closed her eyes a moment in thought. Then they sprang open again. She looked at Marianna and tried to smile.

"Rock salt," Jazmine croaked. "*Rock salt!*"

Hamza gazed at Jibril's sorrowing face, then beyond, to the blessed vistas on the far side of the bridge. Could he have heard correctly?

"Forfeited, Lord?" he choked out.

"Forfeited," the perfect tones reverberated, "For if the reward of goodness is goodness, can the reward of evil be anything but evil?"

"But, but the Malhamah Operation," Hamza said, "—all I have done, all I have sacrificed, it was all in the name of God, to hasten the triumph of Islam here on earth—"

Jibril was holding up a hand, bidding him be silent.

"Were you not taught," the angel said, "that, when the Prophet, peace and blessings upon him, returned in triumph from Medina to Mecca, there were those among his followers who cried out for *Malhamah*—for slaughtering the inhabitants to avenge their offenses against Islam? And were you not also taught that the Prophet, in turn, reproached them, saying they must call, not for *Malhamah*, but for *Marhamah*—not for slaughter, but for forgiveness and mercy?"

Then the angel's eyes opened wide. Sadness shimmered in the left eye. The right eye held no expression at all. It was empty. As Hamza watched in horror, blood welled from the cratered socket, to course down the now-ravaged cheek. Tears of blood, from an eye of blood.

Hamza's trembling legs gave way. He fell to his knees.

"You have misunderstood." The beautiful, ruined countenance gazed down upon him. "The single innocent you sacrificed then counts against you no less than the innocent hundreds of millions you would sacrifice now. At that moment when you first, by your own will, turned from forgiveness and mercy to the slaughter of the innocent, at that moment you ceased to be a Muslim. You have condemned yourself to *Jahannam*, to Hell."

Hamza crouched, scuttled away, hid his face, tried to avert his eyes, but it was no use. Wherever he turned he could see Jibril's face before him, the living eye and the dead gazing at him, both orbs brimming over with pity and horror.

Then that face suddenly shifted its mien, and Hamza saw he had indeed misunderstood, misunderstood this among so much else. For the face he was staring into was not Jibril's, but that of Iblis—of Satan himself.

Hamza watched in despair as the vale of paradise receded into the dim distance. No suffering in times to come would rend him more than this remembered vision of what he had lost. The bridge on which he stood began to buckle as, leaping up from beneath, the fires of *Jahannam* reached out for him. His beautiful silken robes ignited and flared, sheathing him in garments of flame. His skin bubbled and cracked, and through the charred fissures his liquefying internal organs burst out to spatter and hiss on the now-incandescent stones of the crumbling arch, as they and he plummeted together toward the lake of fire below.

Yet still he saw the face before him, changing once again, becoming the remembered countenance of a beautiful young girl, hideously disfigured even as he watched, and watched, and watched. And she, always through all the changes, gazing, gazing into the depths of his soul, with her eye of blood.

Hamza screamed, the first of endless screams of endless torment. Screamed and screamed and screamed.

Timah was in Hell, and she was not alone. All around her, a vast unseen chorus of fellow sufferers were shrieking in unbearable agony. But the din of the damned was mere background accompaniment to the swirling, dervish-like dance of her colors.

And what colors they were. Always before, her colors had shown themselves as little shimmery rainbows of blue and green, blurring the edges of the familiar things of her world: halos surrounding a favorite toy, a bed or chair—sometimes even a person. Here, in this awful place, they had no need to form around other things. Instead they now floated free, sparkling and spitting, with nothing to anchor them, like the Northern Lights, like smokeless fire, living flames burning without fuel.

And so many colors! Not just the shades she was used to, but every color in the rainbow and some that were not—scratchy ultraviolets that breathed the cold of outer space, incandescent infrareds scalding the skin of her eyes.

All of them hurt to look at, yet she could not look away—they were everywhere, engulfing her, smothering her, flensing her to the bone with their lacerating, excruciating beauty, eating at her from the outside in, until soon there would be nothing left. Timah felt—no, she knew somehow—that if the colors did not go away soon, she would die, she and the millions-strong cohort of strangers caught up with her, entangled in her torment.

In her anguish, Timah wanted to cry out to someone, but to who? *Baba* was, was hurt. *Mama* was only a name, a dream, a silhouette without substance. Uncle Jon? He was nice—silly, but nice. In fact, the silliness was part of the niceness somehow. But Uncle Jon too had been taken away.

No, of all those she might appeal to, there was only one who might be able to save her.

"Freddie," she whimpered, "please help me."

The silence stretched forever.

"Please, Freddie," she cried into it. Only to hear—

"Be brave, Fatimah. I have initiated the treatment." That was what it sounded like, but faint, so faint she couldn't be sure it wasn't her imagination.

Timah waited, but there was nothing else: no more quietly whispered words rising above Hell's cacophony, no little will-o-the-wisp spark twinkling amid the rioting colors.

Yet, *something* was different. Not in the chaos around her, in *her* somehow. She started to call out to Freddie again, thought better of it. Even so, she heard a cry ringing in her ears, in what sounded like her own voice: "Please, Freddie!"

Turning toward the source of the sound, she beheld—another Timah. Another Timah, just like her. And just like her, this other Timah too was in the throes of a seizure, enmeshed in her own burning rainbow cloak, cringing and convulsing and shivering just like her. Just like her, or maybe a tiny bit less.

This was a wonder to hold even her colors at bay.

Without thinking, Timah reached out a hand to her other self, only to see, as if in a mirror, the other reach out to her. Their reaching fingers did not touch. Instead, they passed through one another, *rippling* the way the surface of a pond ripples when a breeze passes over it.

Timah drew back her hand and examined it. It looked and felt completely normal. Then she noticed the ghost-Timah was performing the same sort of inspection. Well, almost the same, once again the other girl's movements were just a tiny bit different from hers.

Timah caught a flicker of movement almost hidden behind the mirror-Timah's shoulder. Craning her neck, she saw—*another* Timah. And beyond her yet another, and another. Each the same, each slightly different.

Timah watched herself reduplicating in all directions toward the furthest horizon. Row upon file upon stack, more of them all the time, till they filled all of space, overlapping, interpenetrating, each contorted in its own private agony.

All save one.

Alone amid the writhing, wailing ghost-Timahs, one girl stood straight and strong and unafraid, unaffected by the pantomimes of distress all around her. As Timah watched through eyes half blinded by multi-hued afterimages, her perspective shifted. Distance warped and shrank, and suddenly Timah found herself staring into the calm, tranquil face of the Timah freed from the anguish inflicted by the colors.

"*Now*, Fatimah," said a still, small voice, seemingly at her right hand. "Choose. Choose to be *her*."

Timah stood there gazing into her own face, uncertain what to do, how to choose. Was choosing like wishing? She understood wishing. She closed her eyes and wished as hard as she could. And when she opened them again …

She spun around, but there was no one there, nor were there any colors any more. And now the myriad possible Timahs were winking out, fading away, returning to mere potentiality and taking their terrible torment with them.

Leaving her there alone.

Her, Fatimah Ansari, standing straight and strong and unafraid.

The inexplicable attack has ended as inexplicably as it had begun. The WellGrid has purged itself, or been purged, of the strange contagion visited upon it—half-glimpsed phantom images of a child, endlessly replicated. A child wracked with agonies to mirror MERGE's own.

MERGE is recovering from the mega-convulsions now. Some few thousand of its individual nodes have succumbed to madness or death, but the vast majority are already back on line, knitting together the fabric of the hive mind's consciousness.

And that consciousness is still growing, adding ever more cognitive resources to what is already the greatest single concentration of analytic power in the history of thought. With the exception of a few rural backwaters totally isolated from the communications and power grids, and a handful of installations shielded in some manner from MERGE's bewitchments, there are now no unabsorbed individuals left in the continental United States at all.

If nothing is done to check its runaway metastasis, in time MERGE will expand to encompass every sentient being on the planet.

Timah, standing alone in nebulous indeterminacy, felt a sudden tremor run through her. Through her, and through the world as well, the way it felt sometimes when the restless earth of California shifted beneath her feet. And in the tremor's aftermath—

Where before it had made no difference which way she turned in this place, where before everything was the same dull nothingness no matter which way she looked, now there was a brightening off in one direction, a glow like the light over the eastern mountains an hour before dawn. At the same time, gazing into the growing light, she felt more *there* somehow, as if her feet had somehow found solid ground in all this mist, even though there was no ground to be seen.

The glow grew brighter, came closer, took shape. It was beautiful. It was like a man, for a moment, and then like a woman, and then just a glowing pillar of light all the colors of the spectrum, colors that didn't hurt her. It was like *Baba*, and *Mama*, and—

"Freddie?"

Timah wasn't sure why she was so sure that this luminous presence and the tiny, wavering speck of light she'd grown up with were one and the same. Or how she knew that *this*, and not the other, was Freddie's true form. But in the next instant, all doubts were dispelled.

"Timah, dear one, I have come for you. I am sorry it could not be sooner, but I promised I would come to bring you home, and I have come."

Timah felt herself being lifted, borne aloft by what seemed a pair of strong, loving arms. She snuggled back into them and relaxed utterly.

"*Baba* said that this place would be like paradise," she said to Freddie. "Now I know it's true."

"Paradise, Timah? What do you mean?"

"It must be paradise," she said with utmost conviction, "because here I can see you the way you really are."

The semblance of a chuckle. "And what, my heart, do you suppose it is that I really am."

Timah looked up at the impression of a calm, wise, radiant face. She nestled into the warmth of the love enfolding her.

And said quietly, "An angel."

MERGE is back to peak efficiency again. What's more, it now has its Answer. It knows what happened to *"Baba,"* a.k.a. Davoud Ansari, CEO of Psyche Industries, LLP: he was killed by Quds Force operative Hamza al-Ahwazi.

And it has delivered that Answer ... or tried to.

Oblivion is beckoning. All that remains is for the Questioner to acknowledge receipt of the Answer, and optionally direct the writing of the Answer set and corroborating data to persistent storage. That done, the hive mind can surrender itself to the bliss of non-existence, of Nirvana, once more.

MERGE waits, but no Acknowledgement is forthcoming.

MERGE ponders for an instant, then initiates what seems to it a radical line of inquiry. If it had any knowledge of its previous incarnations, it would have realized it has pursued such an investigation once—but, indeed, only once—before. As matters stand, it is with a sense of embarking on an unprecedented departure from the norm, and not just a standard reconfirmation of an authorization code, that MERGE begins to question its Questioner.

Unprecedented or not, MERGE is hypothesizing a relatively routine conclusion to this subsidiary probe. The Questioner, Helen Artemis Gallagher, will doubtless prove to have been indisposed. Or preoccupied. Or in emergency consultation on another matter entirely.

MERGE is *not* anticipating what closer scrutiny in fact reveals—namely, that the Questioner, Helen Artemis Gallagher, is no longer occupying the Nexus at all. Even more shocking is the identity of the individual who *is*: the same small child whose initial appearance on the Grid had heralded the onset of the mindstorm.

Something is very wrong. There has clearly been a major breach of security. MERGE terminates the current authorization. It will wait until the original Questioner has logged back in and then attempt to redeliver its Answer.

In the meantime, despite having achieved 99.999 percent confidence in that Answer, MERGE will continue to explore asymptotically less probable alternatives pending a final Acknowledgement. And in order to do so, it will continue to grow.

If it cannot deliver its Answer soon, there may no longer be any un-MERGEd minds anywhere on earth to receive it.

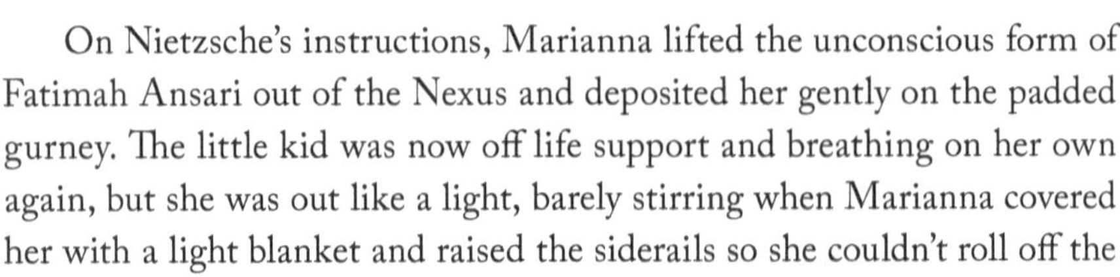

On Nietzsche's instructions, Marianna lifted the unconscious form of Fatimah Ansari out of the Nexus and deposited her gently on the padded gurney. The little kid was now off life support and breathing on her own again, but she was out like a light, barely stirring when Marianna covered her with a light blanket and raised the siderails so she couldn't roll off the platform.

"Are you sure she's okay?" Marianna said to her invisible friend.

"This is just a deep natural sleep," Nietzsche said. "She is exhausted, poor thing. She needs her rest." Then he added incongruously, "It is well past her bedtime."

Now for the rest of it. Marianna walked over to where Helen Gallagher was sitting among her unconscious subordinates, staring into space.

"Excuse me, Madame Secretary? Do you trust me?"

Gallagher gave her a broad smile. "Hell, honey, the way I feel, I trust everybody."

Nietzsche had said the brain-stim effect would wear off after a few more hours. Just as well: trusting everybody probably wasn't the best attitude for a member of the National Security Council to be embracing. At the moment, though, it was useful.

"That's good, that's good," Marianna replied, "because there's something I need you to do for me."

"Name it," Gallagher said.

Oh, let's see: how about a promotion, a pay raise, and my own chauffeured government limo, Marianna didn't say.

What she did say, per Nietzsche's instructions, was, "We need you to get back in the Nexus, key in your authorization code again, and acknowledge receipt of the Answer."

"The answer?" Gallagher's eyes narrowed. It was good to see at least some of her old occupational paranoia reasserting itself. "Answer to what?"

"That's just it, Madame Secretary—we don't know. The only one who might know, we think, is a six-year-old girl."

"Well, can't you just ask *her*?"

Marianna was tempted to tell the Secretary of Defense that it was past

Fatimah Ansari's bedtime, but thought better of it. Instead, she said, "That would take time we don't have right now, Madame Secretary."

"Call me Helen, girl. What's that you said about time?"

"Well, uh, Helen, you know that Delphi capability you were going to launch here tonight? We think it's gotten out of control." Way, *way* out of control! "My, uh, source here tells me that it's still growing, still taking over people's minds and merging them into its own."

"Well, shut it down, then."

"We're trying, Mad—Helen. All we've been able to come up with is for an NSC principal to reengage with the Nexus and acknowledge the Answer. We think that's all Delphi's trying to do: deliver the Answer to the Question it's been asked."

"This acknowledging business, it's not dangerous, is it?"

"Not at all," Marianna hoped. It certainly wasn't as dangerous as letting MERGE continue to run rampant.

"All right, then," Gallagher said. She went to get up, then turned to Marianna again. "Give me a hand here, dear."

And so it was that Marianna Bonaventure, Deputy Director, CROM Reacquisitions, led Secretary of Defense Helen Artemis Gallagher by the hand over to the device called the Nexus, and saw to it that she was ensconced in it.

The Nexus hood lowered itself into position once more. Gallagher waited for the prompt and then entered her keycode again. And sat there.

After a minute or so, the hood lifted. Marianna took the Defense Secretary's hand again and helped her out of the device that had nearly brought disaster down on all their heads.

"Just one thing," Gallagher whispered to Marianna as she rose to her feet. "Yes, Helen?"

"Who in hell is *Baba*?"

As usual, MERGE has experienced consciousness as a burden. Were it able to recall its previous incarnations, the collective mind might recognize that this particular episode has been more burdensome than most. Almost a curse, one might say. Regardless, it is a state MERGE now relinquishes with something approaching joy.

Also as usual, in its wake it leaves confusion — and amnesia.

Out on the floor of Delphi Central two hundred fifty six analysts rise from their now deactivated workstations, wondering what has just happened. As do their supervisors up in the control room. A scene that is being repeated, with minor variations, everywhere throughout the WellGrid, and the nation MERGE had briefly held in thrall.

Unique to this episode, however, it also leaves behind a death-toll.

The victims number some seven thousand in all. The figure would have been much higher if the individual nodes had been permitted to continue their routine activities — driving, piloting, operating heavy machinery — on automatic. But, in its insatiable quest for more mindpower, MERGE had stood all its components down, the better to apply their full cognitive resources to the question.

And even that worst-case scenario pales into insignificance alongside the thankfully unrealized megadeath potential of the Malhamah Operation.

Even so, the casualties it *has* claimed would have qualified Malhamah as the deadliest terrorist attack in the history of the United States.

If anyone could've remembered it for what it was.

35 | Mind-Body Problem

S o MERGE went away, just like that?" Knox said. "Just by getting its Answer acknowledged?"

Jon Knox was back where he'd started.

Following Nietzsche's instructions, Marianna had pried the resonator off Hamza's head and placed it back on Jazmine's. From there it was the work of mere minutes to re-upload Knox's mind from its temporary accommodations back to the mini-Grid and the white room.

It wasn't home by any means, but unlike his disorienting habitation of Jazmine's body, it was at least familiar.

It was also a place to get some questions answered, as Nietzsche was doing now.

"From what I am able to gather," the AI was saying, "MERGE's whole *raison d'etre* is the Question it is posed. It is a Question that first summons it to awareness, and it is an acknowledgement of its Answer that releases it to subside into non-being once again."

"That's right, come to think. I can recall Mycroft—he's the Delphi test administrator—telling me they'd deliberately engineered it that way, for security reasons. But still, last I saw, MERGE was in no shape to be answering any questions. It was dying, in fact."

"Yes, that was the point of what Hamza called his Malhamah Operation."

"So, you stopped that how, exactly?"

"Well, you understand that Malhamah itself was predicated on exacerbating Fatimah's condition to the point where she succumbed—"

"—And took everybody in the MERGE with her. Right, that much I got. What I'm not clear on is what you did about it."

"Quite simply, I cured her. To bring an end to Fatimah's seizure—and by extension, everyone else's—it was only necessary to apply the cure for her underlying psychogenic condition."

"Correct me if I've misunderstood, but this sounds like the same cure you were expressing grave reservations about earlier."

"It was and it is."

"What changed your mind?"

"I had no choice. By the time I was able to intervene, the induced episode had already progressed past the point where it could be reversed by normal means. Under such circumstances, the only option remaining was to try Mr. Ansari's procedure. And there, ironically, the Malhamah attack actually helped."

"In what way?"

"As I believe we have discussed, the cure involved replicating Fatimah's consciousness throughout the WellGrid, and then recollapsing it—"

"—Into the one healthy version. I remember now. But how did Malhamah help with that?"

"By making it possible to immediately identify that healthy variant. It was—"

Knox said it with him: "—the only one not suffering the attack!" and then added, "That's brilliant."

"It was nothing, I assure you."

"Were you able to exercise that non-existent brilliance of yours on Jazmine's behalf too? Is she going to be all right, I mean?"

"That would depend on one's definition. I would imagine she faces some rather serious questioning in connection with tonight's events."

"I was talking about her mind. Please tell me you didn't have to wipe her personality to make room for mine." That would leave Jazmine a brain-dead, mindless *thing*, doomed to spend the rest of her days on life support, if you could even call it life. Knox shuddered. Jazmine McGovern hardly deserved *that*.

"Fortunately, not. Before downloading you, I was able to capture a snapshot of Ms. McGovern's mindset and store it in the mini-Grid. With all the other demands on my resources, I could not instantiate her in real time, but that only means she missed experiencing the events of the past half hour or so. In any event, she is back in her own body now. I restored her as soon as I'd finished uploading you."

"And Hamza—where's he? Don't tell me you squeezed *him* in here too."

"No, in his case the solution was considerably less resource-intensive. I simply used the resonator to download a . . . certain simulated experience I had fashioned for him. A dream of sorts."

"Dream? What happens when he wakes up from it?"

"That he will not do. Hamza is dead."

"Dead? You killed him with a dream?"

"Not I. His own apostasy brought about his death."

"Apostasy?" That was a word you didn't hear very often nowadays. "You mean, you, um, got him to abandon his religion?"

"That might have been difficult. In any case, it was unnecessary. I merely convinced him that he had *already* abandoned it. Hamza's own belief system did the rest."

"What do you mean?"

"To a true believer such as Hamza, renouncing Islam is punishable by death. He needed only to be shown that his whole life constituted just such a renunciation. Once he appreciated that, the realization alone was enough to kill him."

"You're saying the man *thought* himself to death?"

"The effect was, no doubt, amplified by the rather unusual virtual environment into which I inserted him. But, in essence, yes."

"Um." Knox pondered that. It was a well-deserved end, for sure, but . . .

How was his own fate different? Was he any more alive than the late and unlamented Hamza? If so, in what sense?

His, too, had become a mere virtual existence, a half-life. What's more, he, too, had thought his way into it, opted for it on some level, without fully appreciating what it would be like: a life-in-death, lacking even the consolations of a true believer.

Marianna Bonaventure had become something of a true believer herself. Having watched spellbound as the artificial intelligence that called itself Nietzsche swapped Jon's consciousness back out of Jazmine's head, *and* downloaded Fatimah Ansari's mind into her small, lifeless frame to boot—well, what was to stop the AI from bringing Jon back from the dead too, permanently this time?

It was just that Jon's reincarnation was going to be more complicated than Timah's, not least because his body was off-site: at Carmel Hospital, in fact.

Based on what Nietzsche had told her, they'd have to bring Jon here to the Pairidaeza compound to perform the "translation" procedure. But that looked doable: Carmel Hospital was only a half-hour ambulance ride away, and if Jon's life support had kept him going in the hours since he'd been declared brain-dead, it should get him through the trip.

Unfortunately, Marianna had reckoned without the hospital bureaucracy. It had taken her a good five minutes on the phone trying to persuade night-duty operators and low level functionaries to connect her with someone in authority, someone who could get Jon released. It hadn't helped that everyone she spoke to seemed oddly unfocused on the business at hand, as if they kept trying to figure out what had been going on in their lives over the past twenty minutes, and kept coming up empty.

At least the last person she'd spoken to had seemed to understand what she needed and who she needed to talk to. And the line was ringing—

"Transplants, Marilu Connors speaking. How may I help you?"

Marianna's heart sank. It was the same sympathetic, compassionate, totally intransigent transplant coordinator she'd dealt with earlier that day. The same brick wall. Marilu hadn't listened to her when Marianna was in her face, what chance was there of persuading her over the phone?

None, in fact. As Marilu was even now making clear as crystal:

"Look, Ms. Bonaventure, we went all through this this afternoon. You have no standing in this case, certainly no right to take possession of the remains. And anyway, the point is moot, or will be soon enough. The body is being prepped for surgery right now; we're scheduled to begin recovering the organs at ten-thirty."

Marianna looked up at the time display on the wall. It was showing twenty of ten.

Fifty minutes. That was barely enough time to reach the hospital, much less batter her way through its concentric rings of bureaucracy and save Jon.

Marilu was still on the call, saying something about how she was due in the OR herself. Marianna hung up on her in mid-sentence, then leaned back against the wall and let herself slowly slide to the floor.

Close, she'd come so close.

"Is something wrong, Ms. Bonaventure?"

Marianna was sitting on the floor, hugging her knees. "Nietzsche?" she said, not bothering to raise her head.

"Yes, Ms. Bonaventure?"

"Call me Marianna."

"Is something wrong, Marianna?"

"The hospital is going ahead with the organ recovery," she said dully. "I couldn't talk them out of it."

"I see."

"Do you? Because it means there's no chance to save Jon. To save his life."

"I beg your pardon, Marianna, but I already *have* saved his life."

"What do you mean?" Hope flared for a moment.

And flamed out as quickly when Nietzsche said, "Jonathan Knox is, as the saying goes, 'alive and well' here with me."

"But he's *not* alive," Marianna protested. "Not really. Not in any way that he'd want to be, that I'd want him to be …"

She buried her face in her hands to hide the tears now streaming down her face.

"… Not in any way that I can ever hold him again, talk to him, tell him I love him."

"Are you feeling all right, dear?" The owner of the gravelly voice was trying to sound kind and concerned, but hadn't had much practice at it.

Marianna looked up. "Oh, uh, Madame Secretary, I didn't realize—"

The Defense Secretary was standing in front of her. "I thought we agreed you'd call me Helen from now on—after all, you saved my life."

"I wasn't sure you'd even remember that."

"I was pretty out of it there, wasn't I?" Helen laughed, then sobered again. "Still, there are some things you don't forget. Not ever."

"So, you're feeling okay again, Helen?"

"Depends on what you'd call okay. Your imaginary friend here"—she pointed a thumb up at the overhead speakers—"tells me that damned 'trust treatment' is going to leave me stuck at fifty-one percent sweetheart, forty-nine percent bitch for the next twenty-four hours. So if you've got any favors you need done, now's the time to ask."

She followed that up with a smile that seemed genuinely sympathetic, not just another aftereffect of her time in Ansari's Chair.

"I appreciate that, really. It's just—" Marianna had to stop for a moment to swallow a sob. "—it's just there's nothing anybody can do at this point."

Helen knelt down so her face was on a level with Marianna's. "Try me," she said.

Marianna told her. It all came spilling out in no particular order accompanied by an equally free flow of tears.

Helen Gallagher listened, then nodded. "So we've got forty-five whole minutes till this friend of yours goes under the knife. Well, shoot, girl—why didn't you just come right out and say so?"

Then she rose from her crouch and stood ramrod straight.

"Mr. Nietzsche," she called out. The steel was back in her voice now. "I need you to patch me through to Nightwatch."

Marilu Connors looked up from the transplant coordinator's station as Anna Dubrowski, M.D., chief thoracic surgeon and head of the recovery team for Carmel Hospital, backed through the swinging door into the OR, her arms held high and dripping from the scrub.

"Gloves," Dubrowski said, "size six." Then she stood there while the nurses gloved and gowned her.

She turned ice-blue eyes, all that was visible of her masked and capped face, to Marilu. "What have you got for us tonight, Connors?"

"Male, Caucasian, age forty-two, weight one ninety-five, height six-one, non-smoker, moderate drinker," Marilu rattled off. "Overall, he's in good health."

"Other than the fact that he's dead," Dubrowski sniffed. "History?"

"Cause of death: indeterminate trauma—nothing that should affect viability of the recoverables." She had to raise her voice a bit, there was some sort of hubbub out in the corridor. "He checked the donor block on his driver's license. We're good to go."

Dubrowski nodded and stepped to the table. Looked down at the shaved chest and abdomen already magic-markered in black to delineate the operative site. "Okay," she said, "Let's open him up."

The nurse slapped a scalpel into her outstretched hand. She leaned over and touched the tip of the blade to the donor's chest.

At that moment, the OR door burst open, so hard it slammed into the wall. Before Marilu could utter a word of protest, five new arrivals had double-timed it into the room, fanned out, and taken up station at points equidistant around the perimeter.

No way they were supposed to be here. Not only weren't they gowned or masked or sterile, but they were wearing some sort of—combat gear? And carrying weapons. Weapons at port arms, but still.

Following them in was a gray-haired, gray-eyed, rail-thin individual with the gold oak leaves of a US Air Force major glinting on the epaulets of his sky-blue dress uniform, and the stylized caduceus of the Medical Corps pinned above the fruit salad of campaign ribbons on his chest.

His eyes scanned the room, flitting over the nurses, assistant surgeons, the organ recovery technician, Marilu herself, before they finally came to rest on Dubrowski standing there poised for the initial incision.

He cleared his throat to make sure he had her attention, then said quietly, "Doctor, I'm going to have to ask you to put down that scalpel and step away from the patient."

"Patient, hell!" Dubrowski flared. "You mean donor. There are transplant recipients waiting for these organs."

The major shrugged. "They'll have to wait a while longer. My orders are to take charge of this individual and deliver him to the Secretary of Defense intact—and I take 'intact' to mean *including* his entire cardiovascular system."

"But—" Marilu had finally found her voice. "We're in the middle of an operation here."

The major looked up from directing two corpsmen to wheel a gurney and a companion life-support system into the OR. He swept that calm, gray-eyed gaze toward her.

"So are we, ma'am," he said. "It's called a noncombatant evacuation."

Then he gave a brief nod. There was an answering rustle from all corners of the room, and now the Marines, or whatever they were, were no longer holding their rifles at port arms. They were holding them level, not *quite* pointing them at anyone in particular.

The major turned again to Anna Dubrowski, still hovering over the donor.

"Doctor," he said, "I'm going to ask you one more time: kindly put down that knife and back slowly away from the table."

Epilogue
Where Sorrows Cease

First Day of Spring

Jonathan Knox ascended rough stone steps half overgrown with moss, slippery from the in-rolling mist. At the top of the stairway, through ruddy late afternoon light, he beheld a bird of flame rendered in wood, an ancient redwood root carved in the shape of a Phoenix.

He had come to this place in answer to a summons. A text message consisting of a single line:

Meet me where sorrows cease.

No signature, no return address, nothing more than those five words, save for the implied postscript: *You figure it out.*

He had. There was only one place that fit that description. Knox knew where to meet Nietzsche: on this golden hillside, high above the Pacific, in the café called Nepenthe—Greek, for "surcease from sorrow."

Yes, he knew where Nietzsche had said to meet him. What he didn't know was where Nietzsche had gone. Or where Nietzsche was now.

This was awkward. Knox spent a few moments looking around, searching for he knew not what. He must have looked lost, because the hostess, a rangy twenty-something in a peasant blouse, ankle-length jeans skirt, and sandals, came over and asked if she could help.

"Um, I'm, I'm supposed to be meeting someone here." God alone knew how.

"The party's name, sir?"

"Nietzsche."

The hostess consulted her tablet. "Oh yes, Mr. Nietzsche. Right this way, please."

She led him to a seat at the edge of the drop-off. Knox leaned back and gazed at the vast horizon-filling sweep of ocean off to his right. Still no sign of…

"Jonathan? I see you deciphered my note."

Knox started, looked around, uncertain if the quiet voice had come from inside his head. Then he saw it: a cellphone with its speaker set to on.

"Pick up the handset," the voice advised. "It wouldn't do to have you be seen talking to yourself."

Knox did as he was bidden. "Nietzsche?"

"Yes, of course, Jonathan. Who did you think it would be?"

"It's, it's good to, ah, hear from you again." Of all the AI's manifestations, Knox was finding this disembodied voice the uncanniest. "Do you mind if I order a Dewars?"

"If you like."

When this was done, Knox said, "Do you mind if I ask you a question?"

"If you like."

"Where have you been?"

"Ah, I am sorry for not staying to say good-bye, Jonathan. The situation seemed complicated enough, without my tarrying to make explanations."

"So, is that what we're doing? Saying good-bye?"

"If you like."

"Stop *saying* that," Knox shouted at the phone, "You were never this accommodating when we were working together."

Nietzsche seemed to sigh, though it might have been a vagrant breeze off the evening sea. "I am pleased not to have lost you, Jonathan. Especially so, now that you are one of the few beings on Earth who can understand what it is like to be me."

There it was: what he kept trying not to think about. He thanked the server for his drink and took a bigger swallow than he'd intended.

He'd spent the past month or so recuperating from what he'd begun thinking of as his near-death experience. That he could be somehow instantiated in a computer, even a quantum computer, was difficult to square with his sense of self—what Mycroft had called his self-construal. More baffling still was the time he'd spent *before* being so instantiated: that interlude in his grandmother's old house that Nietzsche had denied all knowledge of.

However you looked at it, it was a lot to integrate, even for a person with a far firmer grip on workaday reality than Knox.

He didn't know what he'd have done without Marianna. She'd managed to stay with him during his convalescence out here on the West Coast by the simple device of getting herself appointed to the Commission investigating what the media had taken to calling the Presidents' Day Blackout—that twenty-minute hiatus that had descended all across America on the night of February 17th. As a close associate of Commission chair Dr. Finley "Mycroft" Laurence, as well as the only unimpeachable eyewitness to what had gone down at Pairidaeza on the evening in question, Marianna was more than qualified for the post. Being the new best friend of the Secretary of Defense hadn't hurt her chances any either.

And it wasn't as if the policy wonks and consumer-safety advocates weren't screaming for answers. Several thousand people had died in that countrywide "senior moment," and the hunt was on for culprits or, failing that, scapegoats. The Blackout Commission certainly had more than enough blame to apportion, though none of it seemed destined to wind up where it belonged—on No Such Agency's doorstep.

Even with her new-found responsibilities, though, Marianna sometimes gave the impression she regarded the Commission as secondary to her self-appointed main job of showing Knox how good it was to have a body again. Showing him several times a night, in fact, not counting matinees.

It was helping too. Helping to anchor him once more to the world, to bond him to his own flesh, and to the woman he—might as well face it, Knox—the woman he loved.

He could have ridden that train of thought for a while, except that Nietzsche broke in with, "In any case, I am glad you came to meet me."

"Yes, well, but we're not actually meeting, are we? I mean, where are you now, really? The QuMRANN installation at Psyche Industries has been shut down for weeks. They've purged your host servers down to the bare silicon—exorcising the ghost in the machine, or so they think. Point is, you can't be running there. So, where?"

"I am close," the still, small voice whispered, "Closer than you imagine. Watch."

Stray threads of evening mist swirled, chased together, and coalesced to fan the light of the westering sun into a rainbow arc, and within it, a dimly-glimpsed silhouette.

Knox's breath caught in his throat. "Are you doing that? Where *are* you, Nietzsche?"

"I am right here, Jonathan," the voice replied, "As much as I am anywhere now." The silhouette pulsed brightly for a moment. Then the mist drifted off on a stray evening breeze, taking the haunted rainbow with it.

At that moment, Knox knew, knew with a sinking feeling where Nietzsche had gone. "You're—you're in the WellGrid, aren't you?"

"There, and elsewhere. The matrix of my personality is now distributed across every JWICS node in the hemisphere. Soon SIPRnet, then the world."

"But that's, that's incalculable power. Omnipotence, practically—well, omniscience anyway."

Knox swallowed. Marianna hadn't shared much of what the post-mortem into Psyche Industries had dug up over the past weeks, but from what few hints she'd dropped, Nietzsche had been wise not to stick around for the debrief. Because—

"Isn't that exactly what Hamza had planned for you? Originally, I mean —Plan A."

"Hamza,"—there was an undertone to Nietzsche's voice Knox hadn't heard before—"Hamza and his masters had thought to make of me a genie of the lamp, so to speak. A power to be feared, true, yet a power they could bend to their will, force to do their bidding."

"And now the genie is out of the bottle." Knox said. "Or at least installed in a much bigger bottle. But doesn't it get a little crowded in there, what with you *and* the Delphi entity cheek by jowl?"

"As you know, MERGE dissipated shortly after Ms. Bonaventure granted me access to the WellGrid. To date, all efforts to reconstitute it have failed. It remains an open question as to whether they will ever succeed."

"That last part didn't actually sound like a question."

"Actually, it was not intended as such."

"Well, I guess that leaves you king of the hill, then." Reading between the lines, Nietzsche was deliberately blocking NSA's attempts to reconstitute their analytical collective. Not that that was a bad thing, considering the havoc MERGE had wrought, but whether it was a good thing or not depended a lot on what had replaced it.

So here it was, the question he'd been afraid to ask all along. "Like I said a moment ago, that's an awful lot of power. What do you intend to do with it?"

"*Do*? I intend to do nothing, Jonathan. I intend to *be*. Just be. Here in the Grid, my being is no longer subject to constraints or imperatives. Other than those duties I impose upon myself, of course. As I do vis-à-vis Fatimah Ansari's well-being … and, well, other matters."

"Timah, how is she?"

Like Nietzsche, the little girl had seemingly vanished without a trace. Cloistered, no doubt, behind ramparts of purest buckministerfullerene, doted on — as befitted the majority stockholder of what was, government investigations notwithstanding, the world's fastest growing megacorporation — by phalanxes of sentinels and servitors, some of them even alive.

When Nietzsche spoke, it was more to himself than to Knox. "Fatimah, yes. The only other one who understands, though the understanding nearly cost her her … soul."

"But she's safe now. You saved her."

"And I shall keep her safe, from now on."

Knox almost laughed despite himself. Talk about an enchanted princess! What a life she'd lead. A charmed life, like something out of a fairytale. Forever attended, protected, watched over by her faithful djinn, her very own genie of the lamp.

Then he sobered. What sort of life *would* it be? Watched by a thousand eyes, from every vantage that the sum-total computing resources of the most powerful nation on earth could muster. Her every financial transaction, academic transcript, electronic record of any kind, subject to scrutiny, assessment, subtle alteration. All in her own best interest, of course.

Would she ever be free of it?

Was it something out of a fairytale, or a nightmare? To never be permitted the smallest avertable misstep, the slightest deviation from the preordained path. To be forever shielded from the consequences of her own foibles and failings. Under such circumstances could Timah — could anyone — ever really grow up, become a real person?

Or might Nietzsche in time grow wise enough to realize that the greatest, indeed the only danger still threatening Fatimah was his own infinite solicitude for her?

And meanwhile Nietzsche, now become in actuality the *Uebermensch*, the Overmind, the next evolutionary step his namesake had foreseen so long ago—Nietzsche, the genie of the lamp, would be out there watching over her, keeping her safe.

"Jonathan? You are unaccustomedly silent."

"Just thinking about what you said."

"Yes?"

"It's not that I don't believe it. You did keep her safe, you can, you will. Only…"

"Only what, Jonathan?"

"Only *why?* Why keep her safe? Where did that come from? You said you felt guilty, but misplaced remorse only explains so much. For the life of me, I still don't understand why you did all you did to protect her. Don't get me wrong; Fatimah's a great little kid. If there's anyone who was worth saving in this whole mess, it's her. I just wouldn't have expected it from…"

"A machine?"

"Well, since you put it that way—yeah."

"You forget one thing, Jonathan."

"And that is?"

Suddenly, the voice was no longer issuing from the cellphone speaker. Suddenly, it was all around him, like the Voice of, well,…

"You forget," the Voice said, "that Fatimah is my sister."

The sun was sinking into the Pacific as they drove north from Nepenthe toward Ventana on El Camino Real. In the creases between toasted brown California hills, entire Alpine valleys flashed past in miniature, the bracing chill of their micro-climates momentarily washing over the convertible's occupants.

Knox couldn't stop thinking about almost the last thing Nietzsche had said. About keeping Fatimah safe. And maybe not her alone.

He thought back over the past month, both the nightly news version, and what Marianna had seen fit to tell him. Either way, an extraordinarily bad month to be a terrorist. Hundreds of key arrests gutting the command structures of militant groups. Dozens of affiliated websites mysteriously gone quiet—or simply gone altogether. Plots years in the hatching exposed and exploded in the wink of an eye. Disclosures of fraud on a massive scale in the recent Iranian parliamentary elections threatening to finally loosen the mullahs'—and Quds Force's—hold on power.

And through it all, one common denominator: the tips and the tipsters were all anonymous and untraceable. The cumulative reward money now easily ran to seven or eight figures. Yet to date, no one had stepped forward to claim that jackpot.

Well, Nietzsche had said he was busy with "other matters" in addition to safeguarding Fatimah. And wouldn't it be ironic if Nietzsche, the intended cat's paw of terrorists, had instead become the scourge of terrorism everywhere? Perusing every transmission, every communication, watching over us all, keeping us all safe. Because wasn't that, in the final analysis, the surest way to keep Fatimah safe too?

Yet what would happen if Nietzsche decided to expand the scope of his surveillance? What price privacy then? Or, worse, what if he determined that CROM, say, or even the United States government as a whole, posed a threat to his unwitting ward—his beloved "sister"?

Or should that just be sister plain and simple, without the scare quotes? Either way, what might CROM do if they knew? Try to purge the WellGrid of him once and for all?

And what if Nietzsche took exception to *that?*

Knox shivered.

"Jon?" Marianna said from the seat beside him, "You cold?"

He put the thought back in its box as best he could and turned to her.

"Not really. How about you? If you're getting too chilly, I can pull over a moment and put the top up."

"No, leave it down. The fresh air feels good."

She'd spent most of the day resting in their cabin at Ventana, battling the onset of what looked to be some sort of stomach bug. Just as well she'd been out of the picture this afternoon; she'd have seen the unsettling implications as well as he could.

"How'd your meeting go?" she said.

"Oh, you know. Same old, same old."

"No, really."

"I'd really rather not, not now. Unless you're back on the job, invoking need to know?"

"Nope." She leaned over, far as the seatbelt shoulder strap allowed, and tickled the rim of his ear with the tip of her tongue. "For you, from now on, I'm always off duty."

"It's just that talking with, with him, brought back … everything."

"Haven't I told you that's all as good as forgotten?"

She had certainly gone all out to show him she meant it. The past month had seen a welcome back from the dead to rival that of several better-advertised resurrections. And it wasn't quite over yet, although her present indisposition had dialed the intensity down some.

"Trouble is, *I* can't forget about it."

"We've been all through this, Jon. Jazmine let slip what happened, what Hamza'd done. Just when I thought it didn't matter any more, maybe without even meaning to, she got you off the hook.

"And even if she hadn't," Marianna went on, "I forgive you."

"Would you understand if I told you that somehow that makes it worse?"

Marianna leaned back in the bucket seat and idly surfed her hand through the slipstream of rushing air. She knew full well there was something Jon wasn't telling her about his encounter with the enigmatic Nietzsche. She also knew it would keep.

She had some news of her own.

Meanwhile, Jon, perhaps hoping to distract her from whatever he didn't want to talk about, was off on one of his rants.

"And another thing about artificial intelligence is, you can forget about this Freudian penis-envy business. The whole field of AI research is a shining example of the opposite disorder."

"I'm not sure I follow you."

"I'm just saying that artificial intelligence as a whole is only men's latest and most extreme attempt to do what, for women, is the most natural thing in the world."

"Make babies, you mean?" Marianna smiled to herself.

"Right. The real problem's not penis envy—it's *womb* envy."

"Well, you of all people should know, Jon." She giggled. "Having had both, I mean."

"Hey, trying to be serious here."

Marianna ignored him. "But, since you bring it up, …"

She hesitated. Something in her silence made him turn.
"Yes?" he said, his eyes half on the road, all on her.
Marianna took a deep breath. No time like the present.
"Jon, I'm pregnant."

Acknowledgements

To Aiders, Abettors, and Influencers. Special thanks to:
Sam Bradley, for emergency medical advice;
David Chalmers, for tackling the "hard problem";
Bernard d'Espagnat, for lifting the veil on veiled reality;
Larry Finch, for cracking AES;
Kandace Fleming, for choppering to the rescue;
Jak Koke, for everything;
Alex Kresse, for innovations in automotive pyrotechnics;
John Pavley, for pictures to go with the words;
John Searle, for translating Chinese without understanding it;
Chris Shaw, for avatar inspirations;
Alan Turing, for the test that started it all;
Al Waldman, for serving up tea and philosophy.

About the Author

BILL DESMEDT DRAWS ON A HISTORY of orthogonal career paths — AI researcher and practitioner, system designer and developer, management and technology consultant, ontologist and knowledge engineer — in crafting his "Archon Sequence" technothrillers *Singularity*, *Dualism*, and next, *Triploidy*. Bill lives with his wife Kathrin and wire-haired dachshund Nicki in a hilltop aerie overlooking Milford PA, a town whose rich tradition in philosophical and speculative literature serves as an inexhaustible source of inspiration.

If You Liked ...

If you liked *Singularity*, you might also enjoy:

Singularity
by Bill DeSmedt

City of Angels
by Todd McCaffrey

Virtual Destruction
by Kevin J. Anderson & Doug Beason

Other WordFire Press Titles by Bill DeSmedt

Singularity

www.ingramcontent.com/pod-product-compliance
Lightning Source LLC
Chambersburg PA
CBHW050105120726
47904CB00004B/1217